wanderlust from an early age. She's lived and worked all over the world, from London to Dubai, Sydney, Bali, NYC and Amsterdam. She's written for the likes of *GQ*, *Hello!*, *Fabulous* and *Time Out*, also a host of YA romance, plus three travel memoirs—*Burqalicious*, *Balilicious* and *Latinalicious* (HarperCollins, Australia). Now she blends travel with romance for Mills & Boon and loves every minute! Tweet her @bex_wicks and subscribe at beckywicks.com.

Once at home in sunny Brazil, **Luana DaRosa** has since lived on three different continents, though her favourite romantic locations remain the tropical places of Latin America. When she's not typing away at her latest romance novel, or reading about love, Luana is either crocheting, buying yarn she doesn't need, or chasing her bunnies around her house. She lives with her partner in a cosy town in the south of England. Find her on Twitter under the handle @LuDaRosaBooks.

Also by Becky Wicks

Falling Again for the Animal Whisperer
Fling with the Children's Heart Doctor
White Christmas with Her Millionaire Doc
A Princess in Naples

Also by Luana DaRosa

Falling for Her Off-Limits Boss

Discover more at millsandboon.co.uk.

THE VET'S ESCAPE
TO PARADISE

BECKY WICKS

HER SECRET
RIO BABY

LUANA DaROSA

MILLS & BOON

All rights reserved including the right of reproduction
in whole or in part in any form. This edition is published
by arrangement with Harlequin Enterprises ULC.

This is a work of fiction. Names, characters, places, locations
and incidents are purely fictional and bear no relationship to
any real life individuals, living or dead, or to any actual places,
business establishments, locations, events or incidents.
Any resemblance is entirely coincidental.

This book is sold subject to the condition that it shall not,
by way of trade or otherwise, be lent, resold, hired out
or otherwise circulated without the prior consent of the publisher
in any form of binding or cover other than that in which it is published
and without a similar condition including this condition
being imposed on the subsequent purchaser.

® and TM are trademarks owned and used by the trademark owner
and/or its licensee. Trademarks marked with ® are registered with the
United Kingdom Patent Office and/or the Office for Harmonisation
in the Internal Market and in other countries.

First published in Great Britain 2022
by Mills & Boon, an imprint of HarperCollins*Publishers* Ltd,
1 London Bridge Street, London, SE1 9GF

www.harpercollins.co.uk

HarperCollins*Publishers*
1st Floor, Watermarque Building,
Ringsend Road, Dublin 4, Ireland

The Vet's Escape to Paradise © 2022 Becky Wicks

Her Secret Rio Baby © 2022 Luana DaRosa

ISBN: 978-0-263-30136-6

08/22

MIX
Paper from
responsible sources
FSC® C007454

This book is produced from independently certified FSC™ paper
to ensure responsible forest management.
For more information visit www.harpercollins.co.uk/green.

Printed and Bound in Spain using 100% Renewable Electricity
at CPI Black Print, Barcelona

THE VET'S ESCAPE
TO PARADISE

BECKY WICKS

MILLS & BOON

Dedicated to the Galapagos Conservation Trust, who are working tirelessly to protect the unique species of the Islands, restore their natural habitat, and provide sustainable solutions to issues like plastic pollution.

Rotherham MBC	
B54 061 255 1	
Askews & Holts	17-Aug-2022
AF	£6.99
RTSWI	

CHAPTER ONE

'HAVE YOU SEEN any boobies yet?'

Mike snorted a laugh at the end of the phone, all the way from Galway, and Ivy put her feet up on the gilded headboard. Flat on her back on the soft satin sheets of her honeymoon bed, she sighed at the ceiling.

'You just couldn't wait to ask me about the boobies, could you? And yes, they're everywhere if you must know. You can't walk down the street in Santa Cruz without being accosted by a man displaying his rail of *I heart boobies* T-shirts. Even this hotel lobby has a rack of them.'

Boobies were the blue-footed birds she'd been excited to see here in their native home, the Galapagos Islands. Her business partner, Mike, had probably been storing up the question for weeks, waiting till she was actually here on Santa Cruz—the island known as the beating heart of the archipelago—to blurt it out.

'Pick me up a shirt, will you? That would make some of our clients' day!' he said. Then Mike's tone changed. She pictured him pouting the way he did, elbows resting on the reception desk at their veterinary clinic, thin lips pursed in the thick of his grey-flecked beard. 'And how are *you*, Ivy? You're a brave woman, going on your honeymoon to a couples' resort, all by yourself.'

'It just means more chocolates and champagne for *me*,' she said, doing her best to stay chipper, even as the song from *Bridget Jones* popped into her head: 'All by Myself'.

'You forced me to come anyway,' she reminded him, crossing to the balcony. The heat hit her like a hairdryer. She'd given up on taming her mass of red curls in the humidity on day one. Three long days ago. 'You said I needed a holiday.'

'And you do. I don't think you've taken a break since I've known you—you're a thirty-eight-year-old workaholic and you know it. Are you meditating, like I told you to?'

She let Mike impart his limited spiritual knowledge, most of which he usually spouted verbatim from Oprah Winfrey's podcasts, while she let her eyes trail down to the heart-shaped swimming pool. One couple were enjoying the facilities in the fading sunlight, floating their cares away on matchy-matchy inflatable love hearts. Ugh.

It should be her down there with Simon, living the couple's dream. Only Simon was probably three pints deep into another session at The Smuggler's Nook back home, planning new dreams without her.

She'd always hated that pub.

'You'll be glad you both called off the wedding one day,' Mike said, probably reading her thoughts. He had an uncanny knack for it after launching and working at Animal Remedy Referrals at her side for so many years. They knew everything about each other.

'You both agreed you didn't want kids when you met, and he took *this* long to tell you he's changed his mind. You were only dating, what…four and a half years? What else wasn't he telling you?'

'Nothing, Mike,' she said wearily, watching the sickeningly happy couple lean across the gap between their inflatables for a kiss. 'I know you're trying to be a good friend but Simon's a good man, you know it. I know it. We just want different things. Talk to me about the animals. How's Ollie's little pup doing after the parvo scare?'

Mike dutifully changed the subject to their animal patients, while a familiar twinge of anxiety made her clasp her phone tighter. She shouldn't have left them, really. What right did she have to take a honeymoon when she wasn't even married? In South America of all places. She should be home discussing the potential acquisition with Mike. It wasn't every day some huge private equity firm offered you millions to take your business to the next level—or to a whole new set of standards that would match their national portfolio.

Then again, she would have to think about that wherever she was. Mike hadn't said it directly yet, but she knew he was leaning towards selling…even if she was still unsure.

Anyway, this month-long trip had been booked for over a year. It would have been stupid to waste it. October was the best time to be here, coming up to summer in the Southern hemisphere. Besides, her mother had already paid for it…probably out of guilt, she thought. Then she admonished herself for being snarky. Not working right now meant far too much time wrapped up in her own head.

Sure, Simon *could* have informed her of his burning urge to spawn mini-mes before they'd planned the wedding and honeymoon of the century.

But then, maybe he had tried to discuss it. Maybe she just hadn't been listening. Hadn't wanted to listen.

Sheesh. Being her other half couldn't have been easy. She did like to work. A lot.

Asking Mike to check in with her again tomorrow, just

so she could be sure that things were ticking along OK in her absence, and getting a firm 'no way' in response, Ivy wandered down to the pool.

Maybe meditating in the final streaks of sunset would help her relax? If she stayed in her room, she'd just check her work email again and she'd already done that twice today. They laughed about the workaholic thing sometimes, but it wasn't really funny. It hadn't been funny to Simon.

Sometimes the look in her ex's eyes when she'd come home late *again*...even now it made her cringe. She'd done to him what her mother had done to her all those years ago—worked so hard and so late that she'd barely kept track of the time or noticed the emotional effects of her absence on the people around her.

The more she thought about it from a distance, things hadn't exactly been smooth sailing before Simon's grand announcement: *'I think I do want a kid, actually, Ivy. Wouldn't it be grand...a little legacy?'*

She cringed to herself just remembering how quickly the fear had set in, how quick she'd been to dismiss it: *'I would be a terrible mother, Simon. We both know that.'*

The swimming pool couple were taking cheesy photos in the blue hues of the pool with an underwater camera now. It didn't feel right to intrude; besides, they deserved the couples' pool, being an actual couple.

Ivy veered off the path towards the hotel's private beach, located a sunlounger in the soft white sand and sat cross-legged to meditate.

Deep breath in. Deep breath out. Free the mind, release the ego.

Yeah, right.

With each swoosh of the waves, in swept her ego to chide her.

Children were nice enough, but she didn't exactly know how to relate to them. Most of her own childhood had been spent cooped up in the house with her nanny and her dog, while her mother worked tirelessly, relentlessly, in some office Ivy had only ever visited in her head. Every day after school had been the same after her dad died: she'd been wrapped up in a cocoon, not allowed out to play in case something bad happened to her, too. Pretty soon her friends had stopped calling round altogether.

Thank goodness for Zeus, she thought. That big daft German shepherd had been her whole world. The reason she'd thrown herself into her animal books, then her veterinary studies! Her own career was her baby now. The *reason* she'd chosen a child-free life and future.

She pinged her eyes open, glowering at the horizon over the water.

Why could she not even meditate properly?

Her mind always spun backwards when she didn't keep busy. Oprah would probably give her a right talking-to. How dare she feel even the slightest bit guilty for making her *own* career her baby? She had a big clinic-sized child to nurture and grow as she saw fit. What was so wrong with *that*?

It wasn't as if *she'd* brought an actual child into the world, only to let her other priorities render it invisible.

Ivy bit the insides of her cheeks. It tended to centre the pain somewhere other than her heart. Her dad's death had hit her mother hard, but maybe workaholics ran in the family.

Either way. She wouldn't ever do that; she'd told Simon as much. They'd called everything off seven months ago. All that was left was this non-refundable holiday. Rumour had it he was dating again already.

So now you're alone. Again. Just you. Is that what you really want, Ivy?

Shut up, ego. Breathe in, breathe out...

A frightened squall from the rocks around the water caught her ears and sucker-punched her square in the solar plexus. What the...?

Squinting, she removed herself from her decidedly un-meditational pose and found herself investigating. It sounded like an animal in pain—she'd know that sound anywhere.

'Where are you? *What* are you?'

Navigating around the rocks in her flip-flops, she sent an army of magnificent red Sally Lightfoot crabs scuttling in a scarlet drove away from her.

Sorry, guys, don't mind me.

The Galapagos was no place not to look where you were going; there were more rare species here than anywhere on earth and most of them had a cheerful tolerance of humans, which was exactly why these islands were so special. Already, on her photo expeditions around the island she'd seen more honking sea lions than she could count, and tiptoed around sleepy groups of charcoal marine iguanas, their red underbellies glowing like the embers of a fire. She always thought they looked like little dinosaurs who'd forgotten to become extinct.

It took her less than a minute to locate the source of the noise. She almost reeled, being so close to it. *No way.*

A baby blue-footed booby! Maybe just a month or so old. For a second, she studied it, in awe of its tiny pale body, light brown wings and distinctively sky-hued webbed feet. Like no other creature on earth.

'Wow,' she gushed, frowning at the deep red gash on its white feathered belly. 'What happened to you?'

The poor thing looked as if it must have got into a

fight with one of those marine iguanas that were usually chomping at moss on lava rocks, further up the beach. Both were synonymous with the Galapagos. This was why she'd wanted to come here for as long as she could remember, to witness such native creatures with her own eyes. But seeing one hurt—especially one so young and so small—she wasn't prepared.

'Come here, little buddy, I won't hurt you.'

Careful not to scare it further, she shook off her green T-shirt and scooped it up. Lucky she'd kept her bikini top on underneath. In minutes she was hurrying back up the beach with it.

'I'll…um… I'll have to call Jero.' A stocky, round-faced lady with a name badge reading Nayely had taken one look at the injured bird from behind the reception desk and got on the phone.

Ivy had laid the fledgling out on the pristine lobby floor on her shirt, much to the interest of the couple who'd come in from the pool. They were standing to her left with their inflatable hearts dripping on the marble tiles, watching her swabbing gently at the wound. Nayely's assistant had located fresh towels and an emergency kit, but it looked as though the wound would need stitches. And probably some kind of special antiseptic. She'd warned them—if it was a bite from an angry iguana, the toxins could kill.

'At least it's still moving, fight or flight going strong,' she said to the crowd as she placed her hand over the bird to keep it still. It wouldn't do to have an injured baby booby flitting erratically about, dropping blood all over their rack of prized booby pun T-shirts.

She was just admiring how its cute little head fitted between her forefinger and her middle finger when a rush

of warm air enveloped her. She turned to see a male figure in the revolving doors, and in less than two seconds
flat all six-foot-something of the powerfully built man
was striding towards her, carrying the scent of the evening and a doctor's bag.

Blinking, she stood to greet him, shocked into silence for a second by his presence. Lean. Athletic. Obviously white Latino, judging by the sun-kissed olive
skin stretched over high cheekbones, and charcoal-black
hair shaved almost to the scalp, as though he could have
walked straight off an army base. He was rocking the
hell out of a tight white T-shirt. A wall of muscle flexed
in his broad-shouldered back as he said a quick hi and
crouched at her feet to inspect the bird.

'Where did you find her?' he asked after a moment,
looking up and fixing deep mahogany eyes onto hers.
Faint crinkles lined them like parentheses; what was he,
thirty-eight like her? Maybe forty?

'On...out there...on the beach.' Ivy cleared her throat,
forcing her neurons to fire correctly instead of all over
the place. God, he was handsome, and, judging from his
accent, American?

'You...work here? On this island, with the animals?'
she asked as Nayely appeared again with a cardboard box.

'There's nothing more I can do here; I'll have to take
her to the clinic.' He paused, as if remembering her question. 'I'm the founder, head vet and operations manager
at the Darwin Animal Clinic,' he replied, diverting his
attention back to the bird, which she scooped gently into
the box while he held it. She caught the edge of a black
tattoo—something jagged and tribal-looking—on his
biceps under his shirt.

'That's one hell of a job description,' she said.

'I work with the domestic animals as a rule. Sometimes we help the Galápagos National Park with injured wildlife, like this. Thank you for getting there first and helping this little one. I'm Jero Morales.'

'Ivy Malone,' she replied, self-consciousness snatching her breath as his bright eyes scanned her up and down from under thick black drawn-together brows. She was shirtless, in just her bikini top. *Doh.* At least she had denim shorts on too and wasn't just standing here directly before him in a two-piece. That would have been awkward because this man was gorgeous.

'Where's the clinic?'

'Not too far from here. We're the only one on Santa Cruz. The only permanent one in the Galapagos.'

'There's only one permanent veterinary clinic, across all the islands?'

'It's more like a shack, but he did start it all from scratch,' Nayely cut in.

Jero's eyebrows raised at the look that must have been on her face. He stood with the box.

'I mean, I just find it hard to believe there's only one,' she continued. 'I'm a vet myself. Back in Ireland.'

He nodded and said something quietly in Spanish to Nayely. The two clearly knew each other—the island was small after all. Ivy found herself wondering where he lived and what else he did on the island when he wasn't caring for sick animals.

Stop swooning, woman!

Suddenly, he was motioning goodbye, and she was speaking without thinking.

'Can I check up on this booby, tomorrow? I'll come by the clinic. Maybe I can even volunteer? I have some time…'

'Sure, Nayely will let you know where I am.' He eyed her up and down again, holding the box against him. She knew instinctively that the bird would be safe in his care. A part of her wanted to *be* that bird.

'I should go,' he said, and she shook herself. What the hell was she doing, crushing out like a schoolgirl?

Must be the heat.

His mouth twitched with a secret smile, and something in her stomach did a backflip as his eyes raked over her torso again. 'Nice to meet you, Ivy,' he said, and she allowed herself the pleasure of watching his pert bottom from behind as he made his way back out into the twilight.

CHAPTER TWO

IVY WAS STANDING in front of the paper-strewn desk, smelling of coconut sun lotion. She'd come to check on the baby booby, and now she was trying to offer her services. Again.

Jero folded his arms across his navy shirt and put his face into neutral. He was tired after a late night with the school board discussing plans for Aayla's next class outing and his brain was struggling to keep up. So many words, he thought in vague amusement, spilling from Ivy's lips under the whirring air-conditioning unit.

'I have my own veterinary clinic, near Galway. Well, I'm the co-founder of Animal Remedy Referrals. Look it up. My partner, Mike, and I have over forty years of combined experience working in academic institutions and private referral practices. I can show you references. In fact, one client just left a five-star review this morning. There were complications during surgery on her basset hound two weeks ago, but thankfully I—'

'That won't be necessary.'

She pursed her lips as he cut her short. She'd hardly taken a breath till now. Good thing the accent was so interesting. Kind of mesmerising actually. Did she always wear green? Today the T-shirt tucked into her denim shorts was ocean green...or maybe it was Irish-clover green? The one she'd wrapped the booby in had been turquoise and green. Even her bikini was green. He'd appreciated that a lot last night.

She cocked her head and gave him a look that said, *Well?*

'I don't doubt your qualifications, Ivy, but we don't have any paid positions right now.'

'Payment?' She looked affronted. 'You think I'm here looking for a job? I just told you, Jero, I have my own clinic in Galway. Although I've recently contemplated selling, if you must know; there's talk of an acquisition by a private-equity-backed group, Blue Stream Veterinary Alliance?'

She paused as if he might have heard of it, which of course he hadn't. 'They're very impressed with our...' She trailed off, maybe sensing his amusement.

'Anyway. I'm here on my honeymoon.' Her eyes darted sideways. 'Kind of.'

He felt his eyebrows arc to his hairline. Now, this was interesting. *Kind of?*

'I'm just offering my help while I'm here. It's what I do. You have other volunteers, don't you?'

He perched on the edge of the table, folding his arms again and catching her trace his tattoo with her eyes. 'Why would you want to volunteer here while you're on your honeymoon? Wouldn't that cut into your cocktail-sipping, scuba-diving agenda?'

Ivy's amber eyes drew a line up from his tattoo to his face. When they locked onto his he wondered how she'd stuck a hummingbird in place of his heart already. She'd done it yesterday too, in the hotel lobby, the second she'd looked up at him with that booby fledgling in her hands.

He dragged a hand along his chin, trying not to linger in her stare, or let his eyes drop to her shapely legs in those shorts. Ivy Malone was something to look at with that sharp, diminutive chin and angular cheekbones, and breasts like two squeezable peaches in a green bikini.

She was married, he reminded himself. On her honeymoon.

'I'm pretty sure your husband wants you with him at any rate; hotels like the one you guys are in cost a fortune,' he said. 'If I were you, I'd be horizontal on a sunbed…'

He stopped talking. That might have come out wrong; he'd been distracted.

'My husband's not here.' Ivy swiped her fingertip across a photo of his team, taken six months ago on turtle release day, then swiped the dust off onto her jean shorts. He cringed inside. The reception area wasn't exactly spotless today. *Or any day.*

'I don't have a husband.' She paused. 'Not even a fiancé any more.'

'I'm confused.' Jero rubbed his arms, blindsided. The Aqua Breeze Couples' Resort was famous for honeymooners and…well…couples.

'Don't be. It's really very clear. I have spare time, and you look like you could do with some help around here.'

She motioned with her eyes to the mountain of paperwork on the desk, and the Manila files poking haphazardly from the cardboard boxes on the shelving unit by the wall. He prayed the posters wouldn't start drooping under her scrutiny.

The surgery and storage rooms were spotless, of course, someone cleaned those every day, meticulously, which was why no one had time to sort the reception area out—they were too busy. Always. It was one thing after the other and his team of volunteers were already all in a million places at once.

But that wasn't all he was thinking now. This woman needed a distraction from whatever had happened with her…fiancé?

What went down there? A woman honeymooning alone at the island's top five-star couples-only resort was not exactly an everyday occurrence. Was she a jilted bride, maybe?

What if her would-be husband had dropped dead or something? He'd heard a story like that once from a chambermaid at The Spotted Finch Hotel in town. Some guy had a heart attack the night of the wedding and left his wife of less than eight hours a widow.

A widow at Ivy's age; what was she, mid-thirties? That would be even worse than what had happened to him and Aayla, which the whole island agreed, mostly behind his and his daughter's back, was pretty terrible.

'Just think about it?' she pushed, digging into her denim pocket and producing a business card. He turned it over in his hand, feeling his lips twitch at the cliched pawprint logo above the web address. 'Look me up. I think you'll find I'm legitimate.'

'I have no doubt,' he heard himself say, studying the slightly crumpled card. *Ivy Malone.* It sounded like a song in his brain. He found himself scrubbing a hand through where his hair used to be. He'd shaved it a week ago. It was getting too damn hot again already.

'I'll be waiting to hear from you, then,' she said. Ivy turned to leave, but swung back at the last second, picking up a book that was threatening to fall from the low-level table by the door—one of many Spanish- and English-language books he kept here for Aayla. She was fluent in both.

'I used to love this book!'

Opening it at the centre, Ivy traced a finger over the

hungry caterpillar, and her face lit up like sunshine. 'Ooh, it's in Spanish, of course. I wonder if it's the same as I remember it in English. I used to read this to my dog, Zeus.'

'Really?'

Her eyes narrowed. 'Zeus appreciated it when I read to him.'

'It was one of my favourites, too,' he said, noticing the dust-free streak her finger had left on the team photo—he really should dust it all off. In fact, he was going to do that the second she left. 'I kept it for my daughter—she's six, and now *she* loves it, maybe more than I ever did.'

'Oh, yes, you have a daughter. Nayely from the hotel did mention that.'

He bristled. So, she'd heard the story too, then. Nayely had probably recounted it all when he'd left the lobby, whether Ivy had asked her about him or not. Single father, born in Quito, raised in Texas, moved to the Galapagos eight years ago, married a tourist he assumed, wrongly, wanted what he did—the happy family, the life they went on to build—who then went on to ditch him for another tourist. A corporate overlord from Washington DC, no less. All of which left him raising their 'wild', 'feral' island child here alone.

He'd had various exaggerated accounts of it relayed to him over the years. No one could keep anything to themselves around here.

Ivy flicked through the pages, bobbing her head of curls as if reliving her own childhood memories. 'You can borrow it if you want,' he heard himself say, just as he noticed she didn't look happy in this moment of nostalgia any more.

She frowned. 'I'll leave it with you. Just in case we don't actually see each other again.'

'Retracting your offer to volunteer for me, now that you've seen the state of this place?'

'Is that what you want?' She placed the book back on the table slowly and he kicked himself for highlighting the mess.

'Not necessarily,' he added quickly. The state of things at the clinic had nothing to do with why she wouldn't take the book, he could tell that much by the look on her face. Not that he had time to read into it. He could see a call-out coming in as they spoke.

Ivy forced another smile in his direction. 'Well, thanks for letting me check on the booby, Jero. Do let me know if you need me,' she said on her way out.

Jero thought about Ivy most of the afternoon, and the morning after that as he made his way to the fish market. Maybe he should just let her work with him. He sure needed her.

But maybe he shouldn't.

Why the hell did accepting help from anyone he hadn't personally invited into his orbit still get old wounds stinging?

His trust issues caused him to cut off his own nose to spite his face sometimes, but the way she'd told him how he clearly needed some help…that still stung.

He should be able to juggle everything by now; it shouldn't matter one iota that he was raising Aayla on his own and running the island's only veterinary clinic, as well as a hundred other projects. He should be able to stay on top of his work *and* provide everything she needed. Millions of people got divorced and made it work. Everything should be under control and on his own terms by now: his life, his home, his work.

Except it wasn't.

Yolanda, the National Park vet, was still off raising funds for a new project on the mainland. Zenon, who'd been on Guayaquil time since his arrival six months ago, had taken a second sick day in a row.

Dudders—short for Daniel Dudley—his well-meaning import from Britain via a gap year at a monkey sanctuary in Thailand, had turned up an hour late again, albeit dragging a crate of overdue dog food he'd lugged all the way from the ferry port.

Things were always late. So were people. He needed another pair of hands; someone he could count on. Hailey, the first full-time surgeon he'd managed to keep for longer than a year, was still in New Zealand, nursing her sick father. He really should advertise the position again, but she'd begged him not to. She wanted to return. She just didn't know when she could.

The sterilisation programme they'd started called him all over the place. No one with an unsterilised dog was refused, which meant he'd put out a mobile service to the other inhabited islands too—Isabela, San Cristobal, and Floreana.

It was against Galapagos laws to transport any animals between islands. Cross-contamination was a big deal; they had to go to them. Cats and dogs carried diseases and parasites that affected the endemic wildlife. The result was sadly much animal neglect, homelessness and overpopulation. If *they* didn't keep it under control, more local wildlife would suffer. It was all hands on deck, *without* all the other work on top…

'Fancy seeing you here.' A familiar Irish voice stopped him in his tracks. Ivy's eyes fell to where Aayla was standing at his side five metres from the port, where the Puerto Ayora fish market was as loud and smelly as ever.

Her small hand clutched his tighter as she slurped the last dregs from a carton of orange juice.

'Oh…hi…you.' Ivy looked and sounded kind of uncomfortable.

Aayla swallowed loudly. 'Hi,' she echoed, eyeing her in interest from under her sunhat. 'I like your camera.'

'Er… Thanks.' Ivy refocused on him, squared her slender shoulders. 'So, you didn't call.'

Awkward.

He pulled his sunglasses off his face and…damn, she was striking in the blazing sunlight. The breeze blew in across the crowds and the port and tussled with her red curls; the colour of flames in a wildfire, he thought, watching them lick her shoulder blades.

She was still wearing the shorts, this time with a skimpy white cotton vest top tucked in behind the camera hanging around her neck. No green…except for the headband and dangly emerald earrings. Her shapely legs went on for ever before they hit the flip-flops on her feet. Her pale milky skin was a little red around the bikini straps, not that he should be looking.

'I was going to get in touch. I've just been…'

'Busy?' she finished, just as a sea lion's bellow from behind her made her jump and almost land in his arms.

Aayla giggled. 'That's just Álvaro. He's not scary!'

Aayla was used to things like this. Flapping giant wings, swishing tails like swords and wildlife honking louder than a city-centre traffic jam were normal to most people round here. Obviously they weren't to Ivy. A crowd of locals lining up for their fish sniggered at her 'tourist' reaction. Álvaro—a fish market resident who probably weighed as much as a small elephant—was laughing too; at least it seemed as if he was laughing. Ivy broke contact from where her hand had landed on his other arm.

'Sorry,' she said, flustered, before catching his gaze and holding it.

'Aayla, go see Marsha over there,' he instructed, still glued to her eyes.

Ivy was irrefutably attractive. But *that* look in her eyes…that was it. That was what had rattled the cage he sometimes forgot his heart was all locked up in.

He hadn't felt a pull like this to anyone in a long time. He'd probably, on some subconscious level, turned a blind eye to his needs in *that* department since Mitch, the Washington overlord, sailed up to the island and left seven months later having fully secured Jero's wife for himself. He still couldn't say Suranne's name out loud without it burning like a bad tattoo. She was meant to call Aayla last Sunday. She still hadn't bothered.

'Daddy! Over here!' Aayla was waving at him profusely from Marsha's table, covered with crates of iced yellowfin tuna, groupers and red snapper. 'Daddy, there are seven of them!'

'Seven of what?' Ivy looked primed for involvement in whatever Aayla was talking about now.

Looks like this woman isn't going anywhere.

With a heavy sigh under his breath, he beckoned her with him as he stepped over Álvaro, and a pelican promptly tried to land on his shoulder. Waving it off gently, he led her to Marsha's market stall, where Aayla was already on bended knees, lifting the plastic sheet up and peering into a box on the concrete floor.

'Found them this morning,' Marsha said, stepping around his daughter to hand a paper parcel of hot-pink scorpion fish over to a customer. 'Figured you were the man to call. Didn't have time to drop them off before I had to be here.'

'You did the right thing,' he said. Marsha was like a mother to him, and most people on the island. Her stall at the fish market had been manned—or womanned, as she liked to say—for the last four generations and this sea lion had become somewhat of her surrogate son.

'They're probably only three, maybe four weeks old,' Ivy said as they both dropped beside Aayla to inspect the puppies. Each one was a slightly different colour, their ears still pink and floppy, wriggling and writhing around on top of each other.

'Any sign of the mother?' he asked Marsha. Then he realised Ivy had said the exact same thing in harmony.

'You're funny.' Aayla giggled. 'I like your camera.'

Ivy suppressed a smile. 'You already said that.'

Aayla looked up at her beseechingly. 'Can I take some photos of them?'

'Not now.'

Ivy stepped away as he pulled the cardboard box of puppies out and Marsha swept a fish head off her table of fresh catch, narrowly missing Ivy's head. Álvaro waddled up for his prize. Just then, a battle commenced between him and the pelican in a showdown of wings, squawks and honks, but Ivy wasn't even looking now. Her amber eyes stayed fixed on the pups as he placed them on a nearby empty table. One by one she helped him check them over, while the tourists looked on in interest. No visible signs of injury. But Marsha hadn't seen the mother either.

'We'll get them to the clinic. They'll need de-worming asap,' he told her. 'Then I guess we add them to the adoption register.'

Ivy raised an eyebrow. 'We. Does that mean you want me on your team?'

Now it was his turn to suppress a smile.

Her qualifications were undeniably impressive. He himself had internal medicine and emergencies covered, but Ivy was a licensed orthopaedic surgeon with countless other creds in animal care. From what he'd seen online, aside from the Doctor of Veterinary Medicine, she had more testimonials and glowing accolades and award-winning papers under her belt than anyone he'd ever met. It looked as if she hadn't done anything but work since she graduated vet school…if anything she was overqualified, but she did seem enthusiastic.

Or she wants to distract herself on her solo honeymoon. What the hell happened there?

Why did he even care? He needed help at the clinic, and help was what he'd got, of literally the highest degree.

'Can I take some photos now?' Aayla asked as they made their way back to his car. She made a grab for the camera, and he told her to watch her manners. Aayla pouted. Ivy looked unsure, but eventually she unhooked it from around her neck and handed it over, which made him smile.

'You have to look through here,' she explained, stopping on the dusty palm-lined path to the road to lean over his curious daughter's slight, six-year-old frame and show her the viewfinder.

Something in him shifted as her bright red curls meshed with his daughter's volcano-black locks for just a second. If only he could get a photo from where *he* was standing, but his arms were full of puppies. Aayla had never held a real camera before.

'Don't drop it,' Ivy pleaded.

Aayla tutted. 'Why would I drop it?'

The two of them bantered all the way back to the clinic, in the back seat with the puppies. He listened in, fighting back the odd laugh. Ivy probed him on his role, work, the clinic, the sterilisation programme, while Aayla probed *her* on how to use the camera.

From Ivy's short, not cold, but slightly awkward answers to all of Aayla's questions he got the impression that she hadn't spent much time around kids. At times she spoke like some kind of robot: forced, mechanical. Aayla just found her more amusing for it.

'You're good with her,' he told her later, when they'd settled the pups into their cage in the back room, now thankfully wormed and vaccinated. Seven less domestics to worry about—they'd be put up for adoption as soon as Dudders got back from wherever he was now and entered them into the system. That was his role.

One of them anyway. Dudders had many roles, they all did.

'Did you hear me? I said Aayla seems to like you,' he said again, when he realised she hadn't responded.

He was surprised that a compliment regarding a stranger with Aayla came so easily out of his mouth when normally it would take ages to even think that about a new person. But from her trepidation he sensed it was something Ivy might need to hear. Anyway, Ivy Malone was going to have to get used to Aayla if she was going to be hanging around the clinic, he thought. It was basically the kid's second home, when she wasn't at school or with Nina, her nanny.

'I'm really *not* good with kids,' she replied now, crouching over their little booby fledgling. Aayla had named her already—Pluma, which meant 'feather'.

Jero peered around the door, where Aayla was colouring in a picture book of cats at the little table. 'She's never held a real camera before. Not till you showed her yours,' he told her.

Ivy curled her fingers round the bird's cage, peering inside. Her face got lost behind her mass of red hair. 'I know cameras, that's all. Cameras and animals.'

There was a sadness to her tone again, and he didn't know what to say. Pluma was cooing in her own little cage under the Darwin quote poster, which read: *The love for all living creatures is the most noble attribute of man.* Hailey had scribbled out *man* and replaced it with *woman*, and he was just about to comment on it, to break the awkward silence, when Aayla bounced back in and asked if she could help Ivy feed worms to Pluma, then take more photos.

He shifted a pile of unattended paperwork to locate the worms and tried to ignore the look Ivy shot him. Yes, OK, the place could be a little more organised, he'd been meaning to address that, but calls were coming in already. A tortoise with a cracked shell and flesh wound over on Floreana that he'd have to see to onsite, thanks to Yolanda being off-island. A pregnant dog had also just been found in a rubbish container.

He answered a call from Zenon, who'd finally woken up from his siesta, watching Ivy and Aayla interact around Pluma the whole time.

Poor little Pluma had probably been abandoned by her mother after being attacked, he thought, trying to ignore the way he couldn't stop wondering things about Ivy. She was here to work, that was all, and she was under no obligation to tell him anything else about herself. Just because she'd probably heard everything about him, from the island gossips, didn't mean it was his place to ask what happened with her ex, or why she was honeymooning alone. Or why she assumed she'd never been any good with kids.

She was reserved around his daughter, sure, but a little less awkward now than when they'd first met, a couple of hours ago.

'Look, Ivy, Pluma just lifted her head up!'

'You're right, she did. She's getting stronger already.'

Despite her insistence on being no good with kids, if it carried on like this, the two might actually form some kind of friendship, he thought to himself absently. Aayla was pretty addictive, but maybe he was biased.

Ivy would be out and about all the time, with him more than Aayla—if she wanted to work, he'd give her work. Besides, tourists never stuck around too long anyway.

Especially unmarried, single, highly qualified, strikingly beautiful ones...

Good thing too, he thought suddenly, catching himself. He'd have to start making sure they didn't bond, for Aayla's sake.

There was absolutely no way he'd have his daughter's heart broken by anyone *else* filling her head with possibilities, and then walking out of her world.

CHAPTER THREE

IVY FLATTENED A hand to her hair. The salty ocean breeze was going to leave it looking wilder than ever after this boat ride. She wouldn't care if she weren't with Jero but she'd caught him looking at her as if she were some kind of entertaining alien over the past few days and it was making her self-conscious.

They'd been talking about climate change. How the United Nations reported up to thirty per cent of plant and animal species around the world were at risk of extinction. 'I know islands like this are especially vulnerable,' she said now, over the sound of the engine.

Jero bobbed his shaved head towards the island ahead. The boat was speeding towards Floreana, where a café owner had called concerned about a mystery wound on his dog's hind leg.

'Why do you think I stay out here?' he said. 'There's more work to do than you even know.'

Ivy pursed her lips, training her eyes on the slope of his nose. The sun was reflecting the ocean spray in his sunglasses, hiding those dreamy eyes. OK, she might have told a little white lie to Mike this morning when she said she didn't find her new Galapagos mentor hot, but it wasn't for a man, or anyone, to tell her what she knew.

Then again, he had a point. What did she know? This was her first visit to the Galapagos after all.

'So…how long have you been out here?' she asked, watching the pier draw closer. The midday sun was already scorching her bare arms through her sunscreen; this place was still a shock to her Irish skin. 'I'm guessing you weren't born in the Galapagos Islands, like Aayla was?'

His dark brows drew together. 'Nope. My parents raised me a Galveston boy. We lived one mile from the beach…in fact I haven't lived that far away from it since.'

Ah, that was right, Texas, she thought, remembering what the receptionist at the hotel had said.

Jero tossed the buffers over the side of the boat, and she pretended not to notice how his sunscreened olive biceps glistened like a rock under his black tattoo. Simon hadn't had a bad physique, but he'd been nowhere near as muscular or toned. She wondered, would the magic have lasted longer if he had been more physically attractive, instead of kind, attentive and…safe?

Was there ever really any magic to begin with?

Ivy frowned to herself. Sometimes she had to think really hard about that. Maybe she'd wanted the magic so much that she'd merely convinced herself that she and Simon had it.

In truth, her heart had never really had to heal from Simon, because it hadn't been all that broken by the break-up. She hadn't ever admitted that to anyone—it was hard enough to admit it to herself, let alone everyone else. Her friends all seemed to expect a crumpled mess in her company after it all fell apart. So how could she admit that she'd spent over four long years with someone who, through no real fault of his own, had failed to make her feel the way she truly *wanted* to feel about a partner, a husband? That she'd been waiting for the sparks to suddenly ignite?

She always knew they wouldn't. But safety and security meant more than physical attraction and chemistry. Those things were more important. Those were the things she *needed*.

At least, that was what she'd told herself after the string of man-children she'd met online, who'd disappeared after just one date. Maybe she'd given up, after that. It wasn't something she enjoyed thinking about, but maybe she'd 'settled' with Simon out of fear she'd never meet anyone she really connected with. The kids thing had been a convenient excuse to get out of it, really, in the end. A wake-up call.

What was Jero's tattoo of? She studied it again, while he bantered with the driver in Spanish, and tried to shove Simon from her head.

God, it was sexy hearing Jero speak Spanish. She spoke a little herself, but the two spoke so fast she could barely keep up. It bothered her, feeling left out, no thanks to spending the majority of her formative years all by herself. Well, apart from the nanny.

Maybe it bothered her more because she liked Jero more than she wanted to already, more than was safe to, considering her temporary status here. Best to keep it professional, she decided. A 'look but don't touch' kind of thing. It wouldn't be hard. Aside from his looks, he was still somewhat a mystery.

She knew about his work obviously. And how his full-time surgeon Hailey, had left for New Zealand, leaving him with a team of volunteers who weren't always the most reliable. She'd seen them do things around the clinic that they certainly wouldn't be doing if they worked for *her*.

But he was doing immeasurable good around the islands. Late last year they'd managed to acquire a new licence and had sterilised almost two thousand animals. They'd worked hard to eradicate the threat of parvovirus and stop distemper reaching the Galapagos sea lion population.

Jero had explained how he'd started leading outreach events and doing school talks too. Most people thought the thousands of dogs on the four inhabited islands were harmless. But he'd stressed to her how they were very much invasive animals, who harassed and preyed on the finches and marine and land iguanas, the birds and, Aayla's favourites, the young giant tortoises. It was nothing short of inspiring, how he wanted to educate people and train even more Galapagos community members and give them the tools to secure a sustainable future. All of this was as important to Jero as raising Aayla.

Well, almost.

It was obvious that Jero loved that little girl like nothing else. Aayla Morales *was* pretty cute, Ivy thought now, all big brown, bright joyous eyes, and raven-black hair with a glossy sheen she'd have killed for as a kid. She had crazy curls, and rosy cheeks you just wanted to squeeze. Watching them together made Ivy forget herself sometimes; she just wished she were as good with her as Jero seemed to think she was. Obviously he only said that stuff to be nice.

She swallowed back the bitter taste that always came when she was reminded, in any way, of how bad she was with kids. Even though Simon had argued it was all in her head. He'd said she was calling herself 'unsuitable' and them 'noisy' or 'expensive' or 'time-consuming' as excuses to not have them herself, because she was afraid she'd be a bad mother, as her own was.

Maybe he was half right. Or maybe she just didn't want to go there with *him*.

Ugh.

It didn't matter, she was only here for another couple of weeks. She might as well use her experience to be of use. And learn something too. What else was she supposed to do?

'Relax!' Mike had almost yelled at her this morning, after he'd wound her up unknowingly by mentioning the acquisition again. Blue Stream Veterinary Alliance were coming down hard now, upping their offer, not just for the central location in Galway, but for the reputation they'd spent years building. It meant freedom for her and Mike, to cast their nets wider somewhere else, or to just enjoy a small fortune, but this was her baby!

She was trying not to think about it here; although, if she was honest, this *was* one of the reasons she'd come away. To think. Money wasn't everything.

'Experiences like this are better for my mental health,' she'd told him anyway. *'It's invaluable really.'*

He'd asked if it had anything to do with Jero—he'd looked him up, apparently, called him 'her type', as if she had a type. She'd told him absolutely not.

A big, fat, not-so-little white lie.

Jero was very easy on the eye. Even when the state of the Darwin Animal Clinic gave her heart palpitations, just looking at him made it less relevant somehow.

That place was far from organised. Volunteers were expected to work five days a week and help with being on call on weekends, on a shared rota. They worked seven-thirty a.m. to eleven-thirty a.m., closed for a long siesta, which everyone took but herself and Jero, then reopened in the late afternoon once the temperature had dropped. Sometimes they worked till seven-thirty p.m.

Typically, surgeries including spaying and neutering were performed in the morning, and most walk-in consultations or off-island calls were in the afternoon. No one was fully responsible for filing the paperwork in those ridiculously outdated Manila folders, as far as she could tell. Everyone did their bit, or at least they were supposed to.

She was itching to reorganise. Practically chomping at the bit already, but no.

It wasn't her place to get involved in any of that. She could get bossy and she knew it. Things were different here; they were also working with far less than adequate equipment. But yikes! How anyone could work like that for long was a mystery to her.

'So, what brought you over here?' she asked Jero, realising she'd been watching him, watching the waves, reorganising his life in her head.

'I moved back to Quito to study.'

'Back to?'

'I was born in Ecuador. It was Dad's job that took us to Texas, but I guess I never felt like I belonged there. I opened the clinic on Santa Cruz a couple years before Aayla came along; it was just a shack then. Grew it out from there, had our own place built in town. Home is home, you know? I think your heart knows, anyway.'

Ivy nodded thoughtfully. Her heart had never known anything but Ireland. Was she boring? Gosh, maybe he thought her so. Her pride went down a notch on the spot.

Jero finished swigging from a bottle of water, kicked a foot up on the bench opposite her and gripped the mast with one big hand as they bumped over a wave. 'My ex-wife, she's American. Met her right here. She was on vacation. Never thought I'd marry a tourist but...'

'Your heart knows, right?'

Jero tossed the water bottle into a crate and huffed a laugh that made her kick herself. 'Never thought I'd divorce one either. But we had Aayla. So, I must have done something right.'

She pulled a face. He was divorced, of course, why had she just said that? Why was he making her nervous?

He grabbed up the bag of supplies they'd brought, and she followed him to the front of the boat, where the driver, Nico, hosed their feet, hands and legs down while a big fat sea lion eyed them sleepily from one of the benches by the pier.

It was still weird, this washing process. Jero said it was to eliminate any bacteria and prevent contamination between the islands.

They walked in silence along the sandy cobblestone road towards the café. His butt looked like two more rocks, and she couldn't help wondering if it was as hard as it looked in those black shorts. Was he still single?

She couldn't help but hope he was, even though it didn't matter in the slightest really. Dating a father meant the child came along with him, and for multiple reasons she was definitely not what either of them needed.

Jero was a man of few words when it came to his private life, but his unsettled state about his ex had been more than clear in his clipped tone back on the boat. She did already know *some* of his story. All she'd done was ask Nayely if he'd lived on the island long—out of interest, because he was a vet too, not because visions of his buff body and piercing eyes had struck her like a gamma ray at first sight.

Nayely had told her the whole story. Her version anyway, right after he'd left the lobby. He'd married some younger woman, a tourist. Bit of a whirlwind situation, apparently. Aayla was a mistake, but he'd loved her mother madly; Aayla too when she came along. Then, a few years later his wife wound up cheating on him with some other American guy who'd been visiting the island. She and this new guy lived in Washington DC now. They had another kid and she hardly ever called Aayla. Jero was raising their daughter alone…with a nanny, whom Ivy hadn't met yet.

Aayla was always either at school, where she was now, or in the clinic, trailing *her*, asking if she could use her camera.

Annoying.

Well…not annoying, Ivy caught herself. That was unfair; she was just being a kid. She was more annoyed at herself for never knowing how to act around her. Of course it must show. At least they had little Pluma and the puppies to care for together. Aayla loved that little booby bird; she'd taken some pretty good photos of her too, so far. OK, a few blurry ones also, but the girl was a good listener, picked things up fast. Maybe Ivy should let her use the camera more often, she considered, under strict supervision, of course.

'What are you smiling at?' Jero opened the door to the run-down shack that constituted a café and her stomach performed a little flip at the look on his face.

'What do you mean?'

'You were smiling, ear to ear.'

'Was I?' she said.

Well, look at that. She actually had been.

Luckily the middle-aged island local in the roadside café near the beach just needed an introduction to some of Jero's antibiotic ointment. Ivy covered the wound on the simpering dog's hind leg with a sterile gauze pad and told the portly man in a vest top not to let the dog lick the affected area.

'We need a cone, really,' she told Jero, touching his arm lightly, registering how the heat of him did something to her insides instantly.

'We don't use them—they create too much plastic waste,' he said, swiping a hand across his forehead.

'How did it happen?' she asked the rotund man in the vest. He was sipping from a can of beer with his feet up on a stack of cardboard boxes in the storage room, watching them kneel on the floor in the hot, stuffy room beside his dog. He said he didn't know, which left Ivy more concerned than she thought best to show.

'People don't always treat their animals here like they do in the west,' Jero told her, on their way back out into the sunshine. It was late afternoon now, and she was tired from the long day attending to calls like this.

'I was starting to get that impression.'

'They just let them wander around, or chain them up as guard dogs. At least we got him to bring him to the mobile clinic next week, when we come back to sterilise.'

We. There it was again. She followed him back up the dusty path. It was nice that he was starting to see her as a real valuable team member, and the word sounded inclusive on a level that lifted her heart for a second…but she did have a flight home booked in two weeks' time.

'Wait.' Jero put an arm out. Ivy stopped in her tracks. She sucked in a breath at the almost-contact. 'Look,' he said, and she followed his eyes to the sea beyond the bushes and the tiny beach ahead, framed by dark lava rocks and palo santo trees.

'What is it?' She was intrigued now by the sight of the water. It looked as if a set of special waves were erupting in a current of their own. Jero sprinted across the road to the beach, dropped the bag to the sand and started fishing masks and snorkels out of it quickly. Another sea lion and its calf watched them from the shoreline, then waddled into the water as she reached him.

'This is rare to see from the beach, if it is what I think it is!' His enthusiasm was so infectious she laughed. 'You don't want to miss this,' he said, and swiftly pulled his shirt over his head. She almost staggered backwards. His ripped torso totally tore her eyes from the weird commotion in the water.

Wow.

Was he going to pull his shorts off too?

Nope. He made a hurry-up movement with his hand.

'OK, OK!' Stripping down to her bikini, she didn't even have time to feel self-conscious, even when he fixed the mask over her head and pulled at the straps, being careful not to pull her hair.

'How does that feel?' His deep chocolate eyes searched hers and her brain went blank. His body was everything she'd expected, and his breath turned her insides to fire. It, mingled with his suntan lotion, created an inexplicably delicious tang.

'It feels good,' she managed, and he smiled with one side of his mouth, then shook his head, as if he was battling something he wanted to say all of a sudden. Apprehension pooled in her belly. Then he motioned her into the water.

In seconds his strong arms were carving through the turquoise shallows with her close behind. A green sea turtle gave her the eye from the seabed, but still he pressed on. She had no clue what they were even aiming for... Until she saw it.

The giant manta ray stole all the breath from her lungs as she stopped just short of ploughing into Jero in the water. He grinned around his snorkel as her eyes grew wide. The creature was as huge as a silver satellite dish, gracefully gliding through the blue with no apparent fear of their proximity. Inches from her mask, it was overwhelming to see, but then it performed some kind of spinning move, spiralling up to the surface, sending her and Jero to the surface with it.

'They breach like this, to get the parasites off their undersides,' he explained, pulling his mask and snorkel down to his neck. He found her hand and she gasped, tasting salt at the back of her throat. His brow furrowed as he drew her closer. 'Are you OK?'

She was trying not to show it, because the spectacle was incredible, but they'd swum a little too far out than she was really comfortable with. 'I'm OK. That was… beautiful.' She laughed softly, knowing her nervousness escaped with it.

'You're a good swimmer, aren't you? I didn't even ask.' Jero trod water, right up close; so close his billowing shorts tickled her hipbones and sent a different kind of current rippling through her insides. She studied the droplets of water on his thick black eyelashes as he took her shoulders with firm reassuring hands. The whole ocean seemed to close in around them.

'I followed you out here, didn't I?' confusion made her snap before she swam away from him on her back.

Distance was imperative, before she lost her mind completely. What the heck was that? She'd almost wanted to pull him close, to feel those muscles pressed against her. The way he'd been looking at her; she knew that look. He might not have pushed her away but no…no way.

The guy wasn't in it for some silly fling with a volunteer and she certainly wasn't here for that either. Especially not with a single dad. Her libido was too fired up; she'd been single for the majority of the year, and since she'd got here to the Galapagos she'd been a permanent odd one out around all those mushy couples at the hotel. He probably hadn't felt half of what she'd just felt; it was all in her head. He was merely concerned she might drown.

Jero was already underwater, diving back down to the manta. Reluctantly she followed him back down into the blue, mind reeling. But as soon as she was under, a sense of calm enveloped her and stuck, even when she was forced up for air. The sight of Jero circling the manta as it drifted silently around the coral like a silver spaceship was as mesmerising as the creature itself.

Suddenly, another one appeared from the blue. Then another, until there were five. The commanding creatures were hypnotising, dancing like a synchronised swimming team. Wow. Maybe *this* was how she meditated, from now on.

Back on the beach Ivy got her first glimpse of Jero's full tattoo up close. It wasn't a dragon, as she'd thought from past stolen glimpses. It was actually a giant manta like the one they'd just seen, swimming at an angle, drawn from jet-black blocks of what looked like Mayan symbols.

Sexy as hell on his tanned upper arm.

He caught her looking at it as he stuffed the snorkels back into his bag, and she couldn't divert her eyes fast enough.

'When did you get that?' she asked, to mask the fact that she was now entirely too self-conscious of her wet white shirt over her bikini. He shrugged back into his shirt, swiped a hand over his head and slung the bag back over the other shoulder. Then he pulled up his sleeve again, revealing the tattoo to her, like an art piece he'd spent hours sculpting, as he obviously had his arm.

'I got it after my first visit here, when I came to see if I could really live here.'

She cleared her throat. 'Nice,' she said, wondering if he could tell how he was making her feel, getting half naked and showing her the wonders of the deep. How dared he? Now she wanted to do it again. 'What does it mean?'

He cocked an eyebrow, pulled his sleeve back down. 'It means I got a tattoo.'

'Yes, but all those symbols.'

'Do they have to have a meaning?'

She rolled her eyes but couldn't help match his smile as he led her back to the road and made for the boat.

'I want to snorkel again,' she said when they were bumping their way back across to Santa Cruz. Jero laughed behind his sunglasses, a foot away from her on the bench.

'You're in the right place. I think your hotel runs snorkelling trips, right?'

She frowned at the horizon. 'Yeah, right. Me and a bunch of couples. Sounds like a blast.'

Jero ran a hand along his jaw, and she felt her face redden. She hadn't meant to imply she was resentful or have him worry about her for any reason. 'I mean, I'd much rather spend my time with you...volunteering. For the next two weeks. I'm learning a lot. And that's something I don't say often to strangers.'

'I'm a stranger, am I?' He smirked into his shoulder, and she gripped the mast, feeling herself sliding towards him with the motion of the boat; or the undeniable chemistry she could feel intensifying by the second. Unless she was imagining it? She still couldn't decide, but, really, why would someone like Jero want anything more than her skill set?

'Funny you think that,' he said. 'You know more about me than I know about you.'

She squared her shoulders. He had a point. She hadn't exactly spilled her heart to her newly appointed mentor about Simon, or the break-up, or the reasons behind it. Jero was a father; one who was raising his daughter alone. Besides, he'd never asked her much about herself anyway.

'All by yourself at the Aqua Breeze,' he continued now, making her heart tangle up in her ribs. He reached for two more bottles of water, passed one to her, eyeing her almost cautiously. 'What are you doing tonight?'

Her head sprang up to meet his eyes. She had a date with a treatment and nutrition plan for Mrs O'Brian's senior cocker spaniel back in Galway, which she'd insisted on helping with from afar, much to Mike's very vocal chagrin. 'I did have a plan...'

'Cancel it. There's a beach clean-up we do every week. I usually man the barbecue afterwards for the volunteers. It's a fun time, you should join us.'

Ivy looked to her feet, feeling his eyes still roving her profile. Butterflies fluttered a trail around her navel. 'I'll think about it. Thank you.'

He nodded and took a swig from the bottle that showcased his Adam's apple and his biceps from a whole new intoxicating angle. She resisted the urge to say she'd come.

She probably shouldn't.

She should be gunning the butterflies down one by one, right as they took flight. It would be a very good idea to stay away from all non-work-related events with Jero; picturing him naked when they were supposed to be saving lives together was not conducive to a productive learning environment. If only she could forget this unfortunate, futile crush.

CHAPTER FOUR

JERO FLIPPED A veggie burger over on the grill, feeling Nayely's and Martha's eyes on him from across the beach. They were talking about him; he could always tell.

The sun was sinking lower, and the beach clean-up was well under way; scores of locals and the odd tourist had already filled a pile of rubbish bags with washed up flip-flops and plastic bottles. His eyes found Ivy, deeply involved as he'd guessed she might be if she showed up... which she had done, an hour late.

He'd spent that hour thinking maybe she wouldn't come.

They'd shared something intimate with those mantas. It had gone beyond all physical contact, or even words. Something had changed in that moment, being with her in the water. On the boat after that, the air had felt physically charged. He could have sworn she felt it too—the way she'd avoided his eyes but couldn't keep hers off his body. The secret thrill had made him ask her here, to something that wasn't work-related.

He was regretting it already. The more he found his eyes roving her figure as she followed the shoreline in a long sea-green sundress, the more he felt unsettled. She even looked good picking up rubbish.

He flipped another burger on the grill and served three

hungry customers, irritated at the way he couldn't keep his eyes off her, bathed in the final streaks of sunlight. The woman was leaving in a matter of weeks, and even if he did go 'there' with tourists, which he absolutely did not, she was *working* with him. Around Aayla. The last thing he needed was for things to get complicated.

She was walking across the sand now, making a bee-line for him. Damn, that long sundress was almost see-through in places, with the setting sun behind her. She was a knockout, in and out of the bikini he'd seen her in today.

'Hey, Ivy, you made it.'

She cast her amber eyes up and down his apron and tongs. 'Hey, yourself, chef.'

He was about to offer her his speciality—grilled shrimp and pineapple skewers—when Aayla bounded over, pigtails flying, covered in sand. He handed her a wet towel for her hands, which she ignored. 'Ivy! Did you bring your camera?'

'Not tonight...sorry,' she said, holding her empty hands up while Aayla pouted.

'Ivy's camera is not your toy,' he reminded her, handing her the towel again, and Aayla rolled her eyes, swiping at her dirty hands with it for all of three seconds before handing it to Ivy.

Ivy held the towel at arm's length, as if it were some strange, foreign artefact he'd just dug up from a Mayan tomb. He bit back a smile, tossing it into a rubbish bag for her.

'Ivy, I thought of a new game we can play with the puppies tomorrow,' Aayla said, eyes bright.

'Why don't you go play with Sasha?' he cut in, tossing a sausage in a bun for another customer.

She ignored him, casting her usual beseeching gaze up at Ivy. 'We can teach them to roll over!'

'Aayla…'

'I think they're a little young to roll over,' Ivy answered, passing him the ketchup when she saw he had his hands full. 'Maybe when they get adopted, their new parents can teach them that?'

Aayla frowned thoughtfully. Jero was about to direct her towards her playdate again, but Ivy had another idea. 'We could try teaching them to sit if you like? Most puppies pick that up pretty quickly if we give them treats.'

Aayla's eyes lit up. 'Can we photograph them, while they learn?'

'Maybe. Let me think about it.'

Aayla seemed to think that was an appropriate answer and skipped away up the beach happily. He felt a sigh of relief escape into his barbecue smoke.

For some reason, Aayla seemed drawn to Ivy, even without the camera. She had taken to shadowing Ivy in the clinic after school, and, OK, so they'd been feeding the puppies, and caring for Pluma together, which constituted more as work than hanging out, but still. Aayla got attached easily, no thanks to a lack of a mother figure in her life, and all of this…well, this had been his fear from the start: that his daughter would be crushed once someone else she admired sped off on the tourist boat and never returned.

'You know, I've been thinking,' Ivy said now, scraping a hand through her wild curls and making the orange rays reflect off the silver bracelet around her slender wrist. 'It was pretty impressive, how you got me to switch off down there today with the mantas. You took me out of my head and put me somewhere else. That doesn't happen a lot.'

'Is that so?'

She half smiled at the ocean, then him. 'I didn't think about my emails for at least twenty minutes.'

He laughed and she shrugged. 'Sounds stupid, sure, but that's a big deal for me. I wanted to say thank you, Jero, for taking me in the way you have since we met. It means a lot.'

She turned to face him, and there it was again in her eyes: the look that spoke volumes of abject sadness, and secrets, and some kind of profound loss that had propelled her to escape into her work, even *before* she'd arrived at the Aqua Breeze Couples' Resort all alone. It made her infinitely more vulnerable to him, and he stopped himself conjuring another carnal fantasy about seeing her with that dress off.

He hadn't asked her any personal questions yet that could be construed as getting too close. Hmm. That *was* pretty selfish of him. Maybe she'd been waiting for him to ask and assumed that he just didn't care. The fact that she was here for work, to learn and to be of use was no restitution for his guilt suddenly.

'I'm happy I could help,' he told her truthfully. 'And you're helping *me* more than you know already. Your experience is invaluable.' He put down the tongs and untied his apron as his friend Nige slapped him on the back and offered to take over the barbecue duties.

'Let's go for a walk,' he said, checking Aayla was still under the supervision of Sasha's mum, as was their agreement while he was on grill duty. 'I have something I think you should see.'

She cocked an eyebrow. 'Intriguing.' Then she hesitated on the spot, as if she wasn't sure if she should leave the scene either. Was he making her nervous after that 'moment' earlier today? 'I can't be long,' she said, eyeing the crowd around the shoreline. 'I do have to get back to work.'

'What work?'

'I run a clinic…'

'How could I forget?' he teased, and she fixed her eyes on him with such piercing effect he wished he hadn't said it. 'Are you going to sell up?' he asked her, remembering she'd mentioned some private equity company trying to buy them out.

Her face fell a second. 'I don't know yet. I don't know what else I'd do if I didn't work there. It's been my whole life.'

'Work isn't your *whole* life though, is it?'

'I love my work,' she clipped. Then she sighed and huffed a laugh. 'I know, I know… I should switch off more. Everyone tells me that.'

'I can always dunk you in the ocean again, if that will help,' he offered, and her mouth twitched again.

'I suppose a little walk won't hurt.'

They headed up the beach, and around the rocks and he couldn't tell if he was unnerving her after earlier, or if she really was so into her work that she couldn't be away for more than an hour.

'I guess your partner must be freaking out without you, in Galway?' he asked as they took the narrow pathway that curved around the huge round boulders together, up, up, up towards the sky and what he knew would take her breath away.

'Mike is fine on his own,' she answered, lifting fistfuls of her sundress to walk easier. 'He always has everything under control.'

'So why are you working on your honeymoon? For your clinic as well as mine?'

The question lingered on the breeze for a moment

as a flock of white butterflies fluttered from a shrub between the rocks, engulfing them in a moving cloud. Maybe he shouldn't have called it 'honeymoon', knowing she was alone.

'I guess work is just how I survive...when things fall apart,' she answered, before tripping on her dress and almost slipping off the path.

'Careful!' Deftly he caught her elbow, looping an arm around her waist till she was steady. Her breath came fast as her palms flattened hard against his chest. One second. Two seconds. She didn't move. He didn't let her go.

'What fell apart?' His lips were an inch from her temple. More sunset butterflies swooped on the wind around them.

'We called the wedding off over half a year ago.' She gulped. 'I shouldn't have come here but... I didn't want to waste the booking. I'd also wanted to see this place my whole entire life. Now I know why.'

Jero's arm was still protecting her; maybe unnecessarily now. The ocean sparkled seductively beyond. Her curls were being lifted by the breeze and blown around his own head, trying to pull him under her perfumed spell.

Man, what is happening to you?

'Well, here you are,' he stated, releasing her, hoping she hadn't noticed his manhood rising to attention in his shorts, as it had today, being close enough to kiss her in her bikini.

'Here I am,' she replied, and the statement felt as loaded as a gun.

In minutes the chatter of the people on the beach was silenced by the ocean and the wind whipping up the grass along the ledge above the boulder wall. The pillar-box-red moss and liverwort carpets danced amid vivid purple flowers. This was one of his favourite meadows on Santa Cruz. It was even more magnificent in the sunset light.

The buteries had multiplied now, swooping in a synchronised show around the flowers as if to present each one to them. Beside him, Ivy reached for the camera that wasn't there and then grimaced regretfully.

Her dress flapped around both of their ankles as he watched her taking it in. 'It's so magical, Jero. The colours, the…'

'Butterflies,' he heard her continue under her breath as she shot a sideways glance his way. Amber eyes, flecked with yet more green and earthy browns in the sunset. The depths of them thrilled him and sent a shockwave of fear pulsing through his veins all at once.

'Come. This isn't even what I wanted to show you.'

He considered turning back, introducing Ivy to some more people, anything so they wouldn't be alone, where he'd think about kissing her again. He'd wanted to today in the water when the waves had pushed her close enough to jab him with her hipbones.

But here they *both* were. And he did want to show her Enrique.

He forced himself to carry on up the path ahead of her, right through the meadow. 'So, did your fiancé do something unforgivable?' he heard himself say. Well, how could someone like Ivy go from being engaged, to honeymooning on her own?

'Not really.'

She was quiet a moment, then she caught up to him on the path. The butterflies were parting for them as they walked, he realised now, as if they were royals in a crowd.

'I think it's better if we don't…you know…get into it,' she continued tightly.

Damn. Was that going a step too far? 'OK.'

As if sensing his disappointment, she pursed her lips and sighed through them. 'It's just that it's over, you know... Maybe it was over long before it was actually... over.'

'How long were you together?'

'Four years. We met in the park. I was taking pictures of the wild poppies and I noticed this tall guy, around my age. He was having trouble bending down to pick something up. Turned out his dog had made a mess... and Simon...that was his name...had done his back in, falling off his bike. He couldn't bend down far enough to pick it up. I offered to help him out.'

'You met because you helped him with a poo bag? Now that's romance.' Jero chuckled, and thankfully so did Ivy.

'It actually was, for a while. I took him food to his place while he couldn't bend down to his oven. When he was better, he took me out for dinners, I got to know Bernie, his Staffie. His mum liked me too. We had a nice time.'

He cocked an eyebrow at her. 'Just nice?'

'Nice was what I needed then,' she said tightly. 'It was grown up, you know, none of the mind games you get with online dating, and, believe me, I'd had plenty of that before I met him. It all took up far more time than it was worth, and I was busy, you know? I guess I was ready for someone, something serious, and easy. He told me he loved me after a month.' She looked at him sideways. 'Then, after four years he decided he wanted a family.'

'And you didn't?'

Ivy shrugged and looked in the other direction. He could tell she regretted telling him that already. Because he had Aayla?

'So…how is it, being a single dad all the way out here?' she deflected.

Jero realised he was dying to know more. Did she say she loved him back after a month? Did she fall for him as hard, or as quickly? By the way she was speaking, he didn't think so. The guy wanting a family had killed it… but as she'd said, before that, she'd been ready for something, and *something* had come along.

He knew people who'd settled for 'almost right' and 'easy' and that was their prerogative. Personally, he could never do that. He lived for the fire, the fights and the making up. But then, he'd had all that with Suranne… and that hadn't worked out either.

He frowned to himself, suddenly uneasy. Her question lingered in the air.

'It's not easy doing it alone but I have help,' he said eventually. 'We have a great community here, and Aayla's a great kid. She's a complex being, the most altruistic little creature I've ever met. She genuinely cares about every living being more than herself.'

'I've noticed.' Ivy smiled.

'A lot like you, actually,' he noted now.

Ivy looked nervously at her fingernails, then at the horizon. 'I don't know if we have that much in common… except maybe growing up without one of our parents. Where are we going exactly?'

Jero pointed to the curve in the path and kept them walking. 'You lost a parent?'

'My dad died when I was four. He went out to watch the rugby with some friends. It was raining, the car swerved, I don't really know exactly…' She trailed off while he fought for the right words.

'My mother worked hard to keep us both going. Even

if it also meant I never saw her. I guess I was mostly parented by my dog, which might explain some things.'

She huffed a self-deprecating laugh and Jero drew a breath through his teeth. *Tough childhood indeed.* What could he say?

He led her on towards where he hoped Enrique would still be nesting, and asked if she had siblings, to which she replied no. No aunts or uncles either, so therefore no cousins. She'd had a nanny, she said, and books. Not many peers or friends. Maybe she'd thrown herself into work all these years to feel seen, and wanted?

Sounded kind of familiar. He'd done that too, albeit later in life.

The possibility of Suranne leaving him for someone else had never ever crossed his mind, until he'd come home that day and found her halfway out of the door. Their dates on her holiday here had been a lot of fun and, yes, the pregnancy had been a mistake, but he'd found himself excited by the prospect of fatherhood; excited to make things work with Suranne. He'd been infatuated with her; blind to the notion that he was just a holiday romance that had got way out of control.

The wedding had been fast, and far too soon, her pregnant belly stretching out her mother's old lace dress. He'd thought he'd been doing the right thing. She'd told him she wanted the same things. But she'd been young, eight years his junior. Looking back, maybe she'd just been scared of the alternative. In spite of becoming the mother to his child, she'd soon realised he wasn't her future.

After the birth, she'd suffocated under the weight of the new parental responsibilities, slipped away right in front of him; he'd just been too blind to see it.

He'd taken on a lot after she left. Maybe more than he knew how to handle. At first it had helped him not to dwell on the separation process, but all the nights he'd spent in the dark, battling a screaming hurricane of recurring nightmares in which Aayla disappeared on him, too…those had damn near squeezed his soul out irrevocably.

The whole drawn-out divorce had only hammered home that he'd been replaced by the mother of his child. He'd tried not to take it personally—a woman eight years younger than him was bound to want different things. Someone so headstrong and ambitious—all the traits he admired—was bound to change her mind a thousand times, but he was a proud man. He loathed feeling downgraded. Discarded, like the fishtails left by seagulls after the feast.

For a long time he'd hoped she'd come back, for Aayla's sake, of course. Not his. He could learn to live without her; in fact, he had. He'd risen from the ashes, toughened up and started over. A betrayal of that magnitude had left him no choice. But why should Aayla have to do the same? Why should *she* ever have to feel unwanted?

'What is that?' Ivy's eyes had grown wide, three metres from the huge grassy bundle of a nest, directly on the sandy floor. It was sheltered from the wind by some shrubs. An army of tiny lizards scurried away as they stepped closer. He touched a hand to the base of her spine, registering the way she flinched at the lizards, then inched closer to him all in one second.

'That's Enrique.'

They were less than a foot from the giant bird. The sun gleamed across her humongous yellow beak. 'She's an albatross. Majestic, isn't she? She's built this right here on the path because she trusts no one will step on it. It's like she knows she's protected by humans if we know where she is. It wouldn't happen anywhere else.'

Ivy looked enchanted. 'It wouldn't, you're right. Why did you call a female bird Enrique?'

'The rangers thought she was he, till they saw her with the eggs. She probably fights off iguanas every day, but she seems to like this spot.'

Jero watched Ivy circle the nest, hitching up her dress to her milky white ankles, keeping a respectful distance. She crouched to get a better look at the giant white bird. Its beady all-seeing eyes were scrutinising her just as hard. The light was fading fast now. They'd have to get back before Aayla missed him, but it felt pretty good to show Ivy things only the Galapagos Islands had to offer. Things he and Aayla loved to share.

Which was weird, and a little worrying...

'She's wonderful,' Ivy told him from the ground.

'She's going to be a great mother,' he replied, refocusing on the albatross and not on Ivy's lips. He crouched opposite her, the grassy, tangled stick nest between them. The giant bird shuffled and ruffled her feathers, clearly proud to be showcasing her future offspring still cocooned in their off-yellow eggshells.

'I guess *some* creatures are just meant to be mothers,' Ivy said wistfully, almost to herself. Her face seemed darker in a heartbeat. 'Some, on the other hand, are not.'

He frowned. 'What do you mean?'

'Does it have to mean anything?' she said, standing up. *Touché.*

Wasn't that what he'd said about his tattoo earlier? That hadn't been entirely fair but why get into how the Mayan symbols in the manta ray translated as the lyrics of a song he'd written for Suranne? A waste of a good song, etched on his skin for ever. A reflection of the way he'd failed Aayla in every damn mirror.

'You're doing a really good job with Aayla, if it means

anything,' Ivy said, as if reading his mind, and he grunted his thanks. Maybe it looked as if he were, most of the time, on the outside. He'd failed her, not fighting harder to keep her mother around. Aayla had asked for her incessantly after Suranne left, but Suranne had asked him to keep away. He'd been torn, proud, hurt, but it would have been worse for his daughter if he'd given in to her pleas, if he'd gone to her and submitted Aayla to more rejection, wouldn't it?

He still didn't quite know how to feel; it nagged him, the thought that he should have done *something* more.

They retraced their route back to the beach in a somewhat awkward silence, pretending to be peaceful and tranquil, and he thought about what Ivy had said for the rest of the night.

So, he couldn't be sure, but, from what she'd said about her ex earlier, Ivy didn't want children of her own… or she'd decided motherhood was not for her. One of those assertions was correct, probably thanks to her own mother never being around when she was a kid. Children were scarred by stuff like that; he should know.

What with her broken engagement too, Ivy might have had her heart battered even harder than his over the years—and that was saying a lot.

He could show her how cool kids could be, though. There were all kinds of ways to see the world if you looked at it as children did. As Aayla did, his miracle daughter who had an age-defying understanding of the importance of these islands, and their inhabitants and struggles, even at six years old. Compassionate, empathetic, still awestruck by the beauty and wonders of the universe. His everything.

But you failed her, Jero. You failed to keep hold of her mother. The one thing she needs as much as you.

Tomorrow would be a fresh start, he decided as he tucked his daughter into bed that night. No more getting waylaid. No more falling under that Irish spell. However Ivy did it, he was now rendering himself impervious to her charms. Only a fool would let his heart and mind get tangled up like a dolphin in a fishing net over a tourist with one foot out of the door and more emotional baggage than him.

He'd be polite and present, but he would not get any more personal with Ivy Malone. And he definitely wouldn't let Aayla get too close either.

CHAPTER FIVE

'Where is it?'

'Where is what?' Ivy had to bite her tongue watching Jero and Dudders, the dreadlocked hemp-dressed volunteer from Birmingham by way of Thailand, both rifling through cardboard boxes full of Manila files in the storeroom, which doubled as a caging area. 'The adoption agency paperwork. I swear I put it here. We need the details for a litter we sent over to Quito.'

'Isn't it in the system?' she asked, turning her attention back to little Pluma, who was fluffing up her wings, probably looking out for Aayla.

Aayla was due in from school any minute. The bird had taken to following her around the place whenever she was here, a lot like Aayla followed *Ivy*.

'The files *are* the system,' Dudders reminded her in his thick midlands accent. 'But I wrote the details down myself. I think.'

Dudders' brows met thoughtfully. His loose elephant-patterned pants billowed in the AC as he stood, racking his brains. A tiny growl, not unlike a sea lion's, rumbled at the back of Jero's throat. 'You *think*?'

Ivy scooped up Pluma and held her close to her chest. 'I can help you organise things a little better if you like?' she offered. Then she waited, expecting the usual brush-off.

'It's fine, we're handling it,' Jero huffed as predicted. She bit her tongue, stroking Pluma's soft brown head with gentle fingers, feeling the tame bird nestle its sky-blue webbed feet further into one hand. So Jero really didn't want her help. Fine.

Not fine at all!

He'd been a little stand-offish for the last couple of days. Once or twice, he'd gone out on call without her and taken Aayla for the 'experience'. She'd been left to handle consultations, and had even performed a couple of small surgeries, always with injectable anaesthetic to keep costs down. Always with one of the volunteers close at hand.

Their vet nurse was a twenty-five-year-old guy from Guayaquil called Zenon, with tattoos of flowers all the way up his left arm and right leg. He was an insult to symmetry but wore a smile that could melt butter, when he showed up on time. Which was less often than she'd have liked.

Dudders was reliable enough, after a little gentle encouragement. She suspected at times that he'd done little at the monkey sanctuary in Thailand besides slip his favourites bananas and play them Bob Marley from his hammock. He'd certainly told her 'that was the best part about it, mate,' a few too many times for it to be a joke, but he was here, and who was she to judge?

All in all, it was the rewarding experience she'd hoped for. Not relaxing at all but humbling indeed. And a stark contrast from everything she was used to back home.

It was still amazing to her that veterinary care at the Darwin Animal Clinic was all provided free of charge. They didn't put a price on saving lives as they did— unfortunately—in her part of the world. Families could bring in their animals for free parasite treatments, which helped protect the fragile Galapagos ecosystem. It was all about giving back, ensuring all animals and people lived in harmony.

But she would rather be contributing *with* Jero when it came to protecting the birthplace of evolutionary theory, out there in the field. Not in here all the time. Or…she'd be fine in here actually if he were here, too.

Either way.

Oh, Lord. She was doomed.

Maybe he'd still invite her on the expedition with him later, she thought, training her eyes on his handsome profile in the sunlight. It was an overnight voyage with a conservationist this time, to check on the endemic waved albatross, known for their wingspan of up to two and a half metres. Unlike Enrique, these birds preferred a more remote location on the far south-eastern tip of the Galapagos archipelago. Some twenty thousand pairs were thought to breed and nest on Española Island—an island that was almost four million years old and totally uninhabited.

Hmm. Ivy watched the muscles turn to rocks in Jero's arms as he pulled more files from the shelf. The mysterious manta almost smirked at her from his arm. There was more to all that cryptic lettering than he was letting on. The design was too intricate, the symbolism too carefully considered to be meaningless.

Again. Why did she care?

For the same reason she wanted to go to a tiny four-million-year-old island covered in albatross poop with him, she supposed. But getting closer wouldn't do her any good. The more she cared, the harder it would be to forget him—them—when she had to.

Already Aayla was a little ray of sunshine, who brightened every room they shared. It had kind of sneaked up on her, the burst of surprise joy at hearing her unique, fresh, often hilarious take on things. Hmm. She'd never thought of her life as being anything but childfree, but Simon's words kept coming to her unannounced now:

'You just think you'd be a bad mother because your own mother was. Abandonment is not a hereditary disease, you know, it's a choice. If you chose motherhood, you'd throw your all into it, like you do everything else.'

Of course, she'd always poo-pooed him, told him it wasn't anything to do with abandonment, that she was just too busy to choose that, and too set in her ways. All of which was true, but maybe he knew her better than she thought he did.

Nuzzling Pluma's head to her chin, she watched Jero sink into the worn leather desk chair and swing his big feet up onto the desk. She liked his leather sandals, they were nomadic and comfortable and a little worn, like Jero.

Suddenly, Simon was gone from her head.

God, that moment with the mantas the other day, that had been *real*.

And the other moment, when she'd stumbled on the path up to the meadow and he'd caught her, eyes full of sunset and surrounded by butterflies. A movie moment! But *real*. The kind of real that stole your breath and threatened to lift you clean off the floor, and proved to you that any other encounter before it was only sub-par. It had taken all her strength not to surrender to her impulses and kiss his impossibly perfect mouth…

'Found it!' Jero pulled a file from a box and held it up triumphantly. Ivy forced a smile. How they could live with such organised chaos was still beyond her.

'Ivy! Papa! Did the puppies sit good when you told them to?'

Aayla all but launched herself into the room. Her nanny, a petite Ecuadorian twenty-something called Nina with hair down to her backside, was close on her heels.

'Not yet, I think they're waiting to sit when *you* tell them to,' Ivy said, surprising herself. That had come out of her effortlessly, without thinking. It was the truth, after all. Aayla seemed to have a real gift with the animals.

Aayla whispered to them as Ivy used to whisper to Zeus. She also sat with them for hours in silence, as she'd done with Zeus. She could have sworn that dog's big old heart used to understand every single word she did or didn't say.

Dropping her school bag to the floor, Aayla, in jean shorts and a shirt covered in tiny clouds and rainbows, got to her knees by the box of puppies. Ivy's heart skidded seeing Jero forget about his annoyance over the filing system, or lack thereof, instantly. He got down to her level in his scrubs and asked about her day. So sweet. And sexy, and…extraordinarily patient.

Aayla was getting assigned a pen pal, someone in her grade, but from a different country. Aayla had a papaya smoothie for lunch *and* her class picked the fruits for it. Aayla got top marks in 3D biology, whatever that was to a six-year-old. Aayla wanted to braid Ivy's hair.

'Wait, what?' Ivy sprang from where she'd perched on the desk with Pluma, away from Aayla's little hands. Dudders pulled on a white coat over his elephant pants and made a swift exit out to the reception area to greet the young couple walking in.

'I know how to braid hair. I can practise on you. I like your hair, Ivy.'

How do I get out of this?

Like a gladiator on a rearing war horse, Jero made a human blockade of himself and coaxed Aayla quickly

out of the storeroom after Dudders, where she was for-
tunately distracted by the family's cat in a cage, and
Nina the nanny.

Crisis avoided.

'I'll try and keep her out of your way,' Jero said, turning back to her. His stance was uncomfortable in the
doorway. Suddenly she wanted anything but.

'No, no, she's fine,' she assured him, crouching to
open Pluma's cage, feeling his eyes on her back. 'It's just
the curls, you know. It wouldn't braid all that well. She'd
only be disappointed.'

Jero made a huffing sound, re-stuck a peeling poster
to the wall behind the cages and pulled another file out
for the family in Reception.

Ugh.

Ugh to that no doubt illegible and useless file in his
sexy big man hands, and ugh to the excuse. Jero wasn't
blind, she'd just given him further proof of how incom-
petent she was when it came to stuff like that…physical
contact, motherly kind of stuff.

Her friends used to laugh at her, refusing to hold their
babies. Only now she was realising why she'd refused.
It always felt too risky. What if she liked it? What if she
wanted one? What if one arrived, and she was nothing
but a disappointment?

That accidentally spoken out loud statement, when
she'd told Jero how only *some* creatures were meant to
be mothers—he'd probably thought she'd been dissing
Suranne, his ex-wife, as if it were *her* business to be making observations like that.

Aayla's mother wasn't exactly beating down doors to
see her, sure, but at least the girl had a father. A bloody
good one at that.

'Look, Jero…'

She was about to explain herself and tell him how sorry she was that kids had somehow fallen into the 'strange little aliens that unnerve me' category in her mind. But she was halted by Pluma, who was all but wrestling from her hands.

To her shock, the dozy little bird dived a foot from her crouched stance, waddled right through Jero's legs, and out of the door towards Aayla. Aayla scooped her up lovingly in her arms and kept her away from the puppies, talking to them all as a group like a shepherdess comforting her flock.

'What the...?'

'Ivy, look, she loves me, and I love her.' Aayla's voice was gentle and soft, but she looked elated. Her happiness was infectious. The urge to explain herself shot straight from Ivy's mind.

'A baby blue-footed booby thinks a six-year-old girl is her mother.' Jero scraped a hand across his head. The sleeve of his scrubs rubbed up to hers as she joined him in the doorway. Hopefully her smile hid the way her impossible heart was revving like a race car at the contact.

'She's never going to get rid of that bird now. They've bonded,' he said, so only she could hear. She forced her eyes to stay on Aayla. His warm breath tickled her ear, rearranging her senses. She was back on that boulder-lined path in her head, pressed against him, nerve-endings fraying all over again.

'We should make sure that doesn't happen, really.'

She swallowed. *We.* Which unfortunate bonding were they talking about exactly?

'They're wild,' he reminded her. 'We don't keep them here. You can't keep anything with wings anywhere it doesn't want to be.'

'What do you think cages are for?' she retorted, flustered.

Jero huffed a laugh. 'Nothing needs a cage if it likes where it is,' he said. 'But the thing about wild creatures is, you never know when they're going to change their mind.'

Ivy kept her mouth shut, even as his eyes on her cheek made her hot. Did he mean her?

It could never be a fling with Jero, she realised like a slap to her cheeks. Even if her mounting crush had twisted her daydreams into passionate kisses with him on windy outcrops. Wasn't his ex a tourist, who'd left them both for another life? What was the likelihood he'd go there again, even if he wanted to? *How about...zero to none?*

'So, that conservationist—her name is Dee Whit-field. She wants to know if you're coming with us on the overnighter,' he said now, looking at her sideways. 'She read about your credentials; I think she's keen for you to join us.'

Oh, so now you're bringing it up.

Ivy felt hot under her collar now. How nice that her excellent professional reputation preceded her. That was not entirely surprising, if she did say so herself. But it was definitely best not to tempt disaster on *her* side, with Jero. Remote sailing, open waters, rugged island terrain, Jero's gym-honed body with his shirt off in the sun, administering animal care, maybe some more snorkelling with exotic wildlife...it would be torture.

'I should probably stay here,' she forced herself to say. 'You've been doing a lot of these trips without me anyway.'

Jero's mouth twisted, then he shrugged at the floor. The opportunity hovered between them like a leaden ball on a ceiling chain, and the next five seconds in her mind went something like: *I'll go. I won't go. Oh, why not, I'll go. What? No, I absolutely won't go.*

This is ridiculous. Visiting one of the planet's most isolated archipelagos is an amazing opportunity. Besides, the conservationist will be there. What could you possibly get up to in such close quarters?

'OK, if the conservationist wants to meet me, how can I refuse? Consider me on the voyage, Captain,' she said, before she could think any more about it.

'I won't be steering the yacht tonight,' Jero replied.

Her mouth fell open. A yacht?

He offered her an infuriating smile that only made his mouth look all the more kissable. 'I'm just kidding—we save those for the tourists. I'll bring the seasickness pills. Don't forget your waterproof jacket. Oh, do you have a zoom lens for your camera?'

'Of course, why?'

'It's the best place for bird-watching in the Galapagos. Aayla loves telling the cruise shippers what's what.'

'Aayla's coming?' Ivy swallowed an albatross-egg-sized knot from her throat as Jero glanced at his daughter, then back at her. He looked mildly irritated by something now.

'I just remembered, Nina's off this weekend. She'll *have* to come with us.'

Ivy forced an upbeat tone that still somehow came out kind of choked. 'Well, this will be fun.'

CHAPTER SIX

'ARE YOU ASLEEP YET?' Jero was standing outside her cabin door. Her breathing caught like a kite on a washing line as she pictured him there, one hand poised to knock if she didn't answer.

He'd already asked her if she wanted a nightcap and, while she'd wanted nothing more after such a long, exhausting day in the heat, she'd felt the chemistry bubbling up between them the second Dee, their resident conservationist, a sixty-something-year-old Brit from the Galapagos Conservation Trust, and Aayla had gone to bed. She'd refused the nightcap, but now, just as predicted, she was lying awake, trying and failing to allow the gently rhythmic bobbing of the ocean below them to lull her into sleep. Thinking about him.

'I'm awake,' she answered, somewhat against her will.

'Then you shouldn't miss this!' he replied. 'I'm guessing you don't have this back in Galway.'

Intrigue won her over.

Out on the deck, Jero ushered her behind a long, protruding telescope he'd focused on the stars. No sooner had she pressed one eye to the rounded end than a barrage of shooting stars lit up the sky, right in front of her.

'Woah!' She staggered backwards in awe, right into him, and he laughed as his hands landed on her shoulders, then fell to her hips. Her pulse became a meteor in her veins on the spot. Jero guided her eyes back to the telescope, then wheeled it into a new position before placing his hands right back where they'd just been, over her hips. She could literally feel the heat of him against her back, making her burn. Did he have any idea what he was doing to her?

'Did you know, you can see twice as many stars in the Galapagos as anywhere else?' he whispered softly as she scanned the sparkly skies.

She swallowed and shook her head. Words wouldn't find her; everything was blowing her mind in this moment.

'It's because we're on the equator,' he continued. 'It means the constellations from both hemispheres meet in the middle. On nights like this, it looks like the heavens are literally exploding.'

Ivy caught her breath. After a long moment of silence, during which she willed her heart to stop skidding around like a bumper car, she said, 'I wonder if my dad's up there somewhere, orchestrating this show for us somehow. He was kind of a star when I was a kid. To me, anyway.'

'I bet you were a pretty awesome kid, Ivy,' he said.

She dared to turn around. Jero was looking at her, really looking at her, as if he wanted to say something else but was holding it back. They studied each other's eyes for what felt like far too long before he looked away. Then he said, 'I don't know if I believe in an afterlife, do you?'

She shrugged, stepping back from the telescope. He'd snatched back the magic somehow, as if their closeness had freaked him out, too.

Dragging a hand through her hair, she watched him reposition the telescope and press his own eye to the end. 'I should go, try and get some sleep,' she told his back,

and scuttled off to her cabin before he could respond.
She slept fitfully till the seagulls woke her up at dawn.

Isla Española was, without a shadow of a doubt, the most
beautiful place Ivy had ever set eyes on. The dramatic
setting was even more perfect than the prettiest parts of
Santa Cruz. Her camera just couldn't do justice to the
towering black lava cliffs, the never-ending rhythmic
crashing and rolling of the waves below, and the gamut
of colourful seabirds swooping around them fearlessly
on the wind.

Aayla did indeed know each and every one of them.

'Look, Daddy! Another cactus finch,' she cried out
now, waving the binoculars at Jero from her place ahead
of them on the grassy trail. Little Pluma, who'd come
along for the ride, poked her white fluffy head out from
the tiny Disney backpack that was slung over the girl's
shoulders. Ivy still couldn't believe she'd brought the bird,
but Jero was right, they'd bonded and Pluma wouldn't
have fared well, being left alone. She only ate worms
from their hands now.

They were forty minutes into their walk in the area
of Punta Suarez, heading towards a well-known albatross nesting ground. So far, Aayla had blown Ivy's mind
with her knowledge of the island's habitat. Even Dee was
suitably impressed, which was saying something, because Dee seemed to know everything about everything.
Though maybe not as much as Jero and Aayla.

'Oh, look, there's a Galapagos hawk coming in. Ivy,
you have to take a photo!'

Aayla was intent on capturing everything with the
camera. Ivy caught Jero's smile as he shook something
off the heel of his hiking boot that looked suspiciously
like a clump of lizard poop. He caught her hand as she

stepped back to avoid landing in any other insalubrious debris, and narrowly missed crushing a bird's egg that was nestled in a shrub.

Adrenaline flooded her veins at his touch. 'Careful there.'

'Thanks.' She fell deep into his eyes again as he lifted his sunglasses momentarily. His loose white shirt flapped open in the breeze, framing his broad chest and the faded Texas Longhorns football shirt he'd pulled on this morning, after their swim off the boat.

It hadn't been easy, keeping her eyes off him, or keeping away from him in the water. But she'd managed to swim on her back, metres away, grateful that Aayla and Dee had been there as a buffer. It all felt a bit too close for comfort, especially after last night.

On any other guy, that football shirt might have made her cringe. So would the baseball hat, she mused now, observing flecks the colour of Ireland's autumn leaves in the browns of his eyes. Jero wasn't exactly your typical football fan. He knew every shrub and flower, and every bird's call that came at them on this path. He knew about the various marine and air currents that saw different creatures settling on different islands, and when he spoke, she listened, absorbing it all in wonder, like a child.

She'd never been anywhere as wild. It wasn't all butterflies, birds and perfection, but to witness him and Aayla out here enjoying this purity together tugged at something deep in her chest, a kind of untethering and unravelling. She couldn't quite put her finger on the feeling.

'Be careful with it, but I think you should take the photo,' she told Aayla, catching up with her on the path and switching out her binoculars for the camera.

'Are you sure?' Jero whispered in her ear.

'Why not? The kid is clearly excited to learn photography,' she replied, securing the camera around Aayla's neck by the strap.

A delighted Aayla snapped away at the birds in the trees and Ivy pressed her eyes to the tiny lenses of the binoculars, focusing in on the rare hawk. Hopefully the gadget would hide her flushed cheeks—why did her heart turn into a raging bull every time Jero so much as brushed her ear with his breath?

'What do we have over here?' She looked up just as Jero put a hand on one shoulder and gently prised the binoculars from her with the other. 'Can I see for a second?'

Suddenly Dee was squealing in excitement, squinting into her own binoculars up ahead of them. Aayla started twisting the telephoto lens of her camera in a way that did make her unsure about the loan, actually…but Jero thrust the binoculars back at her, redirecting her attention.

'What are we looking at?' she asked him.

'Just the elaborate courtship rituals of the mighty albatross,' he said through his wide grin. 'These birds mate for life. It's quite something to see this for yourself, look!'

The warmth of his hands clasped over hers made her brain turn to mush. Then her eyes found what he was showing her. She couldn't help the smile stretching out her face, especially as all three of them started laughing and commenting on what they were looking at, as if they'd been thrown into a studio to record a soundtrack on behalf of David Attenborough.

Two giant albatrosses were dancing seductively on the rocks ahead, stopping every now and then to clap and smack their beaks together like swords.

'See how the female tilts her head back and cries out like that?' Jero's mouth tickled her ear again, making her shiver. 'That's albatross code for, I quite like you. I might want to have your babies.'

Ivy grinned and turned her head, almost knocking him on the nose with the binoculars. Swiftly he pulled them from her hands, and she froze to find him less than an inch from her face. 'Sorry,' she said too quickly.

'You're a hazard,' he teased. His narrowed eyes grazed her lips, and she could have sworn, for just a fraction of a second, she literally *saw* him think about kissing her.

Then he turned to Aayla, swiping a hand across his mouth and jaw as if he were physically squishing the thought. Her heart began a steady thrum that was almost too loud. Head high, she smoothed down her shirt and shorts and carried on up the path towards Dee, cursing herself, avoiding his eyes.

That was close, dammit, too close for comfort. *But he definitely felt it too.*

So, her unfortunate crush might not all be one-sided. She couldn't help mulling it over as they all went about counting the albatrosses they came across in a considerate silence for the next two hours. Dee and Jero tagged the ones who weren't yet being monitored, and occasionally time stopped as a frolicking sea lion stole her attention from the task at hand.

She still couldn't quite look Jero in the eye, and he seemed to be steering himself and Aayla away from her at every opportunity.

The sooner they got back to Santa Cruz, the better, she told herself later, watching Jero push the chairs around the table ready for dinner on the deck of their boat. She pretended to be concentrating on some notes she'd taken earlier, but she couldn't stop looking at him from her lounge chair, wondering what he was thinking about earlier.

If he was thinking anything at all, she reminded herself. Men didn't romanticise every little encounter as women had the tendency to do. If only she could stop picturing him with his shirt off.

Never mind, I'll soon be back at the hotel, she told herself. She'd be back in control of her wandering thoughts, there.

'Almost time for dinner, Ivy, are you hungry?' Dee asked her from across the deck. She was setting the forks on the small table.

The sun was setting on their first day on Isla Española, and Aayla was busy photographing the last rays creeping over the wooden boat and the deep ocean they were bobbing on, offshore. *Nowhere to go now. No distractions.* Not even an Internet connection to aid the checking of her emails.

They ate their pasta and salad as the sun sank, and the captain of their trusty vessel, Manny, turned a series of lights on, sending shadows dancing across the deck. The ocean was quickly fading into black. It felt as if they were deep in space, with not another human or boat around for miles.

Aayla started yawning in her seat. Then she ran to her room and returned with *The Hungry Caterpillar.* 'Pluma wants you to read to her, Ivy,' she stated, crossing to the bird's small cage and letting her out to waddle freely around the hardwood floor. Her blue feet left little smacking sounds in her wake, but Ivy shifted in her chair at the familiar blast of discomfort.

Jero seemed to notice. He stood from his chair opposite hers, while Dee looked between them in interest, sipping on the last of her soup. 'Ivy doesn't want to read to anyone tonight. It's been a long day,' he told her firmly, taking the book from his daughter's hands.

But Pluma was waddling straight towards her now and, in seconds, she'd hopped onto Ivy's lap, pinning her in her place.

'I swear, she understands what you say, Aayla.' Ivy laughed, struck with wonder as the bird burrowed into her lap on top of her napkin.

'I told you, she wants you to read to her.' Aayla took the book back from Jero and pushed it towards Ivy on the table. Pluma ruffled her feathers encouragingly and Jero let out a sigh, clearing their dishes and cutlery away as Dee excused herself and went to her cabin for the night.

'Maybe I should read to you, Aayla?' Ivy heard herself offer. Jero looked unconvinced for a second, but she picked up the book and Aayla settled herself down for the story anyway. Ivy read half from memory, and half from badly translated Spanish under several more shooting stars. Jero's eyes burned into her from across the table. She stumbled over her words several times.

There was something unnerving that came with being around just the two of them, she realised. Their little family unit was something quite special, something sacred. Something she'd never had. It was cosy and warm, like pulling on a jumper fresh from the dryer. It made her feel snug and complete… right until she remembered she had absolutely no part in it. Not really. She *was* an outsider here. This thing would carry on without her, long after she was gone, picking up her life alone back in freezing-cold Galway. The clinic was all she had. Maybe she shouldn't sell, she thought suddenly, even if Mike told her he wanted to.

The thought of being without it suddenly made her feel quite vulnerable, like a baby bird left out in the open for the lizards. Her work was literally *all* she had.

* * *

The chemistry with Jero was still burning brighter than the stars by the time he left the deck to carry Aayla to her room. Ivy turned to the moon in its Milky Way hammock, listening to the little girl's sleepy giggles through the wall, watching the ripples across the ink-black water, anticipating his return.

Jero was behind her again in minutes, holding up a bottle of whisky and two glasses. 'How about a nightcap?'

He motioned to two lounge chairs side by side and every inch of her knew she should probably say no again and go to bed, as she'd been planning to since they'd finished dinner.

'OK. Why not?' she heard herself say anyway. *Curses.* She was doing what she'd avoided doing *last* night—immersing too much of herself in his all-too-captivating company—but it wasn't as if she could change her mind. He was already pouring her a drink. She didn't want to be rude.

Silence settled around them as she moved to the other lounge chair, taking Pluma with her. As if sensing the tension in the air, Jero started talking about their day, the albatrosses, the sea lions they'd be tagging tomorrow. He told her about a penguin who'd once sneaked on a boat like this behind him, and how he'd had to sail all the way back with it so as not to cross-contaminate the islands.

It could have been the whisky, but she started to relax.

Until he said, 'So, you told me you didn't want to get into it, and forgive me for asking, but I can't stop wondering how come your ex could have ever let you go.'

Her breath hitched in her throat.

'I mean, I don't know you very well.' Jero reached for the bottle again and, stunned, she held out her glass for one more. 'But I can tell you're smart, you're accomplished, you're beautiful, and you can make up a mean ending to *The Hungry Caterpillar*. Who knew he ended up adopting a blue-footed booby in the English version, like Aayla?'

Ivy rubbed her arms, trying to ignore the way him calling her beautiful felt like hot liquid honey filling the cracks in her heart. 'I told you, Simon wanted to start a family,' she admitted, taking herself by surprise.

Jero nodded, tapping his glass to the arm of the chair. 'And you weren't ready?'

'I don't think I'll ever be ready. I work too hard for all that.'

His eyes narrowed at her words. 'It's not easy,' he said quietly after a moment. 'Raising a kid. It's not something I ever anticipated doing alone, either.'

He swigged from his drink and stood up. Ivy followed him, resting her arms on the railing and noting the moonlight in the water throwing ethereal, shimmering streaks on his skin. 'Why did your ex leave *you*?' she dared. 'You're smart, you're accomplished, you're beautiful.'

He grinned and nudged his shoulder to hers, swirling the ice in his glass until his mouth was a thin line again. 'I guess she wanted more than this island. After she left, I used to wake up in a sweat thinking Aayla was gone too. I used to race to her room at three a.m. just to check she hadn't sneaked away. Between you and me, sometimes I still do. She'll leave me one day, though. She'll want more than this island, too.'

He stole a sideways glance at her. She read his look like a book. He was terrified Aayla would leave him as his ex had. 'I don't think you need to worry about that just yet,' she said, softly, daring to place a hand over his. 'You're a great dad. Aayla seems happy, well adjusted…'

He studied her hand as if it were a rare, untrustworthy

alien that had landed on him from the rings of Jupiter. 'I do my best.'

'She's wonderful. I, for one, enjoy her company. Really, that's the truth. Trust me, that is quite surprising. Coming from me...'

A storm blew over his features suddenly. He pulled his hand away and put his glass down on the deck, eyes like narrowed slits. 'So, when is your flight out of here again?'

What?

She watched him curl and flex his fingers, as if he was still shaking her touch away. He'd just let a wall down, then built it back up higher than ever. 'I... I don't know. I forget what day it is,' she said truthfully.

'Well, you'd better write it down. You don't want to get stuck here.'

'I guess not,' she replied coolly, even as her heart went berserk in her chest. She scanned his profile in the darkness. He was slipping away faster than he'd started to open up.

What had just happened? Oh, God, had she accidentally just insulted Aayla?

'What the hell?' Ivy jumped as, without warning, Jero gripped the railings, his knuckles white. She followed his eyes out to sea. A bright white light she hadn't seen before was flashing on and off in the distance. Even she knew it was far too close to Isla Española than what was allowed after dark. 'I don't believe it. They came back!' he spat, incredulous.

'Who came back?' Her heart was still skipping beats.

Jero darted for the cabin in his bare feet. She followed him in confusion, with Puma waddling after her. Manny was snoozing on a couch, but he sat bolt upright when Jero snatched up the radio and promptly called the coastguard.

CHAPTER SEVEN

'LAST TIME THEY CAME, they filled the hull with thousands of sharks and tuna. Tonnes of it.' Jero kept his eye on the vessel ahead, feeling his temperature rise with every second they drew closer. 'They wreaked havoc on land, too.'

Manny was doing his best to speed them towards the illegal trawler, but it was speeding away from *them* just as quickly. His head was a storm of possible outcomes. 'I probably don't need to tell you, Ivy, that wildlife trafficking is the third most profitable illegal activity after drug and weapon smuggling?'

'I did know that.' Ivy scrubbed her wild red hair from her forehead and held it back with one hand against the wind. 'I appreciate the education, Jero, but what exactly are you planning to do?'

He bit on his cheeks. Good question. Dee was watching Aayla and Pluma, safe inside, but who knew who was onboard that boat? Or what?

'You're not going to try and get on that boat, are you?' Ivy said now. She looked even paler than usual in the moonlight. How the hell was he supposed to answer her? There wasn't exactly a plan.

'All I know is the coastguard won't get here as fast as we need him to—the very reason these illegal traders try their luck out here is because we can't man every island around the clock, especially Española. It's too far away from everything else. Hey!' He yelled out over the roaring engine as the vessel came into full view. Ivy let go of her hair, mouth agape.

Her eyes grew wide and fearful all of a sudden. 'Jero...'

'Hey! Do you have a licence to be here?' he called out as Manny steered them close enough to see the guy on the deck, looking up at them. Of course, no one answered him. Crates and boxes of ice were sloshing water over the ship's deck, and he felt the chill of it run through his veins. They were planning to ice whatever they'd been trawling, which could be tonnes of fish and marine life, as before.

Manny swerved the boat again and it lunged as they caught a wave. Jero's heart stopped as Ivy slipped and almost skidded under the railings into the water. The ability to anticipate her next move overpowered him, as if it were coming from somewhere outside himself. He caught her, wrapped his arms about her waist and pulled her backwards against his chest, gripping the railing tight with his other hand before he could suffer the same fate.

'Don't make me dive in there after you!'

A stocky guy on the deck caught his eye. There were three of them now, leaning over the side, making wide, frenzied gestures at each other. He knew instinctively they were discussing when to pull up the nets.

'They know we would have called the coastguard. Whatever they've been trawling up to here will be destroyed if they pull up now,' he told Ivy over the wind.

Ivy pulled away from him. 'I need to get the camera! We need proof of what they're doing!'

'We need to stop them,' he replied, but she was already scrambling for her SLR. As Ivy snapped away, one hand on the railing so as not to fall again, the men scattered, obviously alarmed she might identify them.

'Nice!' Jero reached for the rope and anchor. Deftly he looped it around his arm and attempted to hook the ship.

'What if they've gone for weapons?' Ivy cried. The camera fell to her waist on its strap.

'We can't think that.' He urged her backwards gently out of potential harm's way and flung the lid off a box of tools. A knife—perfect. Another knife, this one longer and sturdier—even better.

Ivy shook her head as he slid them both into his pockets and attempted the hook again. This time it caught, just below the bow.

'What are you doing?' Her hands snatched the back of his shirt as he approached the railings and studied the shrinking gap between their boat and the bobbing trawler.

'I'm going to cut their nets. I just have to jump onto their lifeboat, see? I can reach them from there.'

Her fingers gripped his wrist. 'Are you crazy? What are you, James Bond of the Galapagos?'

He ignored her. 'It'll be carnage if they bring those nets up. If Aayla sees that…'

Manny was swerving close enough now that he could almost jump onboard. Manny would know what he was intending to do, he thought. They'd been over scenarios like this a thousand times—you did whatever you could to protect this place. The ocean was family, a provider and a friend. He'd taught Aayla that too, years ago. He put one foot up on the railing, ready to jump. To his horror, Ivy was beside him in a second.

'I'm coming with you,' she said now, climbing over the railings completely until she was leaning precariously over the open water, her skirt and hair a billowing flag.

'Get down, Ivy, they'll see you…'

Before he could stop her, she was leaping from the side and landing cat-like on all fours on the yellow-striped lifeboat. His stared at her in disbelief. *What the...?*

'Hurry up, then,' she snapped up at him. There was still no sign of the men on deck, though he could see one head bobbing up behind a window. They'd brave the deck again soon. It was now or never.

The floodlights from their boat just missed him as he took the leap over the thrashing water and landed with a thud beside her. Ivy bit back a smile as their eyes met, then both of them stumbled on the next wave, colliding and righting themselves together. Mutual admiration filled a millisecond window before he handed her a knife and they both got sawing.

They only had to loosen one side to throw it off kilter and ensure whatever these guys had captured would be thrown back into the water, instead of hoisted up onto the trawler. They had to work fast, but Ivy was as determined as him, working the knife with deft cutting movements and focus, even as the ocean spray soaked them to the bone.

'Hey!' A voice, from the deck. One of the men. 'What do you think you're doing?'

A bearded weathered face was peering down at them now, thrashing his arms about.

'They've seen us,' he told her. Ivy didn't stop her sawing. In fact she sped up.

'We're almost there, don't stop!' she urged.

'Daddy?' The voice from behind him, on their boat, was an ice-cold nitro blast to his bloodstream. *Aayla.*

'Daddy! Come back!' Aayla was awake and watching the scene in terror.

'Don't stop,' Ivy yelled again, but the guy who'd seen them was attempting to climb over the side of the trawler now, his yellow jacket a warning beacon. Would he drop to the lifeboat, to stop them himself, with a weapon, all while Jero's daughter looked on?

Suddenly, the net shifted. Ivy jumped backwards, almost tumbling to the floor again as it crashed towards them and swung out again, threatening to take them out with it. Jero caught her just as the tangle of fishing nets folded and collapsed with a heavy groan. Just a second ago it had looked as if it weighed a tonne, but now it was flapping emptily over their heads, blocking the guy's descent. Unfortunately, it also blocked their exit.

Ivy clutched his shirt at the collar, burying her head in his shoulder. He wrapped himself around her, and tried not to picture Aayla up there, watching all this. Her little mind must be spinning in fear.

Just then, a barrage of lights appeared on the horizon like soldiers. Beyond the nets, the sky lit up and whirring sounded above them. *Thank God.*

The helicopters almost drowned out his next words to Ivy. He breathed a sigh of relief into her hair, still cradling her head against him. The Galapagos National Park control centre must have monitored their trajectory and vectored a patrol vessel for an interdiction. Galapagos Park Rangers and Ecuadorian Navy officials would rescue them and see to it that these guys were locked away like the incorrigible scum they were.

Remarkably an emotional yet exhausted Aayla slept through all that followed their dramatic rescue and deposit back on their own boat. The night patrol, the buzz of radios, the clicking of cameras and the onslaught of questions made a wreck of his head. It was several hours before he and Ivy were alone, and their deck was quiet again, but he couldn't sleep.

Neither could Ivy apparently.

She found him on the deck, a blanket wrapped around her shoulders. She was clenching and unclenching her fists with shock and nerves, and he poured her a warm tea from a flask, urged her to sit back down in the lounge chair.

'That wasn't exactly how I planned this night to go,' he told her wryly, and she hugged an arm around herself, eyeing him over her teacup.

'I just hope Aayla didn't get any ideas, watching us chase after criminals,' she said with a sardonic smile. He exhaled deeply and dropped to the other chair.

'So do I. Luckily she seemed to understand we had no choice.'

Ivy held his eyes. Then she put her cup down and took his hand across the gap, sending a warm cascade of comfort over his heart that almost made him recoil from her. 'You were amazing, thinking so quickly about what to do.'

'You jumped over there first,' he reminded her. For some reason, he was remembering the feel of his hand in her wet red hair on the lifeboat, how much he'd wanted to keep her safe, and keep her close.

She screwed up her face, wrinkled her nose, embarrassed maybe? 'I did, didn't I?' she said.

Whatever it was about her that kept drawing him in was equally repellent: a snake around his ribcage, threatening to squeeze all sense out of him. She wasn't here to stay; she'd be on that flight before he knew it; he'd been sure to remind himself of that—and her too—in case *this* moment ever arrived.

Another moment where he wanted to kiss her.

'So what happens now?' she asked him on a sigh. 'They got dragged off that ship pretty fast.'

He cleared his throat, pulled his eyes away with his hand. 'They'll scour the trawler for illegal trade, then the guys will likely wind up in jail. All *we* can do is go to Española at dawn, check for damages. If they made it onto land too, who knows what we'll find?'

'What about Aayla?'

'She'll stay here, with Dee.'

'But this is Dee's trip…why don't I stay with Aayla?'

Her offer danced in his mind, giving him a headache. Fixing his eyes on the black horizon he shook his head. No way was he leaving Aayla alone with Ivy, not even in these circumstances. The kid was getting attached enough as it was to someone who was leaving the second her honeymoon—or whatever this was—was over.

'We might need the both of us,' he said instead, measuredly. 'Like I told you, who knows what we'll find once we make land?'

Ivy sighed through her nose and the guilt rendered him silent, swigging his tea till it burned.

She'd leaped in to help tonight, literally, without him even asking. She'd shown no fear at all when they'd been slashing those nets. She'd probably saved a thousand marine lives alongside him in the blink of an eye. Without her help, it might have been a different story. He bit down hard on his tongue, wishing he could shake the need to tell Ivy how grateful he was that she'd been there. But he couldn't find the words. Didn't want to hear them from his own mouth. Already she was settling under his skin, like an itch he couldn't scratch. He'd needed her just now…a tourist, no less.

'Are you OK?' Ivy stood from the chair and crouched in front of his. 'You seem anxious. You did everything you could, Jero. They caught those guys because of you. Aayla is fine. She thinks you're a hero.'

He watched her lips, and only half heard her words. Just one slight movement and he could pull her in, scoop one hand behind her head again and claim her mouth this time. She'd been giving him the signs all day. He'd felt her fingers clawing his shirt earlier like feeling his clothes wasn't enough, felt her eyes on him ever since they'd boarded this boat. He could have her straddling him right here on this chair, let her melt into him under the moon. It was very clear she wanted it too, even if she wasn't doing anything about it.

For good reason. Get a hold of yourself, man.

He stood, left her on her haunches by his chair, while he busied his fingers with screwing the lid back onto the flask. 'You should get some sleep,' he grunted, turning away so she wouldn't see how much this deplorable desire was unsettling him.

'I'll wake you up at first light.'

CHAPTER EIGHT

IVY'S NERVES HAD been shot all morning, since before they'd ridden out here in the little Zodiac boat, leaving Aayla and Dee behind on the larger boat. They were still waiting for news on what—if anything—had been found on the seized trawler besides fish but thankfully Jero had been wrong about them coming ashore, too.

She watched the ticcing motion of his strong jaw as he scanned the beach for injured wildlife, as if he didn't quite believe their luck. The wind tussled at their clothes. She was already having to squint through the drizzle.

'You must have seen the results of a previous island swipe, from the look on your face,' she ventured aloud, hugging her arms around herself.

'You don't even want to know what they'll do, once they decide what they want,' he replied stoically. 'Why do you think that young orphaned penguin followed me home, that time?'

Ivy swallowed.

The rain was picking up speed and strength by the second, soaking her clothes. Jero's T-shirt was almost transparent. Every muscle cast another shadow under the grey sky. He'd hardly spoken all morning and she was trying not to wonder if the night's events were the only reason.

He'd gone cold on her pretty quickly last night; drifted

away like a glacial front, just when she'd got a glimpse inside his head. *Men,* she'd huffed, when he'd gone. It was preferable to be more annoyed than hurt after all. She'd pretty much called him a hero. Big mistake. Yes, Aayla had said it first, but if he thought she was going to gush over him too, only to be ignored…

'Ivy. Over there.'

She followed his finger just as Jero made for another sea lion pup further up the beach. This one was alone, writhing on the sand, bellowing out little helpless honks that splintered her heart. She crouched at his side to inspect the creature. It was bigger than the last, roughly the size of a medium-sized dog.

'It doesn't look hurt,' she observed. 'Just a little malnourished.'

Ivy saw her reflection in its big, round sorrowful eyes. 'Where did your mama go?' she whispered, stroking a hand along the animal's smooth, almost waxy fur. Usually they weren't supposed to touch the wildlife here, but as a vet, and a woman, some maternal instinct to protect these creatures was quickly taking over. Whatever their species, babies needed caring for.

'Looks like the mother's abandoned him for some reason. It happens,' Jero said wanly. 'Maybe her mother couldn't feed herself and couldn't produce the milk to feed her.'

His jaw twitched again, and she wondered if he thought about his ex whenever he saw a lonesome creature looking around for its long-gone mother, the same way she thought about herself as a kid, sitting on the floor under the stairs reading *The Hungry Caterpillar* to Zeus.

'What can we do?' she asked as the goosebumps prickled up on her arms. The rain and the intensity of this situation were making her colder by the second.

He sighed, offering her a sideways glance. 'The National Park vet would usually see about a bottle-feeding situation, but she can't leave the island and we don't have the facilities to maintain that here.'

To her surprise, he put a hand to the back of her neck under her hair. Instinctively she leaned in for just a second as his thumb made a small comforting circling motion on her skin. The gesture sent a solar flare directly to her loins in spite of their situation. A sob she'd somehow managed to contain since their rescue last night welled in her throat, and she only just managed to swallow it back again.

'Good thing Aayla's not here. She might have tried to carry it back to the boat in her backpack anyway,' he mused.

Ivy didn't trust her own voice now. She might've tried the same thing once. For all the good they did here, they couldn't help every animal. It just made her want to stay longer, try harder. Do more. Suddenly she understood why Jero had arrived here all these years ago and never left.

Flipping back to vet mode, Jero handed her a notebook and pen from his backpack. 'Make a note of the physical characteristics, his size, external earflaps, fur colour...we have to report every animal we come across...'

They worked together for an hour in the rain, carefully scouring the beach for any birds, sea lions and iguanas displaying signs of distress. The only thing that looked distressed, however, was Jero. Was he still thinking about the sea lion pup, or was it Aayla? He probably felt bad for scaring her last night, but the kid was tough. Once she'd learned that they were trying to stop tonnes of marine life from meeting their untimely death, her little fists had balled up and her mouth had twisted at the injustice. She hadn't looked upset, she'd been angry.

Ivy barely knew the kid, but she could see the way Aayla cared for her animals. She'd helped to shield her young eyes from some kind of massacre last night but, at the time, she hadn't even realised what she was doing. Did she really jump on that lifeboat, before Jero even had a chance to?

They made their way back down the winding coastal path towards the Zodiac boat and Ivy focused on his backpack ahead, thinking about Aayla and what he'd said last night, about losing her. It was pretty clear he did still carry the scars from his ex abandoning them, just as she still panicked inside whenever she pictured someone else she loved leaving *her*.

Maybe that was partly why she'd left Simon, before he could leave her, she wondered absently for the first time ever. One of them was probably always going to go eventually, even if she *had* agreed to bear his children. It was awful to think about, yes, but facts were facts. They'd just never really had all that much in common. She should have woken up years before the kids thing forced her to. When did she decide that, just because she'd been ignored before, she'd have to settle for the first man who paid her a little attention?

'Not far to go now. You OK back there?' Jero cut into her thoughts, turning back over his shoulder. His shirt was fully plastered to his form now in the rain, like some kind of island sculpture.

'All good,' she replied, glancing down at her own rain-soaked shirt. The pale minty green and white stripes were kind of see-through already. Had he noticed?

She rolled her eyes to the grey sky—what did it matter how she looked for him? Why was she letting this man confuse her like this? Rather than admit they might have something in common last night, Jero had pushed her away. The way his tone had changed when he'd asked her: *'So, when is your flight out of here again?'* It still made her shiver.

She really *should* check when her flight was, though. Mike was probably dying to have her back…or not. He hadn't called in a while, now that she thought about it. She was getting a little concerned he might be worried about telling her he wanted to sell.

The more they stalled, the more they were offered for the clinic in its prime location, but they could only buy so much time. Mike had a family to raise; the money would mean he could take a few years out from work to enjoy that, but what would *she* do? It wasn't about the money to her. It wasn't about having a man either; she would always need to feel needed.

'How did you know this was what you wanted to do? Live out here, I mean. Caring for all these wild creatures, especially in situations like this?' she asked Jero as they hurried onwards.

'It's not all paradise, like the tourists think,' he replied, clambering over a fallen log and stopping to check she made it, too. The sandy ground was flooded in places now, and lava lizards scurried from their path as they forged ahead.

'On my second day here, when the last surgical light burned out, I had to use a headlamp in surgery for the rest of the week.'

'A headlamp? Really?' Ivy swept a branch out of her face as leaves and thorns threatened to take her out. The action caused a shower of stored-up rain to soak her hair even more.

'That's island life,' he said. He lifted the next branch away from her face so she could make it underneath it safely. 'When a family's dog was knocked down by a car in my first month here, we didn't even have a splint for its broken leg. I had to go to two local hardware stores. Even then, all I could find that would work was some window trimming. It was stiff enough after they cut it to size for me.'

'Did it heal?'

'The dog was fine. But that's when I realised there was more that I could do here on these islands than I could ever do anywhere else. That's when I went about setting something up permanently. There's still so much to do, but we don't have to go to the hardware store for make-shift splints any more, so that's something.'

He held another branch back for her. 'I like how no day is the same, but still, we make a difference.'

'I kind of like your island life,' she said, before she could even register the words exiting her own mouth. 'On days like this, I wish I didn't have to leave.'

Jero stopped in his tracks and turned to her. Her heart lurched as he reached for her face and produced a stray leaf. It must have been caught in her hair. The rain seemed to disappear. Everything disappeared. Her fingers found his hand as it hovered close to her cheek with the leaf... just as a crash of thunder shook the sky and the heavens burst open.

She shrieked. Jero clamped her hand in his and started running. She could barely see where they were going now through the torrent of rain lashing at her face, but suddenly he was urging her towards a makeshift shelter, a box of sorts, which seemed to be made of several wooden upright planks and a straw-covered roof. She found herself inside the tiny enclosure, panting, catching her breath as Jero pushed open a tiny window at eye level, sending a shaft of light in.

'It's for the birdwatchers,' he explained, and Ivy laughed nervously, dropping to a tiny seat as the rain crashed against the roof like bullets. Dry moss and leaves were scattered across the floor. Somewhere, an unseen animal scurried away.

Jero dropped the backpack to the ground. The shelter seemed to shrink to fit them both. 'Are you sure you don't want to leave?' he asked her now, motioning skywards to the torrential rain with a wry smile, shaking out his arms and shirt.

Ivy hugged her arms around herself, watching the manta on his arm in the beam of light. 'I don't know,' she told him, truthfully. Jero, standing here before her like some kind of hunter warrior on this windswept, rain-soaked four-million-year-old island was turning her heart into a dancing circus monkey. Being in a birdwatching box didn't help.

'We both know you *have* to leave,' he said pointedly, inching closer to her still.

'I know,' she managed, lifting her head to meet his gaze, letting her hands close the gap between them, till her fingers were clasping at the hem of his T-shirt. 'I do have to leave eventually, but…'

What was happening to her brain? Every word they were exchanging felt like some kind of nail into a coffin. His eyes were glimmering with desire; he felt it too, this *thing*. Right now, in this moment, two very different lives were merging before her, throwing her off-kilter. Part of her wanted to stay longer, making sure nothing like the horror show out there ever happened again. Helping him.

Helping *herself* to *him*…who was she kidding?

A reckless kind of energy surged inside her.

Ivy pulled him in as if her life depended on it. Jero reciprocated, sweeping down to claim her lips like a wild creature swooping for its prey. Her tummy dissolved into a warm, liquid ball of lust as their kiss deepened and intensified like the rain pounding the straw roof above their heads.

His voice came hard and terse, setting her heart alight. 'Ivy.'

A fizzing current tore through her veins as he pulled her up from the seat to him, igniting every fibre of her being. She squished the voice as it scorned her: *You shouldn't be doing this…you've been staying away from this for good reason, too many reasons to count…*

His lips seared hers possessively. His tongue swirled and ravished her mouth in a hungry dance. She never could have guessed it could feel like this. That she could be this turned on by a relative stranger. *Shocking…but, oh, yes…more!*

A deep moan of pleasure escaped her open mouth as she found herself clasping the bulk of his muscled shoulders. Muscles rippled in her hands. *He's so freaking hot.*

Jero slowed his kiss, and his fingers trailed a pattern up her ribcage to the hem of her bikini top, lifting her wet shirt as he went, making her physically ache for him.

Her breath came sharp as her nipples stiffened. The feel of him caressing the curve of her breast like precious treasure—it was enough to make her damp in places the rain couldn't reach.

Dizzily she melted like butter against him, then gasped in anticipation as his other hand swept her head back, finding fistfuls of her hair at the nape of her neck. His lips rained kisses across her shoulder blades, her mouth and breasts. She'd dreamed of this after all, while wish-

ing the thoughts away, and now, tasting his kiss, reality
was a thousand times better.

*You're going to fall for him now...what an idiot move
this is.* Her ego tried to chastise her again, but she shushed
it away, arched her back and pressed into him, dying for
more.

Then, as if to tease her or torment her, Jero withdrew his perfect mouth, pulled back an inch and trailed
a thumb across her bottom lip, gazing so deep into her
eyes that a shiver shook through her, not from the cold
this time.

'I've been thinking about doing that for days.' His
mouth curled in a half-smile that quickly turned to something like faint admonishment as he caressed her face
with one big hand. 'I've been telling myself not to.'

She gaped at him, too dazed to utter a word. She
needed to feel his lips on hers again before regret took
hold of her too. She wanted this moment to last, way too
much to talk. Reaching a hand to the back of his head,
she pulled him in again, caressing his shaven scalp, tracing his tattoo with her other hand.

His ebony eyebrows drew together. 'See what you're
doing to me,' he half growled, half purred against her
mouth, and she shut him down with another kiss. The
sensual sound of his enjoyment sent new bolts of anticipation rippling through her. She could feel what she was
doing to him; it was pressed firm against her thigh as he
found her lips again.

'I'm safe,' she heard herself saying, finding the zip on
his shorts, kissing him deeply as he shook them aside.
She hadn't stopped taking her pill.

Jero murmured something indecipherable, then
cupped her backside and lifted her off the floor, placing
her back on the tiny seat. Instinctively, her legs wrapped

tight around his waist. His hardness made her damper than ever and when he pushed her underwear aside it took just one thrust for him to slide inside her. She was so ready.

His fingers twined into her hair. Arching her head back, he took her lips again and she forgot where she was completely as he thrust in and out, hard and swift, softly and slowly, filling her up deeper every time. Oh, God!

Deep unrivalled pleasure coursed through her with every move. Every hot, wet stroke and slide took her further into delirious, delicious insanity and she hugged his middle with her legs, feeling her climax building already. The wildness of it had every atom in her body throbbing and pulsating. *This* was the hottest sex she'd ever had!

Time was an alien concept suddenly. They could have spent minutes there, or hours, she couldn't get her brain around anything but the feel of him. When she toppled over the edge of pleasure, crying out into his mouth with the contractions, Jero jerked inside her. His expression sharpened to such fierce intensity as he came that her throat dried up. Together they shook and trembled with a new undoing, and Ivy struggled to find her breath. *What just happened?*

Jero collapsed against the wall, shaking his head. Laughter bubbled in her throat at the spent expression on his face; she felt so naughty, like a bad, bad schoolgirl with her boyfriend in the bike shed.

'The rain's stopped,' he observed after a moment, eyeing her warily as he pulled his shorts back on and scraped a hand across his head. She couldn't read him now, but every blood vessel was still tingling between her thighs. *Did we really just do that?*

Jero swept up his backpack from the ground and elbowed the door open. Sunlight flooded in, sending her crashing back to reality. The sky was blue again. Their path back to the boat was clear. She hadn't even noticed.

The boat ride back to their island was quiet. Ivy read a book, or at least pretended to. She kept sneaking glances at him. He looked distant, distracted. OK, so a lot had happened, and not just between them, but was he regretting that spontaneous sex? She didn't want to regret it, but if it meant things would be weird from now on, she would.

Ugh, maybe that was too reckless. Amazing, yes. Unmatched in every way, but while it was probably inevitable that they'd act on this attraction somehow, she was the tourist here, just like his ex. Her presence, and this closeness, must stir up memories, remind him of what he'd lost before by doing the exact same thing. Was he putting her into the 'big mistake' box already?

She'd walked head first into a tricky situation, but it wasn't just her, was it? Discomfort snaked through her as he averted his eyes the second they found hers across the deck. They'd both crossed a line they couldn't go back from.

CHAPTER NINE

JERO WAS JUST walking into the clinic as Ivy exited the operating room. She caught his eye as she pulled off her surgical gloves and paused in her stride, probably surprised to see him. His stomach lurched with the eye contact as he dropped the box of syringes he was carrying down beside the desk, but she'd never know it, because he'd been doing pretty good at keeping his cool since the other day out on Isla Española.

'You're early,' she said, adjusting the bun of red curls piled high on her head. 'I thought you were out with the mobile clinic.'

'I was, and now I'm back. I have to restock before we head to Floreana later.'

He tapped the box of syringes and she frowned. 'I thought you'd wait for Aayla. She's finishing school in half an hour.'

'She's going on a playdate. I doubt she'll make it here today.'

'Oh. OK.' Ivy looked sideways. 'I haven't seen her, or Pluma, not since we got back from Española.'

'Well, a lot has been going on,' he said as the guilt began to rage around his heart.

The huge black cat squirmed in their client's arms beside her. The short man holding it cleared his throat, looking between them in interest. 'If you don't mind, I should get going,' he said in Spanish.

Jero hurried to open the door for him at the same time as Ivy. They collided in the entrance and Ivy let out a harried sigh. He clocked her flushed cheeks; the way she shook out her arms, then straightened her white coat, all while avoiding his eyes. She was all wound up now, no thanks to his arrival. Or his lie. Could she tell he'd been keeping himself and Aayla at a distance as much as possible since his totally unacceptable, seemingly irrevocable crush got out of hand?

He swiped a hand across his head, knocking his sunglasses sideways and correcting them quickly. *Great job, Jero. So much for keeping it cool.*

'How did the surgery go?' he asked her when they were alone in Reception. Ivy made a thing out of writing something down in a folder he didn't recognise. She started telling him about the cat, and the urethrostomy, or penis amputation, she'd just performed on it due to the sixth urinary obstruction it had suffered in as many months. Watching her lips move took him back to the island...like most things she said now did.

It was very unfortunate. No matter how much he distracted himself he couldn't stop reliving how they'd almost brought the whole damn birdwatching box down with their antics. Man...he hadn't had sex like that in a long time; maybe ever. The way the trembles of her orgasm had rippled through him; that was some connection. He'd been craving the taste of her ever since...

'Jero?'

'What? Sorry, were you talking to me?'

Her amber eyes narrowed. 'I was saying how I've started a new filing system. It should make things a little easier for you all. Should we go over it now?'

His turn to frown now. 'Why did you do that?'

He stepped around the desk and flipped through the neatly labelled patient file, but she was opening the laptop, typing into some programme he also didn't recognise, ticking online boxes, telling him how they should log all their notes here too from now on.

'We don't do things like that,' he told her, shifting on his feet, feeling the lump of coal in his heart drop to his stomach and start to burn.

'Well, you should. It's better this way,' she retorted. 'You need a digital trail.'

'Why?'

'Because it's not 1963, Jero, and the world has moved on. I can't imagine why you're so offended by evolution. What would Darwin say, if he was still here?'

Jero clenched the insides of his cheeks. Changes were not things he particularly embraced, especially when they were initiated by someone who'd come in out of nowhere and messed with his head enough already.

'I don't want a digital trail, Ivy. It's more personal this way,' he said coolly. 'We know where everything is in the *real* world. Why fix what isn't broken?'

'Just give it a chance, will you?' She sighed. 'And I'm not sure you do know where everything is. You're always looking for files. It wastes time.'

He opened his mouth to respond but Ivy was already bashing something else into the computer, a fierce look of purpose on her face. OK, she had a point. His way of filing *was* pretty dated. And maybe it was more than her new filing system annoying him.

They'd both given into their attraction out there on the island. It wasn't all Ivy's fault that his carefully regulated world had just been twisted all out of alignment. He shouldn't have caved in as he had. All he'd done was invite more trouble into his life. Aayla's too. Ivy had cast her spell and burrowed under his skin, which was not a good place for her to be, seeing as she was leaving in just over a week.

He knew she was leaving. And he'd got his heart involved anyway.

'You put the animal's details in this column, and the contact details on this tab...'

He stood in silence as she explained the online system and tried to pay attention over the noise of a fresh litter of stray kittens Dudders had brought in earlier, mewing for attention in the back. This was just one more thing to think about in an endless list—he had to head back out with the mobile clinic in less than two hours, this time to Floreana.

He'd promised Dee an update on the trawler saga, which meant heading to her research base at the Tortoise Station up in the Santa Cruz highlands, where he'd also examine the giant tortoises for new pregnancies. A friend of Aayla's was coming to the house tonight with her mother, to see about adopting a puppy. Did he promise them dinner too? He couldn't even remember.

All he could think now was, why was Ivy going out of her way to help him, when he'd been a total jerk?

Maybe she was just as mad at herself for complicating things, he considered now. *Neither* of them had addressed what had happened out there on Española yet. Instead, they'd been doing some awkward dance around each other ever since, like two courting albatrosses unsure of the next step. Sure, they were busy, but not too busy to have found the time to talk by now.

Maybe they *did* need to talk about it. He should let her know where she stood so she didn't expect anything more while she was here.

Yes, he would tell her that. That way he'd draw a line for himself too. A very distant line from any further temptation...which, come to think of it, was probably why he'd been avoiding her in the first place. Distance meant he couldn't get any closer, even though he wanted to.

Smart, Jero. But not exactly fair.

He flipped the lid down on the laptop, left his hand on top.

'Ivy, about what happened. We should probably...'

Relief flooded her eyes. 'Oh, God, yes, Jero. I was thinking the same thing...'

She swivelled the chair to him, inviting conversation, but the doorbell jingled an interruption and in walked their next client with Bernardo, a huge brown and white dog the size of a Shetland pony.

Ivy tore her eyes from his and stood, while all the words he'd been planning to say dissipated in the air conditioning. They both plastered smiles to their faces. Jero cursed the timing under his breath.

What was she thinking, exactly? What did she think he was going to say? Why did he care so much, dammit?

His phone rang on the desk, stealing the moment completely.

Aayla's school.

His heart sank like a ship even before the teacher spoke. Aayla had gone outside to the bathroom ten minutes ago and she hadn't come back yet. They couldn't find her. He stared blankly at the wall a second, processing it. Every father's nightmare.

Ivy must have sensed the slow-building dread in the pit of his stomach or seen it on his face.

'What's wrong?'

'Aayla's missing.' He could barely believe the words coming from his own mouth.

'Missing?'

'Can you handle this examination?' he asked her.

'Of course I can handle it.' She put a hand to his arm. 'Go!'

He didn't miss the concern that flickered in her eyes before he turned for the door, but he couldn't take it onboard. He couldn't even contemplate that she might have something to worry about.

'She won't have gone far, try not to worry!' she called after him.

Jero bit his tongue the whole way to Rainbow Grove Primary School, as if he might yell his real thoughts to the trees along the sandy path if he didn't. It was a fifteen-minute walk usually, but now he was running, his head a blur. So much for not contemplating that there might be a real problem; his phone was still silent. Which meant no one had seen her yet.

'Aayla!' His voice carried on the breeze, disturbing a chicken pecking the path ahead, and two tourists wielding cameras and giant backpacks.

What if she'd been kidnapped, stolen right off school property?

What if one of those fishermen from the illegal trawler had come to exact revenge? Of course, they probably wouldn't recognise him, or her. They were still incarcerated anyway, awaiting trial as far as he knew.

But what if...what if...what if...?

Telling him not to worry just proved how little Ivy knew him, or anyone else who was trying to be the best parent for their child. You worried all the time. There was barely a moment when you didn't worry. You could worry all damn day and all night if you stopped to think about the dangers your child might inadvertently wander into on the path of life, all while you were looking the other way.

Not that Ivy had any real reason to know that, he reminded himself. She hadn't known much in the way of parenting. She'd barely been around a child before meeting Aayla.

He admonished himself, kicking a pebble in his path and apologising to a sleeping dog as it landed in front of his nose and woke him up. There he was again, being hard on *Ivy*, when really he *should* be being harder on himself. Ivy had been nothing but great for Aayla so far; the rest was in his head. A result of his own guilt over upsetting the status quo, which could in turn, if he wasn't more careful, upset Aayla.

Aayla could pick things up from a mile away, every bit of chemistry and tension. She knew something was up with him and Ivy, now that he thought about it. She'd been adamant that Ivy read to her on the boat, and she'd been asking to hang out with her ever since their return.

He'd told her no, kept her just as busy as him on other things…but he wasn't proud of himself for it.

'Did you find her?' Concern and fear had become a bubbling geyser waiting to erupt by the time the kindly middle-aged Ecuadorian woman, Mrs Ferdinand, took him aside outside the school gates.

It was home time. All around him, parents were collecting their kids and the hot sticky air was thick with laughter and high-pitched chatter. The friendly community he'd seen grow around him and Aayla had never made him feel so alone.

'We still haven't seen her,' Mrs Ferdinand apologised,

as Angie, the single mother of Aayla's planned playdate, approached, looking just as worried. 'But we think she must have gone looking for her bird somewhere.'

'Pluma?' Jero scratched his head, pulling his silent phone out again, as if some random, kind stranger might call him if he watched the screen, and report that they'd found her. Perspiration built at the back of his neck, and he fanned out his shirt. Angie bit her bottom lip, eyeing him up and down.

'She's made quite a name for herself in this place, with that bird,' the principal told them. Angie squeezed his arm and he pulled it away. 'Apparently, she started to try and fly in the classroom, and Aayla got quite upset about it. We think it might have happened again when they were outside…'

'Is anyone looking for them?' Angie asked.

'Of course, every teacher and volunteer, some of the parents too—'

'She doesn't do this. She doesn't just wander off,' he interrupted, heading off alone towards the rainbow-painted outhouse where she was last seen, calling her name. Desperation was making an empty well of his stomach. He hit the beach next. Was it too soon to call the authorities? To make sure no one left the island until she was found?

He called to check, jarred by the wobble in his own voice. They were already on it, of course— the school had alerted them. It made the silence of his phone seem louder.

For the next hour Aayla's name echoed all around him as others joined the search. From the beach to the street, people were gathering, talking, hypothesising under their breath no doubt, all looking for his daughter. It was all Jero could do not to sink to the sand and rock himself into a parallel universe; one where this was not happening.

CHAPTER TEN

'NAYELY?' IVY PRESSED the phone to her ear over the squall of the seabird someone had just deposited in reception. It hadn't been too injured by the child's wayward football to forget how to bring a house down, and the noise wasn't exactly soothing her frenzied mental process. 'Zenon!' she called to the storeroom. 'Zenon, in here, please!'

She'd been worrying about Aayla, and Jero ever since Jero had left over an hour ago. Now Nayely was calling from the hotel reception. *Please, no,* she thought, signalling for Zenon to take the bird with him into the back. Now was not the time to learn her room had flooded, or the ceiling had caved in, or worse.

'Ivy, I think you need to come here. I can't get hold of Jero.'

Ivy's stomach contracted. 'What?'

'Aayla is here. She's asking for you.'

Within minutes, Ivy had left Zenon fully in charge of the squawking flightless cormorant and hurried back across town on the bicycle loaned to her by Aqua Breeze Couples' Resort. She'd never ridden it so fast.

Swinging through the hotel doors to the lobby, she found Nayely sitting with a tear-stained Aayla on the purple plush sofa, snuggling Pluma to her chest. It was

quite a sight: a child and a bird with blue feet. A couple
wheeling suitcases, who looked to be in their sixties,
cooed and ventured closer on their way past, but Aayla
spotted her and leapt to her flip-flopped feet.

'Ivy!'

To her shock the kid ran for her across the marble
floor and Pluma tried her best to ruffle her feathers. She
couldn't quite manage, seeing as Aayla now had a firm
grip on her soft feathered body.

'Jero's on his way. I finally got hold of him,' Nayely
told her, glancing behind her.

The poor woman had a queue of people to attend to
now, but it seemed she'd held them off. They were all
drinking some kind of cocktail, watching Pluma, looking nothing but amused. Ivy thanked her profusely for
not leaving Aayla's side. What a community they had
here! She dropped to the sofa in relief while Aayla bab-
bled on at her, talking a million miles an hour in both
Spanish and English.

'This was where you found her, Ivy. Maybe Pluma
wanted to fly to you?'

'Well… I never thought about that,' she said truthfully.

'I wish we had your camera when she flew.' Aayla
stood between Ivy's knees, and Ivy prised the bird gently from her hands, setting her on her lap. She tried to
keep her voice calm and collected.

'She flew, already?'

'She tried to fly away!' Aayla's lip wobbled. Then
she started to cry again. 'What if she doesn't love me
any more?'

Ivy felt her throat dry up.

'Don't cry, sweetie,' she managed, looking all around
for help. It was deeply uncomfortable hearing her cry.
Suddenly she knew why. It took her back to all the times

she'd cried, alone, convinced that her own mother would rather be anywhere than at her side. Some kind of strange maternal instinct to protect her kicked in again, as it had done back on the boat when she'd kept on slashing those nets, knowing if they didn't break she'd present this poor kid with a sight she'd never be able to un-see.

'Did you actually see Pluma fly?' Ivy asked her softly, right before Nayely called across the lobby to confirm that, yes, Pluma had flown to the hotel entrance and tried to get in by pecking at the door. Aayla had appeared moments later, claiming Pluma had landed several times along the path here from the school. It sounded a lot as if the tame bird had been checking to make sure Aayla was following her.

Unbelievable, Ivy mouthed. The bird was a miracle. This was the first she'd heard of Pluma flying, but it surely wouldn't be the last. Jero's words came back to her: how you couldn't keep anything with wings anywhere it didn't want to be.

Ivy got to her knees in front of the child, wiped the tears from her cheeks with her fingers as she'd seen her friends do to their children. It wasn't as awful as she'd previously expected. Aayla calmed down instantly, which sent a strange rush of warmth to her heart and somehow comforted her, too.

'She's a wild creature, Aayla,' she told her gently. 'She's going to fly sometimes. But it sounds like she came to a place she thought one of us would be. And she brought you here too! That means she loves us both, does it not?'

The sobbing Aayla seemed to contemplate this for a second, while Ivy realised the truth of her own words. Pluma *must* feel a bond with both of them, if she'd come here to Aqua Breeze. She'd rescued her from the beach just outside.

'She's going to miss you!' Aayla sniffed, making the liquid comfort blanket dissolve from her heart on the spot. But then, Aayla embraced her in a huge hug, almost squishing poor Pluma between them again.

'Aayla?' They sprang apart. Jero was here, flying through the double doors towards them, scooping Aayla up in his arms. 'Aayla, you scared me to hell and back. What are you doing *here*?'

Ivy stood slowly, registering how her pulse had sounded in her ears the second he'd appeared.

'I'm sorry, Daddy, I was looking for Pluma. But Pluma was looking for Ivy.'

For a second, as he held her and checked her face for scratches, and asked if she was OK, Ivy felt completely invisible. This was a pure father-daughter moment, in which anyone could see, without a shadow of doubt, how much Aayla meant to Jero.

She found herself blinking back tears as some kind of new, gut-based longing possessed every part of her. Longing for what? She didn't quite know. It had started just now, when Aayla said Pluma would miss her.

Maybe she was destined never to be a part of something this important. Maybe she'd never know this kind of love. She'd always been too busy telling herself she didn't want it. What was wrong with her?

'Ivy?'

She shook herself, dashing a hand across her eyes. Jero was talking to her, asking her something about the clinic. 'Zenon's there,' she answered quickly, annoyed at herself for getting emotional. 'Pluma flew here, Jero…'

'I know,' he said, finally releasing his daughter. His hand found hers, and just his touch sent a shockwave up her arm. 'Thank you for handling things so fast.' His voice was a gentle, warming breeze in her ear. 'My phone was all choked up with other people calling to see if I'd found her.'

Before she could respond he strode across the lobby to Nayely. 'I can't thank *you* enough either.'

'I didn't really do anything,' Nayely started, but Ivy watched her neat black eyebrows rise to the roof as Jero swept her in and hugged her so hard the poor woman floundered, clearly shocked by his enthusiastic embrace.

'These women, both of them, are extraordinary!' he enthused vociferously to the line of cocktail-drinking couples waiting to check in or out. Everyone applauded; some even whistled. The sixty-something woman giggled under her Galapagos visor like a schoolgirl. Her husband cocked a greying eyebrow in sudden suspicion, crossing his arms over his booby T-shirt.

Ivy bit back a smile at the sight of Nayely's flushed cheeks. Maybe she wasn't the only one with a crush on Jero around here. Not that Nayely, or this sweet retiree, had ever wrapped their legs around him in a birdwatching box, in the middle of a rainstorm.

What are you doing to yourself, Ivy?

She forced her eyes away, gathered up her bag from the sofa. Now was not the time to revisit their hot one-day stand or wish it would happen again. Jero had avoided being alone with her ever since, so clearly he regretted it too. Wasn't that what he'd been about to tell her earlier? That he wanted to forget it ever happened? She'd been expecting that, so of course she'd been ready to agree.

Obviously he wanted no part of a 'fling' with a tourist. She'd known that much before they let their impulses take over out on that island, and that was fine by her. *She* didn't do flings either. She was, as Mike liked to say, an all-or-nothing kind of woman. More nothing than all, most of the time, but still. What did she have to offer *these* people, really?

This was their little bubble, their inner circle. Their family.

'I'm supposed to be on Floreana by now, with the mobile clinic.' Jero scowled, scanning his phone when they were outside on the hotel driveway.

She put a hand to his arm. 'Cancel it, we'll go tomorrow. You've just had a pretty intense couple of hours—take some time out.'

Beside them, Pluma was waddling on the sand under Aayla's watchful gaze. Jero had given her a strict instruction in the lobby not to try and hold her back. *'If Pluma wants to fly, let her fly.'*

'OK, but I should still go and see Dee at the Tortoise Station,' he mused aloud to a nearby tree, sliding his phone back into his pocket and making the sexy cryptic manta on his arm come to life for just a second in the sun.

'Tomorrow,' she repeated. Why was he so stubborn? The man had more things on the go than her and that was saying something.

Jero let out a sigh. 'OK, but I think I promised to cook dinner for one of Aayla's friends and her mom. They're coming to pick out a puppy.'

Ivy closed her mouth. She'd been about to protest this plan, too, but she did want to see the puppies get rehomed. Jero had taken them all in as fosters while they looked for new families for them.

'Can Ivy come for dinner, Daddy?' Aayla tugged at the bottom of Jero's shirt, casting her big brown eyes up from her to Jero and back again. 'Pluma wants us all there. If we're all in one place, maybe she won't fly away again?'

'Oh, no, I, I'm busy…' Ivy trailed off, glancing at Jero. He wouldn't want her at their home, would he? Besides, she had to close up the clinic, finish adding the patient information to the new system, check in with Mike…because he hadn't exactly been forthcoming with his recent thoughts on the acquisition in her absence.

She was starting to get nervous. There were huge changes ahead if he wanted to sell and she decided not to…

'Sure, she can come for dinner, if she'd like,' Jero said, blowing all her other thoughts out of the window. He glanced at her sideways and shrugged before pulling his sunglasses over his eyes, rendering him unreadable. 'We wouldn't want to upset Pluma.'

Aayla let out a whoop as if it were a done deal, then gripped Ivy's hand like a vice, beckoning Pluma to follow them on her little blue feet up the pathway, the opposite way to the clinic. Ivy almost expected the bird to fly away again, but she seemed content with her previous adventure for now. Instead, she fluttered up to Jero's shoulder and perched there. The disbelief on her face must have made Jero laugh, and all tension was lifted. But through the hotel window, Ivy saw Nayely still watching them all, pretending not to.

'She wants a ride on Daddy!' Aayla exclaimed, bouncing up and down.

Who doesn't? Ivy thought to herself, feeling the anxiety creep back in again like a toxic jellyfish tentacle up her spine. If she went to their house, she and Jero might be forced to finish their conversation from earlier and talk about what happened. He'd tell her it could never happen again and while she'd have to agree… Ugh. Awkward.

She pushed the thoughts aside as they walked as a trio, with a bird, into the late afternoon sun. Nope. *Not today, insecurities.* She was a grown woman, and he a grown man. If he could do this, so could she.

This evening, and really the rest of her limited time here, was reserved for her duties. And adorable Aayla and Pluma, and the puppies. That was all.

CHAPTER ELEVEN

JERO FELT THE twisty tangle of what he now called Poison Ivy reclaim its grip on him, just at the sight of her administering a simple anaesthetic to the dog on the table before them. Not that Ivy Malone was anything but a remedy, but pretending he felt nothing in the face of her imminent departure was excruciating.

'Almost there, little guy,' she soothed as the adopted male street dog succumbed to the drugs, all ready for sterilisation. The truth was, Jero felt a little as though a part of himself were going under the knife, too.

Ivy was all checked out of the Aqua Breeze Couples' Resort. Her suitcase sat in the storeroom like some harbinger of doom, all ready for her to leave straight from here, straight to the ferry that would take her to the airport.

For days now, since *before* the dinner at his house, when Aayla had insisted Ivy be the one to tuck her and Pluma in and read them a story, he'd been holding back the burning urge to tell her that her being here had meant the world. To both of them.

It was always on the tip of his tongue. But he hadn't said a word.

They both knew what that encounter had been, right? A simple one-off. A very, very pleasurable, memorable one-off, but a one-off all the same. Getting all mushy and emotional about her leaving would feel too serious, too dramatic.

Or maybe telling her would feel too much like admitting he sort of liked having her around, that he needed her.

He didn't *need* her, not in the clinic, not anywhere. He'd fought too hard to get over the last tourist who'd sucked him in, and *married* him, then spat him out, and finally he was fine. No way was he going through that again, or anything remotely similar.

He'd let every single opportunity to talk to Ivy about anything non-trivial pass him by, and now it felt too trite to bring it up. Ivy hadn't tried to talk about what happened, either. If she was embarrassed or regretful about hooking up with someone else on her would-be honeymoon, he didn't know, but between them they'd mastered small talk instead of anything serious. And now, here they were. Counting down the minutes they had left... sterilising another animal.

'Pass me that knife?'

'He's looking pretty good to me.'

'Let's call his human. He'll be awake soon.'

Just tell her, Jero. Just say something nice. It's the least you can do.

That night when she'd joined them for dinner, Angie, Aayla's friend's mother, had done her usual chatterbox thing all night, from openly discussing her ex-husband's affairs at the dinner table, to picking out the plumpest, cutest puppy, to getting more than tipsy while Aayla and her daughter played upstairs.

When she'd finally departed, leaving him and Ivy alone in the house, he'd been about to bring their misadventures up casually again, in a no-big-deal kind of way, so at least they weren't just ignoring what had happened. But he couldn't quite think of how to say it. Then Aayla had called them up to her room for a story. Then Ivy had made some excuse to go home before she'd even made her way back down the stairs.

Maybe it was better this way?

Idiot. You'd rather just let her go now without a word, than actually talk about your feelings?

Of course, being Ivy, she'd insisted on coming in for her shift before leaving, so whatever it was between them that hadn't gone away simply because he'd hoped it might still lingered between them like an impertinent ghost.

It was still there in the car, two hours later.

'You know, you really didn't have to drive me to the ferry,' she said. Her hands were clenching and unclenching the bottom of her seat. Her jeans and brown leather boots, all ready for landing in Galway, only served to emphasise what different worlds they really lived in. He gripped the pick-up's steering wheel, then cut the engine. The car park was busy. The next solar-powered ferry to Baltra Airport was just pulling in.

'I'll come in with you,' he said, catching her eye in the mirror.

'Making sure I actually leave, huh?' she joked, clicking off her seat belt. But it probably wasn't really a joke. There wasn't anything particularly light about this moment; in fact, he was disturbed by the perpetual ache at his core. He didn't want to acknowledge it one bit, but he couldn't ignore it now.

He let her out of the car, let his hand linger too long on the small of her back as he wheeled her suitcase onto the ferry. They made the short crossing over the Itabaca

Channel in relative silence under cloudy, moody skies, and the silence dragged on into Departures.

'Wow, it's busy in here,' she noted needlessly, rubbing at her arms, glancing at him sideways.

Why could he not just say it? He'd loved having her around, he wished she could stay longer. That one-off had left him wanting her more than he'd ever wanted anyone!

Why was he such a damn selfish, broken idiot?

Aayla had worn her heart on her *My Little Penguin* sleeve this morning, hugging Ivy goodbye before school. Ivy had asked him if she could leave her camera with Aayla but he'd refused. He would buy his daughter her own camera. She'd looked pretty hurt at his refusal but presents—aka reminders—weren't necessary here. He hadn't wanted to let her say goodbye at all, really. Goodbyes meant pain and tears to Aayla, no thanks to Suranne. They did to him, too, he supposed, but this wasn't about him.

Was it? He contemplated it for half a second.

'You're kidding me?' Ivy was scowling up at the departure board now. 'My connecting flight from Guayaquil is cancelled. Of all the bad timings. They could have sent a text...'

She stopped talking, then rolled her eyes. 'I know, I know, island life. But seriously, why now?'

Her words made him laugh and he didn't even know why. Instant relief, maybe? She wasn't going anywhere, not yet anyway.

His mind spun at the change of plan as he followed like a Sherpa with her case to the check-in desk. She slapped down her Irish passport. 'I need to get to Galway.'

'Sorry, ma'am, there's been a technical difficulty. The airline has paused all flights.'

Jero listened in as the smartly dressed woman in a red

bow tie explained how one of the airline's international crafts had experienced an engine failure—but only in *one* of its engines—and that they'd put her on the next flight, in five days' time. More or less.

Ivy did a good job of not appearing as annoyed as he knew she probably was, even when they were back in the car, heading back to Puerto Ayora.

'Five days till I can fly. More or less. What will I do till then? I can't go back to Aqua Breeze,' she said, fixing her eyes on the passing scenery. 'Even if they weren't fully booked a year in advance, I'm pretty sure my so-called honeymoon was nothing but trouble for poor Nayely.'

Jero frowned to himself. Maybe he was crazy but he was already one step ahead.

'You know, if you want to keep volunteering, we can put you up at the staff accommodation. It's not so bad, if you don't mind the odd Bob Marley song drifting through your windows at night.'

She turned to him and for a second he thought she might flat out laugh in his face at the notion of prolonging their awkward time together. 'You want to put me in a room next to Dudders?'

He shrugged, but he couldn't help chuckling under his breath. 'I'm just saying, the offer of a room is there, whether you want to carry on working for us or not.'

'Why would I not?'

Jero fell silent, feeling her eyes drill into him. Her question was loaded. 'I guess…you might have decided you're over it,' he tested after a moment.

'Because we never talked about what happened?' Ivy exhaled long and hard next to him. When she spoke next, her voice broke like a glass, shooting shards straight through his hardened shell. 'It doesn't mean I'm over it,

Jero. In fact, if you must know, when I saw that flight was cancelled, I felt a bit relieved.'

Was she serious?

Jero put his foot down. Ivy gasped and gripped the dashboard as he swerved and pulled the car over, leaving the engine running in a cloud of dust. 'Get out,' he instructed.

Ivy stuttered, clutching her bag to her. 'What?'

'Get out!'

Before she could say anything more, he was already out of the car, striding around to her side. He yanked the door open, just as she was placing one decidedly un-beach-suitable boot onto the sandy ground.

'I didn't want you to leave just yet either.' Inexorable surging started up in his loins till he was acting on autopilot. He took her face in his hands, and for a moment, as reality caught up with him, he pressed his forehead to hers, feeling days of pent-up emotions threaten to spill out of him. *To hell with it.*

'I shouldn't have ignored what happened. I should have said something. I'm an idiot.'

'So am I!'

'I haven't been able to get that day, or the taste of you, out of my head.'

Ivy clutched his shirt by the collar and pulled him close. 'God, me neither.'

Just the scent of her tore through his senses, driving him wild. He found her lips, fuelled by the same intensity as before in the storm. Ivy's hands were suddenly all over him, claiming and possessing him on the side of the road like some demon hitchhiker he couldn't get enough of. They were kissing so furiously she was sprawled against the bonnet of the car with one leg hooked around his middle before they came up for air, and only then it was at the insistence of a truck driver, honking at them, trying to get his wide, heavy load of supermarket goods past their car.

Within the hour they were wheeling Ivy's case into the pristine sparkly lobby at the Pelican Hill Apartments. 'We had these built just before our house was built,' he explained, calling for the elevator. 'I lived here with Aayla for a while after...' He trailed off. No need to get into the break-up with Suranne now. 'Mostly I rent them out to the tourists.'

Ivy touched her fingers to her lips as she looked around the lobby with its giant Galapagos marine life wall feature and palms in silver pots. 'You had them built? You mean, you own these?' Her hand slid up and down his arm, as if she couldn't bring herself to break contact. 'Why did I not know that?'

'I guess I never told you,' he said. He found himself smiling at her slightly swollen lips, how they'd felt on his again right as he'd been about to let her go. They'd stopped the car several times on the way here to explore different routes, mainly around each other's mouths. Whatever was going on right now was probably reckless, and clearly everything he'd told himself he *wouldn't* do... but he was trying not to care. Somehow the universe— or a faulty plane—had given him another chance. How could he ignore that?

He pulled her close in the elevator and kissed her, feeling her melt into him all the way up to the fourth floor, where she pulled away quickly as the doors opened. Just in case.

'I'll put you in 401,' he said, swiping his card across the key lock. 'Don't worry, Dudders is on the second floor.'

'You have digital locks here? That's interesting,' she

teased, trailing kisses along his tattoo up to his neck, making him forget what he was doing for a second. 'I'm surprised you don't have to write my name down in a giant fusty-smelling leather-bound book…'

'Oh, we'll do that, too,' he said, hoisting her up over his shoulder. She squealed and laughed and pretended to protest as he pushed her case inside with his foot and kicked shut the door behind them.

Lowering her to the bed, he leaned over her, trapping her with her hands above her head, pressed to the mattress. 'Now what?' he growled, hearing his own desire catching in his throat.

'Now what?' she replied, pulling him down to her. In seconds he was smothering her in kisses, letting his tongue continue its journey into even more delicious places around Ivy's milky white body. Smooth as Irish silk. Sure, he shouldn't be doing this, any more now than when they did it the first time. But something was different now. This time he literally couldn't stop. No logic or reason was enough to make him take his hands off her.

He slid off her ridiculous boots. The rest of their clothes were on the floor in seconds. They both knew the car had been the foreplay. It didn't take long before she was writhing naked against him, sucking, caressing, moaning the way she had that day with the rain coming down hard over their heads. He trailed his fingers along the smooth white flesh of her stomach as she arched her hips to meet him and pleaded for him to be inside her.

'You want me?' he teased, hovering at the edge of her.

'More than I should,' she breathed.

That was invitation enough. She cried out as he bucked into her with one swift, hungry stroke that made clamps of her fingers over his shoulders. 'Oh, yes…'

Nothing had ever felt so damned good to him in his

whole life. He shut down the voices telling him he'd regret this. Nothing had changed at all! He was well aware of that. Ivy was still leaving. Just not yet. And would a little fun before she left for good *really* be so bad?

He had to stop before he came completely undone too soon, so he slowed his strokes, but Ivy was a force to be reckoned with. She rode him expertly almost into oblivion for a second time. It felt like hours they spent there, switching things up and around, trying things he couldn't even remember trying before; or maybe it was just different with her. They fitted, no one could deny it. Her slim frame felt precious, all small and trembling against his, but Ivy wasn't shy. She knew exactly what she wanted.

'Jero, please...'

'Please what?' he mouthed against her as she made an animalistic sound that turned him on more than any noise he'd ever heard, and pulled his lips to hers, then pressed her mouth to his shoulder, looping her arms around him. The sheets were soaked, the palm trees looked positively bashful outside the window at what they were witnessing.

'Please, please, please!'

'Tell me you wanted more of this, ever since last time,' he demanded, clenching his jaw, hovering at the edge of her again. He loved the look on her face, the sheer agony of the promise he was making, and not quite delivering. Whatever had come over him didn't feel quite like him; it was as if she'd unlocked another side of him, something raw he'd never explored, but wanted to. Again, and again.

'I wanted it. I want it.' Ivy half grinned, half gulped a huge breath, and tried to pull him back by the hips. He entered her again with the force she was begging for, memorising her face as the pleasure pulsed through her. She laughed huskily and wickedly, as though she couldn't believe the side of her he was bringing out either.

He couldn't get enough of the noises she made, or the way she shrieked with delight and curled her toes. She gripped the sheets either side of her, turning her knuckles white. By the time he felt his release he could have sworn he'd just been dancing with her soul in a whole different dimension.

'It really takes five days to repair a plane…' Ivy mused, some time later, rolling to her back and catching her breath. He turned to face her on the pillow, studying the flecks of sunlight in her eyes and the giveaway glow of her cheeks. Daylight was still streaming through the window straight onto their damp, slick bodies and crumpled sheets.

'Five days, more or less,' he reminded her, smoothing a stray red curl behind her ear, only to watch it bounce right back. 'Doesn't sound like it's the best plane, if they need to fly spare parts in over the best part of a week.'

'Or a specialist engineer?' She pretended to shudder. 'Maybe I dodged a bullet. Maybe we should just make the most of it. Unless…'

She paused. He could almost hear her think. 'Unless?' he encouraged, but he could already read her face.

'I mean, I'm still leaving, Jero.' She traced the manta ray on his arm with one gentle finger and sighed. Suddenly, the mood was dead.

He echoed her sigh at the ceiling, kicking the cotton sheet from the bed to allow more cool air across his naked body. 'I know.'

'So…this isn't really a good idea, is it?' she followed. Ivy's expression turned pained as he watched her dark red brows draw together. She stroked a finger to his cheek next and the warmth transferred straight to his heart. He got the feeling she was waiting for him to disagree, but how could he, when she was right? He'd done it again, let his animal instincts take over. Reality was slapping his red-hot face already.

Aayla had been all torn up about Pluma flying away, and Pluma was just a bird. The kid was scarred, no thanks to his failure to keep Suranne on the island long enough to help him raise her. He'd be an idiot if he went down that road again with someone else. Saying goodbye to Ivy again would be confusing as hell for him…her.

Her.

He shook himself, dragged a hand across his head. He liked this woman, a lot more than he'd been expecting to, but women came, and women went from his life and when this one left too, for the second time, Aayla would be tortured with questions he wouldn't be equipped to answer. What kind of message was he sending to his daughter?

'Jero?' Ivy narrowed her eyes. He wanted to kiss her again, go in for round two, but he also wanted to grab up his things and go. Let this *really* be the last time they saw each other.

She linked her fingers through his, and pressed his hand to the pillow between them, as if she could already feel him slipping away. Her imploring eyes made him forget everything else except how good it felt to be with her, but she'd said it first, right? This *was* a bad idea. If they kept this up, even for five days—more or less—he wouldn't be able to help involving Aayla. It would be even more complicated down the line.

'I don't regret what just happened,' he started, feeling the weight of his thoughts building up on his tongue. The words felt heavy and cold, like ice cubes crushing out the flames that had just been roaring between them for the best part of an hour. But if he didn't say them now, he never would. He turned to her. 'No regrets, Ivy Malone.'

'No regrets,' she agreed, curling her fingers tighter in his.

'But you're right, Ivy. It's not a good idea. This can't happen again. Maybe you should enjoy however many days you have left. You can stay here, of course, but forget about working with me. Go out, enjoy the islands, take more photos…'

She sat bolt upright, clutching the sheets to her chest. The hurt on her face rocked his core. He'd actually been testing her a little bit, he realised now, hoping she might argue, or confess that she wanted to make something work that didn't mean ending things for ever in five days.

'OK,' she said slowly, measuredly, as his heart pummelled his ribs like a boxer in a cage fight. 'I guess I can understand that, all things considered. Aayla considered.'

He clenched his fists around the sheets. Idiot, of course she didn't want to make anything work. What did he expect? That she'd turn around and announce she was selling her practice in Ireland for him and moving here? With him and Aayla? They weren't enough for her, just as they weren't enough for Suranne. Of course, he'd fallen for another headstrong ball of fire who'd end up doing nothing but burn him, and his daughter.

He forced himself not to reach for her as she left an Ivy-shaped patch of warmth and sunlight on the bed and stood up. Biting hard on his tongue, he stared as she turned fully naked to face him. Dear God, she was magnificent. He couldn't recall the last time he'd wanted a woman so badly, but he'd been stupid enough already, getting involved like this. Not every plane would break, and no honeymoon lasted for ever.

Let her go. Just let her go.

She studied him a second, then reached for her clothes. 'I guess this is the last you'll see of me, then, Jero. It's over.'

CHAPTER TWELVE

THE RADIO CAUGHT her attention from its perch on Marsha's packed fish stall. Ivy stopped with her camera in the middle of snapping three giggling children playing with a ball just beyond the bustling market. The locals were starting to pay attention to the news broadcast too—something about a rare bird on another illegal ship, discovered just outside the Galapagos National Park, tied to the same group of people who'd run the illegal trawler.

Marsha called her over. 'Ivy! I haven't seen you around in the last few days, I thought you'd left.'

'Nope, still here.' Ivy pressed the lens cap back on her SLR camera. She'd been keeping a relatively low profile since she'd found herself stuck here three days ago, mostly because she didn't want to invite questions like this, that might lead on to talking about Jero. By now it was probably rare for people to see her out without him.

Marsha touched a fishy hand to her arm across Álvaro, the ever-vocal sea lion. 'I think his voice is needed, Ivy, as usual. People listen to Jero.'

She stepped around Álvaro and smoothed down her green sundress. 'What?'

Marsha explained how Jero was one of the people who'd been called to give evidence at the trial over on the mainland. It had been expedited thanks to the new arrests, the international news coverage, and the rare bird. 'I was there too,' Ivy found herself saying incredulously. 'I saw it all. Why didn't they call me?'

Marsha blinked at her and rested a hand on her trellis table, just missing a severed fish head with her fingers. 'I don't know. Ask them or ask Jero. Aren't you still working at the clinic?'

'Not exactly.' Ivy drew a deep breath and allowed the moment to be interrupted by the resident pelican as it made a swoop for the fish head. Marsha shooed it away, and Ivy took her leave.

In an instant she wanted to call Jero, but nope. She was not going to do that. Yes, it was a constant stab in the gut knowing she was so close, yet so far from him after everything that had happened. The more she let what happened replay in her head, the more panicky she felt about having overreacted. In her silence, in staying away, she was playing the role of the tourist who was always going to leave, instead of maybe…just maybe, a woman who saw a glimmer of a future she'd never dared to imagine before. When they'd been making love, she'd pictured selling up, moving back here, seeing if they could make it work. But she hadn't told him. Of course, she hadn't told him—she'd been pumped with pheromones again, full of him. Afraid he wouldn't feel the same.

Resuming her walk, she tried to force all thoughts of him from her head. What good would it do to indulge in any more of these arbitrary outbreaks of madness? There was a child involved. She'd done the right thing.

Right?

Jero insisted on flying in on every breeze though, the sound of his voice, the feel of his lips on parts of her body that still burned for him. His passion in the bedroom was merely an extension of the way he conducted himself daily—but she'd never had a lover quite like that before. One who just seemed to fit so effortlessly. The first few times with Simon had taken some getting used to. She'd been left thinking 'that was nice' more times than she'd ever thought 'wow, that took me to another dimension!' In fact, the same could be said for most of her previous sexual encounters. She'd almost come to believe sex was overrated. Now she knew differently.

Just thinking about the positions they'd tried made her hot. Stopping under a shady tree, she answered her ringing phone, and observed two more kids playing on the shore, where they'd done the rubbish clean-up on the beach. That felt like ages ago already. And she was noticing children everywhere, which was weird. She'd barely registered them before.

'Hey, stranger!' Mike's voice sounded strange out of context already. 'Any news on the flight home?'

She sighed. 'Not yet.'

'Aren't there other flights you could catch?'

Ivy closed her eyes. 'Yes, but those would cost extra,' she explained. 'I don't have to pay more if I wait for the same airline.'

'The same airline with faulty engines? That makes sense, I suppose.'

Her mouth twitched at his Irish dryness. 'What's new from the Blue Stream Veterinary Alliance, Mike? I haven't checked my email today.'

'I noticed you'd been taking some time out from that,' he said. 'That's a good thing, Ivy. But yeah, they've given us a deadline for an answer. Six weeks from now. You were supposed to be back by now, so I guess I'll just tell you while we're here. I kind of want to sell.'

Ivy sucked in a breath. She'd known it in her gut, had

felt it coming like an alarm bell on a ticking clock, she'd just been blocking it out.

The parents were cuddling now, watching their happy offspring frolic in neon swimsuits. Her swimming brain took her back to Jero's lovely house the other night, reading Aayla a story, one either side of her bed with its ridiculous *My Little Penguin* bedsheets. They'd matched Aayla's T-shirt. So cute.

In fact, it had felt so warm and loving and cosy in that family unit…like something she'd been missing.

Of course, it had all just freaked her out and she'd left as soon as she could. Stupid really, getting ideas from a man who lived a zillion miles away from her normal life. It wasn't as if the lonely hole she'd spent her childhood in had been filled with anything else, just because she'd met a hot single dad and his kid.

So they'd invited her in—up to a point. Made her feel like part of a family for the first time since her dad died and her mother forgot her existence. They'd also made her forget she had some very adult decisions to make regarding her own baby—her clinic!

'Are you even listening?' Mike seemed to have realised he was talking about the private equity group's aspirations, and Miss O'Reilly's moulting parakeet, to dead ears, and she continued on along the beach, fanning out her shirt, apologising as her mind reeled with all this information.

'You just don't *want* to come home yet, do you?' he said now, making her pause in her tracks. 'You want to see more of this Jero guy. *And* his daughter.'

'Don't be ridiculous,' she snapped back, making an iguana turn its head to her.

'Well, at least you've switched off for once,' he said.

'There's more to life than work. But you do know, Ivy, your life will only rise to the level you settle for.'

Ivy was struck dumb a second. 'Wow, Mike, Oprah did good.'

'It's not Oprah, but she would probably say that if you weren't still so caught up in the past, maybe you would start to see a different future. For this place, for yourself! Listen, no one could blame you for keeping your heart all bolted up, but sometimes you need to let it out of that steel cage you keep it in…just for a little bit?'

Ivy gaped at the ocean, then bit down on her cheeks. Mike didn't know *all* the details. She'd already opened the door to that steel cage twice…well, she'd opened a bit more than a door, if she was honest. And how bed-shakingly brilliant that had been! But she'd be gone from here in a matter of days, back to Galway, where this would all be past tense and her heart would most certainly protest getting back in its cage. She'd never see them again, and she'd have to try and forget them.

She told Mike as much, noticing how the sound of her words made her feel more and more as if she was lying, denying herself what she really wanted. Mike scoffed at her and reminded her how she'd asked him to mail her old camera to the clinic on Santa Cruz, so Aayla could have it. Jero had refused to let her have her newest one, after all, and she'd wanted to leave the sweet girl with *something* to nurture her talent.

'You're single, Ivy, just enjoy yourself! I'll tell these guys they'll just have to wait a little longer. It's decided,' Mike said. 'Remember, just because I want to sell, you don't have to. Or you could work under new management for a whopping huge salary… There's a lot to think about. You could even work on contract and take extended holidays. Anywhere you wanted to.'

He emphasised *anywhere*. Like he actually meant here, in the Galapagos.

Then he told her he had to go. The parakeet needed him.

'Ivy?' Dudders' voice behind her made her spin around, just as she'd hung up on Mike. He was carrying a bag of tiny fish she knew were for the kittens and other creatures in the backroom at the clinic. 'I thought that was you. How's the fourth floor of Pelican Hill treating you?'

'Great, thanks,' she managed as her eyes found an unfortunate hole in the crotch of his well-worn elephant pants. 'How's the Darwin Clinic?'

Dudders dutifully recounted the latest happenings. Then he mentioned there was some kind of bug in the new digital system that they couldn't quite figure out how to fix. He looked at her expectantly over his bag of fish. 'Jero said you wanted to enjoy the rest of your time here away from the clinic, which we totally get. *Totally.* But…if you could find a few minutes…'

Ivy moved her camera to the other shoulder, and felt her face contort into a deep scowl as his words sank in. What was happening today? The universe was testing her for sure. First Mike's announcement, now this. Jero had told the other volunteers she had volunteered *not* to be there. How dared he? She'd done nothing of the sort. He was putting words into her mouth.

Her blood started boiling slowly as her mind churned. Yes, she had ended things, but he didn't have to act as if she was already gone, especially if she was *needed*. He'd told her he had no regrets. He'd been lying. He regretted it so much he was actively trying not to involve her in *anything*.

Before she could project her irritation at Jero onto

poor Dudders she took another deep breath. 'I have a few minutes,' she told him. Then she forged ahead of him on a beeline for the clinic.

'Ivy!' Aayla squealed and ran from her nanny, Nina, and almost ploughed Ivy over the second she walked in with Dudders. 'I thought you were gone!'

'I was but...' Ivy scanned Reception for Jero while her heart leapt and danced. She hadn't expected Aayla to be here during school hours. As far as she could see, Jero wasn't in the building. She didn't know whether to be disappointed or relieved, but all anger dissipated on the spot. What was she supposed to tell Aayla? They'd already said their goodbyes three days ago.

'I have a sore throat,' Aayla said now, putting her hands around her own neck and pulling a face. She was the picture of adorable in a scarlet headband, a red shirt and jean shorts, with her long brown hair flowing about her face in tendrils. But she did look paler than usual.

'Oh, I'm sorry you're sick, honey,' she found herself saying, getting to her knees to look her in the eyes. 'When did you start to feel poorly?'

'In maths class.'

Ivy smiled and pushed a lock of hair gently behind the girl's ear. 'Maths used to make me feel the same way.'

'I brought her home from school early,' Nina explained.

'I'm so happy you're here!' Aayla threw her arms around Ivy's shoulders, just as Pluma fluttered out from under the small table by the door. She flew up to perch on a shelf, right on top of the Manila files Ivy had hoped to make redundant, and bobbed her white head towards her. Was she actually saying hello?

Ivy was stunned into silence by both Aayla's embrace,

and Pluma's reaction. The bird was getting bigger, and tamer every day. She was roughly the size of a giant crow already, and while she was flying freely wherever she wanted, that still happened to orbit Aayla. Incredible!

'So...the computer...' Dudders had dropped the bag of fish on the desk and was looking at her expectantly again.

'Oh, yes, of course.' Remembering why she'd come, she hurried over and took a seat, placing her camera carefully on the desk.

Ivy was just fixing the issue in the system when Jero walked through the door. Her heart pole-vaulted to her throat in his presence. His shoulders were hunched, his handsome face was etched in concern. He was wearing the Texas hat again, flip-flops and a navy-blue T-shirt with *STAR Divers* on the back. Drop-dead gorgeous in that casually oblivious way. *Curses.*

He didn't notice her at first. He went straight to Aayla and got to his knees by the little table, where she'd resumed her reading with Nina. *What to do?* Ivy decided it would be a little silly to try and hide behind the laptop and the desk, so she stood and held up her hand. 'Hi, Jero.'

He turned to her in surprise. 'Ivy.'

She tried not to look affected by the mini clowns doing somersaults in her belly. 'I was just getting your files back up and running. If you'd told me sooner you'd have saved a few days' work. Some of what you entered will have to be added again.'

He shrugged, but he did look kind of sheepish as he glanced at the others and cleared his throat. 'I um... I didn't want to bother you.'

More like, you didn't want me here in case I let on how you screwed a tourist's brains out—twice—and then conveniently forgot she existed, she retorted in her head, but she kept her cool. 'It was a small issue with the server. If it happens again, you can just...'

She squared her shoulders and stiffened her spine, realising that whatever she said, if he cared at all, was probably going right over his head. 'I'll write it all down this time if you want.'

Jero didn't speak. He was still staring at her as if she were some feral cat he didn't know what to do with. Was he angry she'd just shown up here? Angry that Aayla knew she was still here, and had just been keeping away from her, for whatever reason? Ugh. Either way, this was awkward. She shouldn't have come.

'Second thoughts, I just remembered, I have to be somewhere.' She snapped the lid down on the laptop. Better to depart with her dignity still intact.

'Ivy, wait.' Jero made to step towards her, one hand outstretched, but in a second Pluma flew from the shelf and dived between them, making a grab for the bag of fish that Dudders had left on the desk. The determined bird swiped it up with her beak but in a flash the bag split at the seams. Tiny fish rained like stinky hailstones over the entire reception area, and, to her horror, all over their heads.

Nina gasped. Jero swiped at his arms and neck. Pluma started gobbling something up from the top of a pile of books. Mortified, Ivy just stood there, watching something small and silver slither lifelessly from her hand to the floor.

Oh, my God!

It felt as if time froze. Then, out of nowhere, Aayla burst out laughing, clutching her stomach, her sore throat apparently forgotten. In seconds, Nina followed, chortling behind her hand. To her shock and somewhat relief, Jero started laughing too. Just the sound of them all flicked a switch in her, till she was laughing so hard she could barely stand up straight, observing the pool of fish now covering the floor. That bird…

'See!' Aayla cried. 'Pluma just doesn't want you to go, Ivy!'

Ivy shook her head and swiped a hand across her forehead. Jero caught her eye, and she felt her cheeks flame. Maybe the kid was right—who knew how smart boobies were, really? At least being showered in fish had eased the tension between her and Jero. Not that she wasn't still annoyed at him for telling everyone she didn't *want* to be here. That would have to be addressed.

The door behind them swung open. 'Help me, please!'

The laughter stopped abruptly. Ivy followed Jero's eyes to the tear-stained teenager who'd just staggered inside, crying her eyes out. In her arms was something limp that looked far too big and heavy for her to be holding.

CHAPTER THIRTEEN

JERO WAS STILL processing Aayla's sore throat, the shower of fish in Reception and Ivy's sudden reappearance, and now the teen was talking a million miles an hour. Summoning calm, he threw the house keys to Nina and motioned to her to take Aayla home. Ivy was already ushering the girl and the dog she was carrying through to the back.

He met her in the OR, where she tossed him scrubs and gloves and set about injecting the dog while the teen stood watching them with watery eyes. 'You don't have to stay,' he whispered in Ivy's ear, catching her arm.

He'd been about to tell her thanks for the new system, before the fish incident. He hadn't wanted it implemented one little bit, but it had certainly made things a lot easier round here... before it broke down. But she was here again when she should be out there enjoying the island.

'Is that another way of saying you don't *want* me to stay?' she retorted in a hiss, eyes narrowed over the needle she was holding. 'You told everyone here I didn't want to work here any more. We didn't exactly agree on that part, Jero.'

Damn.

He didn't have time to respond before she'd turned to

Dudders. 'Dudders, Jero and I have got this. Take this lady out front, please.'

Jero watched Dudders lead the teen towards the door. His volunteers had come to trust and rely on Ivy almost as much as him, and he'd gone and told her to stay away. He watched her with a frown. He'd had his reasons for that at the time and allowing her time alone to see the island was the least selfish one of them. He didn't trust himself around her.

But here she was, and he did need her. The dog had been run over. It looked like a dachshund/beagle mix, no more than ten months old.

'Degloving to the left paw,' Ivy observed over the table as they inspected the male dog's toenails. They were all but peeling off with his skin and fur—a proper mess. Thankfully Aayla had been too distracted by Pluma and the fish back there to register all this.

'Can you save him?' The teary teen was still hovering in the doorway, looking between them hopefully from beside another cage of mewing kittens that wouldn't have fitted in the storeroom with the others. 'I brought him straight here.'

'He'll be OK,' Jero assured her, meeting Ivy's eyes again and trying not to register the agitation that still lingered in the depth of her stare. This was not the time to be thinking about how they'd left things…or how he'd been practically sitting on his hands every night since, to stop himself sprinting to her apartment to continue where they'd left off.

'The dog…the poor thing…he just stood there and let the scooter hit him…' The teen refused to move her eyes away, even as Dudders continued urging her away.

'We'll take care of him,' Ivy cut in, before he could.

It seemed as if the driver had sped off without even

looking back, which happened a lot. Most of their injured animals came in having been struck by cars or scooters. The poor girl had been right behind the offending scooter on her own bike and seen the hit and run.

'Please, do what you can! I think he was injured even before this happened,' she told them from the doorway, right before Dudders finally managed to coax her out to Reception, swiping a mop and bucket on the way past, to clear up the fish no doubt.

The X-rays didn't look good. 'She's right. He was likely born with a deformed wrist,' Ivy said, studying them alongside him some minutes later. 'I think it was fused in a bent position…it was probably his deformity that led to this paw injury. He just wasn't quick enough to pull the limb out of the way and stop himself from getting run over. Poor little man.'

'I think we have to amputate,' Jero said solemnly.

Ivy's eyes narrowed over the sedated dog. 'Once it's gone, he'll adapt quite quickly on three legs, I'm sure. But right now, he's in too much pain to go on enjoying life.'

'That makes two of us,' he followed.

'What?' Ivy crossed her arms. 'Are you comparing yourself to a dog, Jero?'

A stupid lovesick puppy maybe, he thought, annoyed with himself.

'Let's get on with it, then,' he muttered, wishing his mind and heart would agree on how they felt about Ivy.

Together they attended to their casualty in silence, but he felt it like electricity every time their arms or fingers brushed. He'd missed her presence around here; missed walking in and seeing her fiery curls and pearly smile and the way she was around Aayla, which had left an impression on the kid, he couldn't deny. Aayla wanted to be a wildlife photographer now, amongst other things.

What a woman, messing with his head like this. He frowned to himself, trying to focus on the stitches. Helping the wounded animal was paramount but seeing her again so unexpectedly had mowed him over like the dog. The last few days without her, he'd thought about her constantly, like an itch he couldn't scratch. Aayla hadn't let it go: *'Ivy this... Ivy that... Daddy, Pluma misses Ivy!'*

'Why did you tell everyone I didn't want to be here?' she asked him now, snapping off her gloves. Jero lowered the sleeping, three-legged dog into a crate beside the mewing kittens and felt her eyes on his back. He cleared his throat.

'I was testing myself, I guess, to see what it would be like when you were really gone. It was very quiet.' It was the truth, wasn't it?

'You are *still* going, Ivy,' he added as the familiar tightening started up around his throat.

'You're right. I have a life to get back to,' she said behind him. 'I should be there already really...especially as Mike wants to sell his half of the business. He just told me. Just now. It won't be the same without him. I can either sell out and leave myself or stay on under new management...my gosh.' She made a harangued sound. 'I'm thinking out loud again. I don't know why I'm even telling you this.'

Ivy went quiet, and he tried to ignore the thudding of his heart. He knew a cry for help when he heard one; despite everything, she wanted his input, or advice. He didn't *want* to care what she did next—it was definitely best if he didn't...

He settled the dog on the blankets, took his time locking the cage and heard her removing the coat she'd pulled on, button by button. Once she'd hung that back on the wall, she'd be gone again. Back to her complicated life, which would in no way involve him and Aayla from all the way over in Ireland, whatever she decided to do.

'It all happened so fast, with us.' She sighed, behind him. 'I took offence that you didn't want to see me here, but you're right, it would have been complicated if I'd carried on working with you—this is awkward enough! Me talking about my life like you should even care...'

'Ivy, of course I care.'

She held up her hand as he turned to her. 'It's fine, Jero. We had our fun. I know you're busy, probably thinking about this trial and everything else, and I know you have to think about Aayla and who influences her in what ways, especially after what your ex-wife did—'

'This has nothing to do with Suranne,' he cut in.

Ivy's eyes grew wide. He cursed himself for his defensive tone. He shouldn't have said it like that. He wanted to believe Ivy had been a temporary distraction, a bit of fun, but it had evolved into far more. How was it that he cared so damn much about her with every passing second? That was why he was mad, he realised. He might have developed feelings for Ivy faster than he had for Suranne. Would he ever learn?

'I have to go check on Aayla,' he said gruffly, removing his coat and tossing it onto the laundry basket. 'I have to shower this damn fish smell off me. I'll hand this over to Dudders on the way out.'

She blinked at him, tossed her own coat on top of his with a strength that defied her size, then crossed her arms again, lips pursed. Flames ignited in her amber eyes. He took a step towards her, then stopped just short of her shoes.

'Thank you for your help today,' he said, willing himself not to cross a line, and not to be affected by the perfect storm of hurt and fury on her face. 'And congratu-

lations on having grown such a great business that someone else would like to buy it.' He gestured around them,
just as a poster peeled from the wall again. 'That's not an
easy accomplishment for anyone but you did it. It must be
something incredible, waiting for you back in Galway.'

'What you do *here* is incredible, Jero,' she responded,
stepping away to stick the poster up again with a firm
slap of her palm. 'If you can't see how much I really mean
that, how much you inspire me, how much you make me
think I should just...'

She caught herself and huffed at the floor.

He stared at her, thrown. 'You should just what? What
were you going to say?'

'It doesn't matter,' she mumbled, which implied it mattered very much but she'd decided not to say it anyway.
Then she swept out of the room in a breeze of wet fish,
which somehow still left him wanting her even more.

Jero was reading the latest notes on the illegal trawler
case when the doorbell rang. He tutted under his breath.
It was after nine p.m. and Aayla was sleeping upstairs.
Her throat was still sore. He didn't need her waking up.
Expecting one of the neighbours, he flung the door open,
then did a double take.

'Ivy.'

'I left my camera at the clinic, and I don't have keys,'
she said, too coldly for his liking. He told her he'd brought
it here after she'd stormed out earlier. He would have delivered it to her himself tomorrow. Maybe.

'I didn't think you'd want to see me,' he added, pointing her through to the kitchen, where the camera sat on
the dining table.

She picked it up, looking around the kitchen warily,
and he regretted not doing the dishes. 'Thanks for keep-

ing it safe.' She sighed, clutching it to her chest. He shoved his hands in his pockets. She smelled like flowers and shower cream now and looked sexy as hell in a long flowing dress the colour of ocean shallows.

'I owe you an apology,' he said. 'Want to sit?'

Her lips compressed, sending the flesh around them white. The two remaining puppies scampered around her while he swept a pile of papers and stray clean napkins and Aayla's toy cars to the end of the table.

'You were right, what you said earlier. What happened with my ex changed everything for Aayla, and me... I shouldn't have snapped. I just don't like being reminded of all the ways I've screwed things up for Aayla.'

Ivy frowned down her nose at him as he dropped to one of the wooden chairs. 'What are you even talking about?'

'Well, I failed at providing the one thing a growing girl needs most, for a start—her mother,' he said, wheeling a toy digger towards him and back again with one finger. 'It's a sore point.'

Ivy dropped to the chair beside his and put a hand to his arm, stopping the digger in its tracks.

'The fact that your ex chose another life away from here isn't *your fault*, Jero,' she said on a sigh. 'Island life is tough. It's no reflection on you. Aayla worships you! So does everyone else I've met around this place. You've built a family around you right here. And if you must know...it's one of the nicest things I've ever felt a part of.'

She fixed her eyes on the puppies a second, who were trying to jump onto another chair. 'I never had a mother around me either, remember. But I'm OK. You're enough, Jero, don't tell yourself anything else.'

He felt a smile flicker across his lips. So, she wasn't mad at him any more. This was good—he'd been kicking himself all night for the way they'd left things. As usual he'd stopped himself going to her when he'd wanted to.

'Thank you,' he said. Her lips were so tempting as usual, but he couldn't kiss her. He wouldn't kiss her.

'OK, so your tech and organisational skills have their limitations,' she followed. 'And you would be murdered for wearing flip-flops in *my* clinic…but those are minor issues.'

He smiled broadly as Ivy dodged his play thump. He couldn't kiss her, but he didn't want this to end either. 'I like when you sing my praises,' he said.

'Don't get used to it.'

'You never really talked about *your* mother much,' he tested. 'Or your father.'

Ivy scooped up a puppy, cradling it to her chest. Then she asked for a glass of wine.

Without pause he crossed to the fridge and grabbed a bottle.

Two glasses later, and she'd told him everything.

Ivy had been too young at four and a half years old to understand the meaning of death. She'd only known that a new kind of emptiness and darkness had settled into the house in her father's place. Ivy's dog Zeus had lain on the doormat for a week with his big head on his paws, waiting. She'd sat with him, telling him it would be OK. Knowing deep down it wouldn't.

She told him how Etta Malone—former mother of the year—launched herself like an Irishwoman-sized missile into her work after that. She sounded like a force to be reckoned with. The first female CEO in her sector who'd bulleted through the gender gap in the tech industry, teaching women how to code. A real role model, so everyone said. Late nights, early morning starts… Ivy had barely seen her for the best part of a decade.

'Mum just made work her everything. Like she could possibly outrun her grief if she distracted herself enough. I guess it took me a while to realise that she was grieving the whole time. She probably thought she was helping me in some way, not exposing me to her misery. But kids know things. They know more than we think.'

'Tell me about it,' he said, offering to top up her wine as he led her to the living area. He moved his guitar from the couch, but she sat at the other end from him and crossed her legs under her, eyes fixed on *The Hungry Caterpillar* on the coffee table.

'I could hear her crying in her bed at midnight, she missed him so much. If I ever tried to go in there, she'd shoo me away. I guess I felt shut out, you know? But I didn't want her to feel worse by bringing it up. So we went on like that, quietly existing on two opposite sides of a wall. I don't know who was more closed-off in the end. Me, or her.'

'Are you still in touch now?' he asked, forcing himself not to stretch his legs out, where they might touch her in any way. Should she even be here? Probably not. If Aayla woke up she'd find Ivy here, and Aayla was already starting to look at Ivy as if she was the greatest thing since Lego.

Ivy sipped her wine, and he wondered if she usually talked about all this stuff. 'She paid for this honeymoon. She wasn't a bad mother; she just didn't exactly give me confidence that you can juggle a family with a career. Things weren't exactly perfect with Simon, but the catalyst to the break-up was the fact that I didn't want a family, not with how hard I work... I'm probably just as busy as my own mother was.'

'But you don't have to be that busy, do you?'

Ivy squeezed her eyes shut and shook her head in her palm quickly. 'I can't believe I'm telling you all this.'

He studied her flushed cheeks. Was she changing her mind, after getting to know Aayla? He might be biased but Aayla was a pretty great advocate for spending time with kids. 'You can juggle anything, I've watched you,' he told her, feeling the oddest sense of pride sweep through him for how she'd overcome such adversity, started out on her own and achieved so much already. She herself was a force to be reckoned with. He leaned forwards, his hand finding her knee over her dress.

'I think you'd be a great mother—just look at how much Aayla loves you already.'

The second he said it, he retracted. 'Not that I'm looking for a replacement mother for Aayla.' His wine glass clattered against the coffee table as he put it down. 'I mean...'

'And I'm not looking to be anyone's replacement mother,' she confirmed at lightning speed. Her fingers were white around the stem of her glass. He thought it might actually break. A jolt ricocheted around his heart.

What the hell had made him say that?

'Maybe we shouldn't have had this wine.' Ivy placed her glass down and stood up, but he caught her elbow. This time she landed right beside him, and a small helpless moan escaped her lips. 'I get it, Ivy. You don't *want* a kid. I get it, but what did you just say to me? You're enough.'

'I know that.' She leaned into his palm as he cradled her face, then placed her hand over his, against her cheek. She might know that, but it still looked as if she was fighting some kind of silent battle in her head.

He emphasised it again. 'You're more than enough. But when you go home...back to your business that ap-

parently someone wants to buy for big money, promise
me you'll think about what you really want, and what
really matters to you,' he said. 'I'd hate to think of you
missing out on anything.'

She scanned his eyes, searching, that look of confusion still creasing her brow. Her voice was choked when
she spoke. 'Why do you care so much?'

He traced a finger over her lips, memorising the shape
of them with his flesh. Mixed feelings assailed him as
Ivy caught his other hand. 'You're special,' he told her,
against his own will. His mind, mouth and body were
simply not aligning on how they should act around this
woman any more.

'Stop making me *not* want to go home, Jero,' she said,
lowering her head. He tilted her chin up.

'Well, stop making me want to ask you to stay.'

Rational thoughts became impossible. He couldn't tell
who kissed who first but in seconds they were a tangle of
limbs on the couch, and he was being forced to remember
how addictive her intense sensuality was as she blazed a
trail of kisses from his lips across his throat, hoisting up
his shirt at the same time, straddling him, locking him
down with her thighs.

Ferocious kisses grew softer, guided by their hearts
more than their hands for once. He really was in deep.
Already. He was going to be ruined when she was gone,
and he was probably walking into disaster with every
passing second, but what was he supposed to do?

He couldn't keep away.

He led her upstairs to the bedroom, tiptoeing past
Aayla's door, and a hunger, deeper and stronger than
anything sexual, rumbled in his bloodstream and did
its best to consume him. Pressing into her on the bed,
he wanted nothing more than to satisfy Ivy and share in

her pleasures and pain; to know every inch of her, every cell and story.

He'd never known desire and longing like this for anyone, never dared to imagine anything so intense after... after everything he'd suffered through to get here. Why not just give in and let himself enjoy her, while she was still here?

CHAPTER FOURTEEN

TWO WEEKS LATER, Ivy stared at the email, feeling her stomach sink. The flight home had left twelve days ago without her, and unless she took the next one, leaving three days from now, she'd lose her free seat. So far, she'd procrastinated and made excuses, spending her days and nights blocking out reality in a blissful bubble of hot sex with Jero.

It was more than hot sex, actually. She loved being at their dining table most, listening to them talk over homework. She loved cooking with Aayla and laughing at Pluma, and telling them both about Ireland, watching the looks on their faces, as if it were some strange, distant land she'd invented. Sometimes, her real life felt like a dream even to herself.

But their conversation that night, when she'd come to collect her camera, hadn't left her head. So Jero wasn't looking for a replacement mother for Aayla, which was totally understandable. She didn't want to be one and she'd told him as much. Maybe a little too quickly, in retrospect.

But the jolt to her heart when he'd first said that, and again, when he'd outright stated how obvious it was that she didn't want a child herself, it still stung. It made her feel less than what he needed…which should have been fine. She had a life to get back to after all.

But it was also confusing as hell.

Kids. Ugh. She'd never wanted that in her life before, not at all, but the reasons for that felt at odds with her heart now, the more time she spent around Aayla. Of course, Aayla was great. Maybe it was just *her* she enjoyed; rather than the notion of herself as a mother.

What was this feeling?

It was taking some processing, for sure.

Thanks to a virtual campaign and a new set of posters around town, designed by Aayla herself, they had managed to rehome the last of the puppies together. And several litters of kittens. Projects like this were starting to feel suspiciously like fun, even though they ate into her email time. But while time had considerably slowed since she'd let herself enjoy each moment away from *work*, it had never stopped ticking.

She should really just stop procrastinating and book the flight!

'Ivy, where should I put Tripod? We need the cage for the new puppies.'

Ivy pulled her fingers from the laptop keys. Zenon was looking around him in confusion for a place to put their three-legged dog. He'd just had his final check-up after the amputation two weeks ago, and she felt herself getting rattled again. Zenon had come in late—again—and had missed the stand-up, where she'd already informed the team of volunteers, including a new girl from Australia, of the schedule.

'The girl who brought him in is collecting him within the hour—she adopted him, remember? Just take him for a walk. Then you can clean the cage for the pups.'

He gave her a salute and made to leave for the back room. *Second thoughts.*

She called out after him. 'He's not called Tripod, she called him Alpha. And you know what, Zenon, there are lots of people who'd like to be on the volunteering schedule. If you don't have time for it any more, all you need to do is tell me... Jero. Tell Jero.'

Zenon's shoulders sagged. To her shock he went bright red from his florally tattooed legs up to his cheeks and stammered an apology. He promised to do better, told her how much he respected her for bringing it up. Jero had tried to pull him up on it several times apparently, before giving up and simply delegating more responsibilities to Dudders and herself instead, but it wasn't good enough and she told him so. Not on her watch.

She tried not to let the tension get to her as she continued with her consultations. A flea treatment, an ingrown claw...it all merged into one as her mind mulled over her situation. She *was* leaving. She had to book this flight. Mike wanted to sell, and so did she.

Maybe.

She still couldn't decide. Every day meant a different emotion around that, too. She'd kept it quiet so far, because the thought of giving up her baby—her clinic—was drastic and terrifying, but maybe it *was* time for something else. The thought wouldn't budge; that maybe she *could* spend more time here, sell up and invest in the Darwin Clinic, if Jero would even allow it? There was so much to be done.

It felt too abstract and strange to consider saying out loud. At night, it kept her awake. She'd taken to studying the exquisite lines and angles of Jero's sleeping face on the pillow beside hers, wondering what the hell was happening to her. Simon kept flashing into her mind, too. Simon had never given her these feelings. He'd never given her the sense that, with him at her side, she could make a difference to the world.

Simon was a good man, but he had never left her flailing in the wind, wondering where she stood or what she'd do without him. In fact, she had always been in control. She hadn't wanted kids, and that had been fine with him—till it wasn't. That was why she'd felt so safe with him, for so long.

Safe, yes, but ultimately unsatisfied...

Jero had encouraged her, that night they'd made love for the first time in his bed. He'd got her thinking more and more about what she wanted. That night, he'd let her in, let down his walls, and she'd let herself consider that this might be something real, something worth holding onto, against all odds.

But that was crazy, wasn't it? Intense emotional flings didn't last for ever; they were called flings for a reason! Besides, he hadn't said anything definitive at all along the lines of, 'Stay with me!'

So what if she thought he felt it every time they made love? Even if he did, he was right to be concerned, and work towards an official goodbye. Despite what he'd said about her potentially being a great mother in the future— or the fact that it somehow meant more than when Simon had said it—she was already thinking about new projects to get involved in, filling up her days as she always did. What kind of role model would she be in the long run? He must know that. She was no good for them.

Just book the flight, Ivy!

'Ivy, where's the extension lead?' Dudders asked now. 'I need to plug this new heat lamp in for the lizard.'

He waved a lamp in front of her, and she admitted defeat, and shut the laptop. 'There's an extension lead in the closet over there, I think,' she said. 'I don't know how old it is. You should ask Jero when he gets back.'

'I'm sure it's fine,' Dudders said cheerily. 'Oh, can you help me shift some of the other plugs around?'

Ivy sighed. She'd book the flight later. And it was time to tell Jero she was leaving for good.

That afternoon, Aayla met her with Nina and Pluma following close by, at the community talk Jero was hosting on the beach. Dee, their friendly conservationist from the tortoise sanctuary, waved at her, as did Angie, the lady who'd come to Jero's house to choose a puppy.

It was late afternoon and the sun cast long, spindly shadows across the sand. The light made all the people who'd flocked to hear him look extra shiny and golden. In moments like this, Ivy couldn't help imagining how rainy it would be when she landed back in Ireland.

Aayla led her by the hand to the chair she'd been saving for her, right at the front.

'Daddy's going to talk,' she announced, and Ivy's heart did a silly schoolgirl skip the second he stepped onto the makeshift stage.

He retrieved a kitten from an oversized pocket in his army shorts, and the kids all rushed to the front, kneeling before the stage to get the chance to hold it, while he relayed the importance of the mobile clinic.

'Don't be afraid to bring your cats and dogs to one of our mobile stations. The more we protect against unwanted domestic animals, the safer our islands will be against diseases...'

He was halfway through his speech, and Ivy was growing sicker, wondering where and how she'd tell him she was finally leaving, when Marsha, the friendly fishmonger from the market, made an appearance. She

looked frazzled to say the least. Ivy crept past Aayla and
Nina. Something wasn't right.

'Sorry, I know you're busy…but it's Álvaro.' Marsha
scraped a hand through her greying hair. Perspiration
glistened on her forehead, as if she'd run or cycled here
at lightning speed, afraid for the sea lion.

'What's wrong with Álvaro?'

Marsha explained how he hadn't been at the market
in two days, which was most unlike him. Someone had
just informed her of an injured sea lion that matched
his description. 'He's on the beach around the bay. You
can't get there without a boat. The guys who found him
couldn't bring him in. He was scared, and violent. I need
you to take me to him.'

'Me?' Ivy was stunned.

'You and Jero. He knows Jero. He knows all of us,
maybe he'll let us help him?'

Some people in the audience had turned in their seats
and were watching her and Marsha, instead of Jero. Jero
noticed. With a frown he excused himself from the stage.
In minutes he'd been given some keys to a boat and was
calling Dudders to meet them at the harbour with emergency medical supplies.

It wasn't Dudders waiting at the harbour with the supplies. It was Zenon.

'What are you doing here?' Jero looked suspicious
as he tossed the bag into the boat. He'd sent Nina home
with Aayla, even after Aayla begged to join them. Secretly Ivy was impressed with Zenon. He wasn't usually
available on call, especially this late. He was usually out
on a date with a tourist or sleeping.

'Just wanted to do my bit,' Zenon said, throwing a secret smile her way. 'I hope our old boy Álvaro is OK. And

hey, Jero, I just wanted to apologise if I've seemed a little unenthusiastic about being here. I'm going to change.'

Jero looked as if Zenon had tasered him for a moment, but he slapped his back good-naturedly and told him it was all good. Ivy nodded her thanks in Zenon's direction as their boat sped away. Good. He'd really listened to her.

The wind tussled with her hair as they cruised around the coast with Pluma soaring on the wind along with them. Never one to miss out on anything exciting, the bird had left Aayla, maybe sensing she was safe, and flown with the grown-ups instead?

Jero caught her eye and she felt her stomach clench, knowing she had to tell him she was leaving. How would he react? He knew she was going eventually, of course, even if they hadn't talked about it yet. Maybe she'd been stalling, falling in love a bit more every day… *Setting yourself up for a real fall,* she added in her head.

'Are you OK over there?' Jero's question was directed at her, and Ivy looked to the water passing by in a blur.

Thankfully Marsha answered for her. 'I'm OK, just thinking about poor Álvaro.'

'Me too,' Ivy said quickly. Darn the stupid tears in her eyes. Yes, she was thinking about Álvaro too but the thought of getting on that plane or upsetting Aayla was setting her off again. Her brain felt bruised to a livid purple welt. She should just say it now; tell them both she was booking her flight, jetting out of here in three days.

Why couldn't she do it?

'Álvaro? Oh, my poor old friend!' Marsha was the first to leap from the boat to the shore when Jero pulled into the shallows.

Ivy felt his hand on the small of her back as they crossed the sand towards the giant sea lion. 'He doesn't look happy,' she said despondently, the second they got close enough. Jero's brow furrowed in concern. Fishing netting was everywhere, burrowed hard into Álvaro's fins, where he'd failed to wriggle out of it. The tangle of blue and green mesh and blood tore at her heart.

Jero looked angry and searched for a knife in the supply bag. 'It could be extras from that trawler.' Then he held her back from getting any closer. The poor thing was bellowing in agony.

'We need to get this off you.' Marsha was visibly upset as she made to tug at the fishing nets. Álvaro snorted and huffed, but to Ivy's relief he didn't make a lunge for her. It was quite remarkable, Ivy thought, how trusting some of these animals were with humans. Especially humans they were used to.

'I can't stand all this blood on him!' Marsha was getting teary, and Jero stopped her tugging at the nets again. There was so much netting, it was a wonder the creature could still move. Ivy copied Jero, holding up her hands, shushing and soothing him. Marsha stroked his big silky face gently, all the while whispering that they were trying to help him.

'Maybe he's OK...' Ivy started.

Suddenly, Álvaro turned to them with a deafening honk and reared up like a circus performer. He roared in fright, making her gasp. A scream chilled Ivy's blood. Then she realised it was her own.

'Ivy, get back!' Jero yanked her backwards into him before the sea lion could land on top of her. Breathless, she froze in his arms, before he ushered her away, and urged her to sit down on the sand. She was shaking. He crouched in front of her. 'He would have crushed every bone in your body,' he stated, one hand on her knee. 'You scared the emojis out of me!'

She sucked in a breath as he put a hand to her cheek and brushed her curls aside, in full view of Marsha. He hadn't touched her in front of anyone before and she didn't miss the look of surprise on Marsha's face. Her heart started thrumming even faster.

'What's she doing?' Marsha's attention was on Pluma now. Pluma had flown to the sea lion's head and was making soft, soothing clucking sounds. Bird language for 'calm down'?

Strangely it seemed to work wonders. They watched a moment while Ivy tried to calm herself down at the same time. Eventually, she let Jero help her up to her feet, and Álvaro remained completely still while they set about cutting the remaining netting from his fins with knives.

'He's not as badly hurt as it looks,' Jero assured Marsha. 'Sea lions have very tough skin; they need it to live on land and in the sea, like they do. He'll heal just fine, maybe a few scars.'

'But what about all the blood?'

'It's just blood. Everybody bleeds.'

Marsha nodded, running her gaze between them. 'I guess you both know what you're doing.'

Ivy stayed quiet, wishing she could quell her nerves. Somehow, knowing Marsha was on to them made her anxious. Was she talking about the sea lion, or was she implying Jero might not have thought this through—getting involved with her?

Just then Álvaro swivelled on the sand and slipped loose of the last of the netting they'd been slicing at and waddled into the water. Pluma soared overhead. Marsha started cheering like a football fan in an instant, running behind him the whole way.

'Thank God, he's going to be OK,' Jero whispered, almost under his breath.

He brought her hand to his lips but stopped just short of kissing her when Marsha turned around. He wasn't quick enough. Ivy flushed. What was happening?

'So, you two are…a thing, huh?' Marsha threw Jero a look that told Ivy she was more concerned for him than she'd dare say in front of her. She tensed, waiting for him to say something.

And waited.

And waited.

He said nothing. Jero just shrugged and cleared his throat and kept his eyes on Álvaro.

Shame blasted her from all angles. They weren't a thing; she was a fling. At least that was what he was implying with his silence, right? He was embarrassed to have been caught out, to have slipped up again with a tourist. Maybe she'd been waiting for a declaration of some kind that he would never make.

Ugh. This had gone too far. She was just delaying the misery now. She'd book her flight tonight, she decided.

CHAPTER FIFTEEN

JERO STOPPED HIMSELF from cursing out loud down the phone as Nina's croaky voice apologised profusely. It wasn't Nina's fault she'd come down with gastro, but he was due to leave for Quito tomorrow. The trial was looming and now there was no one to watch Aayla while he was gone.

He stacked a pile of scattered books on the kitchen table, wondering what to do. He could ask Marsha—but Marsha had to be at the market stall at five every morning. Besides, he was a little annoyed at her for sticking her nose into his business the other day, asking if he and Ivy were a thing like that, looking at him as though he might regret it. He'd almost said, *Yes, of course...wasn't it obvious?* But then Ivy had said nothing either and he didn't want to assume anything or turn them into village gossip.

He needed to talk with her privately about where they stood. He couldn't say what he was feeling any more, out of some stupid fear of rejection. Ivy wasn't Suranne, and what they'd built in such a short space of time was special. He'd realised that the second she was almost crushed by a sea lion.

As for now...

Aayla could stay with a friend, he supposed, but he'd

rather Aayla stayed at home—no one in their right mind would want Pluma flapping around their house and the two came as a package deal these days. The bird went outside whenever she wanted, but she was still leaving enough feathers around the place to stuff a pillow with.

Not a bad idea for a Christmas gift, he thought idly, just as the doorbell rang.

Ivy stood there looking gorgeous as usual in another green top and jean shorts. 'I wasn't expecting you,' he said as she stepped past him without stopping to accept the kiss he'd been about to drop on her lips.

He hadn't seen her much since the Álvaro episode. She'd been busy. So had he; but he'd missed her. She smiled weakly and held up a bottle of freshly squeezed orange juice.

In the kitchen she eyed his half-packed bag. 'You pack in the kitchen?' She half laughed, collecting two glasses from the cupboard above the sink.

'I was packing the coffee before I forget. Hotel coffee sucks. Then Nina called me. She's sick.'

Ivy walked around the table, sipping her juice. She picked up Aayla's latest drawings of her new obsession, Álvaro, while he explained what had happened.

The rare bird they'd found on the second detained ship had turned out to be the last of its species. Someone as yet unidentified had stolen it from a sanctuary on Floreana. Now, thanks to new supposed 'evidence' and a stream of outrage from environmentalists worldwide, all of which was being broadcast on more television channels than he cared to count, the trial was an even bigger deal than before. He didn't want to go at all, but he was a representative for the island community more than just a witness to the event itself, and he owed it to everyone to help bring these people to justice.

'I might be gone a few days at least, in Quito,' he explained. 'I was kind of counting on Nina to stay here with her.'

'Poor Nina,' Ivy empathised, still looking at the drawings. She seemed paler than usual and tired, he realised, studying her over his OJ. As if she'd been awake all night. When he asked what was up, she told him nothing was wrong.

She was lying.

Was it them she was thinking about? This *'thing'* they'd somehow fallen into, which now included one of them bringing orange juice to the other in the mornings? Or was she about to tell him she was leaving? The sudden thought was chilling.

'Ivy, we need to talk...'

'Why don't I stay with her, while you're away?' Ivy's eyes were brighter now, searching his.

'Oh, really, you?' He hadn't been expecting that. 'You don't have to do that,' he followed quickly. As if he'd impose like that! She was always so busy, not least with the volunteer duties she was still assigning herself, and the acquisition back home.

'I'm serious, Jero, if you need someone to stay with Aayla, I'd be happy to.'

Oh. OK.

Jero found his hand moving to his mouth. He stroked his chin thoughtfully, staring at the cutlery drawer. Ivy mumbled something under her breath behind him.

'Of course, it's a stupid idea, why would you want me doing that?' she followed, but he was considering it now. If she really *wanted* to...

He trusted her, he realised suddenly. With Aayla. In his home. He couldn't stop thinking how quickly they'd bonded.

How reticent he'd been at first to let it happen, but how it had happened anyway. A lot like their own relationship.

He turned. Ivy was looking at him warily. 'Forget I ever mentioned it. There must be someone else more suitable—'

'No, no,' he interjected, crossing to her. 'If you're sure it's what you want to do, I can get the volunteers to cover some of your shifts. Or all of them. You can stay here with her and Pluma.'

'Whatever works,' she said with an insouciant shrug, looking around the room instead of up at him.

'You know, for a second I thought you were going to announce you'd booked your flight home,' he admitted in relief, resting on a corner of the kitchen table.

Ivy flushed red and looked to the floor. He drew her towards him between his legs, worried now that he couldn't read her.

'I know you must be thinking about your practice back home; all the things you have to do in Galway?' His throat felt dry and tight as he said it, but he squeezed her hands, psyching himself up for the right words to leave his mouth.

'You know, Aayla wants to visit you in Ireland? She says she wants to photograph the Giant's Causeway.' He paused, tracing her lips with his eyes. 'I was thinking maybe… I could come with her, to photograph the Giant's Causeway? And maybe you could come back here with us after. See to it that Pluma doesn't miss you too much?'

Ivy's eyes grew wide as saucers. He watched them fill with joy and relief before she wrapped her arms around his shoulders, flooding him with her sensual scent and the kind of hope he hadn't dared feel until right this very moment. 'That's what you needed to talk to me about?'

He stood, then took her face in his hands. 'You're not

even gone yet, and I miss you. Maybe we can make something work. I know it's a lot to think about, and nothing needs to happen right away but...'

He trailed off. Ivy looked troubled again now, drumming her nails against her side. He held his breath, searching her face. 'Ivy...did I say the wrong thing?'

She shook her head. 'No, no, not at all,' she said, taking his hands again. 'Of course, I want to think about this...it's just, I thought, after you didn't reply to Marsha's question about us being a thing...'

'Why would I confirm anything to Marsha when we haven't even discussed it ourselves? I've been waiting to talk to you. Things have just been so crazy with this trial and everything else.'

She nodded, smiling slightly. 'I suppose I didn't say anything either. It's all been such a whirlwind.'

'I'll only be gone a few days,' he said, allowing a sense of relief to wash over him, finally. 'We can talk more when I get back.' He pulled her against him, till her hips dug deliciously into his flesh. 'But right now... I think I should show you a couple of things in the bedroom, you know, just in case you have any problems while I'm away?'

'I think that's the best idea I've heard all day.' She grinned.

CHAPTER SIXTEEN

DAY ONE OF babysitting. Ivy's mother sounded more interested than she'd heard her in years. 'You're still in the Galapagos? What's going on?'

Ivy pressed the phone to her ear and continued stirring the cake mix, while Aayla did her best to pour the first lot of chocolate gloop into the silicone cups they'd laid out. She'd already managed to get more on the counter than in the cups, and her face was covered in chocolate already.

'Who told you?' Ivy asked, wishing every cell of her body didn't tense up every time they talked.

'I bumped into Mike at the shop, he was on his lunch break. He said you were taking some more holiday time. Are you OK? You're not sick, are you?'

Pluma let out a squawk and zoomed from the shelf behind her, clattering onto a pile of dry dishes. Aayla giggled, waving her chocolate-covered spatula about to a made-up song about cake.

'What the blazes is going on?' Her mother had always said *What the blazes?* and Ivy almost laughed.

'Just making cupcakes with Jero's daughter and her booby, and no, I'm not sick, just because I took some more holiday.'

'Her what?'

Ivy dutifully explained the bird situation as best she could in the midst of the total chaos erupting around her.

'So let me get this straight. Instead of working out the details of a multimillion-euro acquisition with your business partner and equity firm, you're adopting wildlife and baking cupcakes… Ivy, I don't know what to say. Are you sure you're not sick?'

She let her mother berate her decisions as she pushed a stool over to the oven, so Aayla could reach it to turn it on. *That's right, one hundred and eighty degrees,* she mouthed, just as Aayla racked it up to three hundred and Pluma decided to land on the girl's head, making her shriek again and almost fall off the stool.

Ivy caught her, and assured her mother everything was fine, she still had time to talk equity, though Etta Malone was obviously getting worried about her mental health. Which was ironic. It had only been in adulthood, when she'd made a name and career for herself in veterinary medicine, that her mother had shown any interest in what she was doing at all. Although, maybe that was unfair, she mused, considering what her mother had gone through, losing the love of her life.

She'd still put food on the table, she'd still given her a roof and an education, and her animals. She should be grateful her mother stuck around and didn't jet off altogether—as *some* people did.

As for herself, right now she was having a blast, even though time was ticking…*tick-tick-tick*…

'I was about to fly home, Mum,' she said now, sliding the tray of overspilling silicone cups into the oven. She lowered her voice. 'But Jero's giving evidence at an important trial and there was no one to watch Aayla.'

Silence.

Then, an incredulous snort. 'Honestly, Ivy, listen to yourself. She's not your child, and this Javier guy...'

'Jero!'

'Lives on an island. In South America.'

'I am aware of that.'

'And you have equally important things to consider back here! I just want the best for you, Ivy. Have you really thought about what you're doing, or *not* doing...?'

Ivy held the phone away from her ear as Aayla walked back into the kitchen holding half of a crumbled plastic brick castle. 'Pluma crashed into it.' She sighed, as if it happened all the time. 'We must rebuild, Ivy.'

'You're right,' she agreed solemnly. 'We shall rebuild.'

Ivy told her mother she had to go, and hung up. For the next two hours, they burned a batch of cupcakes, made one quite excellent batch that she vowed they'd deliver to poor Nina, and tried not to let Etta Malone's authoritarian agenda pour cold water over her mood. OK, so yes, she had shut up about her upcoming flight the second Jero had mentioned Aayla needed a minder. *Sucker.* And she'd cancelled it in her head the second he'd suggested they might work something out, even though the clinic was playing on her mind—all the unfinished business still left to attend to. But he'd said what she'd been waiting to hear. Finally. What else was she supposed to do? She was in love. Bursting with it, for the first time in her whole life.

Now. In no way was she the perfect babysitter, as demonstrated by the layer of chocolate and feathers where the kitchen counter used to be, but...

'Ivy, pass me that tree!'

She forgot what she'd been thinking. Aayla's sticky fingers had created a sheen all over the brick castle but the look on her face, deep in concentration over their rebuild while Pluma waddled about the living room, was priceless. What was a few more days here, in the grand scheme of things? She'd take a few more days when Jero returned, to iron out the details of his visit to Galway, and the possibility that she might come back here to be with him in the Galapagos. She had plenty of time to talk to Mike and the stuffy men from the Blue Stream Veterinary Alliance—life wasn't all work, work, work!

She paused, letting Aayla stop her from placing a tree on top of a castle turret, where it clearly did not belong.

Life wasn't all work, work, work.

She'd never let a thought like that cross her mind until now.

Day two of babysitting and, Ivy had to admit, she was pretty tired. The day had been jam-packed and she'd even had a visit by a mother from Aayla's school, along with three more six-year-olds. She didn't mind—exactly—but the hair-braiding session that had commenced had eaten into her scheduled call with Mike, till she'd had to postpone it altogether. She was almost asleep on the sofa when Jero called.

'How's the trial going? Are they going behind bars for life?' she asked as his handsome face beamed at her in the video-chat window. She was surprised to find butterflies in her belly as he told her all about it, and pride rushed through her, thinking of him standing up on behalf of the community. But she couldn't wait to get him back here.

'I'm missing you and Aayla,' he said. 'Are you having fun?'

'We sure are,' she replied, thinking it best not to say how exhausted she was. She recounted the trip to the shops, and the book they'd been reading on Irish folklore, but she omitted the guilt trip from her mother, which she'd been trying to forget about.

It wasn't easy. Her mother had a habit of getting under her skin.

'Hailey sent an email from New Zealand,' she remembered now. The first full-time surgeon Jero had had on his books for a while had called in to announce she wouldn't be coming back, which seemed to disappoint him. For a moment she wondered whether she should offer to take her place permanently, but something stopped her. She hadn't even spoken to Mike yet; she was rushing into things.

'Daddy!' Aayla interrupted, leaping in front of her, and she hurried a goodbye, and left them to talk, wishing she weren't suffering such a conflict of emotion. He wanted her here, she knew that now, he wanted to make things work, and so did she…but then again, what if she wasn't what they needed?

An hour later, she'd just sat down to check her emails and finally call Mike back when something huge clattered and thudded to the floor upstairs. Tossing her laptop aside, she sent Jero's guitar crashing to the floor, then raced up to Aayla's room with a pounding heart.

She threw the door open. 'What's wrong?'

Then she saw the dresser on its side and her heart all but stopped. 'Aayla?' One of the drawers had been pulled out and was smashed into a thousand splintered pieces on the carpet.

'I was standing on it,' she admitted sheepishly from the bed, where she was nursing a ginger kitten that she'd picked up from the clinic. Another animal who'd adopted Aayla more than the other way round. 'Lola was up on the curtain rails. Daddy doesn't like it when the animals climb the curtains.'

It took almost an hour for Ivy to sweep up all the pieces of the splintered drawer, and right the dresser. Now she'd have to report this damage to Jero and the thought of his disappointment made her cringe. She should have been watching her more carefully! What if Aayla had been squished under the dresser? It didn't bear thinking about.

Story time was next. She had to finish the book they'd started the night before, and by the time she got downstairs to check her email, she cursed herself at the significant chip on the neck of Jero's guitar.

To hell with emails, they could wait, she was too tired. Ivy poured herself a glass of wine, removed the braids from her hair, and vowed that tomorrow she'd be a shining example of authority and productivity.

That same night, halfway through a TV show about the mating cycle of penguins, she spotted a suspicious Manila file sticking out from under a pile of books on the shelf below the coffee table. She tried to straighten it up—symmetry was everything after all, not that Zenon's tattooist would agree—but then she spotted the words 'renovation plans' on the front, and she couldn't help a peek.

So, Jero had plans, it turned out. Plans to redesign the clinic! She studied them, impressed, and a little awed. It was clear from the apartment buildings that he had money in assets and, despite his humble lifestyle, he had plans to make use of that fact someday, for the good of the island, and the community.

That was so Jero.

The redesign went beyond anything she'd imagined, including open-air kennels with remote-controlled ceilings in case of rain, and a separate outhouse for storage and mobile-clinic supplies. He'd never mentioned wanting to redesign. But he was always so busy with things as they were now. Plus, he always seemed so reluctant to change!

Maybe he was waiting for the right time…or the right *person* to encourage him, she mused.

Day three of babysitting. Mike was in her ear now, and not just about the guys at Blue Stream Veterinary Alliance. He was asking her when she was coming home, and he had decidedly fewer nuggets of spiritual wisdom to impart this time. She was annoyed with herself for letting him down, and she told him so. He just sighed.

'I just didn't think you'd stay *this* long. Business aside, you know I want the best for you,' he said, in the strangest echo of her mother two days before. 'But you're not exactly the maternal type, are you, Ivy? I thought you didn't even want children.'

'She's not my child,' she heard herself say. But the very words from her mouth made her feel quite sick; Aayla felt unwanted enough by her own mother. Thank God she was dancing around the kitchen to Irish folk by The Dubliners—her new favourite—and hadn't heard. She lowered her voice. 'Anyway, why can't I change my mind?'

Mike stuttered a moment. 'Well…that would be great, good for you.'

He doesn't sound convinced, she thought. *He sounds like he thinks I'm losing the plot. Am I losing the plot?*

No…don't let him get in your head. Or your mother. Or yourself for that matter. Maybe you should meditate?

No time for that. Aayla was vying for her full attention again, this time with a dance performance. Ivy pulled her legs up under her on the familiar sofa and tried to ignore her calling laptop, and the chipped guitar.

Just focusing on Aayla's joy, with Pluma and her new stray kitten, Lola, as sidekicks quickly blocked everything out. The kid looked a picture with the hairstyle she'd given her. Ivy got to her knees and snapped a hundred photos with Aayla's new camera, in a hundred different exciting angles that made Aayla shriek in delight at having her own star gig photographer. The camera was the old one she'd asked Mike to post to the clinic; it had finally arrived.

In moments like this, she forgot everything else in the world, but in Jero's bed alone in the dark, she suffered through fevered dreams of missing planes and dodging falling furniture or sleeping in late from exhaustion and missing her shift. She couldn't let Jero or Aayla down. They'd been through so much. And she couldn't do this to Mike—he needed her. The guilt was insufferable. Old insecurities kept piling up like Lego bricks.

She was terrible at multitasking, she just wasn't equipped... She'd been trying to prove something to Jero because she was falling in love with him, but this wasn't her world and she'd never be good enough for him, or this little girl.

What was she *doing*?

CHAPTER SEVENTEEN

THE HOUSE WAS empty when Jero stepped inside. Tossing his keys onto the table, he called for Ivy and Aayla. No answer. He sprinted upstairs, thinking maybe he'd surprise them and walk in on them playing a game or something. Then he saw the smashed-up dresser. Frowning to himself, he scraped a hand over his head—what happened there? Where were they?

He grabbed his bicycle and found them both several minutes later, at the clinic. Dudders and Zenon greeted him with high-fives and Aayla rushed from the storeroom to hug him, abandoning the litter of kittens she was playing with, save for a ginger one that clung to her shoulder like a fuzzy accessory. Ivy pressed her back to the wall in Reception and started unbuttoning her white coat.

'Why didn't you tell me you were here?' He went to kiss her, but something wasn't right. Instincts primed, he took a step back. Her face was a picture of concern in the light from a small lamp shining onto an aquarium with a lizard in it. A tangle of cables was wrapped around the tank, which annoyed him, but he couldn't exactly fix it now.

'It was an emergency, another amputation,' Ivy said, gesturing to a cage with a black puppy in it. One hind leg was bandaged, the other missing. 'Good to have you back.'

Then she tossed her coat to the basket and pulled Aayla into a huge embrace that both warmed his heart and sent a chill straight through him.

'I have to go,' she announced to Aayla, smoothing down her hair. Aayla had the strangest hairstyle he'd ever seen, all backcombed like an eighties singer. 'It was so much fun hanging out with you!'

Aayla hugged her, as if she'd known this was going to happen. 'Bye, Ivy!'

'Bye Ivy? Where are you going?'

'To the airport.'

Jero's heart kicked up a storm and thundered in his chest. Ivy threw him a look he didn't like one bit before making for the door.

'Guys, watch Aayla for me, please,' he said, and followed her outside.

The taxi was waiting down the street. Ivy hurried across the gravel towards it, red hair flying. He called out to her, but she didn't answer. Without looking back, she yanked the door open urgently and climbed inside.

What the...?

Jero sprinted back for the bicycle and sped after the cab. The sun was starting to sink behind the trees and anger prickled his arms like mosquitoes. She was leaving now? Without so much as a goodbye?

He sped up and veered into a narrow lane that he knew would come out right in the taxi's path. Swerving in front of the car, he held his hand up, blinded by the lights. The driver skidded to a halt right in front of him, sending a shower of gravel into the air.

Jero tossed the bike aside and flung the taxi door open. 'What are you doing?'

Ivy squared her shoulders at him in the back seat, but her tears defied the fierce look on her face.

'I thought I'd save us both a goodbye, Jero. I can't pretend this is my life any more.'

'Get out of the car.'

She shook her head. His eyes found the bags piled up next to her; the stupid boots she'd arrived here in and tried to leave in before. 'Not this time,' she said. 'I have to go. I'm sorry, Jero, it's better this way. My flight leaves in two hours. I should have left ages ago.'

He bit his tongue. He should have seen it coming.

You are a total idiot, Jero!

She was leaving the second he'd relieved her of her babysitting duties!

Ivy liked Aayla enough, but she'd only been helping him out because of this little 'thing' between them. Now she'd had a taster of his real life and she was done.

He glowered at her, seeing red.

'How could you do this?' he hissed, gripping the top of the door, turning his knuckles white. He was about to tell her how much he'd trusted her, with himself, with Aayla, but the words were too humiliating to even say out loud. Why had he even let her in, and let himself fall for her?

'I'll pay for the damage to the dresser. And your guitar.'

My guitar, too?

'That's not what I'm talking about! I was falling in *love* with you.'

Ivy's eyes widened.

Jero faltered. Did he just say that out loud?

Ivy just sat there, rooted like a leaden weight, clutching her bag. She couldn't wait to go. The driver cleared his throat. It was all he could do not to kick something.

'Ivy, talk to me.'

Ivy squeezed her eyes shut and, this time, he did kick something—the tyre. The driver told him to back off and he apologised. This was all his fault. He'd let her in, fallen for her, even made tentative plans for a *future* when he should have known better. Hadn't he learned anything? They all left...all the tourists. He knew it and he'd dived right in again anyway and taken Aayla down with him.

'I'm sorry, Jero,' she sobbed, making to reach for him, but he moved from her grasp, gathering the strength he needed not to break something next. He'd already snapped, he had to cool it.

Before he could get his thoughts in order the taxi rumbled off, and he stood there in the fading light, shaken and fuming, willing himself not to go after her.

This wasn't some lame movie; *this* was how it ended.

Ivy heard the explosion as they reached the town borders. She almost hit her head on the car ceiling as the driver swerved to a stop again. What the hell was that?

Glancing behind her, she swiped at her wet eyes and tried to make sense of the tower of flames she could see, roaring out from behind the tree line.

The driver was talking fast in Spanish, asking if she wanted to keep going towards the ferry, but now she could hear screams. Oh, God. Each one froze a little more of her blood. People were running out of their homes. Panic consumed her as grey smoke clouded the horizon. It was coming from the direction of the town, and the clinic.

'We have to go back!'

In seconds they were speeding back the way they came. Her brain was a cyclone tearing through horrific possibilities. The driver's radio buzzed, and she almost threw up as she recognised words: *Darwin Clinic. Fire brigade. People inside.*

No!

'Hurry!' she yelled. 'I'm a trained medic! What if there are injured animals?'

What if there are injured people?

Aayla was in there. Dudders and Zenon. Jero must have been on his way back…after she'd left him there, reeling.

No…

Ivy felt sick to the core as the driver put his foot down harder. Jero's face flashed into her mind…the look he'd given her when she'd told him she was on her way out, without even saying goodbye. He'd been falling in love with her. He'd said it. She'd almost got out of the car to say it back, but she hadn't.

Why hadn't she? *Coward.* 'Hurry up, please,' she urged again in Spanish.

All this time she'd told herself he was in it for some fun with a tourist, but it had meant just as much to him as her. And she'd hit him where it hurt: straight in his own fear of abandonment by someone else he trusted.

She was just scared of him loving her, she realised, almost as much as having no one love her at all. She was scared of loving anyone that hard, in case they left her; in case they decided at any point that she was merely just getting in the way of something better. It was always there in the back of her mind. Jero had told her she was enough, already, and she hadn't let herself believe it.

A siren blared in the distance as they swung onto the street where they'd started, metres from the clinic. It just didn't feel or look like the same place. Heavy noxious smoke formed an ominous wall, blocking her vision.

Leaping from the cab, she made for the clinic—or the place where the clinic used to be. The fire seemed to be raging out of control.

For a second she was shocked still in a whirl of smoke and heat and ashes. Everything was burning. Everything he'd worked for. She gasped at the towering flames licking the roof, devouring the walls. Behind her the driver yelled at her to turn back, but no...*no way.* Aayla was in there!

'Jero!' she yelled. 'Aayla!'

Dudders was behind her now. He grabbed at her arm and made to pull her back, and to her utter relief she saw Zenon holding Aayla to him, metres away by the trees.

'Aayla,' she called, racing over to her through the smoke. She coughed and almost had to stop halfway but Aayla's arms locked around her middle like a baby octopus and Ivy drew strength from nowhere, scooped her up in her arms. 'You're OK, you're OK...'

'I'm OK, but Daddy's inside!' Aayla wailed against her, louder than the sirens, and Ivy somehow made it to the guys and their open arms, fighting for words and her own breath.

'Jero went in there?'

'He went to get the kittens,' Dudders stammered, his face lit up by the orange inferno. Ashes smouldered in his dreadlocks. The black dog in the cage sat at his feet, and more people were gathering on the periphery by the minute, watching in shock and fear, and tears. Some were throwing water feebly at the flames from plastic bottles.

Through her panic Ivy mentally tried to recount which other animals had been inside, but Jero...oh, God, what had possessed him to go in there? And where was the fire brigade? Why were things always so slow around here?!

'Daddy!' Aayla fought her way from her arms and

Ivy blinked in disbelief, just as the crowd started buzzing and cheering.

'What the…?' Ivy squinted into the smoke where the entrance would usually be, and then she saw him.

A huge sob that had been building in her throat almost threatened to topple her. Jero staggered into the light, silhouetted by the blaze. He was holding a box of squirming kittens. His clothes were blackened, his skin ashen grey. He had never looked better. *Thank God, you're alive!*

Running towards him, she was blocked in her tracks by a crew of paramedics who'd somehow arrived on the scene with the fire engine while she'd been fixated on Jero emerging from the building. Ivy was forced to watch it all from the sidelines like a dream as he was wrapped in a blanket without so much as noticing her and ushered into the ambulance with Aayla.

She had no choice but to watch it roll away, while she stood there between Zenon and Dudders, witnessing Jero's empire burn to the ground. The firefighters couldn't save it. Within the hour, the Darwin Clinic was nothing but a pile of rubble and smouldering ashes and all she could think was, thank the heavens and all the angels in the sky that he hadn't been burnt to a crisp along with it.

She couldn't lose him, as her mother had lost her dad. She knew that now; she'd known it the second he'd told her he was falling in love with her, too. He might just be the love of her life.

CHAPTER EIGHTEEN

JERO'S THROAT FELT as if he'd swallowed jet fuel. The hospital room seemed to swim around him as the nurse left. He could barely speak or swallow, and he wanted nothing more than to go home.

He clenched his fists, willing the hellish imagery of the evening to leave him. First, Ivy, all but running for that taxicab, away from him. Then the clinic going up in flames. He'd seen his life flash before his eyes the second the glass shattered in the front windows, right as he'd made it back to the forecourt.

'Can I come in?' Ivy asked from the doorway, making his head turn, and his pulse spike. Every muscle in his body had just tensed up, as if she'd walked in with a cattle prod.

'I thought you'd be halfway to Galway by now,' he managed as she pulled up a seat by the bed.

'Well, surprise, the explosion made me turn around.'

At first his defences were primed. Then he softened in her gaze, as he always did. Already he adored every angle and line of her face. He liked it so much that sometimes even looking at her caused a strange, aching sensation around his heart, in his chest and in his throat and he'd thought about her the entire time he'd been away. Even if this was yet another temporary delay before she left—again—she was impossible to be mad at.

'I'm so sorry, Jero. The whole clinic…it's gone.' She put two hands to his arm, one over his tattoo, and her warmth softened him even more. He must be a total sucker because he was glad, in this moment, that she was here. Almost as glad as he was to still be here.

Zenon and Dudders had somehow made it out with the dog, but he'd had to go back in for the kittens. No animal was going to perish if he could help it, not on his watch. The heat had been suffocating. He'd had to crawl on his hands and knees just to see in front of him, across the piles of blazing Manila folders and melting wall panels. He'd thought of Ivy in there. Wondered for a moment if their angry exchange would be the last thing she'd remember of him.

'Yes, it's gone, but no one died,' he said, aware it sounded too flippant for the severity of the situation but what was he supposed to do? Cry about it? He'd move on, as he'd had to do before. 'What made you come back?'

'Jero, even before the clinic went up in flames, I knew I'd messed up.' Her voice sounded choked now. 'I shouldn't have tried to go without talking to you. I was just afraid of how I'd started to feel about you, and Aayla. I'm not used to this…' She gestured between them, as if there were some invisible forcefield she didn't know how to turn off. He bit into his cheeks.

'Neither am I,' he said stiffly, and she leaned in, pressed a hand to his cheek the way she did.

'I know you trusted me.'

'I shouldn't have been so angry…'

'I wrecked the house, your dresser, your guitar, I am a rubbish babysitter.'

He stared at her, not sure what to say. Did she really

think he cared about material objects more than people, and animals, and her? He hadn't seen the guitar yet, but it couldn't be as bad as the pile of rubble that now constituted the Darwin Clinic.

'I was just convinced I was no good for you, no good with kids. It doesn't mean I don't love them or want them in my life. Maybe I do. I think I probably do.' She squeezed his arm earnestly and he almost smiled.

'I want you and Aayla in my life,' she clarified quickly. 'If you'll still have me, if you meant what you said, maybe we can work something out. You could come to Ireland while the clinic's being rebuilt?'

He laughed to himself under his breath, then coughed again. Ivy looked hurt as she passed him some water, and he shook his head. 'No, no, I like that idea,' he said, taking a huge gulp from the glass. The idea started to take shape in his mind, and slowly it pushed some of the horrors of the night aside. Galway with Ivy... Aayla would lose her mind.

'But we can't rebuild so easily. There's no insurance, for a start.'

Ivy's eyes grew round. She sat back in her seat and dragged a hand through her hair.

'It was built on community funding...every cent went back into supplies. We just never thought we'd need it. I can sell some of my properties, I guess... I have assets.'

He knew what she was thinking. You could never run a clinic in the western world without insurance, but that wasn't exactly the case out here. That place had started life as a shack and treatments were free.

He didn't even want to think about it now. He took her hands in his and brought them to his lips. Everything ached, even his eyes, but somehow the monster started to shift on his chest, till he barely felt its weight.

'We shall rebuild,' Ivy said thoughtfully, almost to herself, tightening her hands around his. A small smile lit up her impish eyes as they locked onto his again. He didn't even have a chance to ask what she was talking about before she leaned across the bed and pressed her lips to his.

'I'm in love with you too,' she said, against his mouth, drawing him closer by the scruff of his blackened shirt and kissing him more passionately than he'd ever been kissed in a hospital bed…right until another knock on the door forced them apart.

Dudders looked at them, his face reddening.

'It's OK, you can come in,' Jero said, still clutching Ivy's hand to his heart. She perched on the bed next to him.

'How are you feeling?' Dudders asked him, stopping by the bedside in another pair of Thai fisherman pants and placing some scrawny yellow flowers wrapped in cellophane on the bedside cabinet.

'Alive. What happened?' he asked now, annoyed at the croak that came out instead. 'What started the fire, do we know yet?'

Dudders looked sideways. 'The fire marshal thinks it was a faulty plug,' he admitted with a wince.

Instantly Jero recalled the wires and cables he'd seen wrapped around the aquarium, where a lizard had been lounging under a lamp. That poor lizard probably didn't make it.

'Ivy told me to ask you how old the extension lead was, but you were busy…' Dudders trailed off, fumbling with his dreadlocks. 'It's no excuse, I totally forgot. I just plugged it in anyway and went back to work.'

'That thing was at least a decade old.' Jero sighed. 'It's not your fault.'

It wasn't, really, they'd all made mistakes with that place. Ivy squeezed his hand reassuringly. 'Ivy was the only one who's tried to make a difference in ages,' he said, to her more than Dudders. 'We should've been more grateful. At least, thanks to you, Ivy, we didn't lose all our data.'

'You need to rest, stop talking,' Ivy instructed now, and his mind churned while the two of them discussed rehoming the animals. What a relief she'd been so adamant about setting up the database. Ivy had technically, or technologically, he supposed, saved the clinic from total destruction. Despite his plans to renovate and remodel he'd let the usual daily grind consume him, till it had all taken a back seat. Those damn plans had been sitting there for months under the coffee table, maybe even years, but he hadn't found the time to act on them. He hadn't even told Ivy he'd met with a design team; she would have tried to push him to do things better, as she always did. Which wasn't a bad thing at all. It was what he needed.

'There's no point beating yourself up over it, Jero,' Ivy said when Dudders left. She knew, clearly, that he was mulling over his mistakes right now.

She leaned in and kissed him again, emptying his head of everything but her as he responded on autopilot, as magnetic as she was. It was no good, getting a hard-on in a hospital bed, but to hell with it. He threw the blankets aside and she scrambled up to the bed, wrapping her arms around him. It was way too small for both of them, and the nurse looked at them in vague disapproval on her way past, but he didn't care. They slept that way all night, his fingers tangled in her hair, her legs entwined with his, and in the morning, Ivy took him home.

EPILOGUE

Eight months later

IVY STUDIED THE new giant bronze statue of Pluma in flight on the Darwin Clinic's new paved forecourt. Aayla had suggested it, the way a six-year-old might also suggest building a pink candyfloss castle in the surrounding trees, but Jero had taken it quite seriously. He'd commissioned an artist from Quito and now it made quite the eye-catching mascot.

Right now, the site was bustling with construction workers, and the electrician was thankfully ensuring there were more than enough electrical outlets to handle everything they might need to plug in. Goosebumps prickled up and down her spine every time they were on site. She had a new baby now—one with Jero.

'Not long to go,' Jero said, walking up behind them. He was carrying a huge potted palm. She jumped up to help him, just as Zenon intervened and took it from his hands.

'Let me, boss,' he said, and he proceeded to struggle with it all the way to the entrance. She bit back a smile. He was doing his best.

'How are my girls?' Jero asked, planting a kiss on her forehead, then another onto Aayla's. He had mud on his face from the trip to the garden centre, and she wiped it off with her finger. He caught her hand and kissed her, and she smiled at the *Who's Your Paddy?* shirt he was wearing; the one he'd thought was hilarious and had picked up in Galway on their trip.

It was crazy the way her heart still jolted in her chest every time he made an appearance. He dropped to the low brick wall and took her hand, watching Zenon place the giant plant down.

She and Jero had worked with an architect and interior designer to take his plans—the ones she didn't think necessary to tell him she'd discovered ages ago—to new heights. They were creating the most perfect space with two consultation rooms, a spacious operating room, plenty of storage and a fully functioning kennel with a remote-controlled ceiling cover for rainy days.

Aayla had chosen seven very specific photos of her favourite animals, all snapped by herself, of course. And why not? She was very talented. They were set to be displayed in frames for all to see, the second their clients walked in. No more drooping posters. No more laptop either, and definitely no more Manila folders.

The morning of the launch Ivy slipped into a new emerald-green floor-length dress and called for Jero to help her zip it up. He didn't answer.

'Aayla,' she called down the stairs. 'Where's your dad?'

'He went out already,' she called back from the kitchen.

Ivy frowned to herself. They were supposed to have been walking down there together, but maybe there was some kind of problem. He could have been called out while she was in the shower, she supposed.

Taking a deep breath and spritzing herself with perfume, she tried not to think that anything was wrong. Whenever he went somewhere and didn't tell her, the old insecurities crept back in...but she channelled Mike and his Oprah quotes, and envisaged her demons being swept into the abyss on the back of a giant flying whale.

Just because her father had gone out one day and never come home didn't mean anything was wrong with Jero. Besides, he was a survivor, just ask the kittens he'd saved by walking into a burning building, she thought with fresh pride.

'We need to go!' Aayla called now, stopping her from trying to call Jero anyway. 'Daddy will meet us there.'

'He'd better,' she mumbled to herself, pinning the golden bird-shaped clip in her hair and taking one last look in the mirror. She looked good, like a head veterinarian in the Galapagos should look, minus the white coat and cat scratches, she decided.

The second she hit the Darwin Clinic's forecourt with Aayla, she could tell something was up. 'What are all these people doing here...?' She trailed off as she spotted Mike, over by the giant Pluma statue. 'Mike?'

Was she imagining things? What the heck was Mike doing here? Adrenaline flooded her veins. Then, she spotted her mother. Etta Malone looked slightly overwhelmed in a fitted pinstriped suit, fanning her face against the heat. Ivy blinked.

What the...?

'There you are!' She barely noticed Jero walking up to her, but he led her in a daze into the crowd, where her mother embraced her and kissed her on both cheeks.

'Hello, darling.'

She lowered herself to Aayla's level. 'Hello again, you. Have you grown since I saw you in Ireland?'

'At least an inch,' Aayla responded proudly, just as Pluma decided to try and perch on Ivy's mother's shoulder. Etta let out the hugest shriek Ivy had ever heard, making Pluma flap her giant wings above her head. The motions sent her mother's red hair in a thousand directions, but as laughter erupted around them Etta saw the funny side, thank goodness.

'You weren't kidding about this thing,' she said, eyeing Pluma warily as the bird settled on one of the statue's outstretched wings.

'What's going on?' Ivy was almost too stunned by all this to construct a sentence. She flicked her gaze from her mother to Jero, but Mike was engulfing her now, in the hugest hug he'd ever given her.

'The place looks incredible, Ivy, congrats. And this island... wow. Now I see why you wanted to stay so much. If I'd come here on holiday I might not have left either.'

Her mother nudged him and smiled sideways. 'I don't think it was just the clinic that attracted her,' she said. They both turned their gaze to Jero, who was now lifting Aayla up onto his shoulders to place a crown of flowers on the giant booby statue's head.

Someone handed him a microphone. Everyone cried out 'speech', and he lowered Aayla to the ground and got up onto the stage. Jero was wearing real shoes for once, a crisp designer shirt and jeans. He was impossibly handsome, not to mention devious, she thought, still dazed. How the heck had he managed to arrange for her mother, and Mike to both be here for the opening without her finding out?

She was surprised either one of them had come; they were both so busy. Although admittedly Mike was busy vacationing with his family. He'd decided to take some well-deserved time off after they'd sold the clinic.

Maybe, just like her, her mother had put work aside for a while, too. She couldn't wait to show them both the other islands, the albatross chicks, Álvaro…

Álvaro?

The crowd erupted into gasps and laughter again and Ivy felt herself being ushered forwards, her mother and Mike on either arm. The giant sea lion had waddled in from the sidelines with Marsha. Ivy watched in amazement as he hopped on his fins right up the steps, onto the stage.

Jero placed the mic in front of him and he honked on cue, making Etta jump and smooth down her suit self-consciously. Ivy felt a rush of warmth for her. She was probably embarrassed to be seen so out of her comfort zone, and being Irish she wasn't used to the heat, but she'd come. She'd made an effort.

'I had no idea he was doing this…' she started as Jero called her up on stage. Nerves gripped her as she climbed the steps. It felt so strange, seeing everyone's eyes on her.

Jero took her hand. 'I'd like to thank everyone for coming here, to the reopening of the Darwin Clinic,' he said into the mic. 'I wouldn't have been able to do this without Ivy Malone.'

'Well, I wouldn't have been able to do it without you,' she added, over the cheers and whoops and claps. They were equal partners, after all. She'd invested in the Darwin Clinic with funding from her clinic's acquisition. At first Jero had been reluctant to agree; he had the funds tied up in assets, and community drives would raise more cash in no time, but to Ivy it wasn't about that.

She wanted to contribute something more meaningful

to a community, to the Galapagos eco-system, something that made a difference. And she wanted to do it with him.

Her mother winked at her now, and Ivy bit back a smile.

'What do you think about it, Álvaro?' Jero asked.

At that, Álvaro rose high onto his hind fins and batted his front fins together. Her jaw dropped. 'How did you…?'

Had the wild creature they'd rescued been getting lessons from some kind of Galapagos ringmaster?

Everyone went wild again, and she turned to Jero, only to see it was Marsha giving the creature a secret set of instructions. She must have been teaching him. *Incredible.* She was just about to say that they had a brand-new tourist attraction for the market now, when she caught Marsha placing something into Álvaro's front fins.

A small red box.

Her heart catapulted straight out of her body and back again. In the crowd, her mother's eyes were glistening. Mike was grinning like the Cheshire Cat. Did they know this was going to happen? Time seemed to slow right down as Jero got to one knee on the stage.

'Ivy…' He trailed off, grinning as the crowd started buzzing with excitement. Ivy felt hot, her green dress was sticking to her already, she wasn't prepared for this… hadn't been expecting this at all. Was he serious?

Now?

In front of all these people?

Oh, my God.

Jero cleared his throat, scanned her eyes as if asking if she was OK. Instantly, with that one look, she calmed down. She was OK. She was more than OK.

Jero looked more serious than she'd ever seen him. 'Ivy. I can't imagine doing this with anyone else. You've changed my life. Will you do me the incredible honour of starting this new chapter as my wife? Will you marry me?'

'Yes.' She whispered it at first. She was still shaking. Then the nervous laughter crept in. 'Yes,' she repeated, louder, into the microphone. 'Yes, Jero, I will marry you!'

Somewhere in the crowd she heard Dudders emit a wolf whistle that could have summoned every dog on the island.

Aayla jumped up and down, clapping her hands together along with Álvaro. Pluma flapped around their heads, as if she were congratulating them too, and Marsha leaned in to hug them both at the same time. Ivy found Jero's eyes amid the chaos and told him without even moving her mouth how much she loved him.

This was, quite possibly, the best day, no, *year* of her life, she decided.

When they finally got a moment alone, she poured all her love into her kisses and tried not to cry. There was so much to look forward to, so many more creatures to care for, so many things to get done…but for now, she decided, she would enjoy her life, moment by moment.

* * * * *

HER SECRET
RIO BABY

LUANA DaROSA

MILLS & BOON

For the real Ana.
Thank you for being an amazing friend.

CHAPTER ONE

WHEN ELIANA CAME down to the hotel bar she hadn't planned on meeting anyone. Especially not the out-of-this-world-handsome man sitting on the barstool one over from her. While catching up on the *futebol* game she hadn't noticed him sit down, until he struck up a conversation about the new manager of one of the teams. Something that threw her off. Men usually assumed she knew nothing about the sport.

At first glance he seemed no more than a well-dressed businessman finding refuge at the bar after a long day. But the longer she kept looking at him, the more her skin tingled below the surface as the extent of his devastating handsomeness coalesced in her mind.

His suit was tailored to perfection, clinging to his body as if he had been born in it. The fabric was the kind of black that swallowed a man not confident enough to wear it. Not him. He dominated every fibre with a quiet but electric sensuality.

The only thing that seemed out of place in this vision was the charcoal-black shoulder-length hair that had been carelessly ruffled on one side to keep it out of his face. Eliana wanted to dig her fingers through the strands of that hair and tug him closer to her.

The fantasy came over her unbidden, intruding on her

already exposed nerves, and she shook her head. It must be her tired brain, she told herself as she bit the inside of her cheek to stop herself from licking her lips as she noticed his eyes dart to them for a fraction of a second.

Eliana had spent the better part of her day travelling from Belo Horizonte to Rio de Janeiro. A bereavement had brought her here. Her father Marco, along with her half-brother Vanderson, had died in an accident a couple of days ago. A fact that had left her numb on the inside.

She had never been close to either of them—hadn't even attended their funeral. A part of her had wanted to… to take that final opportunity to say goodbye to the only family she'd had left. But when it had come to it she'd backed out, staying locked in her hotel room as she got to grips with the new reality she now lived in.

She was now the heiress to her father's hospital and fortune, and that was a twist of fate no one had seen coming—Eliana least of all.

'May I?' the man asked, pointing at the empty bar-stool between them.

Eliana nodded, taking a big sip of her wine as he slipped into the seat. She could almost feel the heat of his body radiating towards her. They were discussing last night's *futebol* match, yet her body was reacting as if he had whispered tantalising words into her ear.

She glanced at her wristwatch. It was late enough not to seem impolite if she left. Her flight was early the next day, and today had already been long and tedious. Going now would save her a lot of energy she didn't have.

Except Eliana didn't want to leave. Not really. The man's casual banter had made her forget about her heavy heart for a moment, and the way his dark eyes looked her over ignited small fires all over her skin.

It was a reaction she didn't expect, but one that also

wasn't entirely unwelcome. This was what people did, right? They met in bars, decided to have some fun.

'I'm Diego,' he said, and it was only then she realised she had been staring at him.

His name sent a cascade of heat down her spine. He had only introduced himself. Why did it feel as if he just said something dirty to her?

'Ana,' she replied and took his outstretched hand. His grip was firm, and his fingers grazed her skin for just a moment as he held onto her hand a flash longer than was necessary.

A spark appeared at the spot where he'd broken their physical connection, travelling down her arm before settling in the pit of her stomach.

'What brings you to Rio?'

A smile curled the full lips, highlighting the distinguished features of his face even more. He wore his jacket open, the linen shirt visible beneath giving her an idea of the pure masculine fantasy hidden underneath the fabric. A thought that dominated her to the point where she had to remind herself that they were in the middle of a conversation.

She'd been a woman at a bar before, talking to men like Diego. But she couldn't remember ever having such an instant and visceral reaction to anyone's proximity.

'The funeral of my father.'

She didn't want to discuss her father with anyone, but she needed something to distract herself from the fire eating her insides. He didn't need to know she hadn't gone.

'I'm sorry to hear that.' Diego's face softened.

'Don't be. We weren't close.' Eliana tried to keep the bitter edge out of her voice as much as she could. But the words tumbled out of her mouth before she could think better of it.

To her surprise, Diego scoffed and took a sip of his drink. 'I know what that's like.'

'Ah, we have father problems in common?'

His eyes darted to hers, darkening as their gazes meshed. A shiver crawled through her as she glimpsed a hint of the vulnerability he must keep hidden away behind his detached facade. The moment only lasted a second, before shutters fell over his eyes, cutting her off from anything that lay beyond the surface.

Which was just as well. Eliana wasn't looking for any attachment here in Rio. The complexity of her father's estate meant she'd need to briefly come back in a month, to claim the hospital and wrap up anything else that needed to be done to have Marco Costa out of her life for ever. She hoped to see as little of Rio de Janeiro as possible. The city bore nothing but nightmares for her.

Diego shrugged her question off, shifting his attention from his own contemplations to her. His pupils were dilated as his eyes darted back to her mouth. A signal that sent fire licking across her skin.

She wasn't imagining the crackling air between them. At least not if she trusted the signs she'd noticed.

'I see how it is. It's fine for me to reveal my secrets, but you won't tell me any of yours.' She took a sip of her drink. Her gaze locked into his. 'I'm always going to be a stranger you met at a bar. What do you have to lose?'

Eliana wasn't sure why she was prying. Under normal circumstances she never would. But Diego intrigued her. Their conversation so far had already differed from the usual bar flirting she knew. Instead of asking about her life or her job, he'd found a common interest to talk about.

Did that mean he wanted to get to know her better?

The thought gave her pause. Hotel bar flirtations

weren't the romances one read about in novels. Besides, such a concept had no place in her life right now.

'Why spoil the evening?' He smiled—only half sincere—but even that was enough to bring heat to her cheeks.

In a defeated gesture, Eliana raised her hands. 'Have it your way, *senhor*, but then I get to know something else. Tell me what brought *you* to Rio instead.'

He relaxed against the bar, with one arm resting on top of it while the other hand came up to his face, scrubbing over the light stubble covering his gorgeous high cheekbones.

'Would you believe me if I said the funeral of my brother?'

He wasn't *really* his brother. There had been no blood relation between him and Vanderson. But, despite Diego having ten siblings, he'd felt closer to that man than to any of his actual relatives.

He'd met Vanderson Costa when they were both eighteen and starting their mandatory military service in the Brazilian army. They'd both signed up for the medical training, their eyes set on med school after their service concluded.

Under normal circumstances the two would never have met. Vanderson had lived in a mansion in Ipanema, Rio's most luxurious neighbourhood, while Diego himself had grown up on the outskirts of Complexo do Alemão, one of the largest slums north of the city centre. But during their service they'd all been recruits, brothers-in-arms going through it all together. Their friendship had bridged the gap in wealth and privilege, teaching Diego so much about himself and his path in life.

And now Vanderson was dead.

Losing his chosen brother clung to his heart as if someone had tied heavy weights to his chest when the news had reached him. To his surprise, he realised that this moment was the first during which he felt he could breathe easier again.

Somehow, this woman sitting in front of him was part of that process.

Diego had lived in Rio de Janeiro his entire life, and the only reason he found himself in a hotel was Vanderson's funeral. He'd attended a small dinner with the surviving family—Vanderson's husband and daughter.

He'd been about to leave when the woman sitting alone at the bar had caught his attention. Red undertones wove themselves through her dark brown hair, which flowed in lavish curls over her shoulders and looked silken to the touch. But what had drawn him in more than her hair, and the sensual curves visible even while she was sitting down, was what she'd been doing. She'd been looking at a nearby TV, watching the sports pundits who were discussing last night's *futebol* game.

Being a *futebol* enthusiast himself, he had felt his interest piqued enough for him to walk over and see what she was doing.

Though Diego hadn't been as subtle as he'd thought, and a few moments after he'd sat down she'd turned her head to look at him. Time had stopped for several heartbeats when their gazes collided, and he'd experienced an unusual twinge in his chest. He'd tried to look nonchalant—as if he hadn't checked her out—but his body had refused to take any orders.

The light brown hue of her eyes was mesmerising. Every now and again the light hit her irises just right, giving them the appearance of pure gold.

She clearly didn't understand the beauty she possessed. He could see that in the way she held herself. More than that, though, her analytical mind and quick wit had jumped out at him when they'd discussed the game. It spoke of passion, and he wanted to get to know her better, to understand what other areas of her life this passion unfolded into.

Which was a strange thought in itself. Diego never got to know the women who entered his life. It wasn't anything personal, and he was upfront about it. He had watched his parents destroy themselves in the name of love, and knew the path of a romantic relationship only led to pain and forced sacrifices.

Diego made sure he got out before things got too emotional and involved. And one way to avoid all that was by not asking too many questions before moving on to the key event of the evening.

So why was he sitting here, asking about her relationship with her father? Or even telling her why he had come here?

Ana's eyes narrowed as she looked him over, a slight frown pulling the corners of her mouth downwards. 'Interesting how this bar is collecting the bereaved.' She paused for a moment. 'I'm sorry to hear about your brother.'

He smiled, feeling the sincerity of her sympathy radiate a gentle warmth through his skin. 'Life is going to suck without him.'

Diego allowed himself to feel the truth of his words with this virtual stranger he found himself drawn to.

He watched as her eyes drifted to the watch on her delicate wrist and saw the signs that she was thinking about leaving. Something he knew he didn't want her to do.

Her lips parted, no doubt to bid him farewell. Not wanting the evening to end just yet, Diego reached out, placing his hand over hers while obscuring the watch. Her skin was soft under his hand, radiating more heat into him that turned into a fiery spark as it penetrated his skin.

'How long are you staying in Rio?' he asked, and noticed a strange huskiness coating his voice. As if he wanted her to stay. Which was ridiculous. Because one night was all anyone ever got with him, so it didn't matter how long she planned on staying.

Ana looked at him with wide eyes. Was she feeling the same intense spark jumping between them when he touched her? She twisted her hand so that their palms were touching, the tips of her fingers grazing over the inside of his hand.

'Only tonight.'

She hesitated for a moment, and Diego saw the wheels behind her eyes turning. There was something she wanted to tell him. For a moment he held his breath in anticipation, but then the light in her eyes dimmed and she remained quiet.

Ana didn't know her assumption about him being from out of town was wrong. He hadn't corrected her. The information was irrelevant. Tomorrow she would be back wherever she came from, while he would be left alone to contemplate a new reality where his best friend was no more.

He hadn't been able to stop himself when he'd seen Ana. Her presence seemed soothing, and it had required only one bat of her long lashes to awaken a roaring fire in his chest. He knew this reaction was different…unlike the usual flings he satisfied himself with. But he didn't care in this moment. His pain faded when that flame spread through his body. He planned on feeding it until exhaustion took him.

'Then I'm glad I spotted you when I did, or I might have missed the opportunity of a lifetime, Donna Ana.'

'You sat down at the bar because you saw me?'

Scepticism laced her voice, and Diego almost laughed at that. There was no way a gorgeous woman like her didn't have men approaching her in bars all the time. Yet she seemed surprised.

'Couldn't help it,' he replied, his voice dropping low as he wove his fingers through hers.

While his mind was still trying to decide his body had taken control, reacting to the attraction arcing between them.

Eliana's heart slammed against her ribcage as Diego's fingers wrapped around her hand, giving it a gentle squeeze. The brown-green hue of his eyes darkened as the attraction that had been whirring around them for the last hour became almost tangible. Their hands touching had created a rapturous reaction within her, and her breath had caught in her throat. How was this even possible?

'An unlikely story,' she said, not able to keep her scepticism at bay.

She knew he was using honeyed words to flirt with her, and yet she couldn't stop the chemicals firing in her brain. Their connection was an intense physical sensation, clawing its way throughout her body.

'You don't believe that I had no choice once I saw you?'

His voice vibrated low, seeping through her pores and into her body, settling behind her belly button with an uncomfortable pinch.

'I think that's a phrase you came up with and that it has proved most successful with all the different women you meet at bars.'

The words rang with the sound of an accusation although she hadn't meant it.

Diego had clearly picked up on the subtle nuance as well, for he arched one of his eyebrows. 'What do you think I'm after?'

His fingers were still entwined with hers, and the tips of them were rubbing against the back of her hand, sending sparkling showers across her arm. Heat rose through her body, entangling itself with the knot his touch had tied in her stomach and colliding with the sparks that were descending through her arm.

Everything about him made her react. He was like a potent magnet drawing at the fibres of her body. Control had slipped from her hands, and Eliana needed to regain it. She wasn't the type of person to let it go that easily. But Diego was shrouding her thoughts in the thick mists of an instant attraction that was unlike any she had ever experienced before.

'You want to sleep with me.' No use beating around the bush.

'Ah, straight to the point. Do you really want to skip the witty back-and-forth?'

His lips parted in a devastating grin, and Eliana caught her breath for a moment.

'I've been told I'm a pretty good flirt,' he said.

She chuckled at the aura of confidence he exuded, not wanting to let him know how deeply it impacted on her. 'I'm sure that's what they've all told you.'

Her words had the desired effect, for Diego took his free hand to clasp his chest with an indignant expression on his face. 'You wound me, Donna Ana. You're not wrong with your assessment, but I make sure a woman feels worshipped and cherished above anything else.'

Eliana raised a delicate eyebrow, thrown off guard by

his bluntness. It matched hers, so she shouldn't be surprised the way she was. His fingers wrapped around hers were creating a luscious fog around her, draping her in a cloud charged with desire and passion.

It made her wonder what else he could do with his fingers if this innocent touch had already raised all the hair along her arms. The soft curve of his lips begged to be kissed… She wanted to lose herself in the delicious promise they wrote on his face.

'What is your usual plan of seduction?'

Maybe she didn't want to skip all the foreplay. Eliana was still telling herself that she wasn't in his thrall, that she could step back at any moment. But the flames of desire uncoiling themselves in her chest had already surrendered to his charms. She wanted *all* of him.

'Normally I would buy you some drinks, and show my appreciation for your taste in alcohol. We'd discuss some unimportant things about our lives, and I would grab at every opportunity to flatter you. Touch you here and there as you tell me about yourself…'

Diego got up and stepped closer to her, forcing her to tilt her head up so she could look at him. His hand wandered up to her exposed arm, touching her shoulder before slipping down, leaving a series of fires under her skin.

'I don't like to talk about myself that much,' she told him. Her voice sounded husky, and she was enthralled by the pure masculine magnetism he exuded. He could have her right this second if he asked.

He dipped his head, his face so close to hers now that the smell of his aftershave drifted up her nose. The scent of moss and earth shrouded her thoughts in an even more alluring mist, and without giving it a second thought she leaned in closer, wanting to close the gap between them.

'Well, it's a good thing you've already figured me out, so we can skip that part, can't we?' Diego whispered in a deep voice filled with promises of desire.

He shifted his head further, his lips grazing her ear and sending a sensual shiver down her spine.

No, would be the correct answer. But why? After the stress of this day, a bit of comfort in the arms of an otherworldly handsome man would be a soothing balm for her battered nerves. He'd made it clear that this was what he did, so there wouldn't be any feelings hurt. And from the way he'd wrapped her around his little finger from the very beginning, she knew it would be *good.* What harm could one night do?

Eliana grabbed her bag before getting off the stool and stepping closer. Her hand trailed down his arm as she leaned in, so her lips brushed against his skin in a small suggestion of a kiss as she whispered, 'I'm in Room 901. Finish your drink and meet me upstairs in fifteen minutes.'

CHAPTER TWO

DIEGO'S NIGHT HAD been restless. He'd thought sleep would come easier now, more than a month after Vanderson's funeral, but rest still eluded him now and then. Sometimes it was due to grief, but more often than not worry kept him awake at night. Worry about the future and the low hum of an unmet need stirring in his chest.

Ana.

The beautiful stranger he'd met at a bar.

He had followed her to her room that night four weeks ago, where he'd had the best sex of his entire life. So good he still remembered how her body had felt on top of him. They had fitted together as if they were made for each other.

That thought kept crawling back into his mind, and Diego had to shake it. They were most definitely *not* made for each other. What had possessed him even to think that? They'd spent the night together and enjoyed an explosive connection. There was no need to attach more meaning to it.

But he wanted more. More of someone he couldn't have. Diego didn't know how to *give* more. His parents had made sure of that. Their constant betrayal of one another had taught him that love only made people do foolish things. He would rather stay single for ever than risk doing to a woman what his father had done to his mother.

His eyelids still heavy with the lack of sleep, Diego threw on some grey scrubs and flipped the switch on the coffee machine in the kitchen. He left the room through the glass door leading outside, crossing a small patch of grass and entering the garage next to his house. He squinted when he flipped on the light, his senses still awakening after his poor sleep.

Instead of a car and other household items, the garage was filled with medical and sports equipment. A big workbench stood on the far side of the room, with a prosthetic limb on top of it.

With a heavy sigh falling from his lips, Diego approached the bench to look at the small leg he had spent most of his free time on in the last week. He was supposed to be fitting it to its owner, a young boy who had visited him last month with a request for a new leg as he had outgrown his old one.

It wasn't often that Diego found patients who needed prosthetics visiting him in the free clinic he ran in Complexo do Alemão. The average person sought him out for the kind of maladies any general practitioner could take care of, as well as wounds that needed stitching. His expertise as an orthopaedic surgeon wasn't called upon very often.

Diego never refused a patient—sometimes at significant personal cost. But he remembered all too well what it had been like growing up in that area, devoid of any kind of hope for a better future. He had escaped his life of poverty, relying on tenacity and just the right amount of luck. And that last thing—along with his memories of his time in the slums—inspired him to work hard and give back to his community.

'Is this the leg for Miguel? I've just seen his mother at your sister's shop, and she told me about it.'

Diego jumped at the sudden voice behind him and spun around. His grandmother, Márcia, had come into the garage with a small tray that held a cup of coffee and some pieces of toast.

'Avozinha, what are you doing here so early?' he asked as he approached her, taking the tray out of her hands and kissing her on the cheek in greeting.

'Pelé likes to be out in the morning, so we took a walk here to check in on you.'

Diego looked past his grandma and into the garden. A large greyhound was sniffing around the grass, lifting his long snout when Diego whistled and bolting towards him with an excited yelp.

Diego went down on one knee and scratched Pelé's throat. The tags around his collar gave a soft jingle as he rubbed his hands up and down the neck of the animal.

'Wait, you went all the way to Aline's shop? You shouldn't walk in that neighbourhood on your own.'

He looked up at Márcia, who frowned, flipping her hand in a throwaway gesture. 'I'm not alone. Pelé looks after me.'

'This little coward? Remember when you had a trespasser in your garden and he hid under the coffee table when he noticed a stranger? He is cute, but that won't save you.'

Diego smoothed the light brown fur flat with one last pat and then rubbed the greyhound between his large, trusting eyes before he lifted himself off the ground to face his grandmother.

'Don't you lecture me on where I can and cannot go, young man. I've looked out for you since you were knee-high and see what you've become.'

Diego tried his best not to roll his eyes as Márcia went for her favourite topic: her surgeon grandson and how she had saved him from ending up on the street mixed up with the wrong crowd. If he was honest with himself, she did deserve all the credit. She had taken it upon herself to raise him when his parents had been too busy sorting themselves out.

'*Sim,* Vovo. You know I worry about you,' he said and raised his hands in defeat. He could never defeat her in a duel of words.

'You'd better worry about Miguel. He needs a new leg.'

Diego turned around with a frustrated grunt, looking back at his workbench and the prosthetic limb that was giving him such a hard time. 'I didn't expect to be doing it on my own. Vanderson had agreed to let me borrow some time from the paediatric specialist on my team.'

'What about Marco's daughter? She will be the new owner, yes? Maybe she won't be against you helping Miguel.'

He turned around to look at his grandmother, a sceptical eyebrow raised. 'I don't know what to expect from her. She and the Costas weren't even on speaking terms for the last seventeen years. Vanderson told me she's a doctor, too. But his father wouldn't let him have any contact with her.'

Diego shook his head. This wasn't just about him needing hospital resources to help one patient. The free clinic he ran whenever time permitted required more support than he could provide on his own. Even if he could hire just one nurse to work there during the daytime, he would be able to help so many more people. But to do that he needed the help of the chief of medicine at Santa

Valeria Hospital. A role that had belonged to Marco Costa until his recent death.

Eliana Oliveira. That was her name. The word in the corridors of Santa Valeria was that she would arrive any day now, to assume the position as chief of medicine.

Outside of the scandal surrounding her birth, no one knew much about her. She was a complete unknown to Diego, who had a lot more than just his staff at the hospital to worry about. He planned on getting the leg sorted out for the little boy Miguel with or without approval from the new chief. Though he'd prefer to do it with her blessing.

'I'm sure she'll be reasonable,' Márcia said, and patted his arm with a reassuring smile.

He wished he could share her optimism about the new chief, but he'd rather prepare for the worst and be surprised.

With a sigh, Diego glanced at his phone's display to check the time, grabbing the toast his *avozinha* had made for him.

'I'd better go. I don't want to be late if today is the day she actually bothers to show up.'

Eliana sat behind the opulent desk that stood in the chief's office—formerly inhabited by her estranged father—and her stomach roiled again, making her hand fly to her mouth. The stress of being back in Rio de Janeiro to deal with the administration of the Santa Valeria General Hospital was taking a lot more out of her than she had expected. She had woken up from an uneasy slumber with nausea cascading through her in violent waves as she'd tried her best to look presentable for the day.

Suelen, the assistant to the chief of medicine, had given her a diary with all her appointments for the day.

Ten people wanted to speak to her today, all of them about an important matter—according to them. Eliana doubted any of them were as urgent as they made them out to be.

Leaning back in the chair, she let her head fall back and closed her eyes for a moment, willing the next wave of nausea away.

She was nervous, and her body was reacting to the tension. She was meant to be a consultant—not the chief. Her training as a general surgeon had not prepared her for all the administrative work she was now expected to do. All the different reports on financial matters only worsened her already troubled stomach.

It was only going to be for a couple of weeks, she told herself as she scrubbed her hands over her face. She would pick a new chief of medicine to do the job for her and go back to Belo Horizonte. Rio held nothing but old pain for her, and she didn't want to be here. Hell, she didn't even want to be the owner of this hospital.

People who had known her father might think she had followed in his footsteps going into the medical field. He had been the prestigious hospital's owner, after all. But he'd only played a small part in her motivation.

Her mother was the one she wanted to be like. She had been a nurse at Santa Valeria when she'd got pregnant. Her parents had been having an affair, and instead of stepping up and assuming responsibility her father had driven her mother out of town so no one would learn about his infidelity.

Time and again Marco Costa had shown himself to be a dishonourable man, and Eliana wanted nothing to do with anything that had once belonged to the man. Not when he had broken her mother so wholly that she hadn't been able to hang on to life. She could almost hear the whispers of the older staff—the ones who had known her mother and what Marco Costa had done to her.

But life rarely considered what someone wanted, so despite her quite visceral opposition in this matter she now had to deal with the inheritance her father had left her. The day she heard his name for the last time couldn't come soon enough.

'Excuse me, Dr Oliveira?'

Her head snapped back to its original position when she heard the knock, followed by the soft voice of her assistant.

Eliana cleared her throat, swallowing the bile she felt rising in it. 'Is it already time for my first appointment?' she asked, glancing at her schedule.

'Ah, no...' Suelen hesitated for a fraction before speaking again. 'A registrar in general surgery has called for help. There are some complications with a surgery, and none of the other consultants seem to be available.'

Her words made Eliana blink slowly for a couple of seconds, unable to comprehend what she had just said. 'There are no consultants to help the junior surgeons? Where are they?'

Suelen looked down at her notepad, a faint blush streaking over her cheeks. She was clearly uncomfortable with the answer. 'It seems one of them called in sick, three are stuck in their own surgeries, and another two are...' she looked down to check her notes again '...playing golf.'

'What?' Eliana got up from her chair and waved the assistant to come with her. 'Move my meetings around. I'll take care of it myself. Just show me to the OR.'

Despite the nerves flipping her stomach inside out, Eliana felt an odd excitement rise within her at the thought of stepping into the OR. That, at least, was a world she understood and felt comfortable in.

They rushed to the general surgery wing, where Suelen pointed her towards OR Three. Eliana wasted no time scrubbing in as fast as she could, and thanked the OR nurse when she stepped out into the scrub room to greet her.

'Do you have a pair of spare shoes around?' she asked the nurse, glancing down at the high heels she was wearing. 'Anything will be a vast improvement.'

'I think we have some *chinelas* for such cases here.' The woman bent down, opening a small cupboard and rummaging around before pulling out a pair of neon green slippers.

Eliana stared at them for a moment, as if she was facing off a venomous snake. They really couldn't have been less flattering if they'd tried. 'Well, I did say anything would be better,' she said with a laugh as she kicked her heels off and stowed them in the cupboard the nurse had just pulled the slippers from.

She received a gown and gloves with a smile, tying a mask around the back of her head as she readied herself to help the surgeon. The doors to the operations room opened with a familiar sound, and a sense of control enveloped her, calming her rioting stomach.

Eliana stepped up to the patient and watched as the registrar struggled to keep the surgical field clear.

'What happened?' she asked, her voice calm. For the first time today, she felt as if she knew exactly what was happening.

'Blunt force trauma caused a tear in the diaphragm. When we went in we found unexpected damage to the kidneys as well. There was a lot more blood than we had expected.' The panicked registrar looked around at her colleague. 'The consultant was supposed to be with us, but we had no time to wait.'

'It's all right. I'm here to help.' Eliana stepped closer to the patient. 'First we want to isolate the bleeding. Clamp, please.' Eliana stretched out her hand and a moment later the cold steel of the instrument hit her gloved palm.

'I think there must be a rupture on one kidney.'

Hesitation was mixed with despair in the doctor's voice and it made Eliana frown behind her mask. They must have spent a lot of time looking for a superior while the situation was unfolding.

She nodded to reassure her. There was no room for panic in the operating room. 'Yes, blunt force trauma strong enough to hurt the diaphragm like that can cause damage to the kidneys as well. Let's clamp the renal artery to see if the bleeding subsides.'

Looking down at the patient, Eliana pointed out the artery in question and placed a clamp there.

'Suction here so we can see better,' she instructed the other junior surgeon, who moved the instrument to where she had indicated.

The visibility on the kidneys soon cleared and a lot less blood was replacing the stuff they suctioned away.

'Good. Always isolate the source of bleeding by clamping the right artery. Now we can work on the repair unobstructed.'

With the blood flow stemmed, they could focus on repairing the damage.

'I think this should be familiar territory for you. What are the next steps?'

The junior surgeon looked at her before dropping her eyes back to the patient.

Eliana listened to her instructions, nodding as the surgeon explained the next steps.

Her hands were itching to grab the scalpel herself. It had been some time since she'd performed any kind of surgery. After earning her general surgeon's classification she'd been asked by her teaching hospital to stay on as a consultant—which she'd agreed to do, with a request for a sabbatical so she could have a break after studying for her board certification.

A break that she had only been able to enjoy for a few days before the news of her father's accident had reached her.

But even with her desire to work on the patient herself Eliana took the opportunity to talk the two junior surgeons through the procedure rather than do it. If these junior staff had been empowered to make their own decisions to begin with, maybe they wouldn't have been so lost in what she considered a rather common complication in a case such as this one.

Eliana repressed a sigh behind her mask, pushing the thought away and focusing on the task in front of her. This was only her first day, and she was already uncovering things that would threaten to extend her stay in Rio de Janeiro when she wanted nothing else but to leave this place behind.

Diego had just left a patient's room when his phone vibrated with a page. The nurses' station in the general surgery wing were asking him to report to their department on an urgent matter. He furrowed his brow, unsure what that meant. As the head of the orthopaedics department, he rarely dealt with anyone outside of his own staff.

He hesitated, staring at the screen of his phone. Something wasn't right. His staff had told him that the new chief of medicine had arrived today. Did it have something to do with her? The orthopaedics head nurse had told him Chief Oliveira had requested a meeting with him next week.

Putting his phone back into his pocket, he hurried towards the general surgery wing and stopped at the nurses' station, looking at the man standing behind it. 'What happened? I got an urgent page to come here.'

The nurse nodded with a heavy sigh. 'Thank you, Dr Ferrari. I didn't know who else to page in this situation. None of the consultants answered my call, and I have two very nervous junior surgeons freaking out in OR Three.'

Diego glanced at the whiteboard with the surgical schedule written on it. There were four surgeries scheduled for right now, with two additional consultants on floor duties.

'Where are those two?' He nodded towards the whiteboard.

This time the nurse rolled his eyes. 'You know them… They were Dr Costa's lackeys and they won't lift a single finger if no one makes them. They made themselves such a cosy nest over the years, they don't know how to do actual work any more.'

Diego had to suppress a sigh at that. Unfortunately for him, and the entire hospital, not every doctor in the building had the work ethic he considered essential. In fact, quite a few of the higher-ranking doctors were friends and associates of the former chief of medicine, and that was exactly the way they acted around the hospital. As if they were untouchable and not bound by the rules everyone else was following.

But now was not the time to think about that. 'You said OR Three?' he asked.

The nurse nodded, but his gaze shifted slightly, as if he was trying to decide whether he should say something more.

Diego arched his brow in a silent question.

'We paged you ten minutes ago. The registrars were freaked out. We weren't sure whether you were coming, so we had to page someone else.' There was mild apprehension in his voice.

'Who did you page?'

'The chief. She came down straight away, so I think they should be done by now. Though I haven't seen them leave the OR yet…'

Diego couldn't keep the surprise out of his expression. It seemed Marco Costa's estranged daughter was not just a doctor but a surgeon. 'I'll go and have a look anyway. Maybe she needs more help.'

He glanced at the whiteboard once more, looking for the procedure that was happening in OR Three. The letters MVA were written on the schedule.

Diego frowned. Junior surgeons shouldn't be operating on a car crash victim unsupervised. With cases like that there was no telling what might await them once they opened up the patient.

He left the nurses' station with a nod towards the nurse who had paged him and arrived at the OR just in time to see the team wrapping up the surgery.

Through the thick glass of the scrub room it was hard to read their mood. One of the junior surgeons was dressing the wound while the other one was talking to the woman he presumed was the new chief of medicine. His eyes glided over her. He appreciated the fact that he had a moment to check her out before she knew he was there.

Her hair was hidden underneath a generic grey surgical cap and her face remained behind the mask. She looked pale under the surgical lights, almost unwell, with a soft sheen of sweat covering her forehead. Was she nervous?

Diego was about to enter the OR when the new chief lifted her head and looked directly at him. Her forehead furrowed for a moment, and he felt an unexpected flash of passion uncoil itself in his chest when their gazes collided. Her golden-brown eyes widened in recognition and he knew it was her. He would have recognised those eyes anywhere.

The woman who had been stuck in his head for the last four weeks.

Ana.

Diego struggled to comprehend this revelation. For a few heartbeats they stared at each other. His thoughts were racing. Ana was Eliana Oliveira. Vanderson's sister. The second the thought manifested itself in his head the puzzle pieces fell into place and he couldn't believe he hadn't seen it the night they met.

They had the same colour hair, that dark brown shade with just a hint of red, and even without seeing the rest of her face he noticed the similarities in their eyes. This was Vanderson's sister. The woman he had spent one incredible night with.

How was this possible? They had spoken about their lives, had they not?

He tried hard to remember what they had spoken about, but the only part of that night remaining vivid in his memories were the hours they'd spent together in bed. He remembered the feel of her skin on his, his tongue trailing down her sternum, her cries of pleasure when his mouth found her essence…

The last memory made Diego shiver with renewed desire and anticipation.

How could he not have seen that she was Vanderson's sister? Now that he knew it seemed so obvious. She had even said that she'd just come from her father's funeral.

Though he now knew that to be a lie. He had been at the funeral, and had kept an eye out for the unexpected heiress of the Costa fortune.

But what were they supposed to do now?

He could see the flame in her own eyes, mirroring the instant desire that flashed through him. It seemed their night together had done little to satisfy her hunger, either. Or was he reading too much into one brief glimpse?

Eliana was rooted to the spot. She blinked once to shake away the shock, and then her eyes found their way back to the surgeon standing in front of her.

From the corner of her eye she saw Diego following every movement she made. Tiny flames were igniting across her skin. For a second, the sight of him even drowned out the renewed nausea that had started up at the end of the surgery. Eliana was glad she hadn't had to operate herself after all. She could feel trembles going through her body. This wasn't just nerves, she thought. She must have caught a stomach bug.

'Make sure you page me if there are any changes in the patient's vital signs,' she said to the junior surgeon, who nodded and left as the patient was wheeled out on a gurney.

She peeled herself out of the surgical gown, pulled both gloves and mask off before removing the cap, closing her eyes for a moment and taking a few deep breaths to compose herself. The last person she had expected to see here—the last person she'd *wanted* to see—had just shown up in the OR.

Diego stood in front of her, tall and handsomely dark. His appearance came with so many questions Eliana didn't even know where to start. He was a doctor. Not only that, he must also be a surgeon if he felt comfortable coming into an operating room just like that. And, even worse, by the looks of it he was a surgeon at *her* hospital.

If he lived here in Rio, what had he been doing at the hotel last month? Eliana had thought she would never see him again.

How to start such a conversation? She didn't even know where to begin.

She opened her mouth and immediately closed it again as another wave of nausea churned her stomach. Her hand flew to her mouth, covering it on the off-chance that something might escape. Standing still, she took another deep breath to steady herself.

'Are you okay?' Diego asked, his voice sounding distant and yet strained with concern.

Eliana tried to speak again, but she only moved her hand away from her mouth a couple of millimetres before feeling ill again. Keeping her palm pressed against her lips, she shook her head, and a second later Diego's muscular arm wrapped itself around her waist as he guided her towards a small stool at the far side of the operating room.

He popped up in her field of vision when he crouched down in front of her, a concerned expression on his face. The warmth she saw in his eyes would have sent her heart rate through the roof in any other circumstances, but the way she was feeling right now she was thankful to have someone there who wasn't a complete stranger.

That thought caused a slight twinge in her chest—something she couldn't focus on. Her mind was too absorbed with whatever illness it was that was making her stomach perform loops within her.

Diego's hand pressed against her forehead for a moment. 'You don't feel warm,' he said. 'But you are sweaty and, from the looks of it, nauseated. Could be a stomach bug. Did you eat anything this morning?'

Deep breaths had calmed her stomach just a bit, and Eliana dared once more to move her hand away from her mouth to answer his question. 'No, just coffee. I woke up feeling like this already, and one glance at food made my stomach turn.'

Diego frowned at her. 'You should know that coffee isn't a substitute for a proper breakfast.'

Under any other circumstances she would not have let him lecture her, but she was feeling increasingly light-headed. The room around her darkened and turned, giving her a sense of vertigo that worsened the nausea.

'I think I'm going to pass out...' she whispered, sensing her impending doom.

She felt his hands grab her shoulders as her eyes closed. He mumbled something to her in a distorted voice, but the meaning of his words didn't reach her mind as she slipped into unconsciousness.

CHAPTER THREE

A BRIGHT LIGHT was trying its best to find a path underneath her closed eyelids. Eliana moved her head to one side to escape the glare. Her temples were throbbing, and her tongue clung to the roof of her mouth as if she hadn't had any water in days. Her lips felt dry as she opened her mouth slightly.

She heard a soft rustling above her, then hushed whispers of conversation, and it was only then that her confused mind realised that she did not know where she was. The thought penetrated the thick fog around her, and she slowly opened her eyes.

An older woman was looking at her with a friendly sparkle in her eyes. She wore a white coat and was putting on some disposable gloves. Squinting at her, Eliana read her name tag: *Dr Sophia Salvador, Accident and Emergency Services.*

'Welcome back, Chief. You gave us all quite a scare when we saw Dr Ferrari carrying your limp body.' Dr Salvador smiled at her before turning to the tray next to her. 'I'll take some blood for a test, to make sure you're okay. But your pulse ox is normal, and pupillary response is also fine. Probably thanks to Dr Ferrari, here, who cushioned your fall.'

Eliana nodded her silent consent, trying to remember

what had happened as the woman drew her blood. She'd woken up this morning feeling rotten, as if she had come down with the flu. She had put it down to nerves about her new job. It wasn't the first time she had felt sick to her stomach because of nerves.

Eliana groaned as she understood what had just happened. Despite her best efforts to look as if she knew what she was doing—as if she belonged here—she had managed to faint. On her first day at work. In front of the incredibly hot almost-stranger she had met at a bar a month ago.

Memories of Diego came rushing back into her consciousness, worsening her headache as a cascade of hot sparks rampaged through her body, igniting her already frayed nerves. 'Wait…where…?'

She looked to where Dr Salvador had nodded, and winced when she tilted her head to the side too fast, causing pain to spear through her throbbing head. Diego was sitting on a chair a few paces away from the bed she lay in.

He got up when she looked at him, his expression still a lot more worried than she'd thought it would be. Snippets of what had happened in the operating room drifted back to her. He'd been holding her when she'd regained consciousness, lifting her off her seat.

Dim memories of him examining her while she was lying down on a gurney came to life in her head. Had it only been a couple of minutes ago? Her sense of time was off kilter. Had he been waiting here this entire time, watching over her?

The thought drove a different heat through her body. Not once in her life had someone watched over her. Being raised by nannies and teachers had taught her early that she was the only person in her life she could count on.

Everyone else had their own agenda and she would only ever be an instrument in their achieving it.

What were his reasons for staying with her? What did Diego want? Those intrusive thoughts crawled into her head before Eliana could stop them. They had only spent one night together. There was nothing more to it.

'Let me expedite your lab results so we can release you as soon as possible,' Sophia said as she picked up the phial with her blood sample. 'From the symptoms Dr Ferrari described, and my own examination, I think a stomach bug is likely.'

The woman left, and when the door behind her fell shut silence enveloped the room for a few heartbeats as she searched for the right thing to say. It seemed it was true. Diego had not only brought her here, he'd stayed to watch over her.

She almost laughed at that thought—at how foreign and unbelievable it felt in her mind. This must be some kind of professional scheming. She was the new chief of medicine, after all.

Yet she could see a hint of concern still etched into his expression as she turned her head to look around her. She paused to look at him for a heartbeat. She opened her mouth, ready to say something, but words wouldn't form in her brain, so she looked back down to her hands, her heart suddenly pounding against her chest at the sight of the worried spark in his eyes.

It was only then that she noticed her surroundings. It was a private room, the interior much more luxurious than she had expected any hospital room to be. The sheets were soft against her skin, the mattress comfortable beneath her. The door to an en-suite bathroom stood ajar, giving her a view of the room which had a large rain shower.

'This is not the emergency department. What is this room?' she asked, forgetting about Diego's dark gaze for a second. How could this be a room in a hospital?

Diego looked around himself, and she saw an expression of contempt fluttering over his face before he regained full composure.

'This is one of the rooms Marco had designed for his various VIP patients. When I arrived with you at A&E they insisted on moving you here once they'd assessed you. They thought you had passed out from exhaustion. Do you remember?' He furrowed his brow.

'Vaguely… The whole thing is just a blur of light and headaches right now.' Eliana looked at the opulence of this place. It was fancier than her hotel room. 'This seems…excessive. I don't want to know what budgets got cut to make this happen.'

She wanted her patients to convalesce in peace and comfort, but this looked more like a room in a spa than a hospital.

Her train of thought stopped mid-track when she looked up at Diego, who had a thoughtful smile on his face as he regarded her. The gentleness in his expression sent sparks flying all over her body.

'I said the same thing when Marco started working on these rooms. Turns out he cut each department's pro bono fund to basically nothing.'

The thought seemed to fill him with renewed resentment for her father.

'You didn't get along with my father?'

As her father had hired all the department heads at the hospital, Eliana had assumed they were his minions. The people he had hired would no doubt also think it acceptable to banish a pregnant woman from the only place she had ever called home. Like Marco had done with her mother.

But it seemed she had found another person who shared her opinion about her father. How odd to think the stranger she'd had a one-night stand with four weeks ago was now her potential ally in this hospital...

Diego snorted a derisive laugh. 'Marco Costa would have fired me ages ago if he could, and over the years I gave him enough reasons to try. But he only ever caught me with my little toe over the line and nothing else,' he said, and shrugged. 'By the time he realised I would be more trouble than my talent was worth it was already too late. If he'd let me go half of his staff would have walked out with me.'

He said it so matter-of-factly Eliana had no choice but to admire his confidence. It took a lot to know one's worth. But there was something else hidden in his words, too. A sense of accountability and belonging. And from those words alone she knew exactly who Diego considered his people.

It was a thought that made envy needle at her heart. Belonging was a foreign concept to Eliana. She'd grown up isolated from the only family she had ever known— which hadn't been much to begin with—and her experience at boarding school had been little better.

'Sorry, I know he was your father—' he started, but she interrupted him with a shake of her head.

'You might remember me saying how I wasn't close to my father back at that hotel bar. Your words are docile compared to what I have to say about him on any given day.'

Understanding rushed over his expression, but it only remained there for a moment before his face slackened again. He was clearly not letting her see his thoughts.

But he must know about her. Everyone in this hospital did. In the thirty-five years since her birth—since her mother had fallen for a guy she never should have—the staff of Santa Valeria had not forgotten the scandal surrounding her conception. From the moment Eliana had set foot in the foyer of the hospital she'd been able to sense the eyes on her, the whispers following her around as she was introduced to different staff members.

Even Diego, who of course hadn't worked here when her mother had got pregnant, must know about her—how she had grown up as the black sheep of the Costa family, escaping her abusive home the moment she'd turned eighteen.

'I'm sorry,' he said, and somehow she knew they both understood in that moment what he was apologising for. Not for something that he'd done, but for the circumstances that had led to him knowing so much about her.

'So, you think Santa Valeria should do more pro bono surgeries?' Eliana asked, going back to what he had said about the budget cut.

'Among other things, yes,' he said, crossing his arms in front of his chest and giving her a view she didn't want to dwell on. She knew the strength those arms possessed. She had found pleasure in them throughout their entire night together.

'What else do you suggest?'

It was a genuine question for the man she'd thought she would never meet again, only to find out that they would now be working together—at least until she went back home in a couple of weeks.

Diego tilted his head to one side, his eyes narrowing as he looked at her with such intensity that her breath caught in her throat. His hand wandered up to his face, stroking over the light stubble covering his cheeks.

'Community outreach. We have some high-calibre donors supporting us. Instead of building private suites and taking those donors on lavish cruises, we could take Santa Valeria's facilities and help the poorer communities in this city when they are most in need of care. God knows there are enough people requiring help right now.'

His words seemed to her to come from a place of experience, with a small nugget of truth shining through.

'Why is that important to you?' she asked, and almost flinched when his eyes grew darker, narrowing on her. Her question seemed to have crossed an invisible boundary.

His jaw tightened for a moment as he stared her down, but Eliana forced herself to meet his gaze straight on, despite the defences she spotted going up all around him.

'It's the right thing to do. I might have got out, but they are still my people.'

'Your—?'

The door opened, interrupting their conversation, and Dr Salvador strode back into the room. The fierce protectiveness in Diego's eyes vanished, leaving his face unreadable.

Eliana's eyes were drawn to the emergency doctor, who stepped closer. She was wearing an expression of medical professionalism on her face that quickened her pulse. She knew that look. She had given it to patients herself.

She whipped her head around, looking at Diego, and whatever he saw written in her face was enough to make him get off his chair and step closer to her side. A similar look of protectiveness to the one he'd had a few moments ago was etched into his features.

'Would you mind giving us some privacy?' Sophia asked him, and a tremble shook Eliana's body.

The nausea came rushing back, her head suddenly felt light, and Eliana reacted before she could think, her hand reaching for Diego's and crushing it in a vice-like grip.

'It's okay if he stays,' she said, in a voice that sounded so unlike her own.

Something deep within her told her she needed him to stay. Whether it was premonition or just a primal fear gripping at her heart, she didn't know.

Diego stopped, giving her a questioning look, but he stayed, and his hand did not fight her touch.

'Well, it looks like it's not a stomach bug, but morning sickness. Or, in your case, late-afternoon sickness.' She paused for a moment, before confirming the absurd thought that was rattling around in Eliana's head. 'You're pregnant.'

Eliana opened her mouth to speak, but no words crossed the threshold of her lips. Pregnant? How was she pregnant? Her head snapped around to Diego, and whatever expression she was wearing on her face seemed to convey to him all the words she didn't want to say in front of the doctor.

The baby was his. *They* were pregnant.

His hand slipped from her grasp as he took a step back. The shock she felt at the revelation was written on his face.

'How long?' she asked, even though she knew it didn't matter.

Eliana had only slept with one person in the last six months, and that was the man standing here in the room with her.

'I can't say without an ultrasound. Do you remember the date of your last period?' Dr Salvador paused for a moment, to give her time to digest the information, before she continued, 'Normally I would get someone from

OBGYN down here to talk to you, but since this is your hospital, and you're a doctor yourself, I'll discharge you. But make sure you start your prenatal care straight away.'

Her last period? She had no idea. Her periods were always irregular and hard to track—something she'd made peace with a long time ago. When she didn't have one, she didn't believe anything amiss.

Four weeks. That was when she'd fallen pregnant. Because that was when she had met Diego.

Eliana didn't register Dr Salvador's words, her mind too busy trying to understand the new and unexpected reality she found herself in. As if her life hadn't been complicated enough, with her father's death. Now she could add an unplanned pregnancy to the pile.

A baby growing right below her heart.

Her hand darted to her still flat stomach.

'All right, I'll leave you to digest this information. But medically you're good to go about your day.'

Sophia Salvador left them, closing the door behind her.

Every muscle in his body was tense with anticipation in a strange fight-or-flight response to the situation. His mind was reeling from the explosive information Sophia had just shared with them, and he was struggling to make any sense of it.

He'd had about a million questions floating around in his mind, but he didn't know how to verbalise any of them now he'd heard her say those words, acknowledging out loud what Eliana's eyes had already told him. How was he supposed to start this conversation?

Diego grabbed a chair from the far side of the room and brought it closer to the bed, sitting down and looking at her. 'Am I—?'

Eliana nodded before he'd finished his sentence. 'It's

yours. There's no doubt about it. I've not slept with any-one else.'

There it was.

A large boulder dropped into his stomach as she said those words. Their one night of searing passion had re-sulted in a child.

'That's not what I expected to hear when I saw you again today,' was all he managed to say, his mind going blank. All he could think of was that life-altering rev-elation.

Eliana gave a short laugh, and Diego wasn't sure whether it was genuine. He barely knew the woman lying on the bed in front of him. It was a thought that made him laugh in return. The mother of his child was noth-ing more than a stranger to him.

'I don't even know how it happened,' she said in a quiet voice, more as if she was talking to herself than to him. 'I'm on the pill…'

Her voice trailed off, and there was a thoughtful ex-pression on her face. Then her eyes went wide with shock and her hand darted up to her mouth, clasping it with a gasp.

Diego stiffened in his chair, reaching out to her. 'What is it?'

'It's my fault. When I came here last month it was after the news of my father and brother's accident. I was nervous and felt ill. I went through my morning routine, including taking the pill, and then…' She stopped and looked at him. 'I threw up. I threw up the medication. But I didn't even think about it because I didn't think I was going to meet someone.'

That explained it. On the night in question they'd had that conversation every responsible adult should have about avoiding unwanted consequences of their consensual encounter. Diego had even worn a condom that first time. Maybe even the second time.

His memories became blurry around the third time, with the night growing longer and the passion hotter, each union burning more intensely than the one before. Her touch had been intoxicating—to the point where he could remember little else about that night.

He couldn't say it was her fault. It might just as well be his. *Theirs.* But the fact was they were now bound to each other through the life they'd created.

'It's not anyone's fault. These things happen—you know that as well as I do.'

He knew that wasn't reassuring, but in this moment—with the shock of discovery still sitting deep in his bones—he didn't know what else to tell her. Or how to ask the question burning on his lips. This was her choice, after all.

Whether it was his expression or the unexpected connection they suddenly shared he didn't know, but Eliana seemed to have read his thoughts, for a moment later she said, 'I don't have a plan, but I'm not abandoning this child the way I was disregarded. The rest I can figure out.'

Something strange bubbled up within his chest at her words. A feeling of heavy responsibility, but with something lurking underneath it as well. A protectiveness unlike anything he had experienced before.

'The rest *we* can figure out,' he said.

Her eyes narrowed as she looked at him. 'Are you up to the task of being a father?' she asked rather bluntly, zeroing in on a vulnerability that he hadn't shared with her yet.

His mind had always struggled to comprehend the enormity of what fatherhood meant. His father had been such an abject failure in teaching him what it meant to be a decent person. Instead of raising him, Ignacio Ferrari had given the young Diego to his mother—*avozinha*—to raise while he went sleeping around all of Rio.

How could he be a proud Latin father in a world where the odds had been stacked against him from the very beginning and his own father had been the worst possible role model? There were things he would have to teach his child, weren't there?

'That's going to be one of those things we'll have to figure out,' he said with a wry smile.

He rested his face in his hands for a moment, pressing his fingers against his temples in a reminder to himself to stay collected. The tension was gone, but it had been replaced by a reality they were both starting to understand.

'Diego, this is a lot to consider. I need some time to think about your...' Eliana didn't finish her sentence, prompting him to raise an eyebrow at her.

Diego straightened his back to look at her. 'My what? This is my child, too. Whatever you may have heard about me from gossiping staff, I don't shy away from my responsibilities.'

He'd made up his mind. For better or for worse, they were in it for the long run. He didn't know how to be a father, but at least he knew how to be around children. His father had created so many offspring, all of them sooner or later arriving at his grandmother's house to get to know their family, that he had experience with all the different stages of childhood.

'What do you want us to do?' he asked, and watched as she shook her head.

'I don't know, Diego. Right now, I can't handle any thought of *us* in this context. I came here to find someone to lead this hospital—not *this*.'

The silence between them grew tense as he watched different emotions flutter over her face, as if she was chasing her own thoughts in her head. He reached his hand out to her—only to stop when a soft buzzing interrupted him.

Diego frowned as he checked his phone. 'They're paging me for a Code Blue. I have to go.'

Eliana nodded, her face blank except for her golden-brown eyes, which were still wide in shock.

'Can we talk about this later?' He didn't want to leave. He wanted to stay and for them to work through this life-altering news together. Especially when she was still so fragile from earlier.

'Go and attend to your patient. I need some time to think. I...' She hesitated for a moment, finally looking at him, and he could see the doubt swirling in her eyes. 'I need some space to work through this. I'll let you know when I'm ready to talk.'

His phone kept on vibrating, and Diego hissed a low curse as he turned around to rush to his patient, his mind still reeling at the way his life had changed for ever in the last two hours.

He was going to be a father.

CHAPTER FOUR

ELIANA SPENT THE better part of two weeks looking for her replacement. The news about her unexpected pregnancy still sat deep in her bones, and she had yet to make a plan. Or talk to Diego about it. Staying locked up in her office interviewing people had made it easy to avoid him, as she didn't know what to tell him. Planning had never been her strength.

'Everything else we can figure out.'

That was what Diego had said. As if they were a team now. Fused together by their one night of passion.

She would have to make a plan with him. Whether or not she wanted Diego in her life didn't matter any more. Eliana had grown up deprived of both parents, so if Diego was willing to be a father she would make sure he could be a part of their child's life. Regardless of how she felt about him.

'Good morning, Suelen,' Eliana said as she passed the desk of her assistant and waited for her to hand her the usual diary full of appointments and a list of important queries she had to attend to as the interim chief of medicine.

But her assistant had only one item on her agenda. 'You asked me to schedule you some time in the emergency department today. Dr Salvador is expecting you.'

'That's right. I almost forgot about that.' She'd asked Suelen to block off some time with each department head so she could observe different procedures. Diego had already alluded to the changes he would like to see at Santa Valeria, and he wasn't the only department head with a wish list.

Even though Eliana yearned for some OR time, her first stop had to be the emergency department under Sophia Salvador. It was the beating heart of their entire trauma centre, and deserved a lot more attention than it seemed it had previously received.

Eliana went inside her office to put down her jacket and bag, and then came out and stopped in front of her assistant's desk again, when a thought dawned on her. There was something she needed to do and had been avoiding for the last couple of days.

'Can you get the obstetrics head up here for a meeting as soon as they have time? I have some matters to discuss.'

Those 'matters' being her child.

She balled her hand into a fist to stop herself from reaching for her stomach. That instinctual protectiveness emerged every time she thought of the tiny being inside her, but she wasn't ready to reveal anything to the world just yet.

Eliana was aware of the looks and whispers following her around, reviving the rumours around her mother's affair with the old chief. Who knew how the conversations would turn when they found out that she was in a similar position—pregnant with the baby of a high-ranking doctor in this hospital? She was still a stranger to everyone here, and didn't dare risk showing any kind of vulnerability. Things had got so bad for her own mother she'd ended up fleeing this place.

An old pain clawed at her heart, and not for the first time she wished her mother were still alive to give her some advice. Had she ever regretted what had happened with her father? Would Diego turn out to be a similar man?

One day at a time, she told herself as she walked to the emergency department. Only time would tell what kind of parents she and Diego would be together.

The second Eliana stepped through the doors to A&E noise erupted around her as nurses and doctors saw to their patients, with ailments of varying degrees of seriousness. She tried her best not to stand in anyone's way as she walked to the far end of the room, looking at a large screen on the wall that held all the information on their current intakes.

'Who are you?' the nurse behind the counter asked her, tearing her gaze away from the screen.

'I'm—'

She was interrupted by Sophia walking into sight. 'Chief Oliveira, I was wondering when you would show up. Our admissions board is already full, so you won't mind getting to work straight away?'

'Work?' Eliana raised her eyebrows.

When she'd scheduled this time she hadn't expected any of the department heads to put her to work. Though she was quite excited at the idea of practising medicine. Being the chief of medicine involved a lot more paperwork than patients—a fact she lamented.

'You wanted to get to know my department. There is no better way than to work here for a day—and we can always use a hand.' Sophia turned around and looked over at the screen. 'Why don't you look at Bed Four? One of our regulars is back, and she'll have lots to say about her time at your hospital.'

'All right.'

Eliana smiled, liking this idea more by the minute. She'd thought she would have to wait until she was back in Belo Horizonte to see patients again. This was an exciting change of pace from her usual chief's duties.

Stepping up to Bed Four, Eliana grabbed the patient chart attached to the end of the bed and scanned it. The intake nurse had scribbled *'shortness of breath and palpitations'* on the form, at which Eliana raised an eyebrow. Why had they left a patient with these symptoms unattended?

The older woman was lying down, giving the impression of sleeping at first glance, but she was actually reading a somewhat tattered-looking book as she lay on her side. Her chest was heaving with laboured breaths, but other than that she seemed unperturbed by her struggle to breathe.

'*Olá, senhora*, I'm Dr Oliveira. Do you mind if I have a listen to your breathing?'

The woman turned her head as if she had only just noticed her. 'I haven't seen you around. Are you new?'

Not a question she had expected. 'That I am,' she answered after a short silence. 'And Dr Salvador has already told me this isn't your first visit.'

Eliana looked at the chart again, but the only part filled out on the admission form was the first name: Selma.

'I'm here more often than I would like, and it takes me a whole day to get here. I usually go to the clinic close to home, but the doctor hasn't been there in a while.' An expression of concern fluttered over her face. 'He said I should come here whenever I need help managing my condition.'

'Condition?' Eliana arched her brows.

Selma put her book down on her lap and grabbed her bag, digging through it to produce a small notebook with torn edges and crinkled paper. She licked her finger to help her turn the pages as she searched for the right one.

'He's such a helpful and kind man, so he wrote it down for me...along with everything the other doctors will need to know. It's called...' She paused, squinting at the words scrawled on the paper. 'Pulmonary hyper...'

'Hypertension?' Eliana asked when Selma struggled with reading the next word. 'Can I see the doctor's notes?'

Someone with such a serious condition should be under the continuous care of a physician. Why had this doctor told her to come to *this* hospital?

If the clinic is closed, go to the Santa Valeria General Hospital. If they refuse to treat you, ask to page Dr V. Costa.

Eliana's heart stuttered in her chest when she read the words written on the piece of paper. She stared at the ink in disbelief. Her *brother* had told this woman to come here.

Selma had said the doctor hadn't been at the clinic for a while. Was Vanderson the physician in question? Her eyes went back to the woman, scrutinising her. She clearly didn't know about his death.

'Have you stopped taking your medication?'

Among the scribbles describing Selma's condition, she could see that she had been prescribed benazepril, a type of medication to treat high blood pressure in older patients.

'Well, yes, I go by the clinic to get my medication from the doctor. But since he hasn't been there for a while I had no choice but to stop.'

'You don't have a GP who can fill your prescription for you?'

Eliana was confident she knew the answer to that question, but she wanted to ask anyway.

They could only be one reason why her brother had instructed this woman to come to his father's hospital's emergency department. Because she had nowhere else to go and she needed to be treated.

Selma's expression faltered for a brief moment. She glanced around, as if uncertain what to say.

Noticing the hesitation, Eliana quickly shook her head. 'Never mind about that. There's probably some built-up fluid in your lungs. We'll treat you for that, and I will stock up your supply of medication. No questions asked.'

She smiled to reassure the patient, before moving away to get a portable ultrasound machine as well as a set of hypodermic needles and syringes to drain the excess fluid compressing Selma's lungs.

Still new to the hospital—and to the emergency department in particular—it took her a couple of minutes to find the right closet and the materials necessary to do the procedure.

The newfound knowledge about the steps her brother had taken to help this patient had unleashed a torrent of different emotions in her chest, mingling with the still-fresh news of her unexpected pregnancy. It was becoming harder for her to focus on just one thing when every day came with a new revelation about herself, her family, or the hospital she now owned.

The thoughts swirling in her head came to an abrupt halt when she spotted someone next to Selma's bed. Diego stood beside the woman, holding his stethoscope to her chest as he examined her.

Eliana froze in place, her senses overwhelmed by Diego's sudden appearance. Her flight reaction kicked in, urging her to turn around and run—as she had been doing for the last two weeks whenever she saw him. But this time her feet didn't heed the command, staying rooted to the spot as an instant and visceral awareness of him thundered through her. The new information about her brother was forgotten as longing gripped her, unexpected in its intensity.

They hadn't spoken since they'd received the news about her unexpected pregnancy, and Eliana knew that was her doing. Diego had tried to reach out, asking for time to talk. Time she had yet to grant him. Because she didn't know what he was going to say as much as she didn't know what *she* would say.

After all, making plans had always been her greatest weakness. And the decisions they were supposed to make together required a lot of co-ordination and planning.

Eliana forced herself to take a deep breath, shaking away the shock of seeing him. There was still a patient who needed her help, and she couldn't get distracted by her personal issues.

She stepped up to the bed, clearing her throat to gain their attention. 'I didn't expect to see you here, Dr Ferrari,' she said as she passed him.

'I can say the same thing about you, Chief,' he replied, and Eliana could swear she heard a hint of reproach in his voice.

Sparks filled the air the second they were close enough to touch, igniting a longing heat just behind her belly button. It was a reaction completely inappropriate, and so out of control it almost made her flinch. The second he came too close to her all her inhibitions seemed to melt away, and she just wanted to be a part of him again.

* * *

With his own wing being as busy as it was, Diego didn't have the freedom to answer pages that weren't work-related as fast as he would like to. So when the admissions nurse in the emergency department had paged him about a patient from the free clinic it had taken him almost an hour to get there and check for himself.

What he hadn't expected was to see Eliana taking care of his patient.

A thrill of excitement mixed with dread in his stomach. While the need to see her pulled at his chest, he didn't want to do it in front of Selma, because he might have to explain some things he didn't know how to.

The new chief didn't know about the free clinic he was running—sometimes using hospital resources like medicine, or time from him and his colleagues. Everyone he'd ever involved in helping out had done so voluntarily, and with the understanding that they might be in a grey zone where the hospital policies were concerned. They were helping people who needed assistance—even if Diego had to beg, borrow and steal from Santa Valeria.

What he hadn't decided was if he wanted to tell Eliana about his side project or if he should lie low until a new chief was appointed and deal with them.

Oblivious to the tension zipping like electricity between them, Selma beamed at Eliana. 'You didn't mention that you knew Dr Ferrari. Does that mean we'll see *you* at the clinic as well?'

A boulder dropped into Diego's stomach. So much for finding his own way of broaching the subject with Eliana.

'I was paged here for a consult when I saw you, Selma,' he lied, and in an almost automated gesture he took the instruments Eliana was carrying into his own hands to start the procedure.

'Do you tend to take a lot of the consultations registrars should be doing?' she asked.

Her voice had an edge to it, but not one of hostility.
Was she amused by his attempt to cover up the true reason he was down here? What had Selma already told her?

Unwilling to drop the charade, Diego shrugged.
'They're better off studying procedures in the OR rather
than looking at every sprained ankle that comes into this
place.' He paused for a moment and couldn't help but
flash a grin at Eliana. 'I'm that good.'

The surprise his shameless innuendo brought to her
face caused the heat of desire to flash through his body.
He knew better than to indulge those feelings by flirting with her, no matter how subtly. But whenever he got
close enough to her, control slipped through his fingers
and he was seduced into forgetting why he couldn't be
with anyone. *Ever.*

Especially not the woman carrying his child.

It had been two weeks since the news broke, and yet
those two words together still sounded strange in his ears.
His child. Diego was going to be a father when he didn't
know the first thing about doing it.

He would never be with someone just for the sake of
a child. Diego would be there for his kid—sure. But that
was as much as he could give.

Eliana was now ignoring his flirtatious attempts at
conversation and was focusing on the patient instead.
'Your pulmonary hypertension has caused fluid to build
up in what's called the pleural space. May I move your
gown down a bit to access your chest?'

Selma nodded and sat up, pushing her feet past the
edge of the bed, while Eliana wheeled a small tray table
around for the patient to lean on so she would have access to her back. Diego had already performed a thora-

centesis on her, with the help of a cardiologist. The thorax wasn't an anatomical space he was familiar with, but in his efforts to providing healthcare to the disadvantaged people of the city he'd had to learn a lot of procedures that lay outside his expertise.

'To drain the fluid we'll use a needle to get to the space between your lungs and your chest wall. That should allow you to breathe easier. This will be cold for a bit.'

She dabbed some cool gel onto the patient's skin and then surprised Diego when she handed him the transducer.

'I will do the procedure—you can assist,' she said, in a voice that didn't leave any room for negotiation, which made it that much harder for him not to argue.

'I'm familiar with the steps of a thoracentesis,' he said, and watched as her eyes narrowed on him, the golden sparks losing their warm light right in front of him.

'Is it a common procedure in your orthopaedic cases?'

Diego had seen the trap he'd laid for himself before she had even opened her mouth, and he cursed himself silently. Some primal force in his chest had urged him to prove himself to her in any way possible. Show her that he could provide for her and their child. Look after them the way his father had never looked after him.

The blood froze in his veins as the jumble of thoughts caught up with him, rendering him mute for a couple of heartbeats. Where had *that* come from? Their night together had altered his life for ever, but that didn't mean they were meant to be anything more than co-parents.

'You know it's not,' he answered in a low growl when he found his voice again. The unexpected depth and chaos of his feelings towards Eliana had thrown him so much he had to remind himself where he was.

'Then you can take the ultrasound while I perform the thoracentesis.'

Eliana prepared the needle and syringe while he sat down on a small stool next to the bed. He made eye contact with Selma as he placed the transducer on her sternum to show Eliana what she needed to see.

'The pressure will be uncomfortable. I'm sorry. I'll try to be as fast as possible,' she said as she looked at the screen of the ultrasound machine for a moment, surveying the field.

Diego watched Eliana's hands as they probed the patient's ribs for a moment before she picked up the needle with her right hand and inserted it in the ninth intercostal space—quick, but precise—her eyes only occasionally leaving the ultrasound screen to look at Selma over her shoulder.

'You're doing great. I've positioned the needle, so we can begin the drain.'

Even though Selma was staring ahead, Eliana kept a gentle and reassuring smile on her face, making him wonder about the work she had been doing before she came to Santa Valeria. The way she'd handled the patient so far was unlike anything he'd ever seen from Marco. He would never have spent his time in any department helping out. He'd valued his own time above patient care.

Diego was relieved to see this wasn't the case for his daughter. Eliana clearly knew how to explain every step of the procedure so her patient knew throughout what was happening. After Marco Costa and his 'money first' attitude towards healthcare, she was exactly the kind of chief of medicine Santa Valeria needed.

Selma winced, and Diego grabbed her hand with his free one, keeping the other steady so that Eliana could do her work.

'Remember to take slow breaths, just like last time. Once we're done, you can rest, and I'll ask the nurse to bring you some books from the library.'

He knew Selma well. Her high blood pressure needed to be controlled with medication, but without medical insurance she could only ever get help from the emergency department when things got as bad as they were now.

'I'll be fine. I need to get back home and pick up my grandson before my daughter has to go to work, so I can't stay too long.'

Diego saw a frown appear on Eliana's face as she listened to their conversation, and he could almost hear the thoughts in her head. She'd want Selma to stay for observation—a wish he shared. But he knew that Selma had no option to stay. Her daughter's work was keeping all of them fed.

He had seen the same thing in his grandmother as well. She had worked herself to the bone to help her grandchildren achieve a better life, to escape the *favelas*, and Diego counted himself fortunate in being able to repay her for her efforts. She had been the only consistent parental figure in his life, raising him after his father had dumped him at her house when he had been busy cheating on his mother. Only to retrieve him again once his parents had 'fixed' their marriage and wanted to pretend they were a family again.

'And we are done,' Eliana said after a couple more minutes had passed, and put her instruments down. She pulled the gloves off her hands. 'I'll ask a nurse to give you the medication as well. Please get as much rest as you can and come back before you run out of medicine.'

She took the notebook that was lying on Selma's lap and stuck her hand in her pocket, retrieving a pen from it. Diego stood up from his seat, leaning to look over her

shoulder. The handwriting on the page was his friend's—
instructions he had written down when Selma had first
sought him out for help.

He watched as Eliana struck out Vanderson's name
and wrote a note beneath it, before handing it back to
the patient.

'Tell them I have authorised all your treatments already, so they can give you your new medication along
with a physical, okay?'

Selma nodded, and a moment later Diego felt Eliana's deep brown eyes were on him, peering so deeply
he thought she was staring straight inside him, past all
the locked barriers he had put up.

But she didn't say anything. Instead, she turned
around on her heel and hurried off.

'Ana, esperar!' This was the first time they had spoken to each other since the bombshell announcement of
her pregnancy. 'Where are you going?'

He caught up to her in three big strides, taking her by
the elbow and leading her into a free exam room at the
far end of the emergency department. Closing the door
behind him, he flipped the lock so they wouldn't be interrupted.

Hot sparks travelled up and down her arm where Diego
had just touched her. Despite his insistence, his fingers
had been gentle as he'd guided her to this empty room
so they could talk.

A talk Eliana knew had been coming—and yet she
didn't feel the least bit prepared. They needed to talk
about their child and what their lives would look like as
co-parents. The strong surges of desire infusing the fibres of her body didn't help in untangling the mess she
found herself in.

She couldn't trust her feelings. Not when everything was so foggy and tangled up.

Diego stood in front of her, his corded arms crossed in front of his impressive chest as he heaved a long sigh. The lines around his eyes told her he had been struggling just as much as she had in the last two weeks. Was he struggling to cope? Or was he trying to find the best way out of the situation?

A sudden fear gripped at her chest when she thought about him running away. Would he really do that?

'What are you doing down here? Shouldn't you be…?' His voice trailed off.

'Shouldn't I be what? Resting?' Eliana scoffed, hoping he had stopped himself from completing his sentence because he'd realised how ridiculous he sounded. Though the protectiveness in his voice had kicked something loose within her that made her heart stutter in her chest.

He was worried about her.

'I'm sorry. I know I'm not handling this situation very well.'

He looked at her, and the spark in his dark brown eyes was so disarming that her breath caught in her throat. She thought she could forgive him anything as long as he promised to look at her like that for ever.

Eliana hesitated for a moment before extending an olive branch. 'I've scheduled some time with each of the department heads so I can get to know their service. The emergency department seemed a good place to start, since I spend a lot of time there at my own hospital.'

Diego dropped his arms to his sides as he relaxed a bit. 'Where is your hospital?'

'In Belo Horizonte. I did my training there, and they asked me to stay on after I got my general surgeon certification. I took a short break between my certifica-

tion and starting my new role and then…well, you know
what happened.'

Diego nodded.

A frown was pulling on his lips and it made her chest
contract. She wanted to reach out and smooth the corners of his mouth up into the self-assured smile she preferred. He looked genuinely sad, which didn't match the
conversation they'd had on her first day. Back then he
had complained about how her father had cut spending
on pro bono surgeries to build lavish rooms for his VIP
patients. Why did he now seem sad at the mention of his
death? Or was something else troubling him?

Her hand went to her stomach in what now felt like an
automated gesture. Even though there was hardly anything to see or feel at the moment, the presence of her
child comforted her more than anything else had in the
last couple of weeks. Their bond was already forming,
giving her strength for the challenges ahead of her.

'I want to go back to Belo Horizonte. With him. Or
her. Which might make things a bit harder if you're planning on being around.'

'If?'

Something in his face contorted—a look of pain she
hadn't expected. Her doubt had hurt his feelings, and
she struggled to understand that for a moment. They
were still hardly more than strangers who were finding
themselves in a position where they had to raise a child
together.

He seemed genuine in his intentions, really wanting
to do what was right. It had been him, after all, chasing
her around the hospital to talk about their child while
she'd been avoiding him. Would he have done that if he
meant to be an absentee father?

'We've never spoken about it, so I wasn't sure how

you feel about your involvement,' she said, and felt his answer coming even before he spoke.

'We haven't spoken because every time I tried to approach you, you ran for the hills as if I had some contagious disease,' he retorted, with an edge of bitterness in his voice.

She deserved that, yet it still made her flinch. She hadn't been thinking about his feelings. The news had sent her into preservation mode for several days as she'd gathered her thoughts.

Because there was more than just the matter of their child to discuss. There was the attraction humming in her blood, flooding her with a sharp awareness every time she so much as glimpsed Diego somewhere in the hospital. It stood in stark contrast to her rational side, which wanted to retreat far away from this way too sexy man and let their lawyers do all the talking.

She wondered what it had been like for her mother to fall pregnant by a man she wasn't in a serious relationship with. If she had lived would she be urging Eliana to find a way to be together, even if it was just for their child?

No, her mother had been stronger than that—even if she hadn't been able to hang on to life at the end. She would have wanted her to forge her own path. It might intersect with Diego's—and she found that she really wanted him to remain in her life in one form or another—but they didn't need to be in a romantic relationship to be good parents. Even though the look he was giving her in this moment was ratcheting up a tightness in her core that she had to will away with a few breaths.

'I'm sorry.' She cast her eyes down, her hands crossed over her still flat stomach. 'I needed some space to think, to figure out what I want to do. I think it's great that you want to be involved. In fact, I was hoping you would.'

Eliana sighed. Her limbs felt heavy all of a sudden as the day caught up to her. Selma's procedure had taken a lot more energy out of her than she had expected.

Diego must have seen her falter, for he stepped up to her, wrapping his hand around her arm. With ease, as if he was picking up a child, he grabbed her hips with his other arm and placed her on the exam room table. Her feet dangled above the floor, grazing along his thighs every now and then, and each contact created a trail of sparks that went shooting across her skin.

The attraction between them was palpable, and the glances they exchanged were heated with desire but underpinned by the gravity of their situation.

'Are you ready to talk now?' he asked her.

Regret tied a knot in her stomach when he took a step back. Even though it had been only a slight brush of her feet against his legs, she didn't want it to stop.

'I still don't have a plan. But, yes, I'm ready to talk about things.'

Only she didn't know what. If it wasn't about her plans for their child, what was there left to talk about? The way every time she closed her eyes she could smell the scent of earth and petrichor as his tongue and teeth had grazed over her neck?

'Have you already had your first prenatal appointment?'

She blinked, finding her way out of the unbidden fantasy. 'I'm actually going to speak to someone today. I asked Suelen to tell them to come see me.'

Diego's lips curled upwards in a grin that made her heart stop for a second before it continued beating twice as fast.

'Two weeks on the job and you're already making people come to you. That's a boss move, Dr Oliveira.'

She laughed, feeling some of the tension draining out of her. 'I had to learn to stand up for myself early on. That habit dies hard, no matter what job I'm in.'

'I know what you mean.'

Eliana looked at him, her head tilted to one side in a gesture of curiosity. She wanted him to elaborate but he remained silent, his face not revealing the thoughts in his mind.

'Do you want to come to the scan in a couple of weeks?' she asked.

This time his expression shifted, and she could see the beginnings of panic bubbling up in the corners of his eyes. A sentiment she understood well. Appointments, scans…those things rooted their surprise baby in reality when they were still coming to terms with the change in their lives.

Her mother had been forced to do it all by herself. Marco hadn't wanted anything to do with his affair or their child. But Diego was already showing himself to be different, wanting to be a part of the whole journey. The thought of going it alone sent terror thrumming through her body, and she wanted to trust him—trust that he would support her throughout the journey. That she could let him be a part of it without her attraction to him burning her alive.

'Yes, I would like that.'

He lifted his hands, and for a second she thought he was going to reach out to her—a thought that thundered excitement and terror through her in equal measures. But he quickly dropped them back to his sides again.

Whatever it was floating between them was affecting him too.

Their one night together had already given her all the comfort she'd get from him. Anything beyond that was never going to happen. A baby didn't change the fact that she didn't want to pursue a relationship—especially not in Rio de Janeiro, when she already had one foot out of the city.

In fact the baby just reaffirmed her feelings about a relationship. Staying together for the sake of a child would only ever ensure that everyone involved grew resentful of one another. That kind of thing never worked out.

'When are you going back to Belo Horizonte?' he asked.

She tried to read his expression, but shutters had fallen over his eyes, revoking the access he had very briefly granted her.

'I don't know. Not for a month or two, it seems. It depends on how fast my father's estate can be wrapped up and how much work needs to be done here. This place is so different from the hospital in Belo Horizonte.'

Diego raised an eyebrow in question. 'How come?'

'Well, for starters the hospital there is part-owned by the local municipality, so the area we service is a lot more diverse than here. Though from our encounter some moments ago I can see you're trying to change that.'

Diego had the decency to look away as her words sank in. It had been obvious Selma knew him, and she had connected him to the free clinic she had mentioned during their initial chat.

'You held yourself well with her. I was glad to see the compassion in your treatment,' he said after a few moments, his lips curving in a small smile that sent her heart rate racing.

'Sounds like you didn't expect me to be a competent doctor,' she replied, willing the heat rising to her cheeks to go away.

'Not at all. I just liked seeing that we're now being led

LUANA DAROSA 63

by someone who thinks of the patients first.' He stopped talking for a second. Then, 'I meant to pay you a compliment. I enjoyed watching you work.'

'Oh…' The heat within her flared out from her cheeks in every direction through her body, making it impossible for her to find the right words to reply.

Silence fell over them and grew more tense with each moment passing as neither of them spoke, each chasing their own thoughts. Eliana was bursting to say something—to set boundaries from the very beginning so things wouldn't get messy. But she didn't know how to start that conversation. Especially not if he was paying her compliments like that.

'I think we should be friends,' Diego said, throwing her completely off track with those six simple words. 'We both went into this thinking it would be a one-night stand. Neither of us wanted more than that. And I don't think either of us wants to get into a relationship just because there's a child. But if we're doing this together, we should be…friends.'

'Friends?' she repeated, as if she hadn't heard right. When she'd been thinking about boundaries, that hadn't been the approach she had thought about.

'Yes. Friends. We're going to be in each other's lives from now on, for better or for worse. Don't you think we should find a way we can be comfortable with each other without…?'

He let the pause speak for itself, but Eliana wasn't sure she understood what he meant. Without sleeping with each other again? Without acting on the intense attraction that wrapped itself around them every time they spoke?

'So, we're going from giving each other multiple orgasms as complete strangers who will never see each other again to being…friends?'

Diego cracked a smile at that, a soft chuckle escaping his gorgeous throat. 'Well, if you put it that way you make it sound like a terrible idea.'

'No, friends sounds good. I only ever had emotionally unavailable parents, so I imagine parents who are friends will be a big step up.'

Friends sounds good.

Doubt crept into her heart the second she said those words, and she fought hard not to let it be visible on her face. At several points during their conversation she had imagined running her mouth along his collarbones. Her desire for Diego was overpowering, firing a heat through her system that left the nerve-ends singed.

How was she supposed to be *friends* with someone who stoked a fire of passion in her with mere glances?

But he was right. They were going to be in each other's lives one way or another.

Was that what her mother had been hoping for when she'd found out that she was pregnant? That she and Marco would find a way to co-exist? Would she still be alive today if Marco had made the same suggestion Diego had?

It was worth a try. She wanted her child to grow up knowing both of its parents' love and support. If that meant she needed to get over her attraction to Diego, she could do that. Right?

'So…how do we go from this…' she raised her hands, motioning around her '…to being friends?'

'Let's start by doing some activities that don't involve a sick patient. Or taking our clothes off. Something like lunch on a Saturday.'

He paused for a moment, the mischievous gleam in his eyes telling her that taking her clothes off was all he was thinking about.

Eliana took the pen out of her pocket again and pretended to take notes on her palm. 'No patients. No taking off clothes. Got it.' She paused for a moment, seemingly inspecting her invisible list. 'Can we talk about work, though? I have some questions about Selma.'

Diego let out a sigh, raking his hands through his already unruly hair. 'I hoped you'd forget about that.'

The discussion about their child *had* made her forget for a moment. When they'd come in here she had planned on confronting him about the clinic, but their attention had quickly turned to other matters between them.

'Did you know my brother? Was he working at a free clinic somewhere in the city? Selma's notes—'

Diego raised his hands, interrupting her. 'Lunch on Saturday. I'll pick you up from your hotel. We can get to know each other. As friends.'

Eliana hesitated, suddenly not sure if meeting Diego outside of work was such a good idea. While they might both be sincere about being friends, their attraction was undeniable—and she could read it in his eyes as well. How were they supposed to dial this kind of visceral intensity back to friendship?

No matter how. They had to do it. Somehow Eliana had to learn to be around him without dissolving into a puddle of need and longing.

CHAPTER FIVE

THE COOL AIR circulating through the hotel lobby did precious little to calm Diego's nerves as he sat in one of the armchairs, waiting for Eliana to meet him. Eliana. The mother of his child and now, apparently, his friend.

Their conversation from a few days ago replayed in his head. He was unsure what had driven him to say that when he didn't mean it. He wanted to run his hands all over her sensual body in various activities that required both of them to take their clothes off.

Except he had to mean it. On a different level of consciousness he realised they needed a tried-and-true framework for their relationship with each other, so they wouldn't be stumbling in the dark while they figured out how to be parents. If his parents had chosen to think about him rather than their own desire and chaotic relationship, maybe he would have had a more stable home.

Diego wanted to do what was best for his child.

The thought still felt foreign to him. Having lived through such a volatile childhood, he'd never thought he would have a child himself. A baby meant stability, a partnership, a family built on trust and love. Two essential qualities he didn't know if he even possessed.

Time to find out, Diego told himself as he watched her come down the stairs.

His reaction to her was instant. The blood in his veins hummed with awareness as he repressed the urge to pick her up and carry her back to her room for a repeat show of that night several weeks ago.

'*Olá,*' he greeted her, his eyes running all over her body as she approached him.

She wore a dark red dress that sat tight around her torso and flared out into a wide skirt that accentuated the supple curve of her hips. Diego had to swallow the dryness spreading through his mouth as he imagined what the dress would look like in a pool around her feet.

'*Bom dia...amigo.*' She said the word 'friend' slowly, as if she was trying it on to see if it would fit.

He prayed that it would. That was the only way he saw to keep on being a part of her life, not just that of his child. Because for reasons Diego didn't dare to examine too closely, for fear of what he might see, he wanted to be a part of her life, too.

'You ready?' he asked after clearing his throat.

Looking at her drove blood to places that needed to remain dormant if they were to become friends. It wasn't as if Diego was particularly rich in friends. Although with his father's innumerable affairs he'd grown up with many half-siblings—some of them a very similar age to him. Being the woman she was, his grandmother had insisted on meeting all of her grandchildren, regardless of her son's stance on the issue, and had always maintained an open-door policy for any Ferrari child. That meant his childhood home had never been empty, but he'd had to grow up seeing his half-siblings' mothers involved in their lives while he only got to watch from afar.

He loved his half-siblings, and was glad to have them in his life, but he still sometimes struggled to see them because their mothers had chosen them, while he had become collateral damage in his parents' disastrous marriage.

His child would have a different life—he would make sure of that.

'What's the plan? Do you just want to have a bite here?' Eliana looked around.

The current passing back and forth between them was almost visible, making him feel ill at ease with their plan to keep things platonic.

'No, you've been living off hotel food for too long. Let me show you a special place.'

'Special?' Eliana asked with a raised eyebrow, but he only winked before he laid his hand on the small of her back to guide her to his car.

The touch was minuscule, so small that it could barely be called a touch, but the heat of it seared the tips of his fingers nonetheless, shooting small fires up his arm and into his chest. He bit the inside of his cheek to suppress the surging desire.

This was not how friends thought about each other.

'It's a nice place by the beach, but hidden enough so the tourists can't find it. I like to go there whenever I have the time—which isn't as often as I would like.'

A brief fifteen minutes later they pulled into a parking garage and walked a short distance to the beach, where they sat down at a small table right at the beachfront.

The expression of wonderment on her face was one of the most marvellous things Diego had seen in a while, and he had to bury his face in the menu so she wouldn't catch him staring at her with unabashed desire.

'See anything you like?' he asked, to distract himself from the unbidden heat rising in his chest.

'I don't know…' Eliana looked over the menu, a slight frown drawing the corners of her lips downwards. 'I like the sound of the steak sandwich, but lately red meat doesn't really agree with me. Or maybe it's the baby who doesn't like it. It's silly, but I think it's already developing its own tastes. As a doctor, I know that's impossible, but… I like to think it doesn't like meat so much. Maybe we're having a vegetarian.'

She paused, looking down at her menu with an intensity that almost made him chuckle. The embarrassment in her voice was incredibly sweet and sexy, and not warranted in any way. Their child was becoming more tangible with every passing day—it was only natural she would associate it with some characteristics.

A smile he had no control over curled his lips, and a warm sensation took tentative root in his chest as he enjoyed the purity of the moment they had just shared. Her care for their unborn child was extraordinary. Already it was so unlike the way his own mother had treated him, ripping him from his home with his *avozinha* whenever it had suited her.

Diego cleared his throat as he felt his chest suddenly constrict. No matter how intense the longing got he would not act on it. Passion faded; it always did. Their co-parenting relationship needed to be built on something more substantial and solid.

'Don't be embarrassed,' he said now, his voice a lot huskier than he'd intended it to be. 'Of course you're putting a lot of thought into what it might like and dislike. One day soon our baby will appreciate that.'

Eliana lifted her eyes off her menu to look at him, and the sparkling intensity of her gaze robbed him of his breath. 'Our baby… It's so strange to hear it, even though I know it's true. When I came to Rio I wasn't expecting anything like this.'

He raised an eyebrow at that. 'What *was* your plan?'

They had never really talked about it. Other than her desire to get back to Belo Horizonte in a few weeks.

'I don't make plans. In the past they haven't worked out for me, so I've stopped putting energy into planning things.'

The warmth in her voice had almost completely faded. Whatever lay behind her aversion for plans was clearly still a painful memory to her.

As someone who carried quite a few of those around himself, he knew better than to probe. If anyone did that to him he would shut them down instantly. Some borders weren't meant to be crossed, and his past was definitely one of them.

'Why is that?' he asked anyway, unable to stop himself.

He wanted to know her—the good things as well as the things that pained her. She was the mother of his child…a baby they'd decided they would bring up together. Surely that meant he needed to know something about her other than whatever Vanderson had told him about his long-estranged half-sister.

Eliana remained quiet, staring down at the glass of pineapple juice the waitress had just put down in front of her. She grabbed the little umbrella sticking out at the side of the glass, stirring the drink as she thought about her answer. Or rather thought about how she could best *not* answer him, he thought with a wry smile.

'Is it safe to assume you've heard all the rumours about Marco Costa's illegitimate daughter?' she asked, without raising her eyes from the glass.

Diego sighed. He abhorred the gossip that was spread in the corridors of Santa Valeria, especially when it involved Eliana. Being from a dysfunctional family himself, he knew exactly what kind of damage it could do to one's psyche, and it could just as easily have been him they gossiped about.

'Yes, I have,' he confirmed, and nodded although she wasn't looking at him.

'Good, so I can skip some things.' She laughed, but it sounded so unlike the laughter they had shared during their night together that Diego almost flinched at the bitterness.

'After my mother died in childbirth, my father did the bare minimum to raise me, leaving it to the hired help. Once I was old enough, he shipped me off to boarding school. A good one—and that's the reason why I was able to get into university—but the spoiled children of Brazil's elite weren't interested in befriending society's latest scandal child.'

She stopped to take a sip of her drink. Her voice had been calm and steady, but when she raised the glass to her lips he saw it shake, the ice cubes softly clinking against the glass. Her visible distress struck at something deep within him, and he reached out underneath the table, laying a supportive hand on her thigh.

'School was awful, and whenever I was home during the school break that was awful as well. Marco had a guest house set up as my apartment, so he didn't have to invite me into the house with his wife and son. Being all by myself, I dreamed of a different life…of parents who actually wanted me. I made so many plans, thinking that one day my father would come around. That one day he would see me as more than just a stain on his legacy. And I watched all those plans crumble into dust.'

Eliana heaved a deep sigh as she took another sip of her drink, finally lifting her eyes away from the glass to look at him. Her expression was guarded, and he couldn't see in it any of the emotion he had heard in her voice just a few seconds ago.

'Sorry, you didn't come here to listen to my sad childhood stories.'

'I'm glad you've said something. Plus, having problems with Marco Costa is something we have in common. You would have had a friend in Vanderson as well. He fought my corner when it came to dealing with Marco.'

He shrugged, trying to lighten the mood that had grown increasingly tense between them. His problems with Marco Costa were dwarfed by the cold and loveless childhood she had gone through.

That was something else they had in common, but he wasn't ready to share that part of himself with her. He didn't know if he ever would be. Probably not. Even friends didn't tell each other everything...

She smiled, but it didn't quite reach her eyes. 'I never saw much of Vanderson. I think our father didn't allow him near me. It's odd to think he disagreed with my father later on, when he obeyed him like that in the past.'

Diego shrugged, trying to defuse the tension still growing between them. He knew how much his best friend had regretted making the choices he had. But was it really his place to tell her that?

'I know Vanderson had to play by your father's rules because he held the keys to everything...hoarding power like he hoarded his wealth. Santa Valeria is a prime example of that. Marco chased profit and prestige above anything else, compromising the ability of his staff to do the good work they tried to do. Building those extravagant rooms, for example, was just one of many decisions he made that showed he was never about helping people.'

Eliana tilted her head to one side in an inquisitive look that kicked his pulse into overdrive. One minute she was pouring her heart out…the next she was sending him looks that made him want to forget about decency so he could have his way with her right here on the beach.

When that was the last thing he should want.

Not with a child between them.

There was too much at stake for any rash decisions, no matter how much his blood was burning for him to touch her.

It wasn't going to happen, and he'd better get that into his head now.

The words had tumbled out of her mouth as if she'd genuinely meant to say them—which she hadn't. Those memories—her father, the boarding school, the score of nannies—weren't meant to be brought to light and examined by anyone. Especially not by this man in front of her.

Eliana had enough problems resisting the fire of attraction sizzling between them without giving herself more reasons to like him. *Really* like him.

But something about Diego's compassionate eyes and the way he had laid his hand on her thigh as she poured her heart out had reassured her that she was in a safe space. That whatever she had to say he wouldn't judge her or make her feel silly for feeling like that. Not like the people she had grown up around, who had told her how lucky she was to be Marco Costa's daughter no matter how badly he treated her.

On the other hand, her half-brother had started to morph into a mystery in front of her eyes. He'd never been cruel to her when she was growing up, but he'd also never stood up for her, and he hadn't ever let on if he'd thought their father was mistreating her. She knew nothing about him as a person, and had always assumed that since he hadn't said anything to make her think other-

wise he was one of his father's minions—just like some
of the other people she'd met at the hospital.

But Diego had started to paint a different picture of
Vanderson. For the first time she began to wonder if he
had been a victim of their father's manipulations just
like her.

'You promised to tell me about Vanderson and how
you two were involved. Did you know him well?' she
asked, watching him with intent. She knew the two men
were somehow connected.

A different kind of expression fluttered over Diego's
face. Not contempt, but something else that hinted at a
wealth of pain and complicated emotions.

'I knew him, yes. We both agreed that we couldn't let
Marco run Santa Valeria the way he did, so we started
working with each other.'

There had been a slight hesitancy in his voice as he
spoke, as if he was choosing his words with deliberation.

'I noticed that Selma came in with instructions about
her medical history written down,' she said. 'A note spe-
cifically asked her to come to Santa Valeria if she needed
to, and to get them to page Vanderson if they had any
questions.' She paused for a moment, tapping her finger
against her chin as she followed her train of thought. 'I
wondered if he was the one who initially treated her. She
said she got her medicine from a free clinic, but that the
doctor hadn't been there in a while. I think that might
be because he died.'

'Not quite,' he said, and glanced away for a moment.
'Vanderson wasn't the one running the clinic, though
he was involved. That note was from him. Your brother
would help me with the free clinic in many different
ways. One of them was covering patients if they came

into A&E for treatments they normally received at the free clinic.'

Her heart stuttered in her chest as she processed his words. He had worked with her brother to bring free healthcare to people in need. A noble effort that was twisted by her unresolved feelings towards Vanderson. She had to admit that she didn't know what she had expected from him—only that what she had got wasn't enough. The picture she'd always had of him didn't quite fit in with caring about the disadvantaged people in the city.

'He helped you?'

Talking about her brother had unleashed a torrent of hurt inside her chest, but she wanted to know. What kind of man had he grown into? Had he regretted staying quiet?

Diego nodded, and she watched his expression as he scrubbed his hand over his clean-shaven face. He looked as if he was trying hard not to give anything away.

'He did, and I probably couldn't have done it without him. I bent a lot of rules so I was able to help people in my clinic, and Marco was suspicious when I…' He shook his head, his voice trailing off into a chuckle. 'I shouldn't be telling you this. You're still the new chief.'

'Oh? Why would you have reason to hide things? I already know you've convinced the emergency department staff to treat uninsured people.'

Her eyes narrowed on him as she thought about that. Was that what he'd been dancing around each time she'd felt him hesitate? How did his role at the Santa Valeria play into the free clinic?

Eliana's mouth fell open when she remembered their interaction with Selma. 'That's why you wanted to do the thoracentesis. Because you'd done it before.' She gasped, replaying the memory in her mind. 'Selma didn't let on a single thing!'

Diego had the decency to look somewhat embarrassed as a hesitant grin took over his face, robbing her of what little breath was left in her lungs.

'She's been coming to Santa Valeria long enough to know the drill whenever she meets a new doctor.'

'And Marco was riled up so much that he tried to fire you?'

Eliana remembered what Diego had told her. How good he had become at toeing the line to keep his job. Was that going to happen to them as well? Were they doomed to become antagonists at work while trying to figure out how to be good co-parents in private?

Was that something her mother had struggled with— co-parenting with a person who held all the power at work?

Diego hesitated, seeming to know what she was getting at. But she wanted to hear everything. A full confession.

'So we're doing it like this, huh?' he said.

She shrugged. 'I'm going to find out sooner or later, no? Might as well get it out there now, as we're clearing the air.'

'You wield a chief's power well, Ana,' Diego said as he leaned forward, resting his elbows on his thighs, giving her a view of the sculpted chest she remembered all too well.

A shiver ran from the top of her head all the way down to her toes, curling them inside her slingback sandals.

'From time to time I would spend some of my working hours in the free clinic rather than at the hospital. Only when there were other senior staff to help out in the orthopaedics department, and only when the patient load was manageable. Also, I would take the samples that pharmaceutical representatives brought and give them out at the clinic whenever someone needed something more than ibuprofen. That's how people like Selma keep their chronic conditions in check.'

He paused for a moment, his brow knit together.

'Most of the time we get general practice patients visiting the free clinic. Though the word has spread, and the lines outside get longer and the cases grow more desperate. Conditions that are very treatable under normal circumstances are exacerbated by the lack of healthcare available to the people living in the *favelas*.'

Diego leaned back in his chair, obscuring her enticing view down his button-up shirt again, and sighed.

'They're my people. I can't abandon them, no matter how difficult it is or how much trouble I might get into. Growing up, I watched people succumb to treatable diseases because families in the poorer parts of the city don't have adequate access to healthcare. So when I needed more hospital resources, I asked Vanderson for help.'

'You and Vanderson worked together to help the disadvantaged community?'

'We did. He would make sure that I got the time I needed with certain specialists. Marco didn't allow any kind of pro bono or community outreach work, but Vanderson was very good at packaging things in a way so that Marco could see a monetary benefit to it.'

Silence grew between them as Eliana took her time to process all the new things she had just learned about her brother, as well as Diego.

The waitress came by to ask about food, and Eliana realised that she hadn't even thought about it. She looked at Diego and he picked up on her silent plea, quickly glancing at the menu before ordering a variety of appetisers so they could have some bite-sized portions while they spoke to each other.

They were only just starting to get to know each other, and Eliana didn't want it to stop. The stranger she had met at a hotel bar on the day of her father's funeral was beginning to take shape right in front of her eyes. The more they spoke, the more she discovered about the compassion that drove him to be an excellent medical professional as well as a good man.

A *really* good man.

Their discussion had been so intense she hadn't noticed the low and persistent hum of awareness coursing through her body with every heartbeat. This was *not* good. She was supposed to find a healthy distance from him, so they could be co-parents without her head getting filled with mists of desire and longing every time she looked at him.

Maybe even friendship was a step too far. What if being cordial acquaintances was all they could manage?

Eliana didn't know what she had hoped for today, but she knew that this strange closeness—the way her attraction was morphing into a deep longing in front of her eyes—wasn't it.

'So, what are you going to do now?'

Diego's low voice cut through her confusing contemplations and she looked at him with wide eyes.

'What do you mean?'

He chuckled. 'I've told you how I regularly misappropriate hospital resources to run my free clinic.'

'Oh, right…' That was the least of her concerns. Or else it was the root of her problem, depending on how she chose to look at it. It was his devotion to doing the right thing, helping the less fortunate, that turned the hot spear of desire piercing her chest into something larger and softer.

He was right. As the chief of medicine she should care about staff members disregarding the rules of the hospital. Whatever the reasons, his confession was a severe breach of protocol and should be met with some form of investigation.

Which was at direct odds with what she wanted to do. He was helping people...doing the right thing. Instead of investigating him and potentially reprimanding him, she wanted to help him. Make it official so he could stop sneaking around.

Was it that simple? Eliana wanted to believe so, although her feelings were getting entangled with business decisions. Did she like the idea because it was good for the hospital, or did she want to do it because she liked *him*?

'Will you show it to me?'

It was a terrible idea to get more involved with him than she already was. Their unplanned child was hard enough to deal with. If she dived further into personal things with him, it would take so much more effort to untangle herself.

Diego furrowed his brow, seemingly in agreement with her internal monologue. 'You want to visit the clinic?'

'Yes. Will you take me?'

He hesitated, his gaze shifting in and out of focus as he contemplated his answer.

'When do you want to go?'

'I'm not doing anything right now.'

CHAPTER SIX

DIEGO TRIED HIS best to watch her without staring as they entered Complexo do Alemão. They had left his car in the parking garage and waved down one of the yellow and green taxis so prominent in the streets of Rio de Janeiro. While the people in the neighbourhood knew him, and his practice, he still didn't dare drive up in anything that looked too expensive. He remembered what it had been like to grow up in the *favela*, and knew he wouldn't be making any friends by flaunting his wealth.

And safety was his primary concern with Eliana— much more than when he was on his own. He knew how to deal with people from his old neighbourhood, but she hadn't grown up here. He doubted that she had ever seen one of Rio de Janeiro's slums.

Her wide eyes as they drove up to the inconspicuous building that housed the clinic confirmed his suspicion. He tried to read her emotions as her expression fluttered and changed, but it was hard to guess what was going through her head.

Diego barely had any clarity in what was going through his own mind. He had shared so much of himself with her that he hadn't planned to—the things he had been doing in the free clinic most of all. She was the chief of medicine—the person holding the reins at

Santa Valeria. He definitely shouldn't have volunteered the fact that he played fast and loose with the rules and hospital resources.

But something within him felt he owed her the truth—about his clinic, and also about himself. He still struggled to talk about Vanderson. The pain of his loss was dulled with every passing day, but every now and then it came rushing back to him, reminding him. Especially when it came to the plans they'd made to expand the clinic.

Was that why he had decided to tell Eliana? Did he want to bring her on board with those plans? She had asked him about her brother, and while he'd felt safe to share what they were doing here, he hadn't said how much he'd meant to him, scared that it might alienate him from her. When she'd spoken about Vanderson he'd seen a myriad of feelings flutter over her expression, and he had known there were a lot of unresolved feelings. Feelings that would now stay that way for ever.

No, he hadn't shared the clinic information with her for his own gain. That wouldn't have rung true within him. He had told her because he wanted her to know him—really know him. Which was a thought so terrifying Diego pushed it away.

He never got to know the women in his life because he didn't ever plan to spend more than one pleasurable night with them. Though Eliana would be in his life always, as the mother of his child.

But he could feel it running deeper than that—further than anything he had felt before. The rising heat inside his chest was messing with his head to the point where he had to use every ounce of self-restraint he still possessed not to sweep her up in his arms and carry her back to his place.

They were not meant to be more than what they were

right now, though. Regardless of how electric her presence felt in his blood.

Diego shook his head, willing himself back into the present as he unlocked the door and held it open for Eliana. She walked through with a small smile on her full lips that instantly reignited the fire within him that he had just stamped out. Her light floral perfume drifted up his nose, making him long to have that scent lingering in his bedroom, the way it had back in the hotel all those weeks ago.

A different lifetime ago, when they hadn't been having a child together.

'Here we go. It's not much, but we don't really need much here. It's rare that anything complicated comes in.'

Diego had been expecting a comment about the state of the place. While it was clean, and furnished to his best abilities, it didn't even begin to compare to any facility her father had built in his long career as a medical professional.

But Eliana didn't comment on the clinic's appearance, her expression veiled, as she pointed at a closed door. 'Is that the exam room?'

'Yes. We technically have one on each side. Though currently only one is in use.'

She opened the door and walked through with Diego following on her heels. The exam room didn't look much different from the reception area. A sturdy table dominated the room, with two chairs standing next to it. There was an old-looking ultrasound machine in one corner, its protective covers gathering a layer of dust.

Eliana looked around with curious eyes, taking everything in as if she was taking stock. She walked past the exam table and looked at the closed cabinets lining the wall. Finally she turned around and leaned her hip against the table.

'I really don't know what I was expecting when you told me about it.'

Her voice sounded thick, and Diego crossed his arms in front of his chest, ready to defend his clinic. 'Do you have anything to say?'

She shook her head, her lavish red-brown curls bouncing around her face and making her look irresistible even in the poor lighting of the room.

'No, I'm impressed with your dedication to this place. You made it sound a lot worse than it is. I thought I'd find an MRI machine you'd stolen from the basement.'

Despite himself, Diego chuckled. 'I think you'd find an ambulance gone missing rather than one of the machines, if I ever dared to go that far.'

While he did technically steal—both his own time and his colleagues', and any pharmaceutical samples the companies left with him—he didn't consider it theft in a moral sense, although he didn't want to seem too blasé about it. Vanderson had given him permission for these things, bringing him close to but never across the hard lines.

But, going by the curious expression on her face, Eliana didn't seem to mind his clandestine activities. Was there still hope for the plans he had for the clinic?

'And you get a lot of people asking for help?' she asked as her eyes drifted around the room once more.

'Why do you think I didn't turn on the light in the reception area? If someone sees the light on there'll soon be a queue of people outside.'

He sighed as he imagined the number of people he would see in the short blocks of time he spent here. Sometimes his *avozinha* would help him triage patients, so that he could attend to the most severe cases first.

The concern sparking in her face kicked something loose within Diego and his pulse quickened. Her next words almost undid him.

'There are really so many people that need treatment? Maybe we should turn the light on since it's the two of us here? I can help.'

Help. That was where her first thought went—to help all the people who needed her to cure them. She didn't ask him about the hours he spent here when he should be in the hospital. Nor did she want to know about the medication he had admitted to misappropriating from Santa Valeria's pharmacy. No, Eliana wanted to know how she could help the underprivileged people in his community.

Diego was speechless, gaping at her as he tried to find words for the feeling erupting in his chest.

Eliana shifted under his stare, raising her brows in a half worried, half questioning gesture. 'What's wrong?'

'You must have received your generous heart from your mother, because there is no way it could have come from Marco,' he said, before he could think better of it.

He reached his hand out, wanting to fix the hurt he saw in her face without knowing how to do it. From the gossip echoing through the corridors of Santa Valeria he knew that her mother had been a nurse there before Marco had pushed her to move. The scandal of her getting pregnant by a married man who was also her boss was still something people liked to talk about—especially now that the result of this particular scandal owned the hospital.

Her brows reached even higher, transforming her expression into a look of surprise. 'Unfortunately I don't know much about her at all. I wish I could have met her.

I'm sure she would have some advice for me about having an unexpected baby with a man who was a fling.'

'It'll be different for us,' he said without thinking, reaching for the first words that manifested themselves in his mind. 'Our baby will have a loving home no matter where it is.'

'Thank you, Diego. That means a lot.'

Her smile for him made his heart stop dead in his chest for a couple of seconds before it kicked back in, driving his blood to all the wrong places.

If she kept up like that she would prove to be his undoing. He felt himself slipping, wanting her right now, but also imagining having her working by his side at the clinic. Eliana cared about the people—his community—and she didn't even know them.

He'd be lucky to have a woman like that on his side. He could learn how to be different from the kind of man his father had been. Was there a world where they could be a family?

The softness in her eyes as they looked at him sparked a longing that pumped through his body with every heartbeat, spreading a heat he didn't know how to process.

He couldn't let himself hope for that. They had agreed not to. He didn't even know how to deal with what he was desiring in this moment. He should step away.

The thought echoed in his head even as he took a step towards her, drawn in by the look on her face.

'So, are you going to turn a blind eye on my clinic dealings?' He wanted to talk about something safe—something to distract him from the longing mounting within his chest.

'I don't know what to do about it. About anything, really. I wasn't ever supposed to be the chief of medicine at a hospital where everyone knows my story.'

He saw a shudder trickle through her body, and pain glimmered beneath the surface of her face.

'It doesn't surprise me that you had to do this behind my father's back. I never saw much of him when I was growing up. He couldn't even take care of the child he'd accidentally created. Sure, I was fed and clothed, but that was the end of it.'

Diego shook his head at the awfulness of that thought. He tried to imagine his *avozinha* rejecting any of his half-siblings for whatever reason, but she would never have gone in that direction. Just as he could never turn his back on his child, no matter the nature of its conception.

'I was raised by my grandmother. My parents weren't around much either,' he said, his mouth moving in a strange urge to share this part of himself with her—so she would understand that she wasn't alone in her conviction to be a better parent than those she'd had.

'What did they do?' She tilted her head to one side, her brown curls sliding over her shoulder, creating a picture of such pure feminine sensuality that he forgot what they were talking about for a fraction of a second.

'They were—are still—very unhappy together. My father would cheat on her, she would kick him out, then he would eventually come back to beg for her forgiveness. Their separations weren't easy. Lots of shouting, breaking things, accusations… And more often than not they'd forget that they had a son to look after.'

He shrugged when he saw the horror on Eliana's face. These memories had stopped bothering him a long time ago. They had done their damage on him, teaching him only chaos and volatility, to the point where he didn't know how to accept calm and love in his life.

'Whenever my dad strayed he would dump me at my

avozinha's place. That went on for a couple of years until my grandmother put her foot down and kept me with her.'

'I'm sorry that happened to you,' she said with a frown of genuine concern for him.

He shrugged again. 'That's why I want to be better with…'

His voice trailed off as he struggled to finish the sentence. The word *us* echoed in his mind, but it would be a ridiculous thing to say to her. They were not anything that could remotely be considered an *us*. As small as that word was, it carried a lot of emotional depth that Diego wasn't prepared for.

'With…our baby?' Eliana prompted him, and he was relieved and disappointed that she hadn't said the word either.

'Yes,' he said, to distract himself from the emotions rising in his chest. 'We should have at least some idea of what we're doing before you leave.'

They were going to be parents, but that would be the extent of their relationship. They would never be more. Couldn't be more than that. He didn't know how.

With the small frown on her face deepening, she wove her fingers through each other, clasping her hands together. 'I know I've been avoiding this conversation, and I'm sorry about that. It probably didn't feel very nice…'

Diego had to smile at that. At least she was aware of what she had been doing. 'It didn't feel great, no,' he replied, letting her know the truth.

But when she hung her head he stepped closer to her, reaching out. He stayed his hand just before he made contact with her and felt heat radiate from her skin.

'This came as such a surprise…' she said. 'I needed some time to process things and—'

Their skin connected when Diego finally laid his hand

on her bare shoulder, interrupting her mid-sentence. He noticed the small shudder run through her body the moment he touched her.

'You will never have to justify your choices to me, Ana. You had your reasons. The important thing is that we're talking now.'

Eliana's mouth fell open as she looked at Diego. The sincerity shining through his words sent hot sparks flying from behind her navel up her spine. Her cheeks flushed, and she could only imagine what kind of pink shade the fire rising inside her had chosen to show on her skin.

It wasn't his touch that sent a tremble through her extremities—though the memory of what his touch could do to her certainly contributed to the overall turmoil rising within her. It was the kindness in his eyes, the gentle understanding that lay underneath his words, that brought forth a whirlwind of emotion she wasn't prepared for.

This wasn't what friendship felt like. Her entire life Eliana had been short on friends, never really forming any kind of attachment to anyone. Yet she was still fairly certain that her feelings now ran a lot deeper than she wanted them to.

'Did you ever think about having a child?' Diego asked into the quiet.

Caught off guard, she gaped at him for a moment, her brain still busy with deflecting the feelings he was evoking in her. 'I… No, I didn't. My father not only drove my mother away from the one place she called home, he also failed to live up to his responsibilities after her death. I thought that once the right person showed up in my life I would tackle family planning with him…hope they would be able to teach me the qualities I lacked from growing up the way I did. But…'

Her voice faltered, and she looked up at Diego when his hand slid down her arm, his fingertips grazing her skin and raising the fine hair on it. His eyes were shining with sympathy, as if he knew the pain weaving itself through her words.

And today she had learned that he did know her pain. Hearing how his parents had dumped him, with no regard to what that might do to him, had broken her heart. He'd been through a lot more than he let on, but was shrugging it off as if it were not a big deal. No wonder he felt so strongly about his part in their child's life.

'What about you?' she asked. Growing up like that must have left a mark on him, too.

Diego stayed quiet for a moment, his eyes drifting away from her face and to his hand, which was still gently caressing the skin of her arm, sending small shivers down her body with every sweep of his fingers.

'I didn't ever think I had what it takes for fatherhood. Still don't—not with how much of a failure my own father has been. A happy family is a foreign concept to me. I don't know how to make one myself, so I never indulged in any thought of having a relationship or children.'

His voice took on a strange quality, as if all of a sudden he had drifted miles away. He seemed to notice, for he cleared his throat.

'That doesn't mean I won't be there for my child every step of the way. I fully acknowledge my responsibility in all of this, and I'm not going to shy away from it.'

An unusual disappointment gripped Eliana. She tried to shove it away almost immediately. She shouldn't be disappointed that he wasn't interested in any kind of attachment—the opposite, really. While deep down inside she wanted to find a person to spend the rest of her life with, this wasn't how it was going to happen—just because he felt a sense of obligation towards her.

'Why do you say that?' she asked, though she wasn't sure what drove her to dig deeper. Somehow she simply wanted to know more about him for her own selfish reasons, if nothing else.

Diego seemed taken aback by her question. 'Do you not want me to be there every step of the way?'

'No, I meant… Why do you believe you don't know how to be happy with someone?'

A flash of something intangible streaked across his expression. An ancient pain and vulnerability. Eliana held in a breath at the sight, as if she was standing face to face with a precious creature that would skip away at any moment if she made a wrong move. If she remained still enough would he open up to her?

'That's a complicated question to answer,' he said after some deliberation.

Despite his words implying a need to distance himself, he stepped closer and leaned his hip against the exam table she now sat on. The increased proximity sparked a fire under her skin, raising the fine hair on her arms.

'Try me. I'm pretty smart,' she said. Her voice was a lot raspier than she'd intended it to be, and she resisted the urge to clear her throat. Maybe he hadn't noticed.

His eyes narrowed, and the gaze gliding down to her lips told her that he definitely had noticed the huskiness of her tone.

'My father took vast liberties with his wedding vows, and instead of seeing him for the man he was my mother kept returning to him every time he came crawling back. I grew up watching my half-siblings—the by-products of my father's countless affairs—have a relationship with their mothers. Those women had been betrayed—just like my mother. But they hadn't shifted the blame to their children. No, I was the only Ferrari child who'd ruined his mother's life just by being alive.'

He scoffed, turning his face away from her and staring at an undefined point at the wall. The pain resurfaced on his expression so slowly that Eliana was sure he was fighting himself on the inside. But he didn't have to hide—not from her. She knew that hurt…had experienced some of it herself. Her father had resented her for existing.

The moment she saw Diego's face contort again she felt her heart make a decision before her brain could caution her to think twice. She reached out to touch him, laying her hand on his cheek and drawing his eyes back to her.

Her thumb rested on his sculpted cheekbone, brushing against it with a slight hesitancy, testing the waters. His expression went blank the moment her hand connected with his skin, nothing but a subdued spark remaining in those dark brown eyes.

'You're too hard on yourself,' she said in a low voice. 'You aren't turning away from your responsibilities. That's something your father would do, right?'

Eliana wasn't sure why she was consoling him, or what had led her to ask such personal questions in the first place. Her upbringing had lacked any parental figure to learn from, making her believe she was missing the special 'something' children got from watching their parents. Why was she so adamant about Diego criticising himself unfairly when she thought the same thing about herself?

But despite her own doubts Eliana's words seemed to reach him—for his eyes grew wide in bewilderment. It was as if he had never thought about his own actions, with his head too wrapped up in what he believed to be true about himself.

Eliana's heart stopped beating for a second when he moved his hand up to his face, placing it on top of hers. He leaned in, and the intensity in his eyes was reminiscent of the night they'd met. The night they had made their baby.

'I'm not the kind of man you think I am,' he whispered in a low voice as he got closer to her face.

He slid her hand off his cheek and over his mouth, brushing her palm with a soft kiss that shot a flare of flames through her system, to settle in the depths of her core.

She wanted to move, to escape this situation. She was getting dangerously close to making the same mistake again. Diego had an incredible talent whereby he could bypass her defences with little effort on his part. Make her feel she wanted him—which she definitely didn't. Shouldn't, really.

Not when there was a child in the middle of it all.

'What kind of man do I think you are?'

'A man who is capable of giving more than I've already shown you. A man who sticks around.' He paused for another moment, his face so close to hers that she felt his breath on her skin. 'I can tell you now that I'm not your happily-ever-after, so don't waste your feelings on me.'

His words hit her with an unexpected ferocity that created an uncomfortable pinch in the pit of her stomach. Was that what she was looking for? Someone who stuck around no matter what? Her father certainly hadn't, leaving her with the bare minimum of attention to survive and little else. Eliana had never been anyone's priority, which had led to her never feeling quite settled wherever she was—never feeling safe.

Did she want that from Diego? Permanence?

She swallowed her emerging feelings as he looked at her. 'We both agreed this would be for the best,' she said, 'so I'm not going to turn around and demand a romantic relationship from you. I want to know you because you're the father of my child, not because I'm pining for you.'

Her words stood as a stark contrast to their actions. Their faces were inching closer to one another as they seemed lulled into a sensual cloud of their explosive desire for one another.

'Good, I'm glad we settled that—so I can do this,' he said, with a grin that brought her blood to a boil inside her veins.

'Do wha—?'

The rest of the word didn't make it past her lips, for Diego had closed the remaining distance between them and pressed his mouth against hers in a kiss she had been waiting for since the day they'd met again.

Her flight instinct melted away under his gentle yet probing touch as his hands wandered over her neck, his fingers creating hot fires underneath her skin as they moved.

This was not what she'd had in mind when they'd spoken about getting to know each other better. But this kind of getting to know him—despite the vagueness of his words—felt so right. She had glimpsed something of him beyond the detached surgeon he let the rest of the world see. It had awakened a need within her that reached far beyond the initial desire that had brought them together so many weeks ago. Could there be something more to their connection?

The thought barely took shape in her mind as Diego's

hands slipped to the back of her head, his fingers weaving themselves through her hair and gently pulling her head back, deepening the kiss as her lips parted, receiving the warmth of his tongue that was sending a shudder through her body.

Her hands clutched at him, holding on to his strong shoulders and pulling him even closer into their sensual embrace. Whatever hesitation Eliana might have felt when she'd agreed to meet him this morning it had melted away now, under the power of his words and the desire his touch evoked in her.

They had both stated their boundaries. Neither of them was interested in a long-term commitment, and they didn't believe in staying together just for the sake of their child. So there was no danger in giving in to the flood of passion cascading through her body, right?

The stakes were clear. She would still walk away from here as soon as her business was done.

Why not enjoy the moment?

He knew he shouldn't give in to the boiling desire bubbling in his blood, but he could not resist the temptation that was Eliana. The second he had seen her in the hotel lobby Diego had known he was fighting a losing battle to keep his hands to himself. Though his intentions had been pure—and he really did want to ease into some sort of friendship with her that would help them raise their child together—he'd soon felt the pull of her unbelievable sensuality tugging at him whenever he'd been able to observe her with her guard down.

Her questions had caught him off guard. While he could acknowledge that closeness would come with getting to know the other person better, he still wasn't sure what had urged him to disclose as much as he had. Other than Vanderson, no one knew about his parents and what kind of damage they had left on him.

His confession about his past had broken the last barrier that had seemed to be keeping his mounting lust in check, and a few moments later he'd stopped resisting and let go of control, his body taking over while his mind was still busy catching up with what they had discussed.

Now Diego crushed her against him, his hands roaming over her back, dipping into every curve of her body and exploring each angle as they were locked in a kiss that spoke of the passion both of them felt simmering between them. Soft moans escaped from her throat, muffled by his own mouth. The vibration of the sound penetrated his skin and set his blood on fire, as if someone had swapped it with a flammable liquid. All his blood rushed to the lower half of his body, pooling in his groin as Eliana's hands slipped under the seam of his shirt, grazing over the skin of his stomach.

But they were still in the clinic—not the best place to do what they were both dying to do…again. It cost him a lot more effort than he'd thought possible to rip his mouth from hers.

A soft gasp escaped Eliana's lips when he drew away, her hands immediately going limp and letting go of the fabric of his shirt. She looked shocked, as if she had just caught up with reality.

'This might not be the right place,' he said when she remained quiet.

There was a small apartment above the clinic, where he sometimes stayed in a pinch, if he was too exhausted to drive. But the look on her face was changing between passion and confusion.

He didn't want to let the moment disappear like that— even though his rational side urged him to take a break and retreat. Their lives were already messy enough… maybe he shouldn't add more sex into the mix.

Yet the beast inside his chest still roared, demanding to fulfil the promise of passion hanging between them. Even now he could see her chest heaving, her flushed cheeks showing the heat coursing through her veins.

'This used to be my grandmother's house,' he said, to fill the silence between them. 'We bought it from her to have a place for our clinic.'

Eliana looked at him, with a sudden curiosity in her face that he hadn't expected. 'Who?' she asked.

Diego stared back with a blank expression, not comprehending the question. 'Who…?' he repeated with a puzzled inflexion.

'You said "we". You and who?'

And just like that the fire in his veins died as if someone had doused him with icy water. He hadn't even realised that he still thought of the clinic as a shared effort between him and Vanderson until she had pointed it out. Even though it had been almost two months since the funeral, the unexpected loss of his friend kept creeping back into his consciousness at the oddest moments.

'Huh… I didn't even notice I'd said that,' he mumbled, and gave in to a sudden urge to share his thoughts. 'I initially started this clinic, but it didn't take long for Vanderson to get involved. He was the one to handle his father whenever we needed to bring one of our patients from here to Santa Valeria. You have your own opinion about him, and I'm not going to excuse anything he may have said or done. But your brother…' Diego hesitated for a moment, not sure how he wanted to end that sentence. 'He cared. And I know he struggled with how he had let things happen.'

'Were you close to him?' Her voice had adopted a strange quality, as if she was afraid of his answer.

What would be worse for her?

The tension of their desire for each other had left them with the mention of Vanderson, to be replaced by an unusual stillness. They were still somewhat intertwined, with her hands lying on his chest while he gripped her hips and held her close to him, their faces only inches from each other.

'Yes,' he said, watching her face for any kind of clue to how that answer would make her feel, waiting for a reaction from her.

She opened her mouth to speak, but a loud knock on the door interrupted her. A moment later the door opened, and female voices filtered through the air.

Eliana went stiff in his arms and immediately backed away from him, freeing herself from his grasp.

'Diego, *você está aqui*?' a familiar voice shouted from the reception area, and he got up with a sigh.

'Yes, I'm here, *Avozhinha*. But we're not open right now.' He glanced at Eliana with an apologetic look. 'Sorry, I'll deal with this real quick.'

He stood up to greet his grandmother. But as he moved towards the door she walked through it—and with her a tired-looking woman pushing a wheelchair with a young boy sitting in it.

'Oh, hey, Miguel. I wasn't expecting you here so soon,' Diego said when he recognised his patient. He went down into a squat to greet the boy, and in a gesture that was more habit than anything else started examining the stump where his left leg had used to be. 'Are you okay? What brings you here?'

'I was just in the area to bring Layla some food,' his grandmother said. And then her eyes fell onto Eliana, who had got up from the table and moved closer with a curious expression. 'Oh, I didn't know you had company.'

'This is Eliana, the new chief of medicine at Santa Valeria,' Diego said as he checked on the boy's leg.

Miguel had outgrown his previous leg quite a while ago, and the ill-fitting prosthetic had caused some damage to his skin and muscle tissue. The scarring was not very visible, but Diego felt it under his fingers. They were lucky that Miguel was so young, or his scars might have prevented him from fitting a new prosthesis.

'How wonderful! Does that mean we can fit Miguel's leg soon?' Layla, Miguel's mother, looked hopeful at his grandmother's words, and both of them looked to Eliana for an answer.

Her eyes went wide with surprise, and she looked at him. 'What's the problem with the leg?'

Diego gestured her to move closer, and had to suppress a shudder when she knelt down next to him, as the floral scent of her perfume danced around his nose, robbing him of his concentration.

'He's outgrown his old prosthetic leg. We see that a lot with patients who lose a limb at a young age. Unfortunately, Miguel doesn't have the privilege of regular check-ups with an orthopaedic specialist, to see when the prosthetic leg has grown too small. The damage to his soft tissue is not too stark, but still noticeable.'

Eliana looked at the boy with a small smile on her face. 'Olá, Miguel, I'm Eliana, and I'm a doctor, too. Are you okay with me examining your leg?'

He nodded, and a moment later she wrapped both of her hands around the small stump where his leg had used to be.

'Hmm, I see what you mean,' Eliana said as she withdrew her hands and looked at Diego, concern etched into her features. 'Can we bring him in? I don't think you have the right facilities here.'

'I...' He hesitated.

The last couple of days he had been making clandestine plans with the paediatric specialist on his team to get Miguel the help he needed. Something that wasn't exactly above board, as he would technically be misappropriating hospital resources to help a patient who couldn't afford treatment.

But Eliana's reaction to this moment was one he hadn't dared to hope for earlier, when he had asked her what she would do now that he'd shown her the clinic. She didn't care about the price tag—she just wanted to help. That fact made the beast roar inside his chest again. If this was her first reaction to seeing a patient in need maybe there were other things they could do together. Maybe even...

'Yes, with your permission I would like to get my team on this case. I've done what I can on my own, but I've reached a point where I need more help,' he said.

Eliana nodded. 'Good, let's get him admitted right now. The fitting will take a couple of days, and Miguel will probably also need some physical therapy before we can release him again.' She walked over to the examination table where she'd left her tote bag and retrieved her phone from it. 'I'll ask my assistant to send over an ambulance.'

'Wait, I can't leave. My work...' Layla looked at his grandmother and then at Eliana, lifting her hands in a helpless gesture. 'I can't miss work or I won't be able to afford any of this.'

Diego watched as Eliana walked over to the woman, laying a hand on her arm to pacify her.

'I don't want you to worry about money. Santa Valeria has a fund for cases like this, so you won't have to pay a single *real*. Miguel needs some special treatment before we can fit his new leg. It will take a few days, but I will ensure someone sends you regular updates. Diego will be supervising his case personally, so you have nothing to worry about while Miguel is away.'

She tilted her head to look at him, and he nodded. 'You know I'll take good care of him, Layla.'

The woman still looked frightened, but she agreed to their plan with a nod. When he had first seen Miguel he had made sure to let her know they were looking at quite a lot of work if they wanted him to regain full mobility with his prosthetic leg.

'It's so nice to meet you, Eliana. My grandson tells me you came to Rio on your own. Why don't you join us for the *churrasco* I'm hosting at my house next weekend? Diego's sister has just graduated, and we're celebrating.'

His *avozinha*'s words launched him back into reality, and his eyes went wide in surprise. What had she just said?

'Oh, thank you, but I couldn't possibly impose on you like that when I don't even know your granddaughter.'

Eliana smiled, but he could see the hint of hesitance bubbling in the corners of her mouth.

'Avozinha, *por favor*… This is my new chief you're talking to,' he said in a low voice. The warning in his words was clear, and he knew his grandmother would make him regret that tone later on.

'Even more important to make a good impression and invite her to dinner, then. I'm not having any arguments about this. With her helping my friend Layla the way she is, that is the least I can do, *querida*.'

Márcia waved her hand in a way he knew all too well. She had made up her mind, and it was going to happen. Which put Diego in a difficult situation. Despite their best intentions, they hadn't got any closer to making decisions about their child today. The only thing they'd managed to do was entangle themselves further into the mess they had started two months ago.

Diego knew better—knew that he shouldn't let his need overpower his rational side. Yet all he could think about was how fast he could get everyone out of here so they could pick up things right where they'd left off. Preferably upstairs in a comfortable bed.

'Well, if I'm not imposing...thank you, I would love to come.'

Eliana glanced at Diego with an expression he couldn't quite read. She looked apologetic, but there was something else mixed into it as well. Was she excited to be invited to his family's barbecue?

'Of course, dear. Vanderson used to come by all the time—everyone will be excited to meet his sister.'

The short howl of a siren interrupted his *avozinha*, and a moment later the ambulance pulled up to the house.

'There's our ride,' Eliana said to Miguel, with a smile that looked plastered on.

The mention of her brother had made her freeze up, and Diego hissed internally at his grandmother's careless words. He had told her enough about Eliana that she should have known better than to mention Vanderson. Especially since they had only really started to speak about his relationship with her brother today, and hadn't got far into the conversation before they had been interrupted.

'Are you coming with us to the hospital?' she asked.

Diego stared at Eliana for a second, fighting the disappointment that was spreading through his chest. He had been hoping they would have a moment alone so they could talk. They had so much to talk about. His re-

lationship with her brother… The child they had yet to
tell anyone about… Their kiss…

But he understood this request was coming from the
chief of medicine and not his…his *what*, exactly? She
shouldn't be his anything, yet the ambiguity of it tightened his chest as if someone was wrapping a rope around
it.

'Yes, of course.'

Miguel had been cleared for treatment, and that had
to be his highest priority at that moment. No matter how
much he wanted to revisit that moment from an hour ago,
when they had been intertwined once more.

CHAPTER SEVEN

ELIANA LOOKED AT herself in the floor-length mirror of the hotel room, turning to one side and scrutinising her profile. Her hand lay on her stomach, searching for an indicator of her baby, but everything remained flat and undetected. This wasn't surprising. She was only at the end of her second month, and most pregnancies didn't start to show until the second trimester.

By then, she hoped to be back in Belo Horizonte, far away from Diego and that fire in his eyes that she wanted to get lost in.

'I'm blaming you for this, little one,' Eliana mumbled at her stomach, even as she felt a prickle of arousal trickle down her spine, settling in her core in an uncomfortable pinch.

Her hormones made this whole friendship endeavour with the incredibly hot Dr Ferrari a lot harder than she wanted it to be. Or at least she used her hormones as a convenient excuse to cling to, because she could hardly believe that she would have been so careless of her own volition. To make out with Diego when they had both agreed to take a step back from the passion sizzling between them.

She let herself fall on the bed with a sigh and grabbed her phone to stare at the screen. She read the message she had typed out to Diego, giving her apologies and telling him that she couldn't attend the party after all.

That was what a smart person would do. Untangle herself from any more situations that weren't strictly necessary and keep any and all conversations centred around one of two things: their work or their child.

But the voice urging her to send the message was weak, drowned out by the mounting curiosity inside her. Despite things not going as planned, Eliana had glimpsed a part of Diego that lay beyond the thick wall he hid behind, and from his reaction she knew he rarely let anyone see that part of him—if ever.

Diego had suffered a lot more than he let on, and even more than that he seemed to think that he was damaged beyond repair. She wanted to know more about him— both about his family and his relationship with her late half-brother. He had hinted that they'd had a close relationship…something his grandmother Márcia had confirmed when she'd said that he would have been invited to the barbecue were he still alive.

Would she and Diego be able to get over their electrifying attraction and be the kind of friends they wanted to be? Diego had shown her a different side of himself—one she understood all too well. And even though she knew he was nothing like her father, the comparison kept creeping up into her brain, making her wonder.

Had her mother at some point believed Marco to be committed to raising their child together?

Even if Diego's commitment was solid, would he really make the time as he'd promised?

Losing her mother even before her own life had begun and being raised by a rotation of employees without ever knowing a loving touch, Eliana wanted more than anything else to be someone's priority. Wanted nothing to be more important than what they had together.

Diego had already picked what was most important to him—his community. She wouldn't change that, and didn't want to either. His commitment to helping the disadvantaged had opened her heart to him more than she cared to admit.

But they couldn't be together. Not when they wanted such vastly different things in life. Diego strived to be of service to his people—those who had brought him up when his parents had failed him. Eliana, on the other hand... For once, she wanted to matter. And if Diego had to split his attention it would be for the sake of their child, and not because of some misguided romantic feelings for her.

'Okay, we can go and meet your extended family. But only if you promise to behave, young one,' Eliana said to her unborn child. 'No mood swings, no hormones that make Mamãe feel things—are we clear?'

She waited in the quiet for a moment, feeling her connection to her child on such a deep level she was almost overwhelmed. It had been nothing more than an accident, and yet her chest was filled with love and affection for this tiny being already. She didn't know how she could have lived her life without that feeling.

'Good, then let's go and meet Papai.'

Diego had texted her the address of his grandmother's place earlier in the week, with a note saying that he'd understand if she didn't want to attend. She had wondered if that was his way of asking her not to come, but the look on his face when he opened the door for her completely wiped that thought from her brain.

Because the way he looked at her, his eyes ablaze

with need the second his gaze fell on her, made Eliana's knees almost buckle.

Or was that her needy mind playing tricks on her? Making her want to believe Diego wanted her as much as she was burning for him?

'I'm glad you're finally here,' he said in a low voice, and Eliana let out a breath she hadn't known she had been holding in.

'You are?' she asked, in spite of herself and her desire to make her composure appear resolute.

'Of course. Talking to you will give me a good excuse to avoid all my half-siblings. Ever since the funeral they've been overbearing.' He paused for a moment and laughed. 'It also means I can stop guarding the door.'

Eliana laughed with him, not letting the information he had just shared show on her face. Vanderson's death had hit him hard enough that his entire family was worried about him. Not for the first time she wondered how the two men had found their way into each other's lives.

'Before I let you in, I must warn you. Almost the entire Ferrari clan is here—including spouses and children. Enough people that I hope we'll become invisible. My family is also incurably nosy, so if they pester you let me know and I'll be your shield.'

Eliana had to laugh at his grave warning. 'Wait—how many half-siblings do you have?'

'Ten,' he said, and stepped aside to let her in.

The moment she walked across the threshold the muffled noise she had been hearing intensified around her.

'Ten?' She tried her best to keep the surprise out of her voice, but knew she hadn't quite managed to do so when she caught a strange expression fluttering across his face. It wasn't shame, but something akin to it. Was he embarrassed about his siblings?

'I told you my father was rather liberal with his interpretation of his wedding vows.'

This time she had no problem understanding his mood. A bitter edge wove itself through each word, and his resentment towards his father clear as day. Clearly while still married to Diego's mother, he'd had ten additional children out of wedlock.

'He's not here tonight, is he?' she asked, even though she thought she knew the answer already.

Diego laughed in derision. 'Not a chance in the world. He might be Vanessa's father, but I would be surprised if he even knew that she's just finished university. Ignacio Ferrari is not exactly...*involved* in any of our lives.'

'Good. Your siblings seem happy enough without his bad energy,' she said, with a playful chuckle underpinning her voice. 'And from the sounds of it, our new *princesa* will have enough aunts and uncles that she won't need grandfathers.' She patted her flat stomach affectionately and noticed Diego's eyes dart to her hand.

'*Princesa?* It's been a long time since my obstetrics rotation, but surely you can't know that at this point?'

Eliana shrugged. 'I'm only guessing from the feeling she's giving me.'

Some of the humour she had got to know so well over the last couple of weeks entered his eyes again. She much preferred this Diego over the one agonising about his painful past.

'Feeling? *Querida*, you are a woman of science. Next thing you'll tell me you've had the tarot read to determine the future of our child.' He tried to sound outraged, but his wide grin gave his true feelings away.

Her reply never crossed her lips, for a fire had suddenly burst to life right behind her navel, pumping heat through her entire body until her fingers felt tingly.

Querida.

A perfectly innocent endearment of familiarity. People used it all the time, to the point where it meant very little. But hearing it from his lips had catapulted her desire for this man in front of her up to the surface, despite her best efforts to keep her growing feelings buried.

He wasn't interested in her. No, he was here only because they were having a child together. It was their child that was behind all his interactions with her. She needed to get that into her head.

'Are you okay?' he asked when she remained quiet, but before she could say anything they were interrupted by a woman's voice calling for Diego.

'Diego! The meat is almost ready. Can you…? Oh, who do we have here?'

Eliana saw that the woman stood almost as tall as Diego when she stopped next to them, and although her ebony skin stood in stark contrast to Diego's tawny hue, the high cheekbones and bright brown eyes immediately gave them away as siblings.

'This is Eliana Oliveira, the new chief of medicine at Santa Valeria. Avozinha thought it appropriate to invite my boss to the *churrasco*.'

His sister raised her eyebrows to look at him with a scepticism that intrigued Eliana. She didn't seem to believe him.

'She must have seen you two together if you got an invitation. You know Vovo doesn't like it that you always come to our family dinners on your own.' She turned to face Eliana. 'It's nice to see Diego has made a friend. I'm Gloria, his little sister.'

The woman stepped closer and air-kissed each of Eliana's cheeks before stepping away again.

'It's nice to meet you,' she replied, feeling a redness

coat her cheeks at the way Gloria had emphasised the word 'friend'. Up until this moment she hadn't even thought about what her presence here might look like to other people. Would they think something was going on between them?

But there was, wasn't there? The memories of their kiss rushed back into her consciousness and she pushed them away.

'Well, don't hide away the first person you've brought home since Vanderson. Let me give her a tour.'

Eliana looked at Diego for a moment. He gave her a look of equal uncertainty before his sister took her by the arm.

By the time they sat down for dinner she had met every single Ferrari sibling, as well as their spouses and children.

Diego had groaned each time one of his family members had started to ask too many questions, or insinuated that he was usually not seen with a woman. But although he seemed exhausted by all their thinly veiled suggestions about their relationship status, Eliana saw the genuine connection he had with all of his siblings. Despite his father's wrongdoings, somehow his offspring had pulled through to the other side, forming a unique and beautiful family unit where they cared for each other.

Everyone seemed beyond excited to meet Eliana, which was a new feeling for her. No one had ever expressed this kind of enthusiasm on meeting her before. And what confused her the most was that they seemed excited she was here simply because Diego had brought her. Even though they didn't know anything about her, or their relationship, they wanted to get to know her.

It was that that caused a painful twinge in her chest. She had never known what it was like to be part of a family dynamic. Would she be able to give her child everything it needed even though she didn't know the first thing about family herself? Or was that where Diego came in?

She glanced to where he was sitting next to her, listening to the partner of one of his siblings. He seemed to know how to form close bonds much better than she did. His father hadn't spread his toxicity to his children, though clearly not for lack of trying. In Diego's interactions with his siblings she could see some hesitancy, though—as if he didn't dare let any of them get too close.

But they were all gossiping and laughing with each other without a care in the world. They had managed to pull through their rocky childhood. How come Diego believed himself incapable?

They wrapped up after dessert by toasting the woman of the evening, Vanessa, who had apparently just finished veterinary school, and then the Ferrari clan broke out into smaller groups again.

A warm sensation trickled down her spine when Diego laid his hand on her shoulder, prompting her to look up into his breathtakingly handsome face.

'Let's find a quiet spot. I think we both might have had enough questions and inquisitive looks.'

The smile spreading across his lips made her knees feel soft for a moment, forcing her to reach for the hand he was offering her. The contact didn't help with the weakness, and her heart was sent into overdrive when he didn't let go of her hand as they walked away from the noise to the other side of the garden from where the table had been set.

Only when they turned a corner did he let go, and point at a periwinkle-blue wooden bench that stood against the house's exterior wall. They sat down together, and the few inches of space between them felt like a cavern as Eliana raised her eyes to look at him.

Though she had enjoyed the conversation, and all the questions thrown at her, she'd noticed one particular topic was missing.

'You haven't told anyone about the pregnancy?'

'No, I haven't.' Diego stared straight ahead for a couple of breaths. 'I felt like that wasn't a decision I should make alone.'

He hadn't wanted to make that decision on his own because they were in this together, she thought. Diego—though still surrounded by thick walls and shrouded in mystery—considered them a team.

Not a couple—he had insisted on that previously, and Eliana had forced herself to agree, even if she found resistance inside her. But a faint voice in her head kept calling out to him, tempting her to forget about the boundaries she had set.

He had made her a priority in that moment. Thinking about how she would feel before telling people news that was just as much his as it was hers.

'Thank you, I appreciate that,' she replied into the quiet, and smiled at him, giving herself permission to feel the warmth pooling in her stomach despite knowing that it couldn't ever be more than a fleeting emotion. But he cared about her—something she was not used to from anyone. Maybe she could trust him with more than she was giving him credit for…like her thoughts about Vanderson.

'I want to know more about my brother. You said you were close.' The words tumbled from her lips before she could decide against them. 'You still haven't told me much about him.'

He'd been near invisible in her life, but maybe Diego could shed some light on him. Had he grown up regretting his past actions?

The pain fluttering over Diego's face made her regret speaking those words, but as she took a breath, ready to take them back, he nodded.

'I know I've been avoiding the topic. His death was so...unexpected. It still leaves me numb sometimes. But you never had the chance to meet the real Vanderson, and I want you to know about your brother. How he opposed your father and how much he wanted to be reconciled with you.'

Reconciliation. A concept Eliana had thought about a lot when it came to her brother. And apparently, he had thought about it too. But then why had he never reached out?

She put those thoughts away for now. There were other things she wanted to know first. 'How did you meet? You didn't know him as a boy, or I would have seen you around.'

Diego shook his head. 'I met him during our mandatory military service. We were both training as medics, planning on attending med school afterwards. Our assignments often put us together, and we spoke a lot about what we wanted to do...how we planned on helping the less fortunate. Me because I had grown up poor, and him because he had seen what greed had done to his father's hospital.'

He paused for a moment, his hand balling into a tight fist, and Eliana resisted the urge to reach out to him.

'We decided we wanted to make a difference—which was when our idea for a free clinic in my old neighbourhood was born. Through his...your father, Vanderson was well connected, and he recommended me for a position at Santa Valeria once I had finished my medical training. We were waiting for Marco to retire, so Vanderson could take over. And he was also waiting for your father's retirement before reaching out to you.'

Eliana's mouth went dry and she swallowed hard. 'What had my father's retirement to do with Vanderson reconnecting with me?'

Diego sighed, a rueful smile on his face. 'Marco was a sad and spiteful person. From a young age Vanderson was forbidden to talk to you, and even after your brother had become an adult Marco threatened to disown him if he went against his wishes. Vanderson would have been ready to take that chance had it not been for the ownership of the hospital.'

This was information she had never heard before, and it stood in direct contrast to what she had believed to be true almost all her life. She had believed her brother to be her father's minion at worst, and apathetic at best.

'He really wanted to know me?' She didn't know why she'd asked that question. It had sounded so desperate.

'Not being strong enough to be the brother you needed when you were growing up was the biggest regret in his life, and it pains me that he'll never get the chance to make it right.'

That confession took all the remaining air out of her lungs. She had never known what kind of person her brother was. A small part of her had always hoped that he would want to know her, but with each day that went by without her hearing from him, her hope had grown slimmer.

'Did you know he was married and had a child?' Diego asked, and grinned when she shook her head. He had his own family? Maybe those were the people the lawyers had spoken about. Marco and Vanderson's estates were closely linked. The estate lawyer had told her that there were other, unnamed beneficiaries of the will, which had made the estate complex enough to force Eliana into staying in Rio longer than she'd intended.

He reached into his pocket, retrieved his phone and unlocked it with a swipe before going through his camera roll.

'His husband's name is Alessandro, and their daughter's name is Daria. He owns a recreational facility near the beach, renting out surfboards and such. Daria has just turned five. They adopted her when she was a couple of months old.'

The picture had been taken on a gorgeous summer day, with blue skies unfolding behind them. Diego, Vanderson and his husband plus child were seated at a round table, all of them smiling at the camera that, judging from the angle, Diego must have been holding.

Eliana's throat suddenly felt tight as she looked at the picture. It was serene, and full of the affection those four people had shared with each other. But more than that it made her realise that she had something she'd never known.

'I have a niece? And a brother-in-law?'

Her voice sounded strained in her own ears as she struggled with the sudden revelation. She had never even thought that her brother might have been married and had children.

It reinforced once more how close Diego had been to her late brother. How much did he already know about her? Was he nodding along as if he was hearing new information when he had already heard it from his best friend?

'So, did Vanderson tell you about my childhood? You must have already known about me before we met.'

Her voice was free of accusation, but she saw that he winced, nonetheless.

'He didn't tell me much. I think the guilt over his own behaviour sat too deep. But he told me how Marco had rejected you and kept you away from the family. That you grew up alone.'

An icy shiver clawed down her spine. That was a lot more than she usually told people. But Eliana found she didn't mind that Diego knew. With any other person the mortification would have been too much to cope with. But things were different with him. It was as if she wanted him to know.

'I can see he meant a great deal to you. No wonder you brought him here to meet your patchwork family.'

He'd not spoken about his half-siblings since they'd sat down. Now his gaze became distant as he looked up to the night sky.

'I like my siblings…even though I sometimes envy them for the relationships they've been able to build. While suffering the same father, at least they had their mothers to look out for them. My mother didn't care enough.' He heaved a drawn-out sigh. 'But Vanderson understood me like they never will.'

Diego envied his siblings? As she glimpsed more and more of the fragments of himself he hid behind those thick walls, she felt their connection solidify beyond the shared necessity of being parents together.

He understood her. He had made her the priority tonight and empowered her to make her own decisions. And he'd given her something of her brother she'd never thought she'd get.

'I wish I could've known him,' she said, and laid a hand on his thigh.

The small touch was enough to make him look up at

her. 'Me too,' he replied, with a smile so sweet and full of longing it made her breath catch in her throat. 'He would have been excited about us. Shocked to his core, but also excited.'

'Since Vanderson was helping you, does that mean you now need *my* help to keep the clinic going?'

Diego's expression slipped for a second. A hopeful gleam entered his eyes, mixing with the intense fire she'd seen the moment he'd opened the door for her.

'That's not something I can ask of you. Not with everything between us being so...'

'Messy?' she asked when his voice trailed off.

'I would have phrased it with more delicacy if you'd given me a chance.' His voice was stern, but a smile was pulling at the corners of his lips when she glanced at him, chuckling herself.

'We'll find out soon enough when we need to compartmentalise work and parenting stuff. This can be our first test.' She paused, looking at him with intent. 'I think my father strayed very far from the path of putting patient care above anything else. If you tell me that Vanderson meant to change that, I'll want to continue on with that.'

She watched his entire demeanour change with each word she spoke, his posture relaxing and opening up, his expression one of such profound happiness and relief that Eliana almost gasped at the intense look he gave her. With a smile on his face, he wrapped his hands around her face and planted a short and hard kiss on her unprepared lips.

'I can't tell you how much this means to me—to my entire community. People like Miguel will be able to get the care they need when they need it.'

Shocked by the unexpected kiss—which she knew was a sign of gratitude and not of the burning desire she sensed coursing through her veins—she stared at him with a blank expression, blinking multiple times as she struggled to regain her composure.

Fires had erupted within her, starting in her core and spreading searing tendrils into every corner of her body. Their lips had touched for barely more than a second, but that was enough to thunder an almost impossible need for Diego through her.

His hands dropped from her face and he looked at her with wide eyes, seemingly surprised by his own action. 'I'm sorry… I shouldn't have,' he mumbled, although the narrowing of his eyes as his gaze darkened didn't show any of the regret he professed. Only the untamed hunger she'd seen in his face before.

It was a want that mirrored her own—and one that had led to the very reason they could never give in to one another. Not with a child involved between them. It would only lead to so much more heartbreak when they inevitably fell apart. Eliana wanted him. Everything deep inside her called out to him. But she needed safety more than anything else. Needed to matter to someone, to be their priority.

Though hadn't Diego shown her he'd made her exactly that today? Was it possible they could be something else even when they'd said they couldn't?

An awkward silence spread between them—the first one of the night—as they both grappled with their undeniable attraction to one another and their steadfast belief that they couldn't go there ever again.

Even though it kept happening.

'Have you told anyone yet?' he asked.

At his question Eliana looked down at her flat stomach, covering it with one hand and breathing a sigh of relief. The sooner they could move on from the tension brewing between them, the better.

'No one outside of the obstetrics department head. The first scan is soon.' She paused for a moment and looked up at him. A spark had entered his dark eyes, and his gaze was almost hypnotising her. 'Do you still want to come?'

'You want me there?' His voice was low, vibrating through her skin right into her core, raising the heat.

'You're the father—you have just as much right to be there as I have.'

'I'm not asking about my rights. Do you *want* me to be there?'

The tension between them came rushing back as he spoke those words, and she saw his eyes fill with an intent to conquer her.

'If you want to—'

'Ana.' He interrupted her, his voice low, filled with promises that made her heart beat fast against her chest. 'Do you want me?'

Eliana's mouth went dry and she swallowed. They had stopped talking about the scan. They were back to the tangible electricity filling her stomach with flutters. Did she want him? Want him how? At the scan? In her life? *Right now?*

What frightened her most was the fact that all those questions had the same answer.

'Yes,' she whispered, afraid that her voice would give out if she spoke too loudly, and watched him come closer...

The beast of unbridled desire within his chest had simply watched for most of the evening, rearing its head occasionally when he'd caught a glimpse of Eliana's smile or when her luscious scent had drifted up his nose.

From the moment she had walked through the door Diego had known that he would kiss her, that they would pick up where they had left off at the clinic. And this time he would make sure to follow through.

Kissing her in the back yard of his *avozinha*'s house had been a tactical error. He should have invited her to his place before drawing her into his arms. But he'd found himself unable to resist her any longer. Not after she'd said the one word he had been dying to hear from her lips.

Yes.

She wanted him. Just as much as he wanted her. That was all he needed to know to forget about where they were and who might potentially walk around the corner and catch them.

Eliana's warm breath trembled against his skin as he pulled her into his arms, his lips brushing against hers in a sensual invitation for her to get lost in the moment. It was an invitation she was clearly eager to receive, as she balled her hands around the fabric of his shirt and pulled him closer.

The passion swimming through his blood roared to life with that one kiss, sending heat cascading through his body. What was it about this woman that drove him over the edge with little more than a kiss? That made him keep coming back for more? That had allowed him to let his grandmother actually invite her to meet his family?

No woman ever got to meet any of the Ferrari clan.

Eliana opened her mouth and caught his lower lip between her teeth, giving it a short but intense squeeze that drew a groan of desire from his throat. She pulled back to look at him, an expression of want on her face. Her breath left her in an unsteady staccato, her chest heaving with anticipation.

Diego pulled her close again, deepening their kiss. This time Eliana let his tongue pass, moaning her mounting pleasure against his lips. His hands wandered over her back, finding the exposed flesh and brushing her with his fingertips. He remembered the softness of her skin beneath his hands that first night together, her taste as he'd explored her body at his leisure, drawing mewls of delight and release from her full lips.

How long had he been waiting for this to happen again? And how often had he told himself that he wasn't allowed to go there—ever? Only in this moment he couldn't remember why he'd been so against it. It was clear now that something special connected them—something that went beyond his understanding of relationships.

Was that why he always struggled to give in completely? Because he'd always be confronted by that crucial bit of information that he'd missed out on as a child? How to form a healthy and functioning relationship where both partners were equal. That wasn't what his parents had shown him.

This was lust burning in his chest—not some misguided emotional attachment. They had both said so themselves. Neither wanted a relationship that went beyond the way they would share custody of their child. If his parents had sought an arrangement the way he and Eliana were trying to right now, maybe things would have turned out differently. Maybe he would have known how to appreciate a tremendous woman like Eliana in more than one way.

His mouth left her lips, feathering light kisses down her neck and caressing her there. Need cascaded through him, reaching a boiling point when another enticing moan fell from her lips. They needed to go.

Diego brought a minimal amount of distance between them to look her in the eyes. They were smouldering with the same intensity he felt.

'My place is down the street,' he murmured, and excitement thundered through him when she grinned.

If it hadn't been for the fire in her core, Eliana might have forgotten why she was there when she entered Diego's house and took in the view. The hallway was almost as large as the hotel room she was staying in, with polished stone surfaces and tasteful decoration in the few places it was needed.

But Diego had other plans for her. The moment they got through the door he slammed it shut behind him and was upon her not even a heartbeat later, capturing her mouth with his.

He pressed her against the cold wall and she felt his fingers leaving exquisite fires as they roamed her body. She let her head fall backwards, surrendering her entire self to Diego and his caresses.

This wasn't supposed to happen… But the voice that kept on warning her about it—about their relationship getting too messy—was growing faint and easy to ignore.

What was the harm? As long as both of them remembered that she would soon be leaving and that they weren't looking for anything permanent, maybe they could loosen the leash on their desire for just one night. At least this time there wouldn't be any accidents.

His hands had found the zipper of her dress. With a twist of her shoulder he turned her around, and she pressed her front against the wall while he pulled down the zipper with agonising slowness, leaving a scorching kiss every time he uncovered more skin.

'*Deus*, Diego, *por favor*…' she whispered, as unreserved need cascaded through her, bringing an intensity and wetness between her legs that made her knees buckle.

'What do you want, *amor*?' His voice was deep, filled

with the restraint he was practising by undressing her bit by bit, taking his sweet time on this journey down her body.

'This is too much. I need you…*now*.'

The zipper stopped just above her bottom, and Diego peeled the dress from her back, folding it over at the front before flipping her around again. With one smooth motion he pulled on the dress again, making it fall from her body and pool around her feet.

The fire in his eyes made her breath catch in her throat. This was different from what she had seen in his face when they'd slept together all those weeks ago. Something about this moment was different from before, and it made her need for him burn all that brighter.

He kissed her, long and deep, tasting her mouth as if he had never kissed her before. Her thighs trembled when he pulled her against him, and the full length of his erection was pressing into her, urging.

'No,' he whispered when she slipped her hands down to start removing his clothes. He took her wrist, wrapping his fingers around it. 'I want to be deliberate this time. I want to savour every moment, taste every part of you, until you have no more to give.'

'Diego…' Her breath came in bursts as his hands caressed her hips. He stopped for a moment when he stroked her stomach, drawing both of them back into the moment that had changed them for ever.

He glanced down, as if to check to see if he could find any trace of their child, and when his eyes came back to hers they were filled with a warmth that sent her pulse even higher.

'I was too focused on my own pleasure the first time around. I need to make it up to you,' he said close to her ear, raising the fine hair at the nape of her neck and on her arms.

Eliana looked at him for a moment, and in the next instant felt her feet leave the ground, making her yelp as she wrapped her hands around Diego's neck. He lifted her into his arms, carried her through the hall and down a corridor, into what she could only presume was his bedroom.

He let her drop on the bed, pouncing on her like a jaguar would jump on its prey, pinning her down. She shivered under the pressure of his body, writhing as his erection pushed against her again. It wasn't just her that wanted this. She was making him feel the same way, filling him with need and urgency. Eliana could see it in the tightness of his jaw as he lifted himself off her to trail gentle and warm kisses down her neck to her sternum, where he came to rest.

Eliana arched her back, pushing closer to him when his teeth gripped at the fabric of her bra, pulling the garment aside to expose her breasts to the cooling air of the Brazilian spring evening. The straps fell down from her shoulders as Diego found the clasp on the front, drawing the bra away from her body and throwing it on the floor.

Diego stopped for a moment, as if plotting his course, and a hungry growl was loosed from his throat. She propped herself up on her elbows, wanting to see what he was up to, but immediately fell back down with a long drawn-out moan when he sucked one of her peaked nipples into his mouth, rolling it around with his tongue.

A firework exploded in the pit of her stomach and her hips arched against his strong frame, as if begging to find any kind of release as the lines between pleasure and pain began to blur.

'Diego…' she whispered, unable to form any other coherent words, trusting that her voice would carry enough meaning for him to understand.

Please, don't stop.

He didn't.

His mouth left one breast to go to the other, lavishing it with the same attention and pleasure he had given the first one, before moving on down over her stomach, his lips and tongue leaving featherlight traces on her skin as if he was mapping her body so he could remember every detail.

Wasn't that what he'd said? That he wanted to remember everything about this moment? Eliana had thought it no more than a line from a man who had seen many women before her and would see many after her, too. But that was not how he made her feel in this moment— as if he was a trained lover going through the steps he had taken many times before. No, to her it seemed all of his attention was focused on her and on what made her writhe in pleasure. That thought alone was enough to renew the need inside her that settled into the wetness at her core.

What made this moment different from that night two months ago? It couldn't be that it was simply because they had started to get to know each other. To build a tentative friendship upon which they wanted to build the foundation of their co-parenting adventure. Was that enough to have such an impact?

Her thoughts were catapulted back into the present when the silk of her underwear scraped against her thighs as Diego moved them down in one smooth motion of his arm. His fingers brushed over her mound as he lowered his face to kiss her thighs, each time slipping just a bit further up, until she felt his breath right next to the place his hand had been caressing.

Her anticipation of what was going to happen next transformed into an eruption of untold pleasure when Diego parted her with one stroke of his tongue and lavished her with its attention.

Eliana fisted one hand into the linen underneath her as a trembling shook her body, and the beginning of a climax was already building inside her as her breath left her mouth in ragged bursts, mingling with the moans he coaxed out of her. Her other hand found Diego's as he caressed her stomach, and she gripped him as if she was holding on for dear life.

'Please, don't stop.'

This time she managed to articulate the words as the waves of her climax started to build, crashing through her with a ferocity that wiped any thought from her brain.

Diego's name clung to her lips as she gave in, losing herself in the pleasure that rocked through her. The muscles in her thighs tensed for a moment before they relaxed again, her breath still unsteady and coming out in bursts.

She felt him smile against her thighs as he kissed one and then the other, trailing small kisses up her stomach until he was on top of her, looking into her eyes with an intensity that brought a new surge of need to her core just as the first one was receding.

Eliana opened her mouth, wanting to say something, though she wasn't sure what. But he stopped her, laying a gentle finger on her mouth, tracing her lower lip before bending down and kissing her. Her mouth was filled with his taste, the warmth of his tongue, and she gripped at his shoulders so as to not drift away in the luscious cloud of ecstasy he had conjured around them.

'You are incredible, you know that?' he whispered against her neck, before his mouth trailed down again and goosebumps made all the little hairs rise on her body.

* * *

Her expression had changed for a fraction of a second, doubt clouding her eyes. Diego halted, looking at her intently, keen to know her thoughts. But before he could say anything her hands had found their way past his waistband. His button popped open with one flick of her finger, and one of her hands pulled at his T-shirt while the other wrapped itself around his shaft, stroking…

A low growl escaped his lips—a lot more feral than he'd intended to be. The moment he had seen the dress drop from her shoulders, exposing her incredible strength and a grace that shone from inside out, Diego had known he wanted to worship her all night. And that even then he wouldn't be worthy of a woman like Eliana. She had endured so much loss and rejection in her life, but instead of letting that experience harden her heart she had emerged from the pain with a softness and a kindness that brought him to his knees.

But now he was enjoying a glimpse of the other Eliana. The one he had met at the bar. Who knew exactly what she wanted and wasn't afraid to take matters into her own hands.

And what incredibly skilled hands she had.

Diego groaned again as she pulled his trousers down, and hardly noticed when she pulled his shirt over his head and threw it onto the pile of clothes already on the floor.

'Hang on,' he said, when Eliana hooked her leg around his waist and flipped their bodies so that he was lying on his back.

A wicked grin appeared on her face as she sat on top of him, his taut length straining against her. 'No. We've done it your way. Now we do it my way, Ferrari,' she replied.

And Diego closed his eyes with a primal moan when

she released the tension in her thighs and let him sink into her in his entirety.

Her nails scratched along his bare chest as they moved their hips in harmony, and Eliana's small cries of pleasure were already threatening to undo him when he wanted this moment to last for ever.

Because this moment was perfection. They were permitted to be who they were—two people attracted to each other, who were finding their path towards their true feelings for each other. As long as they remained like this, they were allowed to be these two people.

The moment they finished Diego knew the spell the evening had woven around them would break, leaving them to cope with the reality of their lives. With the fact that they were not built for the type of relationships others had. Not after everything that had happened to them.

But right now he just wanted to feel this incredible woman crushed against his body as they lost themselves in their burning passion for one another.

With another groan, Diego pulled his upper body off the bed, slinging his arms around her torso and hugging her close to his chest before turning them around once more so he was on top of her.

'Ana, I—' He interrupted himself, pressing his mouth on hers again, wrapping her in an indulgent kiss as he sensed their shared climax approaching.

And with that kiss full of promise and tenderness he felt the release wash over him, as Eliana, too, cried out his name, writhing underneath him with a sob of pleasure.

CHAPTER EIGHT

THE GENTLE BRUSH of fingers against her exposed back coaxed Eliana out of her slumber. She felt warm breath on the back of her neck, and she stretched her legs and toes as she enjoyed Diego's caress.

'Bom dia, meu amor,' he whispered near her ear, and sent sparks flying down her spine.

'You shouldn't call me that,' she mumbled back, but instead of pulling away she snuggled closer into his hard and warm chest.

My love. Such an endearment was way too intimate for what they were…which was something they hadn't defined. She had spent every night of the last week at Diego's, entangled in his sheets most of the time, but also talking with him about anything they could come up with.

Now he didn't reply, instead nuzzling into her neck, the kisses he traced on her skin making her shiver with renewed need.

'Don't you need to be somewhere? I'm sure I told Suelen to make sure your surgical schedule is full.'

Through the thick fog of desire, Eliana grasped at straws. Anything to make him move away, even though that was the last thing she wanted him to do. And he knew she didn't really want him to go.

Diego chuckled into her hair, pulling her even closer to his chest. 'It's Sunday. We don't have to be anywhere if we don't want to.'

No, don't say that.

She needed him to be busy so she could find enough distance to get away. To think. Right now, all her emotions were tangled up in the visceral and deep connection they shared on more than just a physical level. While the sex was mind-bending, Eliana could see a pattern beneath it. There was a reason for it, and it had precious little to do with skill and everything with how she felt. For him, in particular.

And she must not feel anything for him. That wasn't part of the plan. The plan was to find an easy-going friendship so they could make decisions about their baby together.

As if he had read her mind, Diego slipped a hand down to her naked stomach, gently resting his palm on the smallest of bumps that was forming where their child was growing. It was that little bump that she should remember whenever her feelings for him were getting messy and tangled. Her baby deserved a stable home, even if it was only with one parent.

'You haven't felt anything yet, have you?' he asked.

Eliana shook her head and laid her hand on top of his. 'No, it's too early at the end of the first trimester. But at least I'm done with morning sickness.'

He hummed low, the vibration seeping through her pores and into her body, awakening a new wave of want for this man.

'I'm going to have to tell Avozinha. She'll be thrilled, and probably won't leave you alone once she knows.'

Diego had meant it as a jovial threat, but she actually found herself excited at the prospect of someone else partaking in the joy she had so far kept to herself. Even though everything leading up to her baby's conception had been an accident—and the situation with her Dr Dad was not in the least bit clear—she was genuinely excited to meet her child, and had felt sad that no one would be there to share that happiness with her.

Except now there was Diego, his *avozinha* and, by extension, the entire Ferrari clan. Her child would be able to know its extended family—people who cared about knowing their new niece, cousin or great-granddaughter. Despite Diego's claim that he wasn't close to his siblings, she could see they genuinely cared about one another. And now about her, too.

'Márcia was the one who raised you?' she asked.

Behind her, Diego stiffened for a moment, his lips still touching her skin. He relaxed after a few heartbeats, mumbling his response into her hair.

'She did. After one of my parents' countless break-ups and subsequent reconciliations, they wanted to bring me back home after I'd spent several months with my grandmother. She refused to hand me over and instead told them to come back if they managed to go a whole year without splitting up again.' He let out a humourless chuckle. 'They didn't last half as long. So my *avozinha* ended up raising me and made sure to involve herself with my half-siblings too, so I could get to know them. It's thanks to her that I turned out the way I did.'

'You can tell her if you want,' Eliana said, wriggling around in his arms so she could look at him.

'Are you sure? She'll probably start making baby clothes straight away and drop them off at the hospital.'

She laughed at the thought of her office being transformed into a nursery. 'Maybe wait until I'm back in Belo

Horizonte. Save the new chief the madness of finding baby sleepsuits in every drawer.'

They chuckled together, though this time she thought there was a strange sense of loss mixed into their laughter. Her departure was looming, and would take her an eight-hour drive away from Rio de Janeiro. She would leave soon, and they hadn't got any closer to understanding how they would work together as parents. Were they trying to put the cart in front of the horse? Was that why it was so difficult even to talk about it? And she knew a part of her yearned to stay here so her child could be close to its family.

'When are you leaving?' He tried to sound casual, but she sensed the tension in his muscles.

She shrugged. 'Soon. I've made my choice as Chief of Medicine, we're just finalising the handover, and then I'll have no more reason to stay here.'

Except you.

The words echoed in her mind, daring her to speak them, but they turned to bitter ash as she swallowed them. She couldn't let herself go there—not with all the mess around them. Diego was a man of enormous calibre and skill, and his compassion for his community ran so deep Eliana could only hope to feel so strongly one day.

But, especially after last night, she knew she could never be a part of his world. Despite all the adversity he had witnessed as a child, he had managed to find his family, bond with them in a significant way that she never would.

Having grown up isolated from everyone around her, Eliana didn't know how to be a part of a family and doubted she could ever learn. Watching the Ferrari siblings interact with another had filled her with a yearning so deep, and it had hurt to know she would never have what they had.

'Who did you pick?' Diego asked, interrupting her thoughts mid-stream.

'Sophia.'

He arched his eyebrows in a surprised look. 'Sophia Salvador? The head of A&E? That's…actually a really good choice.'

'I spent so much time agonising over this decision, so your approval means a lot.'

Diego shot her a grin that made her heart skip a beat. She felt the heat rushing back to her core.

'Why was it a hard decision?' he asked.

'Because the hospital is infested with my father's people, who would be perfectly happy to stay the course it's on when what Santa Valeria really needs is a change for the better,' Eliana scoffed. 'The hospital should be known for the incredible talent of its medical staff—not for how nice the en-suite bathrooms of the patients' rooms are.'

She had made that exact speech in front of the board of directors as well, though they hadn't been impressed.

To her surprise, Diego laughed. 'You would get along well with Alessandro, Vanderson's husband. Vanderson could be a bit timid around his father, not wanting to draw too much attention to himself. Alessandro had no such reservations.'

'I would love to meet him,' she whispered.

She had only learned about him last week. With Vanderson's death, she'd believed her only link to her family was dead too, until Diego had dropped the bombshell around her brother-in-law and her niece.

Her child's cousin…

'You would?' There was an edge of surprise to his

voice. 'I can take you to his shop. Daria might even be there, since it's the weekend.'

Her pulse quickened and her mouth went dry. She'd meant that wish to be a quiet desire, but had blurted it out before she'd been able to stop herself—something that seemed to happen way too often around Diego and his disarming smile.

Meeting her brother-in-law? The thought both terrified and excited her. But after seeing the dynamic between Diego and his siblings she wanted to see whether her child could have something like that as well—even if it was with a cousin rather than a sibling.

'I would like that.'

By the time they arrived at the Copa Cabana, where Alessandro ran his store, Eliana was a puddle of nerves, and Diego was fighting the need to chuckle by biting the inside of his cheek. Normally so confident and sure of herself, she seemed to be struggling with the thought of meeting a family member she hadn't known she had.

Although if he put it in those words, he could understand why she felt nervous. Diego himself had met so many mystery half-siblings and cousins he had never previously heard of that the situation bothered him very little—which was probably more a statement about his father's promiscuity than anything else.

They stood on the beach, a few paces away from Alessandro's store. A small café was attached to it, with some tables sprawled around the entrance. Behind the store was a five-metre-high climbing wall that made Diego smile when he looked at it.

When he'd been a more frequent visitor here, he'd sometimes do his workout by climbing that wall. Daria had often egged him on, asking him to climb faster and higher.

As if his thoughts had summoned her, a small girl burst through the doors of the shop and bolted towards the pair. Diego smiled, going down on one knee so the girl could run straight into his arms.

'Tio! Where have you been? You said you would visit more often.'

Daria launched into a flood of sentences that he barely understood as they hugged each other, and he felt a twinge of guilt in his chest. He had only come to visit them once since the funeral.

'I'm sorry, *meu anjo*. You know how I get busy with work sometimes.'

Daria nodded gravely, as if she knew exactly how difficult the life of a surgeon was. Then she noticed Eliana, who now stood next to him.

'Daria, this is my friend Ana,' he said, and closed the gap between him and Eliana. 'Where is your *papai*?'

'Never too far away when she runs out of the store,' a low male voice said.

Diego set Daria down. She ran over to her father as he got closer to her. Alessandro came to a halt a couple of paces away from them but didn't even look at Diego. His eyes went straight to Eliana, and from the surprised and pained expression on his face it was clear that he had immediately spotted the similarities between her and Vanderson that Diego himself had missed that fateful night at the hotel.

'You're…his sister?' he asked, and Eliana nodded.

Tears sparkled in their eyes as they fell into each other's arms in an emotional display that robbed Diego of any remaining air in his lungs. He had thought that meeting Alessandro might be important to Eliana, but he had never imagined how emotional it would be for everyone—him included.

'Do you have time to sit down for a bit?' asked Alessandro, and Eliana looked over her shoulder to Diego, who shrugged.

He ushered them to one of the café's tables, where they sat down together, quiet for a moment.

'You could have given me a warning,' Alessandro said as he crossed his arms in front of his chest. 'You know I hate surprises.'

Diego smirked. 'That's why I didn't tell you.'

The man scowled at him, but his expression immediately softened when he looked over to Eliana. 'You really shouldn't put up with him…he's bad news.'

'Well…' She hesitated, her hand slipping to her stomach as she looked at Diego with a silent question: *Should we tell him?*

It was something Diego had thought about since he'd found out about her pregnancy. Eventually he'd need to tell the people around him that he was going to be a father. But their journey had been such an unconventional one he didn't know how to start explaining that he was having a child when he hadn't been in a relationship with a woman…ever.

Once someone outside of the two of them knew about the baby it would change everything. But Alessandro and Daria were the only people she had left that resembled her family; it was only natural that she wanted to connect with them by sharing their news.

Were they ready for that step?

There was only one way to find out.

Diego took a breath and gave her a small nod, which she acknowledged with a smile. Was she excited to be telling them?

'I know I've only just met you, so this may sound a bit strange. But Diego and I are actually having a child.'

Alessandro's eyes went wide with surprise, and his gaze darted between them as if he couldn't understand what she had just said. 'You two are…?'

'We're not together, no! This is an accident. We met some months ago now.'

She'd voiced her denial so rapidly it took Diego a few moments to register the hurt blooming in his chest. Which was ridiculous, since he *knew* they weren't together. He had set that expectation from the very beginning, so it shouldn't surprise him that she believed him.

Had *his* feelings changed?

They couldn't have. He didn't know how to love with every fibre of his being. Didn't know how to behave in the kind of family he secretly wanted to have. Alessandro and Vanderson had been the role models for something he knew he would never be able to achieve, no matter how much he desired it. So he had contented himself with watching from the side lines as their family came together and grew.

Being a minor character in their story was better than becoming a tragic failure in his own, right?

Except now here they sat, their roles reversed. He had made a child with this woman next to him, who had endured so much injustice and loneliness without letting it affect her heart.

She always tried to appear strong and independent when people were paying attention—a reflex no doubt born from the neglect she'd experienced during her childhood years. But whenever she thought no one was looking the guards came down and she became a much softer person. A person who would call their unborn child 'princess' because she felt a connection strong enough to know with certainty it was a girl.

He'd seen the same woman this last week as their passion had been transformed into something much more profound right in front of his eyes. He'd seen her come apart and put herself back together right under his hands, heard her whisper his name in the dead of the night as he pulled her closer into his embrace.

Everything in those moments had made sense in a way he hadn't experienced before. It had all just felt right, suddenly, and he felt like a fool for ever believing he couldn't have what he'd sensed last night. What he felt right now in this moment, as they told the first other person that they were having a child together.

Only she had rejected all those feelings with one phrase.

'I can't believe it. Of all the men you could have found in Rio, you've tied yourself to the eternal bachelor. That's material for a telenovela right there.' Alessandro looked at Diego. 'How do you feel?'

As if his world was falling apart right underneath his feet. Everything he'd thought to be true about himself had shifted since he'd met Eliana, and now he couldn't go on without her—didn't want to know what it felt like to be without her. She had found the thing Diego had thought he was missing. It had been inside him all this time, waiting for the right person to find it. Waiting for her.

'Better than you give me credit for,' he said, to distract himself from his own inner turmoil. 'I have you to show me how to be a good father.'

Alessandro laughed at that and looked down at Daria, who was sitting on a chair next to him and was busy enjoying her milkshake. She stopped drinking when she noticed her father looking at her and tilted her head,

clearly oblivious to the discussion that had gone on between the adults.

'I think you're not giving yourself enough credit for
turning out to be a decent man despite all the obstacles,'
Alessandro said with a pointed look. 'I can think of a lot
of different reactions to an unplanned pregnancy.'

Diego glanced at Eliana, who had gone quiet during
their exchange, her hand still resting on the tiny bump
that was starting to form.

'It wasn't how I planned to have a child, but I'm glad
it happened the way it did,' she said. 'Diego hasn't shied
away from taking responsibility. We're just trying to figure things out as we go along, while I'm still wrapping
up things with Marco's estate.'

There was a softness in her words that caught Diego
off guard. Was it affection? After she had rejected him
so resoundingly he hadn't expected to encounter such
warmth only a few moments later. Was she *glad* they'd
had an accident on their first night together? That it had
been with Diego?

'I mean, how else would I have met you?' she added,
looking at Alessandro with a wide smile.

Their connection had been instantaneous, and Diego
was happy for her. After the way Marco had isolated his
own daughter from any kind of family life, she deserved
to know some of her roots.

She halted for a moment, her eyes trailing over to the
sea for a moment. 'I didn't see your name on any of the
papers in my father's will. Vanderson was his only ben-
eficiary, but after the accident...'

Alessandro shook his head with a sad smile. 'You're
sweet to worry. But Vanderson had his own estate and
that went to us as his next of kin. Me not getting along
with Marco didn't affect us as a family.' Alessandro

smiled, reaching over the table to grab Eliana's hand and squeeze it. 'Make sure Diego gives you my number so we can keep in touch. Daria will be thrilled to meet her little cousin in a few months. Isn't that right, *anjinho*?'

Daria beamed at all of them and nodded. Her excitement to meet her new cousin was palpable in her face. Diego heard a soft gasp coming from Eliana, and saw the shimmer covering her eyes as she looked at her niece with a big smile.

'I can't wait for you all to meet this little one.'

A noisy group of tourists walking towards the shop interrupted their discussion, and Alessandro stood up with a sigh.

'I have to take care of this.' He walked over to Eliana and pulled her into another hug. 'Let's grab some coffee when it's less busy, so we can have a chance to chat. I'm sure there are a lot of things you would like to know about Vanderson, and it would be nice to relive the memories I have of him.'

She nodded in agreement before hugging Daria as well and waving as they both scurried back into the store. When she sat down again, her face was unreadable.

'How are you feeling? Lots to process?' Diego asked, and looked at her for a moment before laying a hand on her thigh to give it a supportive squeeze.

'I like him. It's good to know that at least Vanderson had the chance at a normal life. Although no doubt my father left a lot of damage on him as well.'

At least. The words hung between them like a dark fog, suddenly rushing in to envelop everything around them. It sounded as if she had given up.

An invisible band had been constricting his chest since she'd spoken those words about her pregnancy, and he had now got to a point where his chest felt heavy under the crushing sensation. He couldn't hide his mounting feelings for Eliana any longer and had to admit to himself that he wanted more from her. More than he had ever wanted from anyone before and more than she was willing to give.

Which left him with no choice but to forget about how he felt. How he had fallen so hard without even noticing? She didn't want him the way he wanted her, and maybe that was for the best. How could he promise her a happy family when he had no idea how to make one? Better to make the best out of what they already had rather than try for something new.

'What do you want to do now?' he asked. 'The climbing wall is a lot of fun if you're feeling brave.'

She laughed. 'Making a baby from scratch has left me a bit exhausted, so I'll pass on the extreme sports for now. How about a walk on the beach instead?'

He smiled as he took her hand, their fingers weaving into each other's as they started their stroll, and a warmth rising in his arms from where their skin connected.

She would leave any day now. Eliana had said so herself. And Diego was determined to enjoy the time they had left, even if he was dreaming of what might have been if they had grown up differently.

The water sparkled in the light of the afternoon sun as they walked down the beach in a comfortable silence. The meeting with Alessandro had healed a part of Eliana's heart in a way only he could have done. With him she had regained a connection to her brother, and even though he wasn't here to explain, she was glad to know someone who could tell her who he had been besides what Diego had already told her.

Diego's support had been essential in this endeavour. It

showed her he cared not just for his child but for her. Getting to know Alessandro—that would be for her alone.

She felt her already bleeding heart squeeze even tighter. Diego's affection meant so much to her when it really shouldn't. At some point would she have to admit that they might have gone too deep?

Eliana shook those thoughts away, instead focusing on the beach around her and the warmth his hand created where it touched hers, radiating heat through her entire body. It might be the last time she got to enjoy such a tranquil moment before she left Rio behind.

'Have you been here before?' Diego asked as they stopped to watch two people zip past them on a pair of quad bikes with frightening speed.

'Not really.' Her eyes followed the bikes as they wove through people. She heard excited laughter trailing after the drivers. 'I didn't like going out by myself when I lived here, and by the time I was older I had already moved away.'

'You haven't missed much. The Copa Cabana gets so many reviews online every visitor comes here.' The bikes came zooming around again and he raised his hand, underlining the point he'd just made. 'I know a private beach that I—'

A loud bang drowned out the rest of his sentence and Eliana clasped her hand over her mouth as one of the quad bikes collided with a palm tree, sending the rider flying over the steering wheel and into the trunk before he fell on the ground unmoving.

Diego swore next to her and sprinted towards the person lying in the sand. She quickly followed him, scanning the people who were moving closer. When she spotted someone holding a phone, she pointed at them.

'Please call for an ambulance and say to the operator

that there has been a motor vehicle crash on the beach.'
Eliana didn't wait for a reply but turned around to find
Diego kneeling beside the man, who had regained con-
sciousness and was moaning in agony.

'What's the status? Anything I can do to help?'

Both the man's arms stood at unnatural angles. One
had a dislocated shoulder, the other a potential fracture
of the lower arm. A quick glance showed her the skin was
still intact, though that didn't mean the breaking bone
hadn't done some damage to the muscles and blood ves-
sels in the arm.

Diego looked at his patient, assessing the damage before bending over the man again. '*Senhor*, do you hear
me?' he asked, and the man nodded with a wince. 'We
are both doctors and we're here to help. You've had an
accident and crashed.'

Eliana knelt down as well, waiting for Diego's plan
of action. Whatever the man's wounds were, she knew
he'd been lucky that Diego was here to help with stabi-
lising the fracture.

A small part inside her felt excited to be working with
him. As chief at the hospital she'd spoken to many people
working with Diego, and none of the other department
heads had received such high praise. The compassion
and care he gave each patient, no matter the severity of
the case, was unparalleled, and after seeing for herself
his interaction with Miguel, as well as the man in front
of him now, she could see his staff had not exaggerated.

'We can't set the bone without an X-ray, but we can
pop the shoulder back in and stabilise the arm with a
sling until the ambulance arrives,' Diego said to her before turning back to the patient.

'Is he going to be okay?' His friend had stopped her
bike a few paces away and now came running over.

Diego stood up for a moment, laying a hand on her shoulder. 'We have to get him to a hospital, but he is conscious. What I'm about to do will hurt without anaesthesia. Can you sit next to him?'

She nodded, her face as pale as the sand surrounding them, and dropped to her knees beside him.

'Have you relocated a shoulder before?' Diego asked Eliana as he came down next to the patient's head.

'I've watched several, but never done it myself.'

'Can you kneel behind his back once we prop him up? This will be rough on him, but it'll make things a lot easier for the ambulance.'

When Eliana nodded, he pushed the man's torso off the ground and she settled behind him, holding him upright while Diego took the arm with the dislocated shoulder between his hands.

'Most of the time you'll find that the tendons in the arm help the shoulder find its way back. All you have to do is pull.'

Eliana watched as he tightened his grip around the man's arm and pulled at it with a sharp but precise motion that sent a tremble through the patient's body accompanied by a stifled shout.

'Then follow the pressure of the tendons to bring the shoulder back into its socket.'

He got to his feet, asking one of the onlookers if he could borrow her towel and fashioning it into a makeshift sling, into which he carefully lifted the broken arm to stabilise it for transport.

'I know you're in a lot of pain right now, and the last thing you want is some doctor asking you questions,' he said, in a soothing voice that even managed to set Eliana at ease. 'But I have to ask one so we can make sure we're not missing anything. Are you feeling any nausea or sickness?'

The man's chest fluttered with each laboured breath, but he shook his head from one side to the other.

'We can't rule out a concussion, but at least he was wearing a helmet,' Eliana said, and Diego nodded.

His hand slipped inside his pocket, fishing out his smartphone. He turned the torch on with a flick of his finger, shining the light into the patient's eyes. 'Pupillary reaction looks good. Fingers crossed we have no spinal or head injuries.'

They both looked up when the sirens of an ambulance came closer and a red and white vehicle came into view. Two paramedics came running, with a gurney in their hands.

Eliana watched as Diego updated them on the patient's status and then took a step back as they readied him for transportation to the nearest emergency department. Her eyes flickered between the patient and Diego, who was now talking to the patient's friend.

'They're taking him to Copa Memorial for treatment. The ambulance can take you along if you want to accompany them.'

The woman's eyes were shining with tears at this point, and she looked around to the bikes. 'I want to, but…'

Diego followed her gaze. 'Did you rent them from the store with the climbing wall behind it?' He smiled when she nodded. 'The owner happens to be a good friend of mine, so don't worry about it. We'll sort it out. Go with him.'

The woman thanked them both with a sob in her voice and they watched her climb into the ambulance.

'You were incredible,' Eliana said, giving voice to the

brewing thought within her. Not only had he kept the patient calm under chaotic circumstances, he'd been able to help with very limited resources.

Diego looked at her in surprise. 'I don't think so...'

Eliana laughed at the denial. 'I'm glad I got to watch you work before I leave. Now I know why your staff keep saying such nice things about you. Santa Valeria is lucky to have you to teach its staff the right way.'

He crossed his arms in front of his chest, raising his eyebrows. 'Did the doctors in your hospital never help in emergencies?'

'Of course they did. What I'm trying to say is that I love your compassion and your dedication to doing the right thing. And after speaking to everyone at Santa Valeria I know that more people who think and act like you are needed.'

His brown eyes grew darker, narrowing on her and sending a shiver crawling down her spine. There was an unspoken desire written in them, something neither of them wanted to acknowledge. Speaking of it would undermine every boundary they had established between them—every agreement they had made for the good of their baby.

So Eliana bit her lip, swallowing the words rising in her throat, and looked at the quad bikes instead.

'Let's get these bikes back to Alessandro,' she said, needing to break the sudden intensity between them.

CHAPTER NINE

THE MORNING LIGHT filtering through the half-drawn curtains fell onto Eliana's face. She tried to turn around but met surprising resistance in the form of Diego, who had his arms wrapped around her waist and was pulling her into him even as he slept.

She looked down at herself. Her naked body was wrapped up in his sheets, her bare back hot where it connected with his chest. Their one night together, which should have been a one-off lapse of judgement, had extended into the last three weeks, with them spending both days and nights together.

The way they had been living was so far removed from what their lives would look like once she left—which would be soon. And they were nowhere near figuring out the arrangements for their co-parenting journey. Instead of focusing on that, they had given in to the tension that had been building between them for weeks.

Misguided tension.

Nothing about their situation had changed. Eliana was still going to leave, handing the hospital over so she didn't have to be involved any more. The city reminded her too much of Marco and what he had done to her. And although spending time with Diego opened her heart in ways she had never experienced before, there was still a

sneaky voice in her head, whispering words of caution
and poisoning these moments they were sharing together.

He'd shown incredible kindness and dedication to his
community. But she'd also glimpsed the ruthlessness with
which he had gone about it—taking resources from the
hospital as well as smuggling people in. Diego had always acted for the right reasons and was ready to put his
own career on the line for it, but would he do the same
for her? Would he consider her part of his people when
her struggle had been so different?

The doubts gnawing at her heart with their sharp claws
and teeth did little to help her relax back into slumber.
Every time she closed her eyes her thoughts started to
whirl around in her head, corrupting what had been three
weeks full of pleasure, laughter and closeness.

With a soft sigh on her lips Eliana turned around—and
gasped when she stared right into Diego's warm brown
eyes.

'Good morning,' she said, when his eyes narrowed as
if he had caught every thought that had just wandered
through her head.

'Do you want me to let you go?' he asked in a calm
voice, and Eliana got the impression that he wasn't necessarily talking about his arms around her waist.

She took a breath to steady herself. His gaze was
throwing her off balance, to the point where she couldn't
quite remember exactly what she had been afraid of.

'I have to go to the hospital. My first scan is later
today, and I need to get some things done before that,' she
said, to wriggle out of telling him about her thoughts. 'As
a matter of fact, you need to be in the hospital, too. The
mayor's wife is getting her hip replaced today, and she's
insisted she will only have the best surgeon touch her.'

Diego groaned, but the sound was very unlike the

sounds that had filled her ears throughout the night as he came back for more of her.

'It's a hip replacement. Any second-year registrar can do that. You're just wasting money, putting the head of orthopaedics on this.' He sighed and released his grip around her to scrub his hands across his face. 'That money would be better spent on something ground-breaking—like fixing curved spines. A doctor from Peru has contacted me about a patient who has a fifty-degree bend they can't fix with steel rods.'

Eliana took the opportunity to roll out of bed, stepping out of Diego's range so he couldn't grab her again. 'Write down a proposal and we can talk about your curved spine. But until then I expect you to give the mayor's wife the very best care. From what the accountants tell me, she's a huge benefactor of the hospital.'

Eliana bent down to pick up her clothes, and when she looked back up Diego's face had changed. The humour in his eyes had died, leaving nothing but an icy tundra where she had just seen warmth and compassion.

'Don't tell me you're putting people with deep pockets ahead of patients who actually need help?'

The accusation came out of nowhere, and Eliana's chest constricted for a moment. She was surprised by the ferocity with which he'd spat those words at her.

'You know I'm not. But big donors are part of the ecosystem, too.'

Diego snorted in derision. 'That phrase comes straight out of Marco Costa's playbook.'

The ice in his gaze took over her body, trickling down her spine and through her body as if someone had poured cold water all over her.

'Do not compare me to that man,' she said, fighting to keep her voice even. 'You don't know what he was like as a person. You only ever interacted with him when you were trying to bend the rules in your favour. Any chief would be annoyed with you over that.'

Her chest heaved as she stared at him, looking for the man she had got to know so much about in the last few weeks, believing she might be able to trust him with the thoughts dwelling inside her. But his expression was unreadable.

'The same goes for you,' he said. 'If you're suddenly so concerned with profits I might have made a mistake showing you my clinic.'

His voice had dropped low, but instead of it causing the usual goosebumps of pleasure to coat her skin she felt the hairs on her arms stand on end in warning.

'Where do you think the money for expensive Peruvian surgeries comes from? All this because you think yourself too good to do a hip replacement?'

Eliana stared at him, waiting for a reply that didn't come. How could Diego accuse her of being like her father when she had worked so hard to support his vision of Santa Valeria's future?

'I don't want to waste my time appeasing rich people when there are others who need my help,' he said, with such quiet fury that Eliana glared at him.

Sprawled out in the bed like that, he would have been a breathtaking picture of masculine sensuality if she'd been able to see past his almost irrational response to one surgery. It wasn't as if she'd cancelled his entire surgical schedule and asked him to focus only on the mayor's wife.

'You are helping the hospital by doing this. The hospital you have, in essence, been *stealing* from for the last few years.'

He sat up, opening his mouth to speak, but she stopped

him with a shake of her head. She knew she would regret letting this conversation go any further than she already had.

'I'm going to leave and let you contemplate who you just compared me to.' She paused for a moment; her hands balled into tight fists at her sides as she sensed the anger rising in her. 'I have the scan today, at two in the afternoon. It's at the hospital, so I'll see you there.'

Despite feeling wholly justified to uninvite him, she realised she needed to be the bigger person. He was still the father of her child.

Without giving him a chance to rope her into any further argument, Eliana took her clothes and fled the room, getting dressed in a hurry before leaving the house with tears of deep hurt stinging her eyes.

'You're an idiot.'

Diego looked up when the voice of his sister Gloria ripped him out of his contemplations.

He had been ready to leave for the hospital when his *avozinha* had called, asking if he could take her along. Miguel had just received his new leg, and she wanted to pay him and his mother a visit.

In typical Márcia fashion, she had been nowhere near ready when her grandson had pulled over to pick her up. So he had come inside to make himself some coffee as he waited. He'd need a lot of caffeine if he wanted to get through the day in one piece.

'Good morning to you, too,' he said, in a low voice that conveyed his overall annoyance with the way his day had started.

'I can't believe you finally bring home a woman and then you mess it up within a month.' She paused to look at him.

'How could you possibly know about that?' The accuracy with which Gloria had pinpointed the source of his annoyance was bordering on spooky.

'You were happy when we last saw you. Not just content, but actually smiling and engaging. None of us had ever seen you that way, so it was easy to guess what was different since you did us the favour of bringing her here.'

Diego crossed his arms, narrowing his eyes at his sister. 'Did you call the council of siblings to discuss this?'

Gloria chuckled—which didn't help his sour mood. He didn't need anyone butting into his affairs.

'No, Albert saw you two interlocked. He said it looked like you were eating something off her neck.'

Diego glared at her, the exasperation in his chest fading away as he was confronted with the truth he'd been struggling with. He wanted to pretend that Eliana's exit that morning didn't mean anything to him.

'Our nephew saw us?' he asked.

Gloria nodded and couldn't hide her grin. 'You made out with someone in Avozinha's garden while the whole family was here. You couldn't have done a better job if you'd wanted to be caught.'

He hadn't thought about being caught when he had kissed Eliana in the garden. That moment had been about releasing something that had been dwelling inside him ever since they'd met during that surgery. Just moments before they had heard that they were having a child together for the first time. Such news should have made him wary of the woman involved, but instead they had grown closer.

'I'm still waiting to know why I'm the idiot here.' He cast a suspicious glance at his sister, who shook her head with a click of her tongue, as if the answer was the most obvious in the world.

'Because I was out walking Pelé when I saw Eliana leave your place in what looked like a hurry. Now, a woman you take to meet your ridiculous family must be special, because in all the years of our urging you to bring someone the best you could do was Vanderson. And no one ever caught you two making out.'

Diego grimaced, his thoughts still catching up with what Gloria had just revealed. The night at his grandmother's house had not gone as he had planned—which might be something of an overstatement. There hadn't been much planning going on after he'd kissed her. All he'd known was that he had to have her in his house. Not just to sleep with her, but to watch her fall asleep. To have her warm body next to him while he drifted off.

In a completely uncharacteristic move, Diego had found himself yearning for more than just a physical connection. And throughout their nights together, he had started to think about their future—if there could even be a future for them together. He had been close to talking to her about it, to discussing with her the blooming feelings in his chest that he had never felt before.

Until Eliana had mentioned his scheduled procedure on the mayor's wife and a wave of deep-seated anger had come rushing into his chest, banishing any other emotion that might have been there for the duration of a few heartbeats. Marco had done that sort of thing—constantly cancelling essential or even urgent surgeries so he could do a routine procedure that any registrar could handle on people who were important and brought in significant donations. They had been put ahead of people with genuine needs who needed his steady hands and exceptional skill to help them.

It wasn't a trend Diego wanted to see continue under

the new leadership, so when she had mentioned it something inside him had snapped.

He'd stared at the ceiling after she'd left, his rage subsiding with each breath and being replaced with a feeling of profound unease.

His words had hurt her, and he had meant them to have that effect, but as he'd lain there regret had crept in. The hospital needed big donors to keep going—he understood that well enough. And none of his urgent patients had been bumped further down the line for him to do this procedure. Had his anger been an overreaction because of the issues he'd experienced in the past?

'She's pregnant, Gloria,' he said now, letting go of the weight he'd been carrying around. 'We're having a child.'

Her eyebrows shot up. 'Then you'd better get your act together, big brother.'

A thought occurred to Diego that made him shiver. 'You haven't told Avozinha that we've fought, have you?'

'I'm not that cruel. I didn't tell her about the kissing *or* the falling out.'

He looked over his shoulder when he heard rustling coming from the house and spotted his grandmother packing her bag. 'I don't know which would be worse. And don't tell her this either,' he whispered at his sister, who shot him a grin before he got up and ushered his grandmother to the car.

He glanced at the clock as they drove, wondering if he would be able to see Eliana before his surgery. He didn't want the shadows of this morning haunting them throughout the day, and he needed to let her know he hadn't meant to sound as harsh as he had. That it had been no more than a reaction from the past.

He didn't know how to handle the feelings he'd started

to have for her. For the family they could surely have together if they wanted to.

Diego shoved his thoughts aside as he went into the scrub room to change for surgery. Whether he liked it or not, the mayor's wife was now his patient, and she deserved him to be on top of his game just like anyone else.

Nerves made Eliana's stomach turn inside out as she settled down on the exam table. When she'd arrived in the obstetrics department the receptionist had asked her to go through to a room immediately. A fact she was grateful for. While her pregnancy wasn't exactly a secret, she didn't want to invite any questions from the staff if they happened to pass by and see her there.

She had told the receptionist to keep an eye out for Diego and send him through if he arrived, and was glad that she hadn't had to specify why she wanted to see him.

Dr Felix sat on a stool next to her, looking at the patient chart on a tablet in front of her and asking all the routine questions. Eliana answered them, her eyes darting back to the door, hoping that at any moment Diego would burst through it, apologising for his delay.

A small voice in her head told her that he wouldn't come. Not after the way they had parted this morning. But she ignored the doubt growing inside her, wanting to believe that he wouldn't not show up just because they'd had an argument. As co-parents, that would probably happen more often than they wanted. Would he always bail when they were standing on opposite sides?

That thought struck fear in Eliana's heart. The thought of getting to know his family—and getting to know her own family through him—had filled her with a warmth that made her heart beat faster. Somewhere along the line her feelings for him had become a lot more tangible than she had anticipated. Wanted, really. But would she even fit into his life? Did he want her to? Her intention to leave Rio remained the same. And Diego hadn't asked her to reconsider, either.

She had found a replacement chief of medicine. The lawyers were all but finished dealing with the estate of her father. After that she would be heading back to Belo Horizonte, leaving Rio and all its painful memories behind her. She'd need to forget about whatever feelings she had for Diego because they clearly were not meant to be.

She couldn't even count on him to come to the scan of their unborn child.

'Both you and the baby are in perfect condition, Dr Oliveira,' Dr Felix informed her, bringing her thoughts back into the room. 'I'm having a look at the results of your prenatal blood tests right now, but unless I see anything concerning you can just come back in a few weeks for your sixteen-week check-up.'

'Oh, I probably won't be here by then. I'm heading back…back home as soon as my business here is done.' She stumbled over the word *home*, her heart skipping a painful beat. She had grown more attached to this place than she was ready to admit.

'I'll make sure to send you a copy of your file so your new doctor has all the information you need.' Dr Felix smiled at her, then looked back at her tablet. 'Are you ready to know the sex of the baby?'

Eliana's eyes went wide with surprise. She had forgotten that they had done a blood test that would tell her the sex of her baby even at this stage. Again her eyes darted to the door, which remained stubbornly closed, and her chest constricted. He really wasn't coming.

Dr Felix noticed her gaze, following it with her own. 'Waiting for the father?'

'Yes, but I think he might be stuck in surgery.'

She didn't believe that, but it was a better excuse than the fact that he'd bailed because they'd argued and he didn't want to operate on the mayor's wife. The surgery must have ended hours ago.

'We can keep this information from you a bit longer if you want to wait.'

The problem was that Eliana wasn't sure.

Part of her did want to wait—desperately. Despite all the barriers, all the walls and traps she had set around herself, Diego had danced around every single obstacle and planted himself in her heart. She wanted him to be a part of this moment, to be a part of her family—wanted to share the highs and lows of her pregnancy with him.

But he had accused her of putting profit over patient care, just as her father had done. And to hear that he thought so little of her after all the time they had spent together had crushed her heart into tiny pieces.

Dr Felix had clearly sensed her hesitation. She picked up a small piece of paper from her desk, writing something on it before putting it in an envelope, which she handed to Eliana.

'These are the blood test results. You can open it together if you want to find out.'

Eliana took the envelope with a grateful smile and jumped off the table, pulling her blouse back into place.

As she walked out of the obstetrics department she grabbed her phone to look at the surgical plan for the afternoon. Perhaps Diego had been pulled into an emergency surgery...

Something was definitely off when Eliana arrived at the orthopaedics department. The staff's whispers died down the second she got close enough to decipher some words, and picked up as soon as she was far enough not to overhear their chatter. A pang of terror grabbed at her heart. This had something to do with Diego. She had known that the instant she had arrived, even though there was nothing to indicate that.

'Where is Dr Ferrari?' she asked a passing nurse, who looked at her with wide eyes.

'He's in the VIP room. It's the mayor's wife. She…'

The young woman's voice trailed off, and Eliana shuddered, her suspicions confirmed.

Something had happened during surgery.

All thoughts of him missing her appointment were wiped from her brain, all her attention immediately on the critical patient they had in their care.

Whatever she had feared finding in the patient's room, the reality was a lot worse than she had imagined. The sound of a flat beep drifted into the hall before she arrived, filling her with a sense of dreadful foreboding. A flat heart monitor was never a good sign. Neither was the fact that the room beyond was too quiet.

Eliana braced herself as she entered the room, analysing the scene in front of her. A female patient lay in a hospital bed, her chest cracked open in what looked like an emergency thoracotomy—something a surgeon would only do if they had no other option and other measures to stabilise the patient had failed.

What had happened that Diego had needed to crack open her chest? Blood clot? They were common in women her age and could happen at any time.

A junior physician hovered around the bed, picking up the different instruments that had been used in the emergency procedure and putting them on a cart. And behind him, slumped in a chair, sat…

'Diego?'

His face looked hollow. With his head tilted backwards, she could see the blood that covered the front of his scrubs as well as parts of his arms, where the gloves had stopped. In the hurry of the emergency he didn't seem to have put on a gown for extra protection.

Eliana looked at the registrar, still fumbling with the instruments. 'Are you from the cardio department?' she asked. He nodded, clearly intimidated by the presence of the chief. 'Tell the head of Cardio I'll need to speak to her before we break the news to the mayor.'

She dismissed the young doctor with a nod of her head before turning back to Diego, who had sat up slightly.

'What happened?' she asked, doing her best to sound unemotional. Seeing him covered in blood had sent pangs of terror through her body until she'd realised that it wasn't his.

'Are you here to admonish me for letting your VIP patient die?' he said in a quiet voice, resentment giving his tone an uncomfortable edge.

Eliana remained silent, not rising to the bait he'd laid out. Instead, she squatted down in front of him to be on the same eye level.

Diego took a few breaths. Tiredness was etched into every feature of his body. She could tell that he had fought tooth and nail to keep his patient alive.

'My best guess? Pulmonary embolism. Even if we'd have caught it early, it would have been too late. I was about to leave when the post-op nurse paged me to check in on her.'

Eliana glanced back at the patient. That had been her first thought as well. A blood clot that had travelled all the way to the lungs, blocking off the flow of blood. She would have probably cracked the chest open too, and tried to manually aspirate the heart.

Looking back at Diego, she put her hand on his knee.

The emergency had clearly taken a lot of energy out of him, and she suspected he might have tried even harder knowing the patient was important to her. Or did she simply wish that to be true?

Whatever the reason, the Diego in front of her looked utterly broken, and no matter how angry she was at him for missing their appointment, the part of her that cared for him a lot more than she was willing to admit wanted to take care of him.

They could have their difficult conversation later.

'Come on, let's get you cleaned up.'

She took him by the hand, and together they walked back to her office, where she shoved him into the adjacent bathroom so he could shower.

Diego heard two muffled voices on the other side of the closed door when he stepped out of the shower after what seemed to be hours. He stopped, listening and trying to understand what was being discussed. One of the voices belonged to Eliana, but the other one was harder to pinpoint.

His question was answered a few moments later when he heard a third voice coming out of the speaker of a phone. The mayor. So the other person must be the head of cardiology.

Dread came rushing back into his system when he thought about the surgery. Hip replacements were routine work. Diego had done hundreds in his career, and his mortality rate lay way below the already tiny rate of hip fractures and related surgeries.

Low, but not zero.

Diego leaned against the door, closing his eyes as he shook off the thought of the last couple of hours. Losing a patient was never easy, but this one really bothered him—mainly because he hadn't even wanted to do the surgery, but had had to concede in the end that Eliana would have to ask for his time in such cases to garner support from wealthy benefactors.

It was something Marco had done constantly as well. The difference between those two, though, lay in what they'd intended to use the money for. Eliana wasn't lining her own pockets with the funds she'd drum up through such procedures—a fact he now realised.

He hoped it was not too late to apologise for his barbed words earlier today.

If only he could have given her a good outcome.

He'd let her down.

Diego knew this wasn't really true—that he had done everything he could to save the patient's life, and sometimes that wasn't enough. Despite knowing all that, he felt like an abject failure.

'You can come out now.'

Her voice rang a lot clearer than before, and a moment later the door opened. Eliana stood in front of him, holding a fresh pair of folded scrubs.

'I brought you some spare clothes.'

He took them with a nod of gratitude and slipped into the clothes before stepping into her office, where he stood for a moment.

'I just spoke to the mayor. He's still processing the news, but thank you for all the effort you put into saving his wife,' she said, and sat down behind her desk, pointing at the chair across from her.

Diego didn't take her up on the invitation but instead elected to stand, leaning his hip against her heavy desk. 'I'm sorry for how it turned out.'

'I know.' Eliana smiled half-heartedly and shrugged.

'He'll come to understand…just like every other spouse in such a situation.'

'Except he was more important to you.'

Eliana let out a sigh. 'He wasn't any more or less important than anyone else. There's a difference between rolling out the red carpet for someone and blatantly preferring them due to their status.'

'I know. I realise that now. And I don't know why I brought it up again. You don't operate in the same way Marco did, and I shouldn't have said otherwise.' He stopped for a moment, relaxing the arms he had been crossing just a moment ago. 'I apologise.'

His apology seemed to throw Eliana off guard, for she stared at him for a couple of heartbeats before finally nodding. 'Thank you. I appreciate that acknowledgement.'

They stayed quiet for a few moments.

Then, 'You missed the scan.'

The sharp tone in her voice was back, though he could see the restraint on her face.

The scan? Diego hesitated for a moment as the sequence of events this afternoon came back to him. With the urgency of the moment her appointment had completely slipped his mind. Guilt bloomed in his chest, mingling with the already heavy shroud of losing his patient. How could have forgotten about the first chance to see his child?

'Are you angry I missed the appointment? Ana, I had to attend the Code Blue of my patient.'

Eliana huffed, her eyes narrowing with a dangerous sparkle. 'I'm not angry that you had to see to your patient. What concerns me is that I had to remind you about the scan now. You didn't even ask if I'm…if *we* are okay.' She took a deep breath, seemingly steadying herself as she looked away for a second. 'I thought we were in this together.'

He paused. Her answer had not been quite what he had expected. She wasn't angry that he had missed the scan. She was angry because he hadn't asked about it.

'This isn't the last time I'm going to miss things,' he said slowly as he collected his own thoughts. 'If you take our kid away from Rio I won't be there for a lot of things. I want to be involved, and I'm sorry I couldn't make it this time, but you're the one carrying our child away from here.'

Diego's pulse quickened, his mouth suddenly dry as he stared at her confused expression. The truth of his feelings for her had started to coalesce—to the point where he could no longer deny it. He wanted her to stay— wanted them to be a family. Because he had fallen for her without even realising, and the thought of watching her leave hung over him like a dark fog.

'Diego…' She looked away, scrubbing her hands over her face. 'I'm still leaving as soon as my business here is done. I can't stay in Rio.'

'Why not?' He knew she struggled with her past, growing up alone and isolated. But was that enough to rob them of the chance of becoming a family? Wouldn't she try for him?

'Because there's just too much pain here. Even being back at this place brings unease to my stomach.' She lifted her hands, indicating the hospital around her. 'Everywhere I go I can feel the stares, hear the whispers about what Marco Costa did to my mother. I hear what a good woman she was or what a poor woman she was, depending on the person I speak to. That's all she'll ever be—a scandal. And that's all I'll ever be here as well.'

Diego's heart broke in his chest as the flood of words

escaped her lips. Words she had spoken for the first time, judging by the sad but also strangely relieved expression on her face. So that was where her insecurities came from. She didn't believe she was good enough to be here, when nothing could be further from the truth.

'You've already shown yourself to be way more than the circumstances of your birth,' he said into the silence spreading between them. 'The mayor's wife just died in your hospital. You knew exactly what to do and you did it calmly. Like the true leader of a hospital would.'

Eliana scoffed. 'I wouldn't be so sure about that. Internally, I've been freaking out ever since I saw her in that room.'

'But you didn't let that affect you. Despite feeling overwhelmed, you remembered to care for the immediate family of the patient first rather than let yourself be carried away.'

Seeing the flaws in someone's actions rather than acknowledging every right step they took was something he was very familiar with, and he knew it took a lot of energy and self-confidence to snap out of it.

She looked at him with furrowed brow, digesting his words. 'I was never meant to be in this position.'

'You don't know that,' he replied, and reached out to brush his knuckles across her cheek. She didn't move away. 'Maybe this wasn't your plan, but neither was this baby—and look how that's turned out. You care so much for it that you want to carry it away from the place that caused you so much pain.'

His hand slipped down her neck over her arm and finally reached her stomach, where he rested his palm, fingers splayed across her abdomen.

Eliana looked down, taking a deep breath. 'You want me to stay?'

'I do, yes,' he said in a low voice.

'Why?'

His heart slammed against his chest as the truth rang clear in his head. 'Because I'm falling in love with you and I want us to try and have what we both weren't able to have growing up. We can be a family.'

It had taken him this long to realise that he wasn't doomed to repeat the mistakes of his past. Just because his father hadn't stayed true to his mother, it didn't mean that needed to be *his* life, too. He was free to love Eliana to the best of his abilities. Showing up to do his part every day. Choosing her and their child until the end of eternity.

Her eyes went wide in surprise, and he saw a slight flush colouring her cheek at his unexpected confession. Well, when he'd come in this morning, he hadn't thought they were going to have this conversation either. Hell, he hadn't even made up his mind whether to tell her about his feelings or if he should just let her go.

'Diego... I thought we had agreed to be friends,' she finally said after an extensive silence—and all the air left his lungs at once, as if someone had kicked him in the stomach.

Despite feeling utterly deflated, he managed a chuckle. 'I think we left the friend zone behind when we started making out whenever no one was watching.'

The blush on her cheeks intensified, and under any other circumstances Diego would have enjoyed the sight. If only she hadn't just rejected him.

An invisible hand reached inside his chest and squeezed his heart to the point of physical pain. Any more and he knew he would break.

'I'm not going to stay here,' she said. 'I can't. Not when I don't even know if you'll ever be able to put me first.'

'What? You doubt me because I missed this one appointment?' The accusation hurt in the depths of his chest, pulling the already suffocating band even tighter.

'No, I doubt you because you've kept things from me. Important things about your dealings in this hospital,' she said in a strained voice, as if she was willing herself to remain calm. 'But your motives are pure, and I've been working hard these last couple of weeks to give you the funds you need. I love how much you care about your community. But you're so used to doing things only the way you do it. I don't know how I would fit into that— how you see us as a family.'

She paused and shook her head.

'I'm not even sure you would have told me about the clinic if I hadn't stumbled upon Selma in the emergency department.'

Diego lifted his eyebrows. He opened his mouth to defend himself, but closed it again after a second of silence. Eliana wasn't wrong, and he didn't have any intention of stopping. Didn't feel bad about it either. Those people out there needed his help, and it wasn't *his* problem that the system was so fundamentally broken that he needed to resort to these tactics.

'I do what I have to do to help my people,' he said through gritted teeth, and saw her recoil.

'I'm not saying that anything you do is wrong. If more doctors were like you we wouldn't even need a free clinic. I just wish I could see the same tenacity in you when it comes to me and our child. But between your work and your mission I don't think we're as much of a priority as we should be.'

An icy shiver trickled down Diego's spine as he grappled to understand her words. 'You don't think you're a priority for me?'

The implication of those words shook him to his core.

If his actions had made her feel that way, he really wasn't any better than his father. He truly didn't know how to be a part of a family, no matter how hard he tried.

His face must have shown the darkness of his thoughts, for Eliana lifted her hand to reach out to him, but stopped a few inches before their bodies could touch.

'I'm…sorry.'

He could see the conflicting feelings in her expression, and it was those warring emotions that almost made him believe she didn't mean what she'd said. But he had no choice but to believe her, even though he wanted the opposite to be true.

He pushed himself onto his feet. 'Don't be,' he said curtly, as the pain of rejection started to well up inside his chest again. 'Let me know about the baby. I can drive up for the next scan.'

He turned around, but stopped in his tracks when Eliana called out to him. 'Are you going to the dinner tomorrow? I've invited all the department heads to talk about the future of the hospital. I need you to be there.'

The future? Diego had rarely been less interested in the future than in this moment.

'If it's about work, sure,' he said with a throwaway gesture, before leaving the office and closing the door behind him.

CHAPTER TEN

THE DINNER WAS the last thing Eliana was in the mood for. Diego's unexpected confession had rocked her to her very core, and she felt the entire world had changed around her.

It couldn't be true. How could he love her when no one had ever done so in her whole life?

What had he been thinking, asking her to stay?

Her heart had been shredded into a million tiny pieces when she'd rejected him. Everything inside her had wanted to shout yes, to wrap her arms around him and never let him go. She'd wanted to be the kind of brave person who could forget about all the dangerous and hurtful things looming in the shadows of their romantic relationship.

His focus was so singular, she was afraid to find out what would happen if he fully focused on her, as she had demanded. But with the needs of his community, the grand plans he wanted to achieve, would he even be able to look out of her? For their child?

All the years of only depending on herself, without her father's love and support, had thickened the walls around her to the point where she could not trust anyone to come in. What if she let him in, let him see everything inside her, all the pain and chaos, and he realised what he was in for? What if he left? Eliana couldn't do that to her child—not when she had grown up on her own.

As much as she wanted to accept his love, to dare to hope, she couldn't be selfish. Her child needed her father more than she needed her lover.

Eliana took a deep breath, pushing the thoughts away. Tonight she had to be the chief one last time.

Her dinner for the hospital's department heads was being held at a restaurant Suelen had selected. They were to be seated in a private dining room so they could all talk freely with each other. But the first thing Eliana noticed was the empty chair and who it belonged to—Diego.

Her nerves lay blank from the conversation they'd had yesterday, and dread turned her stomach into knots when she sat down next to Sophia, who was looking at her with a degree of concern. Outside of Diego and the obstetrician, she was the only other member of hospital personnel who knew about her pregnancy. She also knew that it was Diego's child.

'I'm fine,' she said to the older woman, who had raised an eyebrow at her.

'Doctors make the worst patients—especially when it comes to high-ranking ones such as yourself,' Sophia murmured, her voice audible only to Eliana.

She smiled at the words. 'Thankfully, I will have you to deal with all my work very soon. Just send me an occasional email with updates—that should do it. I trust your judgement, or I wouldn't have picked you.'

'Should those emails contain a detailed Ferrari Report, or would you rather not read about him?' Sophia's tone was playful on the surface, but alluded to a lot more than Eliana wanted to discuss.

Was he not going to show up after her rejection yesterday, even when she had asked him to come?

Her mouth went dry and she reached for her glass of water, taking a big gulp. She had arranged this dinner in an attempt to reach out to him one last time—even though she was rejecting him she still cared for him, and she wanted him to know how much their time together had meant to her. How much she admired his indomitable spirit and sense of community.

One last gift for the man she loved but couldn't be with.

'I want to say that won't be necessary, but I don't want you to call me a liar,' she said with a sad smile.

'What happened?' asked Sophia.

Such a simple question, and yet Eliana didn't know how to answer it. What *had* happened?

'At the beginning we were just two people who met in a bar and never planned on meeting again. Until we got the news of my pregnancy from you. Then everything changed. We thought we could be friends but...' Her voice trailed off. But what? They'd fallen for each other when they really shouldn't have done?

Eliana still wanted to give in to his lure. She was standing at the edge of a cliff, ready to fall for him. But what if he didn't show up to catch her?

'For what it's worth, I've known Diego ever since he started working at Santa Valeria. He's a good man, and does great work with his pro bono efforts. But he takes himself a bit too seriously.'

Sophia shrugged when Eliana raised her eyebrows in a silent question.

'I don't know how to say it better. He just…gets too much in his head sometimes, and that leads to impulsive decision-making. It makes him a brilliant doctor in times of crisis, but I'm not sure how well that works in personal matters.'

Eliana went quiet for a moment, thinking about what she had said, and then the waiting staff arrived with the wine she'd ordered for the table—excluding herself.

The twinge in her chest resurfaced as she looked at the empty chair one more time. He really wasn't going to come. It shouldn't surprise her—not after she had rejected his advances. But she'd really thought that he would come, for the sake of what they had and in spite of what they wouldn't have in the future.

'Thank you for joining me, everyone,' she said, and drew the attention of the room to herself. 'I guess I could have sent an email, but I didn't want to miss the opportunity to talk to all of you personally before leaving. As you all probably already know, I have finally made my choice for the new chief of medicine.'

She paused and raised her glass.

'I'm pleased to announce that Sophia has agreed to become the new chief of medicine and will usher Santa Valeria into a great new future.'

Glasses clinked all around, followed by a brief silence as everyone sampled their beverage. Eliana cleared her throat, suddenly feeling tight and constricted. She had practised these words believing Diego would be there to hear them, and understand their significance. Did it even make sense for her to say them?

'On top of that, I've also worked on establishing a more robust way of enabling you and your teams to help the less privileged communities here in Rio.' She paused to look around the room, her eyes once again resting on the empty chair. 'When speaking to you, I've heard many of you express interest in doing more pro bono work. So, starting immediately, a percentage of Santa Valeria's profits will be put into a newly established charity whose leader you can petition to release funds for pro bono projects. It will be led by Diego Ferrari,' she continued, and paused when she felt her voice wavering for a moment, 'who sadly could not be here tonight.'

Glasses clinked again, and Eliana sat back down on her chair. The cheerful atmosphere in the room was not managing to penetrate her gloom. But at least she had done something good while she was here in Rio, even if things hadn't turned out as she'd expected. With the new charity, Diego would have the right tools to keep going with his free clinic and help his colleagues bring in a significant number of cases from less wealthy patients.

She had done it because it was the right thing to do, but he had been the one to inspire her action. And now he couldn't even show up at the dinner.

'All right, this should be enough to hold you over.' Diego handed the patient a small paper bag with the required medicine in it and sighed with relief when the man closed the door behind him.

He let himself fall into the rickety chair behind the reception desk, burying his hands in his palms as he let out a groan of exhaustion. The plan had been to quickly stop by here and drop off some supplies someone had donated before heading to the dinner Eliana had organised for the leadership team at the hospital.

But when he had arrived at the clinic some people had already been waiting, needing to see a doctor right that instant. The patient they'd brought had been struggling with a nasty infection on his calf that Diego had needed to lance straight away, or he would have risked going into sepsis. By the time he had drained the fluids and packed the wound with antiseptic paste, hours had come and gone. But at least the patient had been saved and wouldn't lose his leg.

Diego glanced at his wristwatch, the weight of it still unfamiliar on his arm. He had worn it for the occasion of dinner tonight, along with a suit—the jacket of which he had tossed aside without much care when the patient's brother had hauled him in.

Just before midnight. There was no chance they were still at the restaurant. Another emergency had prevented him from fulfilling the promise of his presence.

Maybe it was for the best. After all, hadn't he proved Eliana's point by skipping her dinner? When that patient had lain down on the table, a quick glance at his wound had told him the infection was severe enough that he needed immediate treatment and nothing else had mattered.

Should he have sent a message to let her know he was held up? The thought had swirled in his brain as he'd started the procedure, but he'd decided not to act on it. She would just see it an excuse after the way they'd left things. Hurt had stopped him from picking up the phone, and he had chosen instead to immerse himself in the urgent patient waiting at his door.

But he cared so deeply for both Eliana and their child. Hearing from her mouth that she didn't think he considered them a priority had thrown him into a dark pit.

Diego wasn't someone to give up. Ever. That was why he'd managed to keep the free clinic alive for as long as he had.

What was different with Eliana that he felt unable to pick himself up and fight? Their conversation yesterday had crushed him. He'd left her office feeling numb, as if walking through fog, trying to understand what had just happened. Why had he not stayed and argued more?

Because she was right.

Tonight would have been the perfect opportunity to

prove her wrong, to show her that he cared about her above all else. But even though the thought had been on his mind he hadn't picked up the phone to get in touch with her.

Why?

Because Diego was afraid to feel how deep his love for her ran…how much it would destroy him to truly lose her.

Or might he resemble his father, after all? What made him think he could love her when he knew nothing about the concept? Fear paralysed him. What if he really was like his father? Maybe it was best she learned now before they got in too deep.

He pressed his palms against his eyes, willing his thoughts to stop chasing each other. The door of the clinic opened again. Diego swore under his breath. Had he not locked it after the patient and his family had left?

'We're not open right now, so if it's not an emergency please come back in the morning,' he said, without taking his hands off his face. Profound tiredness was digging its vicious claws into him, and he just wanted to rest.

'I thought I might find you here.'

Eliana's voice was coated with ice, sending a shiver down his spine.

He sat up straight, looking at her with a surprised expression. 'What are you doing here?' he asked, before he could think better of it.

'Me? What are *you* doing here?'

She looked at him, and there was a different kind of fire burning in her eyes than the one he was used to seeing.

'But of course you're here. Because you are Diego. You would give an arm and a leg to help your people, but you can't show up for me when it counts.'

Diego rose from his chair, meeting her gaze and not

flinching at her bitter tone. 'I don't get to decide when emergencies come in,' he said, with a veiled expression. Agitation flared in his chest, mixing with the guilt he'd been carrying around since yesterday and creating an explosive fire.

'That's not the point. I was never angry with you for looking out for your patients. I know what it's like—I've been in your place.'

'*Have* you, though? Have you *really* been in my place? Have you watched friends die and families fall apart because of the inadequate health care that exists for people who live in the *favelas*? Because that's what I see every time someone comes through these doors. I clawed myself to the top from the very bottom so I could help them avoid such a fate. How could you possibly know that when you grew up in the best private school in this country?'

The words burst from him like a geyser that had been blocked by a boulder for far too long.

Eliana stared at him silently. The only indicator of her emotional state was the raised pulse he could see hammering against the base of her throat as she swallowed.

'You don't even know half the things I had to go through, growing up the way I did. I might have had plenty of food and clothes to keep me looking the part, but I was alone. You had your community to bond with and carry you through the hard times. I had no one.'

The last words came out as a whisper, and regret wrapped itself around Diego. He hadn't meant to throw his own internal turmoil at her.

'Why don't you tell me?' he said. 'You no longer have no one. You have no idea how much I—'

'No,' she interrupted him in a voice made from stone. She took a shaky breath, her golden-brown eyes trained on him. 'You do *not* love me. If you believe that I don't understand your pain because I grew up surrounded by my father's wealth, you cannot truly know me. I've told you so much already, but you still don't understand.'

Hurt was etched into each of her words—a pain that resounded so intensely within him that it stole his breath. How had they got to this place where they had stopped understanding each other? It seemed as if the last few weeks had only been a mere dream of two people who were too different to tread the same path.

'Don't say that I don't love you,' he whispered, feeling the weight of her words settling on his chest and breaking his already crushed heart into pieces. 'I know it's true, whether you want to hear it or not.'

He might deny many things, but his feelings for her were genuine—even if they had landed them in this painful place.

'I thought I could do it,' she said. 'I really believed I could be in your life without hurting so much…without all this pain. But I don't think I can—'

Her voice finally broke, after wavering throughout her sentence, which prompted Diego to get off the chair and take a step closer to her.

She immediately shook her head. 'I waited for you at dinner, praying that you would show up despite the conversation we'd had. I wanted to be wrong about my reaction yesterday. I let you in…told you what it was like being on my own, having no one to trust.' Her throat bobbed when she swallowed a deep breath, her voice straining with each word. 'I asked you to show up when it counts—and you didn't. And you still haven't even asked about the scan.'

Her words hit him like a blow to his solar plexus, knocking the air out of his lungs as he slipped deeper into the dark pit he'd thrown himself into last night. After everything they'd discussed, all the things they had been through, he hadn't asked her about their child. He really wasn't any better than his father.

'I don't know what to say,' he rasped, his throat thick from the onslaught of emotions mixing in his chest. 'How is—?'

Eliana shook her head. 'I don't need you asking any more. I think we've reached the end of our road here, Diego.'

Her hand slipped into her handbag and retrieved an envelope. It looked bent, as if she had been carrying it around for a while.

'What is it?' he asked, flipping the envelope to examine its back. There was nothing written on it.

'Something you should know,' Eliana replied, with a rueful frown pulling at the corners of her lips. 'I'm leaving tomorrow. I know we have yet to figure out how we want to do things with the baby. I will be in touch as I get closer to my due date. But for now, I think I need some distance.'

'Ana, *por favor*...' He put the envelope down and circled the reception desk with two large strides, wrapping his hand around her upper arm as she turned to leave. 'Please don't go.'

'I have to—don't you see? Things shouldn't be so painful if they're right...if they're meant to be.'

She turned her head to look at him, and the pain in her eyes almost made him recoil.

'Maybe we were just kidding ourselves from the very start.'

'Ana...' He whispered her name and his hand went up to her cheek, only for her to flinch away before he could touch her.

'I have to go,' she said as they looked at each other, and she freed herself from his grasp, fleeing through the door before he could find the words that might persuade her to stay.

With a sigh that didn't even contain half of the pain and anguish welling up in him, Diego fell back into the chair and buried his face in his hands, his entire being crushed by what had happened in the last hour. She was gone, driven away by his inability to find her the space in his life that she deserved.

He was just like his father.

In the end, he had failed to be different.

A heavy blanket of sadness fell on his shoulders and he sat up straight again, his eyes falling onto the envelope he had put down as he'd tried to stop her leaving. He picked it up, turning it around in his hands a few times before opening it.

Inside he found a small flashcard with one word written on it: *Princesa*.

CHAPTER ELEVEN

DIEGO LOOKED AT the equipment being unloaded off the truck and taken into his clinic and felt the familiar twinge of regret in his chest. He had gone back to the hospital the day after that night in the clinic to find a summons to the office of the new chief of medicine.

There, Sophia had told him what he had missed when he'd skipped dinner—the announcement that he would oversee a new charity dealing with everything related to community outreach and pro bono procedures at Santa Valeria. It was a position he wouldn't have dared to dream of even with Vanderson in place. And Eliana had made it come true without even thinking twice about it.

Thinking about her still felt as if a searing hot dagger was being poked between his ribs, leaving him feeling hollow. Weeks had passed since he had last heard about her, although he'd tried to get in touch with her to thank her for the new job and to hear about their baby. His daughter.

That was the only thought that managed to pierce through the darkness he surrounded himself with, making his chest swell with unbridled joy and anticipation of the day he got to meet her.

A lot of the things said that night had been born out of fear—he realised that now. Fear of the unknown. Fear of trusting his heart over his head. Fear of losing the only woman who had ever meant something to him.

She alone had managed to sneak around his defences, making herself a cosy nest inside his heart. But his first reaction had been to treat her like an intruder, and the result of that reaction would be something he would regret for the rest of his life.

'Could you at least try to look pleased about this?'

Diego turned around when he heard his *avozinha's* voice behind him. 'I'm thrilled. With the extra staff and equipment we can service a much wider area of the Complexo do Alemão. We've even got our own patient transport van now.' He pointed at the roomy van parked near the entrance.

'You'll need to sound more convincing for me to believe you,' his grandmother muttered, while shaking her head at him. 'But you've been moping around like a sad puppy for the last four weeks. I guess you'll tell me it has nothing to do with Eliana and your baby girl being so far away.'

Diego sighed, rubbing his temples in a futile attempt to stop the emerging pain. 'I'm not moping. Am I sad she's gone? Yes, of course. I missed the first scan, and I wish I could be there for the next.'

Eliana had left almost four weeks ago, meaning she was well into her second trimester now and would soon have her next routine check-up. It pained him to think that he had yet to see his daughter, even if it was only through the screen of an ultrasound.

Throughout his life Diego had made many questionable choices and mistakes, letting the shadows of the past haunt him to the extent that it had sometimes immobilised him, rendering him incapable of deciding. It was that kind of primal fear that had made him stand back as Eliana walked out of his life for good.

'Have you told her you'd like to be there?' Márcia asked, and he scoffed at that.

'She's not taking my calls.'

'Can you blame her after the things you said to her? To think that you didn't even ask about the baby...' Avozinha clicked her tongue with a disapproving head-shake.

He drew his gaze away from the X-ray machine now being delivered to look at her. 'What? Who told you that's what happened?'

'You should know by now that your grandmother knows everything. I really thought I'd raised you better, my *netinho*.'

Diego's ears suddenly pricked. Little grandson? She had stopped calling him by that diminutive ages ago... only used it now when...

'Okay... I'm in trouble, apparently.'

'Of course you're in trouble!' Márcia raised her voice at him. 'How can you believe you are *anything* like your father? My son turned into a selfish and egotistical man, despite my efforts to raise him as a good person. But he used to be kind and sweet—qualities I see in you to this day.'

Diego stared at her, his mouth slightly agape. How could she possibly know that this was what he had been struggling with? That these were his innermost thoughts—the fear that he would turn out precisely the same because he hadn't been taught any better. But...

'He didn't teach me anything,' he whispered, and the revelation struck him like a ton of bricks falling on his head. 'He wasn't around enough for me to learn *anything* from him. He didn't teach me.' He looked at his grandmother in disbelief. '*You* did. You raised me to be better than him.'

Márcia shrugged, but gave him an encouraging smile. 'Glad you got there in the end.'

Diego froze, unsure what he should do next. How could he ever have believed he would turn out like his father when that man hadn't spent enough time in his life to influence him? No, all the things he had learned had come from his grandmother and all the half-siblings he'd grown up with.

His mistake seemed so incredibly foolish now, and his outburst in the clinic a couple of weeks ago silly. He was in love with this woman—what else was there to know?

'She has her next scan tomorrow. If you leave now you can get to Belo Horizonte with time to spare,' his grandmother informed him.

He grabbed her by the shoulders, planting a kiss on her cheek before realising what she had just said. 'How do you know that?'

'Just because you were having issues talking to her it doesn't mean I missed out on bonding with the mother of my next grandchild.'

She said it so matter-of-factly that Diego had to laugh.

'Text me the name of her doctor,' he said as he turned around to leave, heading straight for his car so he could be in Belo Horizonte just after nightfall if all went well.

Eliana sat in the empty waiting room, softly talking to her growing bump. She had her hand draped over it, as if wrapping it in a protective cocoon as she waited to have her scan.

Even though she was well into her second trimester she had yet to feel any movement from her tiny daughter. A fact that—according to the several online pregnancy communities she had found—wasn't anything to worry about. Most women in their first pregnancies didn't notice anything until the twentieth week. Eliana was just past sixteen.

It was at moments like this, when her nerves got the best of her, that she wished Diego was here. At least she could have shared the worry with him, if nothing else.

The thought that she had made a mistake gnawed at her more and more. Their last encounter had been charged with her fears—driven by them as she pushed him away and in doing that losing any chance of a future where they might have been a family. Where he might have sat here with her, holding her hand, as they found out more about their child.

And why? Because her insecurities had overwritten sensible concessions in those moments. For her entire life she had been irrelevant, with no one caring where she was or how she was doing. The damage caused by her father's neglect ran a lot deeper than she'd understood before she'd met Diego and got pregnant.

Because of her past pain she had demanded to be prioritised over things he didn't have any control over. For the first time in her life she'd had someone who truly cared for her, cherished her beyond any doubt, and instead of taking his feelings and actions at face value she had pushed him away—too afraid to deal with a reality where Diego wasn't going to abandon her.

It was an action that seemed so foolish now that she'd had time to process it. Why had she felt the need to leave Rio de Janeiro behind her as fast as she could? It wasn't the city's fault that her father had been a neglectful wretch. And Alessandro and Daria lived there—the only family she had remaining. Along with Diego's big family. All her daughter's aunts, uncles and cousins lived there, and so did Márcia, who was already more involved as a grandmother than Eliana ever could have hoped, and checked in with her almost daily. Not to mention Diego himself—the man she loved with all her heart.

Eliana had made a mistake, running away. She was at the point where she had to admit that.

Not for the first time in the last couple of days she took out her phone, checking flights back to Rio. She was still fine to fly, even with the pregnancy, though she'd have to choose soon.

Would Diego even take her back after the fight they'd had? Her heart squeezed inside her chest, sending a stabbing pain through her body.

She could sit here and wonder if he would, or she could go back and find out.

Her finger hovered over the flight, ready to buy the ticket, when the receptionist came into the waiting room to call her. 'Dr Oliveira, we're ready for you now,' she said, in a soft voice that sounded almost swoony. 'Dr Ferrari has just arrived and he's gone through. Your husband is…'

The receptionist waved her hand in front of her face, but Eliana's mind had gone blank after hearing his name so unexpectedly. *He was here?* Her mouth went dry and she suddenly felt both heat and chill rising within her, creating an intense storm as they met in her midsection.

She held her breath as she opened the door, and gave a soft cry when she saw Diego sitting in a chair with the sort of casual nonchalance she was so used to seeing from him. As if he belonged in this chair, in this place…

'Diego, you—'

He stood up from the chair and took a step towards her. 'I made it this time. No emergencies or last-minute patients.'

Her mind was still reeling from his sudden appearance, her lips parting without any words leaving them. She stretched out her hand, wanting to touch him, to kiss him, and tell him what a fool she had been.

But they were interrupted by her obstetrician Dr Porter entering the room, and after some brief introductions he started the scan and check-up.

Diego slipped his hand into hers when she winced at the chill of the gel on her stomach, and they both looked at the ultrasound picture in awe as Dr Porter showed them their daughter. He squeezed her hand as they looked at the screen together, feeling the magnitude of this moment. They had made this little life. Together.

'Okay, both mother and child are healthy and looking good. Have you experienced any discomfort? Unusual bleeding? Anything?'

Eliana shook her head, still speechless from seeing her daughter through the ultrasound, overwhelmed by the unconditional love she'd experienced at the sight of their child. Glancing at Diego, she saw he had a similar expression, and they looked at each other with a small smile, knowing each other's thoughts without having to say anything.

They walked out of the doctor's office and into the car park in silence, only stopping when they got to Diego's car. Then they turned to each other, deeply lost in the other one's eyes for a few heartbeats, before they hugged each other.

Tears started to coat her eyes, falling down her cheeks as relief washed over her. How could she have let him go?

'I'm so sorry, Diego,' she whispered into his neck, prompting him to take her face in both of his hands so he could look at her.

He swiped over her cheeks with his thumbs, brushing the tears away. '*You're* sorry? I have to apologise for *everything* I said. I was hurt and confused. I wanted to be with you, but I didn't know how. I lashed out. But if you let me I will try to make up for that for the rest of our lives together.'

'I thought you were putting me in second place. I couldn't deal with being part of a family. I didn't think I knew how to be with someone like you...someone who has radiance and love all around you. I'm still not sure I know how to be a part of it, but I want to try. If...' She swallowed the lump that had suddenly appeared in her throat. 'If you'll have me back.'

Diego looked at her for a moment, the brown of his eyes darkening. He looked like a predator that had just spotted its next meal. She held her breath as he remained quiet, then he dropped his head towards hers, brushing his lips against her in the kiss Eliana had been longing for since she'd left Rio de Janeiro a month ago.

'I love you, Ana. There's nothing in this world that can change that—nothing anyone can do or say to change my mind. And I promise to show you that every day until for ever.'

Eliana smiled as relief and joy collided in her chest, igniting the firework in her heart that had been waiting to explode ever since she'd met him that night at the hotel bar all those weeks ago.

'I love you, too—*ah!*'

She suddenly went rigid, and concern washed over Diego's face. 'What's wrong, *amor*? Is it...?'

But then she smiled again, even bigger than before. 'I can feel her... I think she just kicked me a little bit.'

Diego's eyes went wide in wonderment and he looked down, placing his hand on her protruding belly. '*Eita, princesa*, that's not very princess-like,' he said with a grin, and pulled her closer to him again. 'Oh, I almost forgot. Avozinha gave me this to give to you,' he added, and his hand vanished into his pocket, retrieving a small velvet box that he handed to her.

'She wants me to have her jewellery?' Eliana raised an eyebrow—and gasped a second later when she flipped the small box open. Her eyes snapped back to Diego, who was now kneeling in front of her.

'She thought her engagement ring would look good on your finger, and I think she's right. Will you let me show you how much I love you by becoming my wife?'

The tears she had just managed to get under control started to fall down her cheeks again as she nodded with a sobbing smile, pulling Diego off his feet and into her arms. 'Yes,' she whispered in his ear, and squealed as he wrapped his arms around her even tighter.

Eliana knew they still had challenges ahead of them, but whatever was coming at them they would deal with it. Together.

EPILOGUE

ELIANA FOUGHT TEARS as she looked in the mirror. The day was finally here: she was going to marry the love of her life.

She was surrounded by his sisters, who were laughing with her, and sharing advice from their own weddings, as well as cooing at her daughter Alice, who was lying in a small cot in the room, observing the proceedings through wide eyes.

She and Diego had debated for a long time whether they should get married straight away or wait for their child to be born. An urgency to tie the knot had filled them both, and neither had wanted to show any patience, but in the end Eliana had decided to wait. As a first-time mother she'd found the stress of pregnancy challenging, and she hadn't wanted to add to that.

The same day he'd come to pick her up in Belo Horizonte they had returned to Rio together, to forge a better future for Santa Valeria.

Eliana had been happy to leave Sophia to deal with the daily task of being the chief of medicine, freeing up her own time to help Diego build on the clinic, sharing the burden and the joy with him. She much preferred practising medicine over sitting in a stuffy office with endless paperwork. And bit by bit they were building the hospital they'd envisaged.

Now the day she had been so looking forward to had finally arrived, and she was sharing it with the people surrounding her. The Ferrari clan had welcomed her to the family with open arms, as if she were a long-lost sister, just waiting to find her family again.

'Don't cry! We've just got your make-up done,' Gloria said with a laugh as she put her arm around her shoulder, squeezing her full of sisterly love.

'Pick a random point on the ceiling and focus on it. That's what helped me,' chimed in Bianca, another one of the Ferrari sisters.

Eliana tilted her head backwards and looked at the ceiling above her head, willing the tears of joy to recede at the very least until they'd had all the pictures taken.

The door behind them opened, and all the women whirled around. Alessandro entered the room, followed by his daughter Daria, who was wearing the same dress as the bridesmaids.

'Is he ready?' Gloria asked, giving voice to the question everyone wanted to yell at him.

He nodded. 'I'm here to pick up my lovely sister and take her to the altar.'

The tears she had just managed to fight off started to well up again. It was finally happening. She was going to get married to Diego.

She took Alessandro's arm and let him lead her down the stairs, through Diego's *avozinha*'s house and into the garden, where they had set up chairs for the guests and a beautiful wedding arch. Her heart skipped a beat when the arch came into sight and the guests rose from their chairs.

And there he stood, at the end of the silver-white carpet they had rolled out, looking at her with an intensity she had got to know so well over the last year. His excitement matched hers as she walked down the aisle to meet him, her soulmate. Alessandro kissed her on both cheeks when they got to the end, before handing her over to Diego with a stern but warm look in his eyes.

'Are you ready for the rest of our lives?' she whispered when Diego leaned in to kiss her as well.

He smiled and grabbed her hand. 'Since the day I met you.'

* * * * *

COMING SOON!

We really hope you enjoyed reading this book.
If you're looking for more romance, be sure to
head to the shops when new books are
available on

Thursday 29th September

To see which titles are coming soon, please visit
millsandboon.co.uk/nextmonth

MILLS & BOON

MILLS & BOON®

Coming next month

A FAMILY MADE IN PARADISE
Tina Beckett

The elevator doors opened, and he was dumped onto the fourth floor. Rounding the corner, he pushed through the glass door to Neves's waiting area. He frowned when he spied Rachel in one of the chairs. He glanced around. No one else was here.

Hell, he hoped this wasn't about what had happened between them last year. In all honesty, he'd been waiting for that to catch up with him. But after a year?

You're being paranoid, Seb.

They'd both been consenting adults who'd agreed to remain mum about the night they'd shared. Not that the hospital really had any rules against colleagues sleeping together, although the unspoken consensus was that it could be a sticky situation. But it evidently worked for some. There was at least one pair of surgeons at Centre Hospitalier who were married. And his and Rachel's encounter had only been one night long.

Rachel didn't even look at him. Dressed in a gauzy white skirt and a blouse that was as blue as the ocean, she looked almost as inviting as the warm currents a short distance away. And when she crossed her legs—that slow slide of calf over calf was reminiscent of… He swallowed. Okay, don't go there.

But at odds with his thoughts were the tense lines in

her face and her refusal to glance his way. It couldn't be a coincidence that she was here. Did she know why they'd been summoned? Was this about the girl at the beach yesterday?

He glanced at Neves's administrative assistant, who must have guessed his thoughts, because she nodded. "He hoped you were in the building so he could meet with you both together."

His eyes went back to Rachel before returning to the desk. "About?"

"Hey, I just work here." Cécile raised her hands, palms out, in a way that said she had no idea why they were here. And he couldn't very well ask Rachel if she knew. Not in front of Neves's assistant.

Cécile picked up her office phone and murmured something into it. Then she looked up. "You can go on in."

When no one moved, she grinned. "Both of you."

Continue reading
A FAMILY MADE IN PARADISE
Tina Beckett

Available next month
www.millsandboon.co.uk

Copyright © 2022 Tina Beckett

MILLS & BOON

THE HEART OF ROMANCE

A ROMANCE FOR EVERY READER

MODERN
Prepare to be swept off your feet by sophisticated, sexy and seductive heroes, in some of the world's most glamourous and romantic locations, where power and passion collide.

HISTORICAL
Escape with historical heroes from time gone by. Whether your passion is for wicked Regency Rakes, muscled Vikings or rugged Highlanders, awaken the romance of the past.

MEDICAL
Set your pulse racing with dedicated, delectable doctors in the high-pressure world of medicine, where emotions run high and passion, comfort and love are the best medicine.

True Love
Celebrate true love with tender stories of heartfelt romance, from the rush of falling in love to the joy a new baby can bring, and a focus on the emotional heart of a relationship.

Desire
Indulge in secrets and scandal, intense drama and plenty of sizzling hot action with powerful and passionate heroes who have it all: wealth, status, good looks…everything but the right woman.

HEROES
Experience all the excitement of a gripping thriller, with an intense romance at its heart. Resourceful, true-to-life women and strong, fearless men face danger and desire - a killer combination!

To see which titles are coming soon, please visit

millsandboon.co.uk/nextmonth

JOIN US ON SOCIAL MEDIA!

Stay up to date with our latest releases, author news and gossip, special offers and discounts, and all the behind-the-scenes action from Mills & Boon...

 @millsandboon

 @millsandboonuk

 facebook.com/millsandboon

 @millsandboonuk

It might just be true love...